Dark Cheer
CRYPTIDS
EMERGING

Volume Blue
Edited by Atlin Merrick

Improbable
PRESS

First published by Improbable Press in 2021

Improbable Press is an imprint of:
Clan Destine Press
www.clandestinepress.com.au
PO Box 121, Bittern Victoria 3918 Australia

National Library of Australia Cataloguing-In-Publication data:

Improbable Press
Dark Cheer: Cryptids Emerging (Volume Blue)

ISBN: 978-0-6452899-1-6 (hb)
ISBN: 978-0-6450426-9-6 (pb)
ISBN: 978-0-6452899-0-9 (eb)

Cover artwork by © Pixie Ink
Cover photo "The Photographer At The Dark Hedges Northern Ireland
(94758811)" by © Giuseppe Milo, on Wikimedia Commons
Typesetting & Layout by Dimitra Stathopoulos

Improbable Press
improbablepress.com

Dedicated to everyone who's ever walked along water or wood,
who's seen shifting shadows there and wondered...
what if?

And for Joseph Carey Merrick, always

Contents

Emerge...

This book is for all of us who never outgrew wanting the chilly warmth of goosebumps.

It's for everyone who devoured stories about Nessie and chupacabras, about mokèlé-mbèmbé and yeti. It's for those who love the endless allure of *what if?*

What if there's truth behind tall tales? What if we take the time to look in the gray between shadow and light? Would we see wonders?

Of course we would.

Because remember, when humans first discovered fossils in swamps and stream beds, ice sheets and tar pits, in caves and bogs and hillsides, we literally discovered *unimaginable giants* – long-gone dinosaurs that made elephants and whales seem teapot tiny. Why not *more* creatures hiding in our hillsides and caves and tar pits? Alive and, perhaps, waiting for *us* to become the fossils?

Think about *this:* people have caught squid over fifty feet long. Those fifty foot squid leave sucker marks on whales that are four inches across. But guess what, guess what, *guess what:* we've caught whales with sucker marks *eighteen inches wide.* How big is *that* squid? Can you imagine it? Why haven't we seen it yet? What if that squid isn't the only thing living wherever that squid lives?

"It has always seemed very curious to me," wrote zoologist Gerald Durrell, "that anybody faced with reasonably good evidence...as to the possible existence of a creature as yet unknown to science, should not throw up their hands in delight at even the faintest chance of such a windfall in the shrinking world."

That is what the stories in this book are about: the darkly cheerful delight of you and me, *you and me* getting to live in a time of such windfall. A time of discovering that lake monsters are real, gargoyles can fly, and mothmen are ready to stop hiding. These stories are about what's under the bed (an argumentative bogeyman), what happens when cryptids move into your neighborhood (you find your Frisbee, finally), they're about what happens when at last we trust (we find safety).

This book isn't about murderous monsters peckish for human flesh, though there *are* stories of tooth and claw, of creatures taking back what's theirs. These are stories of what's in the dark, and an acknowledgement that it may be happy to help and just as happy to devour. After all, to a cow destined for a plate, the farmer is a monster, though she'll possibly never see herself that way. Neither do most of the cryptids in this book, even if they do quite like the taste of you.

This anthology about emerging includes writers, too, many appearing in print for the first time here. We're so especially excited that *these* creatures have emerged beside us. Welcome, you creative cryptids.

"Never make the mistake of thinking life is now adjusted for eternity," wrote naturalist Loren Eisley. "There are things still coming ashore. There are other things brewing and growing in the oceanic vat."

Brewing just there, at the edge where ocean waters turn dark *enough,* but light enough too, just enough for us to glimpse fins or fangs or great big eyes looking back at us.

I bid you cheerful welcome, cryptids. Come up out of that sweet dark.

Atlin Merrick
Winter 2021

The Name of the River
BAILEY BAKER

Always, it had been the River, slipping under the thick moss and through the murky currents, with an occasional visit to the End to look out at the wide, lonely Sea. The Sea was beautiful, but there were risks in the edgelands, where there was no cover, no depths. The daytime brought the sun, which made skin red and painful, and the salt in the water made the burn hurt even more. The fish and bug things tasted strange there, too, made the belly turn and the throat dry, and the plants turned to mush in the mouth. The Sea was good for Thoughts – they grew bigger, brighter, something felt in the body instead of locked in the head – but the days after were difficult.

Besides, most of the Sightings happened near the Sea, and they caused a salt-hurt of their own, but in the eyes.

Inland, there were trees, and trees brought shade. Everything around was green and cool, except for the flowers, which tasted sweet, sunshine in the mouth that didn't burn. *Nothing so beautiful should be eaten* was a Thought, but sometimes the longing for sweetness was too great. After, there would be sadness, but that was all right. Sadness could be survived.

Over time, humans had started building their dens closer and closer to the River. It was concerning at first, but the humans didn't seem to want to be in the water, usually, just to look at it. They also seemed to like the trees, and if they did take them out when they were building, they'd put more in later. It seemed wasteful, but the new trees would grow over time and sometimes would even have flowers.

One day, an especially beautiful yellow flower bloomed just at sundown, and the smell of it, sweet and pure, drifted on the air down to the River. It smelled like longing, teasing the nose, making the mouth water. The den was dark and quiet, the grass long like when the humans were away hunting. The stretch of the long neck wasn't enough, the tongue could not reach. It smelled... so...good...

A sudden, frustrated heave of the body, and the flippers had grass beneath them for the first time. The tail coiled up and pushed against the ground, and then again, and the body moved forward, and the world grew much larger.

The flower tasted especially delicious. Sadness came after, as always, but the flippers rippled against the soft, smooth green, and this time, the hurt passed quickly.

Humans watched things.

Once, it had been fire. The humans had gathered in a circle around some wood and made flames. There would be singing, talking, laughing. Sometimes they would sleep around the fire, curling toward it for warmth. These humans had hunted, had shown how to eat the plants. This had been a long time ago, when there had been Others in the River.

Now, they watched a box with lights and sound in it. It didn't seem to create warmth, but people gathered around just the same. They would sit in their dens, and not talk, not sing, only laugh a little. Sometimes there was music, and music was good. The flippers-and-tail were quiet on the grass. On nights with no night sun, it was easy to watch through the wall glass.

The humans in one den, the one with messy plants and the rattling move-box, watched shows about Thoughts. They didn't always make sense, but new words were good. Outside was Nature. The night sun was Moon. The light box was Tellyvision. All the land animals, the ones who always ran away, had names: Deer, Raccoon, Rabbit, Fox. Foxes were like dogs but also not. Snakes lived in the River, of course, so they were known, and Otters, and Fish, though not as many as before. Birds flew over during sun time, but not moon time. Some Birds ate Fish, but not so many it was a problem.

And the River…one night, Tellyvision said that the River, too, had a name. It rolled around in the head for days after, danced up and down the throat and across the back of the tongue, though of course words didn't work that way for the creatures of Nature.

The River was called Altamaha.

Knowing the name made the River feel alive. It made it both bigger and smaller, new and familiar. There were many Thoughts about the name, Thoughts that made the belly feel warm.

Names were good.

It would be good to have a name.

New humans moved into the den next to the house with Tellyvision, four days before the night without Moon.

This den was set back away from the River, on a wide piece of land with especially thick, smooth grass. The flippers-and-tail made almost no sound on grass like this, but new humans still called for caution. It was old habit to hide behind trees, to watch, to listen. The den had large walls of glass, so watching was easy. There was lots of activity at first, many humans, loud and clompy and rustly, but then the den got calmer, quieter. Two days passed, and the same humans walked back and forth in front of the glass. Three humans, two big – *adults,* another word from Tellyvision – and one smaller, *child.*

The child had red hair down to the chin and carried around the squares that made them quiet. *Books,* Tellyvision had called them. The child was alone most of the time, even when eating, but the adults would come through every once in a while and sometimes share a meal. One adult was wide, hairy, and deep-voiced. The other was quieter, harder to see, a flash of yellow off to the side of the glass, an occasional hand passed over the red hair of the child.

Watching, thinking. Air between the lips, not quite a hiss.

Child could be a problem. Children liked to *do.* Children liked to swim, and bug things and murky water were not enough to stop them. Children liked to climb, to seek, to find, to touch. Children screamed at Sightings, brought adults, threw rocks and sticks. One child, long ago, had been kind. Many more had not. It would be best to leave, at least for a while. The River was long, other places were safe.

But Tellyvision, the next den over. *This week on Nature at Your Doorstep. Live from Symphony Hall.*

The child had settled with a book behind one of the walls of glass. Again the flash of yellow, this time a drink offered, pink like a flower. Another touch to the hair, a touch that made the child look up and smile, understandable. Even watching that touch made the flippers wiggle a little.

More watching, thinking. That den finally went dark and quiet, but in the next den, oh. Tellyvision that evening brought a new word and a new wonder: *Opera.* Sleep was late in coming, as sound and color and *magic* continued to thunder in the head and heart long after the screen went black.

The eyes opened to find the sun already high in the sky – a new experience – and the red-hair child wide-mouthed and staring from just a few feet away.

A Sighting. Oh, no.

"I won't hurt you," the child said slowly, holding two hands up. "I won't tell anyone you're here. Okay? I promise. I'll just–" The child's feet turned slowly toward the den, even as the eyes – green, like the grass – stayed locked firmly on the face. The little body tensed and prepared to run as the head shook the sleep away.

Wait. Don't go. From the heart place. *Won't hurt you either.*

The child froze. "What…how did you do that?"

Do what?

"That." The child lifted one hand, pressed the palm into the forehead. "I can hear you. In here."

Really?

"Yeah." The child lowered the hand slowly. "Say something else."

Like… There was no word for it, so the eyes stared at the child's feet. They were wrapped in a leather material, bright purple and sparkly like the sand by the sea, tied with a bright pink tie. *Pink. Purple. Feet.*

The child followed the line of sight. "My shoes? You like my shoes?"

Shoes. Yes.

A small smile came to the mouth. "Thanks. I do, too."

Shoes. This was followed by a waggle of one flipper. *No shoes.*

"Well, I guess not." The child's feet stayed rooted on the ground, but the head stretched to examine the flipper more closely. "You look like a giant seal."

!!!!! Images: seals flipping over nets, flirting with trainers at shows, balancing beach balls on noses, snapping fish from the air in payment for tricks. *Tonight on SeaWorld TV: Seals, Nature's Comedians!* A little indignant chuff came from the back of the throat.

"Oops." The child laughed. "Sorry."

Back at the den, the creak of a door. "Charlie! Charlie, it's lunch time! Where are you?"

"I'll be right there, Mom!" The child turned back, the smile still on the face. "Man, my mom is going to love – wait, what's wrong? No, stop! Don't go!"

The body slid into the River, but the head stayed above the surface. Images of men with lights in their hands, long sticks that shocked, dogs, nets, guns, *guns,* cages…

"No!" The child ran to the River's edge. "Please don't go, *please* don't. Okay? I won't say a word to Mom, or to anyone. I promise! Just…" The child held out a hand. "Stay for a while longer, won't you? *I promise.*"

A drop of water ran down the child's face: salt-hurt.

An image from Tellyvision: a piece of an old movie. *Sorry, kid.*

The Thought of losing Tellyvision made the belly drop, but it was too late. The body dove beneath the current and headed upstream, the tail sweeping hard and fast.

Sometimes it rained. Rain was good.

Fish liked rain. The droplets looked like bug things on top of the water, would bring the fish to the surface. Eating was easy in the rain, and the belly would be full for days. The water would taste better too, like air, like nothing. The River and the ground around it would smell fresh and clean. Colors would be more colorful, the greens even greener, the flowers even brighter. And best of all, if the rain went on long enough, the River would grow deeper, wider, and the current would move faster. The body could float, twist, turn, race.

A word from Tellyvision: *fun!*

The rain had been falling for three days. The moss in the trees was heavy with water, the sand of the River bottom was swirling and shifting. Just after sunrise, a storm had come, thunder like the drums in the Opera and lightning that made the eyes burn and skin tingle. The rain hit the trees like an angry tail, but the light through the gray clouds was enough to swim by, to hunt by.

A Red Dot Fish swimming near the surface caught the eye. Red Dot Fish were *delicious.* The body stilled, the neck tensed, the mouth open and ready to bite. The fish saw the body, though, and started to swim away, downstream, as fast as a fish could move. The body followed, diving, chasing, the mouth wet with hunger, the tail splashing with effort.

The Red Dot Fish was caught, finally, and swallowed (yes, *delicious*), and the body surfaced, water streaming down the head and long neck, blinked out of the eyes. Directly across the River was the den of the red-hair child. The eyes looked at the thick grass, the new box of blue water surrounded by gray, hard ground. A row of red flowers sagged from the rain, their petals dropping wasted to the ground. Another flash of lightning, another blink to clear the eyes, and the red-hair child was standing at the wall glass. The eyes met.

Not safe! Upstream! was a Thought, but the child was already out of the den, running past the flowers and water and gray, toward the River. "Wait, wait! Please! Wait!"

Stop! An image: the racing current of the River, a tree branch sweeping quickly by, dipping under the water and out of sight.

"All right, all right, just—" The child stopped a River's width away and bent over, breathing hard. "Just please, don't go. I've been watching for you." Another few breaths, and the child straightened, brushing the now wet red hair back from the face. The green eyes shined like the sea. "I wanted to apologize. For scaring you."

An image: the child at the time before, hair dry, purple shoes, eyes wide, holding two hands up.

"Well, yeah," the child said with a huff. "I was scared too, but that was before you said you liked my shoes."

Shoes good.

"I didn't tell anyone," the child said in a rush. "About you, I mean. Not a living soul. Not even my mom."

No?

"No. I mean, it was…obvious. That you were frightened. That you had been…hunted before."

The belly dropped. Images from before: a spear. A net. A dog. The mouth roaring with pain. Not shared with the child.

A word from Tellyvision: *private.*

A deep breath drawn in. *All right now.* An effort: the corners of the mouth pulled up, toward the sky. *Thank you.*

The creak of the door. "Charlie!" From the den, through the steamy air. A flash of yellow. Mom. "What are you looking at out there? Get in here before you get soaked! You'll catch your death of cold!"

"It's like two hundred degrees out here," the child muttered. "Coming, Mom!" over the shoulder, then, "Will you stay?"

Not safe.

"It *is* safe. It will *be* safe, I promise. I won't say a word to anyone, and there's nobody around here to tell anyway." The child again pushed the hair from the face. "You can trust me on that."

The child's eyes were wide. A word from Tellyvision: *hopeful.* The heart turned over.

Yes. For a little time. Will that do?

"It's a deal." The child smiled. "I'm so happy you came back."

The child turned and ran toward the den and the yellow flash by the entrance. The body moved back to the River and slipped into the cool water. A Thought: a few more fish in the mouth, then

Tellyvision in the den next door. A rainy night would make good cover, as long as the lightning passed.

Learned: early to sleep, and a resting place back and away from the far side of the River, where the green was thickest. The rain had stopped overnight, and the River was buzzing with sound and light early.

One fish and two bug things, one drink of water (fresh, from a puddle, refreshing), one good stretch before the creak of the door and the slap of human feet across wet grass.

The child, *hopeful*-eyed, a long, thin stick in one hand and a carry-bag in the other. A long watch from behind the trees as the child's head turned from side to side, eyes searching. No other humans, no voices. A cautious flippers-and-tail from behind the trees, one eye on the River and safety.

"Oh, there you are." The child held out the stick. "I told my mom I was going to try fishing today. She was over the moon. 'Glad to see you getting outside more, Charlie.'" The child's voice was higher than normal now. "'No more stunts like last night, mind.'"

Fishing. An image: diving beneath the water, grabbing a River eel with the mouth. *Why stick?*

The child laughed. "I'll show you." The tail part down on the River bank. "This is called a fishing pole. This is the line and this is a hook. You use bait to lure the fish to you, a worm or something, and then when they go to eat the bait, they catch on the hook and you pull them out of the water with the line." The child leaned in closer. "But I'll tell you a secret. I don't use the hook and the bait. It's not fair. I just put the pole like this—" The child pushed the end of the pole into the ground. "And I let the line trail into the water, and there! The perfect excuse to sit next to the River all day. Look, I brought a book, and a sandwich." The child smiled widely. "We can spend the day together!"

The eyes blinked. An image from before: another child, white-yellow haired, also smiling. Blue eyes, like the sky, not green. A piece of sandwich, held out in small digits. "I made it for you special, 'cause you like fish. It's tuna!" Not shared with this child.

Private.

The body slipped into the water, the head surfacing just down from where the line teased the water. *What is in the book?*

The child's smile even wider, bright like the sun.

"You haven't asked my name. It's Charlotte."

The next day, the pole by the River. Another book, another sandwich.

The mouth turned down. An image: "Hey, Chuck, what do you say we go out after supper and throw the ball around? We need to build up those muscles." The wide, hairy adult.

The child's mouth turned down, too. "Yeah. That's my dad. He still thinks I'm a boy. My mom fights with him about it all the time."

Another image: A flash of yellow. "Charlie! It's lunch time!" Mom.

"Well, she's trying to keep him from getting mad, you know? It's just a nickname. They called me Charles when I was born, after my grandfather. I changed my name last year, on my birthday. My teachers use it now at school, and all the other students do too, except for this one guy, who's a real shithead." The child covered the mouth with one hand. "Oops, sorry."

A scene from Tellyvision: *I'm going to wash out your mouth with soap, young lady.*

The child laughed. The body was close to the child on the River bank, and the child leaned to one side and bumped the arm against the flipper where it rested on the grass. The flipper tingled from the touch. "So, what's your name?"

The mouth turned downward. There had been Thoughts about names, but how to get one?

No name.

"Wait, really?" The child's head tilted to the side, the eyes narrowed. "What do your friends call you?"

The throat grew tight. *No friends.*

"Okay, well, what about your family?"

The eyes burned a little: salt-hurt. An image: a morning on the edgeflats, no creatures around. No Fish, no Birds, no creatures of the River, no humans. Not even bug things. Only the body.

"Oh," the child said, quiet. "You're all alone then."

Sadness came then. *Yes.* A new word, *alone.* Heavy in the heart.

"I'm sorry." The child sighed. "But…you have me now, right? We're friends."

An image from Tellyvision: two humans, walking side-by-side down gray, hard ground, looking at each other, laughing.

The child smiled. "Exactly."

The edges of the mouth up in reply. The heart, not so heavy. *Yes. Friends.*

"Good." Tail parts on the River bank for a while, quiet. A Bird in the trees, black, loud. The child thinking. "So…do you want a name? We could come up with one, if you like."

Yes. The word fast, like the current. *It would be good to have a name.*

"Okay. Is there something you especially like, a flower maybe? Or do you want me to make a list? There are lots of names out there…I had a friend named Rain once. Or you could pick a season, like Winter or…"

The eyes looked down. *From the book.*

The child blinked. "Like, choose a character? From this book? Well, okay. Sure." The child opened the book, pushed the papers. "How about…Jordan?"

Jordan. The word floated in the mouth, sounded like a flower tasted. *Good name.*

"I like it. It's pretty. And I think it's the name of a river, too, in another country. Israel, I think." The child scratched the head. "I should know that, actually."

The eyes opened wide. *There is another River?*

"There are other rivers, yeah. All over the world." The child leaned back on the arms against the River bank. "But they can't be as good as ours, right, Jordan?"

The lips turned up, and the long neck slid slowly closer until the nose was almost touching. The child smelled like Fish, and dirt, and friend. *Right, Charlotte.*

Charlotte felt sadness. That was a Thought. The eyes were wet, salt-hurt, and the nose was...the nose was...

An image from Tellyvision: Got a snotty nose? Try Softies brand tissues!

Charlotte did a big sniff, but not of flowers. The nose was definitely snotty.

What's wrong?

"It's my dad. He's just...he wants me to be someone else, you know? Someone big and tough and − oh, I don't know." More snotty. "He and my mom had a big fight last night. She told him she wants to have my name changed legally, which would be great, you know, but he...he wants to send me to boarding school. A *boys'* boarding school."

Alarm. *Charlotte is not a boy.*

Charlotte sniffed again. "That's the thing. He thinks you can just wish for something and make it happen." The head shook. Jordan knew now that this meant *no.* "I mean, I know I'm just a kid, but even I know better than that." Charlotte looked down at her hands, twisted in her lap. "I just...I just wish he could love me for who I am. You know?"

Jordan sighed. *Charlotte is good.*

Charlotte smiled, watery, snotty. "Thanks, Jordan. You're the best." Stood, brushed clean the tail area. "Listen, my mom is sending me to my grandma's for a few days. Time for everybody to cool off, she said. They only live in the next county, but the house isn't on the river. Will you be okay without me?"

Okay, yes. The head nudged the arm. *But sadness.*

"I'll be home as soon as I can, I promise." Charlotte turned toward the den and walked away, shoulders down and eyes on the ground. Jordan's heart place ached.

Then the River was quiet.

It had been a long time since Jordan had had time to have Thoughts, other than the ones shared with Charlotte. The body slipped into the River now, sinking down until only the eyes and nose were out of the water. It felt good, restful. A few bug things floated by, and the tongue slipped out lazily, sliding them into the mouth without effort. The body was peaceful, but the head was unhappy.

Charlotte, the friend, was unhappy.

A deep breath in through the nose, and the eyes closed. An image: another child, smaller than Charlotte, white-yellow hair, blue eyes, quick smile. A laugh like a bird. "We'll be best friends!" Tuna Fish sandwich held out in stubby fingers. Chasing birds on the green grass while the eyes watched from the River.

Another image: "It's my birthday next week!" Swinging from a tree branch. "Birthdays mean parties! And cake! And presents! All my friends are going to be here. It's going to be great!" A drop to the ground. "Can I bring them back to meet you?"

A soft smile on the lips. *Not safe.*

"You'd never hurt me," the child said seriously, before running inside, and there had never been time to explain that the risk actually ran the other way.

Another image: The worst Sighting. Children, screaming, red-faced and terrified. Rocks hitting the body, the neck, the head. Adults streaming from the den, this one closer to the River. Lights, spears, nets. "This way!" "I think I see it!" "Christ, it's huge!" The click of guns. The barking of dogs, the teeth of one deep in the flipper. "Kill the scaly bastard!" Fire in the neck, in the back. The mouth roaring with pain. The desperate dive. The churning tail. The days of hunger, barely able to hunt. The nights spent in the edgelands, jumping at every sound, letting the salt into the wounds. The sparkle of blue seaglass, seen by the eye as the body, smaller, weaker, dry, turned at last to return Inland.

Another image: The white-yellow hair bowed, the voice choked and low. "We're leaving today," in a soft, sad voice. "Dad says it's not safe here anymore. We're moving in with my grandma."

Watching from the deepest part of the River, body poised and ready to run if needed. Heart place aching.

"I know you probably hate me now. But I want you to know that I'm sorry. I didn't mean for you to get hurt. I just...I wanted everyone to meet my special friend." The hands wiping at the eyes, salt-hurt. The voice dropping to a shush. "I'll miss you."

The slow, silent lift of the neck from out of the water, still hidden behind the trees. The toss of the head, the release of the seaglass from the mouth. Blue, like the eyes. A present, for a birthday. For a friend. It landed at the feet.

The child stooped to pick up the stone. Wrapped it in her small hand, held it over her heart place. "Thank you," in the quiet voice, a small smile on the lips. "Good bye."

The eyes opened on the now day. A present. Charlotte needed a present.

Once the sun had left the sky, it was off to the edgelands.

The den was dark and quiet. Flippers-and-tail moved the body across the grass. The blue water rippled in the square, and despite the worry, the body paused, curious; the nose wrinkled at the smell. Too clean to be fresh, not for drinking. The gray, hard ground soothed an itch on the underside, though, and the body did another quick shimmy before inching up to the wall glass.

The body had never been near the den at night. It was darker inside than outside, though not by much. The eyes couldn't see into the den, but could see...could see...

A word from Tellyvision: *Self*.

The eyes could see Self, then: large, larger than the body felt, and green, like grass, like trees. A creature of Nature. The eyes, dark, wide, curious; the face, sharp, but also round, soft. The head turned, one side and then the other. Water sometimes showed Self, but not clearly, not like this. This, then was Jordan, Self, Charlotte's friend.

Flippers-and-tail slightly closer to the house, leaning over to drop the treasure on the gray, hard ground close to the den entrance. A perfect piece of seaglass, green this time, like Charlotte's eyes, like the trees, like…the body. Like Jordan.

The long neck had just pulled back, the body just starting to turn toward the River, when too-bright lights flared from the den, shining out onto the grass, onto the blue water in the square, onto the gray, hard ground, onto the *body*.

Jordan, heart-place quivering, jerked the head around to look back into the wall glass, only this time to find a flash of yellow, yellow *hair*, Mom, staring back at Jordan with wide blue eyes.

Mom's hand, reaching out to touch the wall glass, her mouth working.

From above in the den, the deep voice of the wide, hairy human. "Goddamn it, what's gone and set the lights off now? Another deer? Jesus, can't we get five minutes in this hellhole without something digging through our damn trash or drinking from the pool? I swear to god, no wonder the kid's such a freak."

Jordan reared back, looked around wildly. Mom started to shake her head, mouthing "No, no," through the glass, but the body turned sharply on its midpoint and flippers-and-tailed faster than ever before, back to the River.

Jordan knew it was time to leave, to go upstream, to hide. A scene from Tellyvision: the rounds of a move-box squealing, the tail part swishing like a fish, side to side. Black marks on gray, hard ground and the humans in the move-box *getting the hell out of Dodge*.

But. Charlotte.

Wait until morning was a Thought. At least, to try. The clouds were thick overhead now, the air cooling; it would be raining soon anyway, and probably most of the day tomorrow. Difficult to see the body in the River in the rain, but maybe, just maybe, the eyes could see Charlotte in the wall glass one last time. Salt-hurt at the Thought, but Self must be safe.

The body hid on the farside under the trees. The eyes didn't close at first, the body didn't rest. The lights were on inside the den and the voices of the adults, angry, loud, carried across the grass and the width of the River throughout the darkest part of night. Finally, the eyes, too heavy to stay open, slid shut.

"Are you…are you here?"
The voice, adult, soft, from the other side of the River. A word from Tellyvision: *gentle*. Rain, not hard, not cold. Early light of morning.
The eyes opened, but the body very carefully didn't move.
"I can't believe you're real," the voice continued. "I mean, I *can*. I remember you. I remember everything about that night, the night we chased you off…but, I don't know. My dad refused to talk about it, and my mom would just say I had an overactive imagination. And over time…well." A hand held out, a red flower. "Do you still like flowers? I brought you one." The hand released it, dropped it to the ground.
The white-yellow hair, yellow now. The body, bigger. Older. Mom to Charlotte, but first friend to Jordan.
A rustle, the tail parts settling down on the River bank, the back leaning against a tree. The yellow hair going flat with rain.
"I…wondered. When I saw Charlotte spending so much time by the river. She's not the outdoorsy type, not at all." A little laugh in the throat. "I thought maybe she was just doing it to shut Joe up, but then, Charlotte's never been the type to do what she didn't feel like doing. Um, I mean. Obviously.
"I kicked him out last night. Charlie's…no. *Charlotte's* dad," Mom continued. "Told him to pack his shit and hit the road. He was pissed as hell, but my folks left *me* the house, so…" A sigh. "He turned out to be a right bastard, in the end. I'm sure she told you. Anyway. She deserves better. We both do."
An image from Tellyvision: a human, tight curls, silver. *You bet your sweet bippy*. Shared.
Mom's head jerked up. "I'll be damned," said in a breath. "Will you come out? Can I see you?"
The body tensed, but stayed still. Nets, spears, dogs.
"I kept mine, you know." Mom twisted so she could reach into

the blue part of her covering. "All these years." The hand held out and opened, a piece of blue seaglass in the middle, clean and bright, shiny. Mom swallowed. "If you can't see clear to forgive what… happened, what we did, I'll understand. I will. And I promise, I'll never say a word. Just – please keep being a friend to Charlotte. We've got some rough times ahead, and she'll need you." A drop on Mom's cheek: salt-hurt. "She'll be lucky to have you."

Mom waited for a long minute, but finally a nod of the head, a deep breath. She stood and brushed off the tail area. "She'll be home soon. I'm going to go make some cookies now, but I'll send her down to do a little fishing later. I'll make sure she finds your gift."

Mom turned to leave. *Wait.*

Mom's body stopped, the head turned back toward the River. A word from Tellyvision: *anticipation.*

Hopeful, on both sides of the River.

The body took a deep breath, stretched the long neck to full length, and started to flipper-and-tail out from under the brush.

Jordan's lips curved upwards on their own.

What We Become
JOANNA GERBERDING

I don't have a name.

More accurately, most children don't give me one. I am the one that runs alongside cars on long trips. The one that the children watch when their games lose power or their book ends. My rules change with each child, but there are always rules. Sometimes I hop over intersecting streets. Other times I slide under the cars that pass. Occasionally I will change size as my backdrop does. Oftentimes, I'm not on the road at all, but keeping pace with the car. I like these best, because I get to feel the grass. It's much more alive than concrete…though I do enjoy getting to run up those sloping telephone wires.

I don't know how I really look.

I appear differently to each child. Sometimes, I am a horse, galloping through the plains and fields. Other times, I am a pale being, a twisted version of the children's companions, but run on all fours. I have even been a fox that flies. It doesn't matter to me how I look, though. As long as I am there to keep them company.

I don't know from whence I came.

I doubt it matters. After all, I am just here for company. For entertainment. For them. Perhaps enough of them imagined me that I became real; perhaps I have always existed, and once kept pace with horses. Perhaps it is a bit of both, or a bit of neither. Regardless, I am here.

And I am not alone.

This is new to me, a child standing in front of me. Why is it not in a car, watching me keep pace as I feed off its boredom? As I consume that which I cure? Why is it looking up at me with eyes red and feet dirty? Does it not know that children belong in cars?

Yet I cannot leave it alone.

It clings to my back as I run. I do not know what to do with it, but taking it with me seems to be a better option than letting it stay where it was. Its grip is surprisingly strong. I had never given thought to their strength before, but it seems that children are very hearty. This gladdens me. I would hate for it to get hurt. I just wish that I knew what it eats. Somehow, I don't think that children feast on boredom the way I do. Maybe they eat leaves? Or bugs?

I am starting to understand what it says.

It likes the daytime. That works for me, as I am less often needed then. We find food, and the child goes where I cannot. I fetch the tastiest fruits from the highest branches for it. It smiles at me, then, and thanks me. I am full, but not from boredom. This is strange. But never mind that now. Dusk is soon to fall, and I must prepare the child to ride.

I am a horse tonight.

That makes things easier. And if I morphed a bit on my own (or did the child on my back do it?) to make sure it could not fall off, no one would mind. The ones who watch me will not care. If anything, it will entertain them more. It's not uncommon, after all, for me to look like I have a rider in this form. It is a win-win; the child with me stays safe, and the child in the car is entertained. I run. I am content.

I wonder if the child notices that it has shifted form with me.

I suppose that it makes sense that we are Made. I do not remember my Making; I doubt the child will remember theirs, once it has run long enough. That must be the way of things. Or perhaps this child (can I still call it that?) is an exception. Perhaps it will always remember, because perhaps those that are Made, rather than Created, are different. Only time will tell, and we have enough of that to go around.

I wonder if I was Made like the child.

Or perhaps I simply Became. It does not matter, but I wonder still. The child wonders, as well. It has noticed its changing, and is pleased by it. It says that it hated its old life, that it was one of fear and pain. This new life, this new form, is less stationary but far more stable, it says. I am not quite sure what that means, but if the child is pleased, then so am I. After all, I exist to make children happy.

I don't think I can call it a child any longer.

It is a young one still, but it is no longer a child like the ones who ride in cars. Its transition was swift, and from what it tells me, painless. That gladdens me. This young one has known enough pain. I hope that in being Made, it has been freed from that...or at least led somewhere with less pain. I hope that keeping it by my side is right for it. The young one seems to think so.

I have a name.

It calls me Nobi. It is my Sprog. And even when there are no children for whom I can run, I do not hunger. My Sprog and I keep each other entertained. It eats what I eat, now. I just wonder when I stopped surviving off of boredom and started living off of affection. Perhaps I always have.

Tonight, we will run again, my Sprog and I. Tonight, and evermore.

Gargoyles of Prague
SHERRI COOK WOOSLEY

Toby slid off the bed and wheeled his IV pole in front and to the side. Some of the tubing was too long; it got caught under the pole's wheels if you didn't drive it just right. Toby looked to the window while his mother, Sami, spoke with the doctors. Pulling on a string to raise the blinds, Toby first saw his reflection. A boy wearing a blue robe over pajamas. Unsettling, though, was his bald head, oddly egg-like. But, if he peered through his reflection, Toby could see a corner of Prague. His mom had moved them here from Utah right before 5th grade because of his stepmom. She'd said he could call her whatever he wanted, "Even Theresa."

Theresa was part of a team to set up a new corporate office in the Czech Republic. His mom had promised they'd explore Prague during the days while Theresa was working, but there hadn't been much time for that before Toby had got sick.

The sound of the door closing – the doctor leaving – made Toby turn around. His mom looked tired, the pale skin sagging under her eyes. She wrapped her arms around herself and tried to smile. "The doctor says you're doing great," she said. Her voice wavered.

"What does that mean? More medicine? How much longer do I have to stay here?"

"Don't worry, sweetie. You just try to relax."

Anger flared inside Toby. She was talking to him as if he were a child, instead of telling him everything the doctor had said.

A knock on the door and Theresa came in, putting her hands under the hand sanitizer dispenser and rubbing them together. She wore what she called her 'professional costume:' slacks and a bright top with a jacket. Chunky jewelry. Black hair in tight braids. She waved at Toby and greeted Sami with a kiss.

Sami whispered, "He's got to take steroids for five days straight again. It makes him so emotional. I don't think I can handle it."

Toby folded his arms across his chest, resenting the closeness between his mom and stepmom. Resenting that this was how he learned he'd have to take the stupid steroids again.

"You've got to keep being strong." Theresa leaned her dark forehead to Sami's pale one and they both took a deep breath. "We're going to keep taking one step at a time."

Toby made a growling noise. "I have cancer; I'm not deaf."

Pulling away to look at Toby, Theresa said, "I'll bring in those candied nuts you like from the street vendors. And the smazeny smyr."

"Whatever." Toby shrugged, acting as if he didn't care. Smazeny smyr. Forget mozzarella cheese sticks. Here they took a whole rectangle of cheese and fried it. Served it with pommes frites. French fries. It sounded gross, but Toby craved the saltiness when he was on prednisone. By the end of the five days his face would be round and he'd be a big baby, angry and sad in uncontrollable tantrums. The worst part was that in the middle of a tantrum he knew he was being unreasonable, but he had no control over what he said or did. Toby thrust his hands into the pockets of his robe and looked out the window. The sun nestled into clouds of rose and purple. In the distance the Charles Bridge straddled the Vltava River.

"Theresa and I are going to get dinner. Will you be all right?"

Toby nodded. His mom had been with him all day. She needed a break. He understood that. He wanted a break too.

When the hospital door closed behind his mothers, Toby stepped closer to the window. In the gloam, the urban landscape had morphed from buildings, into mysterious shapes. Grit – rock against brick – scraped outside his seventh story window. Curious, Toby leaned his forehead against the cold glass to see better. No locks on windows this high; only solid panes.

Suddenly gray claws came into view and dug into the brick wall to find purchase. Wings the same shade smacked against the window.

Then a gray face, chiseled, filled the window. A feline face with carved nose, eyes, and whiskers. Wings pressed tightly to its back. Sharp teeth and a tongue that hung out in mid-pant. A statue. One of the creatures that decorated so many of Prague's ancient buildings.

"Come out," the gargoyle said. The voice sounded like it looked: coarse and solid.

Toby's hands trembled. "I don't know how."

"Yes, you do."

Toby placed his hands flat against the glass and pressed. His fingers spread and melted through the window. Toby gasped. The window surrounded his wrists, but his fingers wiggled in the chill autumn air. Marveling, Toby stretched his index finger to touch the gargoyle's foreleg. Stone. Yet, the stone moved as the gargoyle shook its leg, the way a horse might react to a tickling fly.

His stomach knotted with anxiety, Toby stepped forward – into the window. The moment lasted longer than it should have taken. Time to smell the glass, feel it melting around his body like warm plastic wrap. And then Toby stood on the narrow brick ledge outside the hospital window. His IV pole stood inside, abandoned, the tubing coiled on the floor.

"Climb on." The gargoyle shifted down the wall to present its back to Toby.

Toby's heart thumped as he looked down. "I can't move."

Still holding the wall, the gargoyle stretched out wide wings. "Hold on to my wings while you find your balance."

Toby grasped a wing first gingerly, but then with more confidence when he felt the stone instead of membrane. He threw his left leg across the creature's body and settled in the saddle area in back of its wings.

"Where are we going?"

"Wherever you want."

Toby didn't have to think. "Old Town. With the Tyn church."

"Grab hold."

The stone flesh emanated warmth from the day's sunshine as Toby pressed his face to the gargoyle's neck and wrapped his arms around. With a leap the gargoyle pushed off from the hospital wall and spread its wings. The night air had smells, real smells of car exhaust and trees and the meat on a stick that street vendors sold. Inside the hospital the only smell was disinfectant. The chemical smell of bleach on sheets and towels, the acrid smell of the solution used to mop the floors, the smell of the hand sanitizer used by everyone when they entered his room.

Toby gasped. His robe flapped in the wind. Tears formed in his eyes. *This is the best thing ever, so much better than an airplane.* Flying was freedom from gravity, from worry, from being sick. Within minutes Toby recognized Wencesles Square below with the statue of the saint on horseback right in front of the metro opening, the National Museum to the left. The same picture on the front of his Fodor's *Travel Guide.*

"What's your name?" Toby screamed through the wind.

"I have no name." The gargoyle folded its wings and shot through a narrow corridor between buildings and emerged into Old Town Square, alighting on a café roof across from the Astronomical Clock.

"But, don't you want a name?" Toby felt confused. Everything in his life was named, sorted. "I could give you one. Are you a boy or a girl?"

"I am the way I was carved. I do not need a name to make it so." Together they watched the elaborate clock gears shift. This was a popular tourist area. His mom and stepmom had brought him here, before he got sick, but the crowd had bunched so tightly he hadn't seen anything. Toby sighed with pleasure and absentmindedly rubbed the gargoyle between the shoulder blades.

The gargoyle tilted its head to the side. "Do you want to go higher?"

"Yes, but wait." He pointed. "What's that statue? The circle in the middle of the square over there?"

The gargoyle turned its feline face to follow Toby's pointing finger. The answer rumbled from a stone chest. "That's Jan Hus. He was betrayed and then burned at the stake. His words are on the bottom: *Love each other and wish the truth to everyone.*"

Rock muscles bunched and the gargoyle launched from the

café, swooping down toward the statue and then beating wings so that they landed on one of the dark gables of the Tyn church. Toby slid off and sat down on the roof. Up this high, he shivered in his robe and pressed against the gargoyle's leg.

"How old is this church?"

"As it looks now, 14th century. An older church was here before that." The gargoyle shrugged a massive shoulder. "BC."

Toby yelped. "Before Christ?"

"Before Carving." The gargoyle tilted his head. "I only know what I've seen."

"I get it." More questions poured through Toby's mind like when and why the gargoyle began moving around. More pressing though, "Where else can we go?"

"I have all night."

"What happens then?"

"I must be back in my place at St. Vitus before the sun comes up and you must be back in your place a moment before then."

Toby nodded. The gargoyle would return to the castle's cathedral and then turn back to stone. Which meant Toby would have to go back to the hospital. To the IV pole. To the prednisone. To his mothers' anxious faces.

"No, I won't go." Toby crossed his arms over his chest. "Leave me beside you. I'll hide in the castle and then, at dusk, we can travel again. We'll see the world every night."

"It doesn't work that way." The gargoyle didn't sound angry. "There are too many children in need."

Toby shook his head. "You don't understand what they do to me." He pulled up his shirt and turned his back to the gargoyle. Toby's fingers groped for the two pieces of medical tape that made up an "X" as if the spot on his lower back was a treasure map. "A needle injects me there. Again and again." He tapped the hard place in his chest. "The doctors put a plastic port inside my chest for the chemo. Feel it."

The gargoyle lowered its feline face and the stone whispered across flesh at Toby's chest.

"They don't even ask. That's the thing." Toby swallowed. His voice came out in a whisper. "The medicine makes my hair fall out. They make me look like a freak."

The gargoyle's eyelids blinked, particles crumbling down its face. "What is 'freak'?"

Angry, Toby waved an arm in the air. "You know. Different. Unwanted. Left out."

"Ah." The gargoyle nodded his head. Light glowed across the horizon promising that dawn would soon follow. "Then we are all freaks."

Toby looked across the rooftops of Prague and saw other hunched stone shapes with a child nestled beside each one. A flash of recognition came when he saw a shape on the nearby gable. This gargoyle looked like a man wearing a monk's cowl over his head with tongue hanging out, panting. It was easy to imagine the rainwater rushing out of the open mouth. A little girl sat next to him, her hand holding onto the gargoyle's. Her brown hair was in uneven pigtails and she wore a pajama top and pants that were too short. She looked up and said something in what Toby recognized as the strange vowels and hard sounds of the Czech language.

Translating, the feline gargoyle said, "'Every night I've waited for you to come. My family ignores me. For them, I do not exist. I'm so happy you finally came, but now I have nothing to look forward to.'" Her mouth quivered and she leaned into her gargoyle.

Toby frowned. His moms treated him like a baby, but they'd never ignored him. Even before his cancer was diagnosed, he'd been loved. An important member of the family. Sometimes he got in trouble, but was never ignored.

Perched on the astronomical clock, a gargoyle that looked like a bat sat with a boy who couldn't have been older than five or six.

"His house burned down last week," the feline gargoyle said. "He goes to live with his uncle in Moravia tomorrow. Tonight he went to look at his uncle's house."

Toby sighed, a heaviness filling his chest where the anger had sat. He pictured his mother's face and Theresa's. No, he couldn't hide in the castle. That was a coward's plan. And his moms would be sick with worry.

"I brought you from the hospital tonight, but you are still unhappy. I did not do enough."

Toby looked at the gargoyle, saw the grit tumbling down the cheeks. "You're crying. Because of me." Tenderly Toby wiped the gargoyle's cheeks and then threw his arms around the stone creature. "It's not your fault."

"Maybe there is time to visit one more place. Hurry."

Toby mounted and they winged away until the river came into sight. The Charles Bridge, seen earlier from the hospital window, looked different up close. The gargoyle landed. "There is a golden double cross on the railing in the middle of the bridge. If you put your hands on it and make a wish they say it will come true. Quickly. Before the sunrise."

Robe flapping in the wind, Toby leaned forward. Walking so quickly made him breathless. The crosses were easy to find, burnished from countless hands being placed for wishes. His lips moved with his words. A glance at the sky showed he didn't have much time.

The gargoyle launched as soon as Toby was on. The trip was brief and Toby eased through the stickiness of the window, turning to catch the speck in the sky that was his friend.

Hours later, Toby awoke to the sound of voices. His mom and Theresa and the doctor whispered together by the door.

"I'm awake," Toby called. He struggled to sit up, his body so tired. He swung his legs over the side and hung onto the bed's rail for balance as he got to his feet.

"Stay there," his mom said. She sounded alarmed.

"I'll get back in bed, if." Toby breathed hard. "You, all of you, come over here to talk. You have to include me."

His mom frowned. "Honey, you're sick—"

Toby fought for balance and then released the bed rail. He thrust his hands into his robe's pockets. Little somethings scratched his fingertips. Gargoyle tears.

"Yes, I am." Toby had to catch his breath. "But I'm old enough to know what's happening to my own body."

Sami's mouth quivered the way it did when she was about to cry, but her head nodded. She was agreeing. "You're right, Toby."

Theresa squeezed Sami's arm and then gave her a little push. Sami moved across the room and gave her son a gentle hug, making sure not to unbalance him.

Toby lowered himself to a seated position on the hospital bed. "And when the steroids are over, can we go up to the castle? I'd like to see the St. Vitus cathedral."

"I can drive you and your mom up there so you don't have to take the tram." Theresa still stood by the door. She folded her arms across her chest and swallowed. "I can stay in the car and read a book so I won't interrupt your time together."

Sami looked to the doctor. He said, "As long as Toby wears a mask to prevent germs from the crowds and keeps the visit short, that would be all right."

"All of us," Toby said. He met Theresa's eyes. "We'll all go."

The doctor and Theresa joined Sami beside the bed. Toby looked out the window and hoped that somewhere in Prague his wish was coming true and a family was seeing, really seeing a little girl with uneven pigtails and too-small pajamas.

Investigating the Sea-Hag Menace
CHERYL SONNIER

We all have our stories.

Children frighten one another with tales of women with wild silver hair and scaled skin, and webbed fingers and toes, who stand on jagged rocks and call up the sea to swallow those who displease them. Superstitious fishermen leave offerings outside caves in thanks for a good catch, or in hope that their boat will escape the sea-hag's wrath. Eyes wide with reverence and fear, they place their gifts and hurry away. When I try to ask them why, they shake their heads and turn their backs. Men and women from further inland laugh awkwardly when locals warn of their sea-hag, and forbid them not to disturb her rest. They are, however, careful to avoid her cave. Just in case.

Whispers, in homes and bars and at bus stops, suggest that these hags were once ordinary women. That they came from the land, called by the sea to guard our shores. Not from human invaders – the sea cares nothing for the borders it touches – but from those who would further harm nature's delicate balance. Who can forget last year's headlines? Damaged trawler nets all around the coastline. Oil rigs that mysteriously stopped working. And when the mob came together to drive the hags away from their caves, as they have always done, the mob drowned in sudden high tides.

Sometimes, on an empty beach, you will meet a man who stands forlorn outside a sea-hag's cave. I spoke to one of them.

"I want to catch a glimpse, see if it's her," he said. "I came home from work and my tea wasn't ready. The breakfast dishes were still in the sink. That was a month ago. I haven't seen her since. I need her to come home. I miss her."

In hushed conversations, where women come together, we ask one another how any one of us could turn into a sea-hag, how a being of comfort and compassion could grow as cold and cruel as the ocean herself. We reassure ourselves that it could never happen to us but in those moments when we are at our most honest, we look in the mirror and our eyes betray our fears.

I set out one morning with my notebook and camera, to ask the only people who know for sure: the sea-hags themselves. Many refused to speak to me at all, and none would speak on camera or be photographed, but some agreed to be interviewed. What follows is in their own words.

Sarah from Folkstone – 53

[Sarah is the first sea-hag to grant me an interview. I must admit to a trembling in my knees as I tread the pebbled sands towards her cave. If I incur her wrath, I may find my fate in the ocean's depths before the day is out. I take a gift of bread, as the fishermen do. Instead of leaving it outside and hurrying away, I hold it before me like a talisman and step inside her cave.

Sarah doesn't look like much of a sea-hag at first glance. Her nails are trimmed and filed, she wears a cozy dressing gown that covers her scaled body, and her silver hair is swept up into a bun that looks more unkempt librarian than wild hag. But her eyes flash with an inner storm when she speaks, and I can't help but wonder what brought her to this point. My voice has a tremor, but I ask her.]

Looking back, there were lots of things that could have nudged me towards the edge, but the final push was trivial. Alan came in from the kitchen to announce, with his usual fanfare, that he had done the dishes. Normally, I would have said, "Thanks, love," and carried on reading my book, but this time the words tumbled from my mouth before I had a chance to think them over.

"Want a medal?" I said. I put my hand over my mouth afterwards, that's how shocked I was.

Alan went from smug to affronted in the time it took for the blood to redden his cheeks. "I beg your pardon?"

At this point, I could have lied and said I was joking. But no. Something had changed and there was, I realized, no taking those words back.

"Look, love," I said. "Do I make an announcement every time

I wash the dishes, Hoover the carpet, clean the loo?" There was more, but I felt that listing every single chore I did that he ignored might be overkill.

"No, but—"

"But nothing, Alan. I work full time as well. I shouldn't have to give you a pat on the head every time you get off your arse and wash a few dishes."

Alan stood blinking at me for a moment – I don't think he'd ever heard me swear once in thirty years of marriage – and then he shook his head in that infuriating way he has that makes me feel like a naughty child who has disappointed him, and stomped off upstairs. I tried to go back to my book, but an itch began behind my left ear that soon grew to annoying proportions. I rubbed at the skin, which felt dry and in need of moisturizer. A piece flaked off and caught in my fingernail. When I held it up to the light, it shone with an odd, iridescent quality, like a dragonfly wing.

I didn't think much of it at the time. A bit of psoriasis perhaps? Dry skin brought on by menopause? I made a mental note to let the doctor have a look if it didn't clear up in a few days. It never did get better, though. I simply grew accustomed to my new moisturizing routine. Of course, that was only the start of it all. I know better now. [*Sarah turns her head and pulls her ear forward, revealing gills. I am both horrified and fascinated as they open and close*].

Katrina from Flamborough – 42

[*Katrina has embraced the sea-hag appearance, it seems; her white hair flows in thick, heavy curls and tangles over her tanned shoulders and down her back; her fingernails are long sharp claws, and she wears only a pale, translucent shift that she claims is made from the shed skins of sea serpents. The effect is stunning, and I find myself wondering what it would be like to stand so unabashed before the eyes of a stranger.*]

My change began the night our Anna came home from a pub crawl with her mates. She was sobbing her heart out, bless her, and clutching her coat together at the front. She wouldn't look at me at first.

"I didn't see him, Mam," she said. "He'd been hiding in the

doorway of the butchers on High Street. He jumped out and grabbed me, and before I knew what was happening, he'd shoved me against the wall and tore my frock open. I tried to fight him off, but he was too strong." She held a trembling hand over her face. "Mam, I was so scared."

I wrapped my arms around her and held her against me, and she buried her face in my neck the way she did when she was little. Hot tears soaked into the neck of my t-shirt as I held her tight, my fingers smoothing her hair until her sobs quietened into soft little hiccups.

"Did he…are you…" I didn't know how to ask the question, and dreaded the answer.

"No." She pulled away and rubbed at her eyes with her fists. "A taxi turned onto the street. The headlights lit us up and he went running off before…you know."

I knew all right. I closed my eyes and gave silent thanks to whoever was driving that car. At least she didn't have that particular memory to harrow her dreams, although the attempt would haunt her.

"Come on." I put my arm around her shoulder and led her into the kitchen. "I'll make us a cuppa and then we'll call the police." She sat on one of the stools at the breakfast bar while I got busy with the tea. As steam began to pour from the kettle's spout, rage boiled within me. How dare he, this bastard man, put his hands on my daughter? On anyone's daughter? How dare he frighten her, try to take away her choice of who she would and wouldn't share her body with? I wanted to kill him. No, I wanted to torture him. To make him feel the powerlessness that caused my beautiful lass to weep, even now she was safe at home with her mam.

At that moment, as I poured boiling water into the teapot, an itch came upon me so hard and fast that I had to set the kettle down and search the kitchen drawer for some cream. Perching on the stool next to Anna, I pulled off my shoes and socks and peered down at my toes.

"Ew, what's that?" Anna said, as I massaged cream into both

feet. The skin between my toes was reddened and flaky, raw in places. Why had I not noticed any of it that morning?

"I don't know," I said. "Athlete's foot, maybe? Whatever it is, it's doing my head in."

Of course, I know what it was now. *[At this point, Katrina holds up her left foot and wiggles her toes, which are connected by a fine web of iridescent skin. I can't help but smile at the sheer delight in her eyes. I wonder about what she's given up, left behind, and what will become of her daughter without her. Feeling brave in the face of her good humor, I ask.]*

Our Anna will be fine. She's strong and capable and if she ever needs me, she knows where I am. But she must find her own path. I hope it doesn't lead her here, of course. I want things to be better for her than they were for me. What mother doesn't? *[She turns from me then, and walks back into her cave, her mood changed. I am, I suspect, dismissed. I pack up my notebook and begin to climb the path that winds up around the cliffs towards the lighthouse, and wonder what kind of mother I would have been, given the chance.]*

Viv from Aberdeen – 65

[Viv wears no clothing at all. Her whole body is covered in small, pearlescent scales and her shortish hair stands out from her head in a luminous silvery nimbus.]

Eric left me on my sixtieth birthday. I'd known something was wrong for a while. We hadn't been intimate in more than a year. He'd said it was because he'd lost his libido, put it down to his age; he's sixty-five. It seemed like he'd lost his ability to show affection too, because I couldn't remember the last time he kissed me goodnight, or hugged me, or even reached for my hand when we were watching a film. All those nights he'd be shut in his study. Working, he said. Turns out he was actually chatting online to Sally, aged thirty-five, whose hair had not gone white and whose body bore no marks of motherhood. I asked him what a thirty-five-year-old in her prime found interesting about a man with no libido who was old enough to be her da. He didn't like that at all.

He said, "For your information, I do have a libido, just not where you're concerned. Look at yourself, woman. You don't even bother to dye your hair anymore, your boobs sag, and your idea of getting dolled up for a night out is putting on your good jeans. It wouldn't be so bad if you at least tried to look sexy now and then."

That's when the itching started.

"Oh yes?" I said, trying desperately not to rake my nails across my belly. "Have you looked in the mirror, lately? You're not exactly a picture o' youth with your pot belly and your bald spot."

He flinched at that, and pulled down the bottom of his t-shirt. I hardened my heart against the hurt in his eyes. The truth was, and this cut deepest of all, as his body changed with age I had continued to love and want him as he was, moobs and pot belly and all. Of course, things were different than in our youth – it had been a long time since a mere flirty look from his twinkly blue eyes had made me want to drag him off to bed right then and there – but given the right mood I still fancied him as much as I always had.

I ran upstairs and locked the bathroom door and turned to my reflection in the mirror above the sink. My hair wasn't that bad, was it? A wee bit wild perhaps – the white hairs were thicker, coarser – but I kind of enjoyed the way it kinked and waved around my face. My complexion wasn't bad, I thought. Yes, there were lines and crow's feet but no more than he had collected over the years.

The itch reminded me of its presence, and I unbuttoned my blouse to find my belly all red and scaly. Not just flaky skin but actual scales. They shone like mother of pearl on the inside of a shell and as I smoothed the cream over them it felt as though my skin was covered in sequins. My breasts hung down over the scales, and I remembered how disgusted Alan had looked when he spoke of them. These breasts that fed and nurtured three babbies, only to be dismissed as old and saggy by a man who had no more use for them. They were a part of me. Why couldn't they be good enough for him? Why couldn't I be good enough?

Now, I don't care. I think they're magnificent. Don't you? *[Viv places her hands on her breasts, which are covered in the same blue-green pearlescent scales as those on her torso. They catch the sunlight as she moves and are, I agree, magnificent. I wonder what the scars from my mastectomy would look like, covered in those glimmering scales, and whether Tim would be able to look at them without pity clouding his eyes.]*

Mina from Heysham – age unknown

[Mina sounds like a girl in her teens but refuses to give me her age. She wears a full body swimsuit and face covering to sit in the ruins of an old chapel, and to any passer-by does not look any different to any other devout woman of her faith enjoying the scenery. To prove her authenticity as a sea-hag, she shows me the scales on the back of her hand, and her long, claw-like fingernails.]

It was a shock, yeah? You only hear about it happening to older women. Although I think there are more younger ones appearing now. My mum and dad are heartbroken. They wanted so much for me, you know? College, a good career, family, everything. And what do they get? A daughter who looks like a monster from an old science fiction B-movie. They come and see me sometimes, bring me things, home cooking and books. I keep the face-covering on, so they don't have to see how bad it's got now. I think they believe that maybe it's just a rash and, when it's gone, I can go back to being their little girl again. It's not going to go away, though, is it?

At first, I thought it was a punishment for losing my temper. Mum and Dad always told me, "Ignore them. They're just trying to get you to react. Don't give them the satisfaction." And I'd try, yeah? I'd pick up my books when they knocked them out of my hands. I'd put my hijab straight after they tugged it crooked. I learned not to take it personally when they called me names. Their behavior is on them, not a reflection of me. That's what I'd tell myself. But it gets to you, after a while. You get so sick of it all that you can't ignore them any longer.

It wasn't that bad. What I did, I mean. It's not like any of them were physically hurt. I just filmed three girls yapping at me and calling me names, and put it on social media. It went viral. One of them got expelled and the other two were suspended for a month each. Some people stopped talking to them but mostly that was it. Nobody cared after it died down.

When it first happened, the scales I mean, I thought that was

34

my consequence for shaming them. How bad is that? Now I know better. Me. These women. We are the consequences. I try to tell Mum and Dad that, but they don't understand.

My favorite part is the lightning. Shall I show you? *[Mina's eyes spark as she points to a large stone jutting out near the entrance to the ruins. When I nod, she closes her eyes and I watch with stilled breath. I'm not sure how she does it, but it looks as though she pulls a bolt of lightning from the air and aims it at the rock. A flash, a crack, the smell of ozone and a piece the size of my hand breaks off and falls to pieces on the rocks below. I applaud, and imagine the crackle of electricity in my own fingertips. Though I can see only her eyes, I feel Mina's grin and can't help but return it.]*

Impressive, eh? And that's only a bit of it. Takes a lot out of me though, bringing up a storm at sea. You should see us when we all get together though. There are a few people I'd like use it on, but I won't. It's tempting, but that's not what it's for. There's so much more at stake. We have to save her. *[Mina shifts her gaze to the horizon, as though listening to something. I sense that my time is up and, thanking her, I leave. She smiles but doesn't answer or look my way.]*

Beth from Cardiff – 24

[Beth is perhaps the most comfortable in her new skin. When she grins, she allows her sharp teeth, reminiscent of a shark's, to show. She grins a lot. I am mesmerized.]

I was working for a housing charity when it first started. You know, one of the big ones with offices and call centers all over the country. Big enough to afford ads on the telly. Anyway, I was sitting in the boardroom taking notes in one of their meetings. All they seemed to do was have meetings; they even had meetings to discuss other meetings. One of the executive team started talking about single mothers. She said it was funny how they couldn't afford to pay their rent but were quite happy to pay predatory interest rates to buy their kids a video game console for Christmas.

"But we mustn't judge," she said, with one of those self-satisfied little smiles they always have when they're talking about us plebs.

"I know," one of her henchmen chimed in. "There's a mother at my daughter's school who claims every benefit going. Free school meals, housing benefit, council tax benefit. You name it, she gets it. Last week she dropped her daughter off at school wearing the same trainers as my kid. How can she afford those when I barely can, and I work for a living?"

"Perhaps she works, too," a small voice said.

Mine, I realized. I had done that thing where I would speak my thoughts aloud. Something I tried to avoid at work.

"Don't be ridiculous," the boss said. "People like her don't work. She probably got pregnant the minute she left school. I bet she's never had a job."

"My mum does," I said, a little more loudly than my first remark. "She works full time and still has to claim housing benefit because she doesn't get paid enough to cover the full rent. She scrimps and saves and goes without to buy my little sister the expensive trainers, so that your kids won't pick on her for being poor."

"Wait a minute," another henchman said. "Doesn't your mother work here, in our call center?"

This time, I let my face speak for me. He abruptly found his notebook fascinating.

You'd think at this point they would have realized that since the daughter of one of the objects of their derision was sitting right in front of them, they should maybe have changed the subject and been more charitable. But no, big boss doubled down.

She gave me another of those smiles. "I'm sure there are some exceptions, like your mum. And she saved up for the trainers, didn't she? That's great. You should be proud of her. But there are lots more out there who know how to game the system and they get themselves into piles of debt rather than save up."

"Game the system?" At this point, I had stopped caring about the looks they were giving me. "The system only works for people like you. You sit here in your designer suits and judge the people you're supposed to be helping. Meanwhile, you use your executive salaries to gobble up cheap housing and rent it out for three times what it's worth to people like my mum, who can't get on the mortgage ladder because she works full time for little more than minimum wage."

I stopped talking at this point because I'd run out of breath, and the room had gone deathly quiet. Everyone except the boss was looking down at their laptop, or their phone. Anywhere but at me, or her. She had gone this deep shade of pink and she clutched her pencil so hard that there was an audible snap when it broke.

"Actually," she said, in this calm, detached voice. "Actually, Beth, I don't think we need you for this meeting. In fact, you're looking a bit peaky. Perhaps you're coming down with something. You should go home and do something about that unsightly rash on your cheeks. No, leave your laptop here. I'll make sure it gets put away properly."

I picked up my things and rushed out of the room before my mouth could get me in any more trouble. In the toilets, I checked out the rash she mentioned and found both cheeks covered in flaky, dead skin. Underneath the flakes, shimmers of blue. I was horrified. I'd always had such a good complexion. I put on my coat, wrapped my scarf around my face to hide the rash, and rode the bus home.

Later the same day someone from HR called and said that due to my 'outburst,' it would be in everyone's best interests if I sought employment elsewhere. They gave me a month's pay in lieu of notice. Probably for the best.

I'd already started to transform. *[At this point Beth runs her long, clawed fingers over the scaled cerulean ridges that follow her cheekbones and up around the edges of her ears. I'm captivated by the sheen. "You should stay with us. Become one of us," her feral smile seems to say, and I have to admit, I am tempted. I think of my boss and the way he looks at me sometimes, as though I'm only there under sufferance, because he has to keep at least one woman journalist on staff for the sake of 'political correctness.' I think of the way he says those words, 'political correctness,' as though their taste disgusts him. Yes, I am tempted.]*

Bernadette from Scarborough – 38

[From my research, I learned that Bernadette was the first to succumb to what many now call the 'sea-hag menace.' She is certainly the least human-looking of the women I've spoken with; even her eyes have changed, the pupils

slitted, the irises and whites combined into reflective yellow orbs. Her alien appearance in parallel with her stature and confident manner, is both beautiful and frightening.]

Someone had to do something, didn't they? Have you seen what washes up on the shore these days? When I was young, we found shells and crabs and little fish in these rock pools. These days you're more likely to find plastic straws and used johnnies. One time, I came down here and found a hermit crab, and do you know what it was using for its house? A doll's head. No, I'm not kidding. How messed up is that? Made me proper furious.

I knew this woman. She was a mystic or some such. I mean she knew all the old stuff, from before men took charge, you know what I mean? Call them witches, hags, whatever you will but they could do things. Big things, like change the weather, heal the sick, make the land fertile. Before the Romans came and put men in charge, these women were a big deal. You get me?

This woman, she knew all that ancient stuff and more, and we got to talking about how, if only us women were in charge, we'd put a stop to all this plastic waste, and those huge mega-trawlers, and burning fossils for fuel, and all that. And she said, "I think we can do something about that." *[At this point Bernadette grows silent, staring out to sea as though searching for something. After a while, she seems to forget I'm there. I ask her, "And what was that?" and, startled, she turns back to me.]*

I don't exactly know what she did. I mean, obviously she did something, right? Because look at me. I woke up the next morning and I had this terrible, scaly rash everywhere. Scared the hell out of me, I don't mind telling you. I went round to her flat to ask for some kind of salve – she was good with home-made ointments and cough syrups and stuff like that – but she was gone. Everything. Her furniture, her books, her cats. All gone. I asked the woman in the flat next door what happened to her and she said the flat had been empty for months. Strange business. Very strange.

I eventually reached a point where I couldn't go out in public without wrapping myself up in heavy clothes and gloves, and a hoodie. And even then, once my eyes went like this, I had to resort to dark glasses. I'd still come down here though, do my litter picking around the rock pools. I couldn't go to work, so I eventually lost my job. Lost my flat, everything. That's when I decided to move into the cave.

Sometimes, when I look out to sea, I fancy I can feel her close by. I never see her, but every time I get that feeling, I see the minke whales cresting the surface of the water way out there. Funny that. I only ever notice them when I'm thinking of her. *[At this point, Bernadette catches sight of a large mega-trawler off the coast. Without a word, she runs to the edge of the water. From my place amongst the rock pools, it looks as though her brown skin is covered in pearls and gems that sparkle as she moves. As she runs into the water and begins to swim, several more women join her from the various caves and alcoves along the shore. They swim towards the trawler. At the same moment, several whale tails break the surface close by.]*

I travelled back to London by train and used the time to write up my interview notes. Two different men, at two different stretches of the journey, told me to smile. A third stood close enough for me to feel his breath hot on my ear as we waited to disembark at St. Pancras. I found my thoughts drifting back to Mina and her lightning. I wouldn't need much, just enough to make him stop pressing his erection against my thigh.

I went out amongst the sea-hags to try to learn how the phenomenon began and found my answer everywhere and in everything. My editor, Andrew, refused to publish this article because he felt it was too damning towards men.

"It's not all men," he said.

Andrew was disappointed that I had failed to bring back pictures of the sea-hags to go with their words. He reassigned the article to John, a twenty-two-year-old intern, who said he would talk to them and persuade them to let him take their pictures. John believes himself irresistible. John is in for a revelation.

Tomorrow morning, through the fog of hangover, Andrew will learn that he underestimated me. Perhaps he should have decided against after-work drinks with the boys, leaving me alone in the office on the night the magazine goes to print. Perhaps he thinks I'm not smart enough to add a few pages.

An itch begins to burn, deep beneath my skin. I hear her call. I know what must be done.

Perhaps we should not ask ourselves how a woman becomes a sea-hag, but rather the opposite: how do we not?

We all have our stories.

Stitches
B C FONTAINE

My father ran away the day I was born. Never even bothered to name me.

I spent years searching for him, for the certainty of self that only family can bring. When I realized there was none to be had, I mourned him for years more.

Finally, I realized that if I couldn't escape his legacy, the least I could do was improve it. I wanted to have a better impact on the world than he did, a better impact on the next generation.

I started a business making and repairing toys. It comes naturally to me. I inherited, somehow, his surgical precision. He'd given me gentle hands.

Now, a little girl beams up at me as I hand her a newly-mended teddy bear. It means more to me than his approval ever could. "Thank you, Mr Frankenstein."

I smile back. "Please, call me Prometheus."

Slide
KAITEE YAEKO TREDWAY

Kiku clutched her baseball glove against the handle of her family's food cart. She thought her greenish skin looked weird against the oiled leather, but she quickly pushed that away. Instead, she reminded herself how right it felt to have the glove on her hand. Every step brought her closer to the park, every minute closer to sometime-after-lunch. Today could change her summer.

Her mom said something, but Kiku hadn't been listening. "Huh?"

Rather than repeat herself, Mom just laughed and reached out to pat the braid atop Kiku's head.

"Mom!" Kiku jerked away from her so violently that she nearly sent herself and her cart toppling. She could feel the water sloshing around in her *sara*, the little divot at the crown of her skull. Kiku stilled immediately to let the water settle.

All kappas had a *sara*. Mom disguised her *sara* beneath layers of blue-black hair, thrown over her head in a side part. Dad wore a baseball cap. At school, Kiku had relied on wide headbands and hoodies, but not today. A thick braid coiled around the edge of Kiku's *sara*. She ran her fingers along the braid and checked the rest of her hair. Dry. No water had spilled. The braid had done its job. Kiku rolled her eyes at herself. Of course it had. She'd have known if it hadn't, since she wouldn't have been able to move if even a single drop of water had spilled.

As Kiku fussed over her head, Mom exhaled, nostrils flaring gracefully. Everything about Mom was elegant. With her high, wide cheekbones and aqua-tinted skin, Kiku thought her mom could be a TV star. Or, if not the star, one of the other main actors. There was always one not-quite-human on a show, and Mom was prettier than all of them. Kiku had inherited her Mom's blue-black hair and cheekbones but not her aqua skin. Nor did she share her dad's rich, olive coloring. To her lasting dismay, Kiku's skin was the pale green of faded cucumbers. Definitely not made for TV, but maybe made for baseball.

Impatient, Kiku surged ahead, wanting time to move faster. They would set up the *kappa maki* carts just in time for lunch, and she would help Mom until the baseball game started. And then, instead of just watching like normal, Kiku would bring her glove over to the field. She would ask to play. She swallowed, her stomach bubbling with uneasy excitement. If she didn't lose her nerve.

These pickup games in the park had started as soon as the weather had warmed up. The games had been on Saturdays while school was still in session, but it had always been a race to stake out the field. As soon as summer vacation hit, the newest class of eighth graders had shifted their baseball game to Thursday afternoons.

Mom caught up with her. "I watched you practice this morning. You've gotten very good at keeping your head upright. Maybe just don't sl– " Their clattering carts filled the silence as Kiku clenched her teeth against what might come next. Mom squeezed Kiku's shoulder when they reached the picnic area. "Never mind. You'll be great."

Nodding carefully, Kiku rolled her cart into place, making sure she had a good view of the baseball field. She'd wistfully watched her classmates play week after week, never feeling like she could go over. Though she recognized a couple of the kids from homeroom and the rest from the cafeteria, she didn't remember any of their names. Her family had moved to town in the middle of the school year. New place. New people. It had been easier to keep to herself. Pulling long sleeves down over her ghostly green hands and a hood over her *sara,* she'd just waited for the school year to end.

Now, Kiku wished she had made one acquaintance, that there was one person who could invite her to play. The thing she liked best about these baseball games was that it never seemed to be about who won. Home runs or miraculously-caught fly balls drew cheers from both teams. Everyone went home grass stained and laughing. They played for the love of it rather than to win. Kiku desperately wanted to play, but her *sara* complicated things.

She'd learned the dangers of nodding her head too enthusiastically early. A nod could send water splashing out of her *sara*, and as soon as that happened, every part of her body would freeze. All Kiku could do then was blink until someone refilled it. She did her best to move carefully, not wanting the embarrassment of immobilizing herself at school or the grocery store. Running, jumping, fielding a baseball...none of that was easy for a kappa.

Even now, Kiku kept her head steady as she fussed with the cart's awning. A part of her screamed that she needed to be more careful. Another part insisted that there was no time for 'careful' in baseball.

She'd known that if she wanted to play, she had to learn how to run without spilling her *sara*. She'd started by walking briskly between four makeshift 'bases' in the yard. She'd made a lot of mistakes at first, sloshing water out of her *sara*. She'd freeze until one of her parents came out to refill it, and then she'd try again. Kiku had learned to move steadier and faster, until she was sprinting around the bases without losing a drop of water. She'd spent her allowance on a baseball glove, and to Dad's dismay, turned the side of the house into her teammate. Kiku's practices fell into a steady rhythm. Throw the ball against the house. Catch the rebound, or let the ball roll. Squat. Scoop it up from the grass. Shift. Wind up. Release. Catch the ball. Again and again. After weeks of practice, Kiku could do everything a baseball player needed to do without spilling her *sara*. Everything but slide into a base. Feet first, hands first, it didn't matter. Sliding always ended the same way.

The edge of the "Kappa's Kappa Maki" banner chaffed Kiku's sore palms as she started to fasten it to the front of the carts. Her hands stung from this morning's attempt at sliding. She'd made a dive for second base, sure that this new head position would work. It hadn't. Water sloshed down her face like always. Frozen, Kiku hadn't been able stop herself as momentum slammed her into a tree. Whatever. She just wouldn't try to slide.

As soon as she fastened the banner, Kiku's gaze darted frantically around the picnic area. Only one other vendor had arrived. All the tables were empty. Sweat dripped between her shoulder blades and down the backs of her knees. Sometimes, when it was this hot, people stayed inside. They didn't come to the park. She gulped. No, that wouldn't be today. The game would happen. It always happened.

Kiku kept her eyes on the tables as she finished setting up, hoping to see some of the early birds: the red-haired pitcher, or the twins with springy, black curls who always played in skirts. She sighed, wrestling the menu stand into place. The unwieldy thing felt like overkill for a food cart with a two-item long menu:

Kappa Maki (Cucumber Roll)
NEW: Cucumber Ice Cream

The cucumber ice cream wasn't exactly new any more, but Kiku liked that her bubble letters were still on the menu. She'd drawn them carefully a couple of weeks into summer vacation, hoping the bright, big letters would catch people's attention.

They had.

None of the kids had ever come to the cart on Baseball Day. They always made a bee-line for the field, and Kiku couldn't blame them. She wouldn't be interested in sushi if there was baseball to play. Halfway through the game, when Mom had gone for a walk, someone said, "Hey, can I get one of those ice cream things?"

Lost in the game, Kiku hadn't turned around right away. One of the twins was sprinting towards third base, and the centerfielder had just scooped up the ball. She didn't want to miss what happened, but she also didn't want Mom to scold her for ignoring a customer. Trying not to groan, Kiku turned away from the game and reached into the freezer. "Three dollars, please."

When she exchanged the ice cream cup for a five-dollar bill, Kiku finally looked at the customer and nearly choked. It was Captain Shortstop. At least, that's what Kiku called her.

Captain Shortstop was one of the best infielders. She was always easy to spot in her neon-colored shirts. Today, a vivid magenta glowed against her copper skin. When Kiku handed back the change, Captain Shortstop smiled at her. It was a bright, excellent thing, all the more excellent for the gap between her two front teeth.

The girl grabbed a plastic spoon and tossed the lid into the nearest trash can. "You ever thought about getting those wooden stick things?" she asked, pointing the spoon at Kiku.

Kiku could only manage to shake her head.

"Bamboo utensils would work too." Captain Shortstop took a bite of ice cream, continuing to talk around the spoon. "They're way better for the environment. This is good!" She looked at Kiku intensely, eyes squinting as though she was trying to remember something. "Your hair is different than it was in school."

Kiku nodded, stunned that anyone would notice. The idea for the braid had come when she'd started to dream of joining the baseball games. As soon as summer vacation started, she'd done her hair like this every day. Just in case.

Captain Shortstop flashed her another smile. "Looks super cool. See ya!"

Tucking the menu awkwardly under her arm, Kiku checked her phone. 11:03. Not even close to lunch time. Mom banged a large, cloth-covered bowl onto one of the carts. The smell of sweet, vinegary rice punched into the air. Out came the bamboo rolling mats, the shiny sheets of *nori*, the wooden rice paddles, and the crate of cucumbers.

Mom tapped a knife on a cutting board to get her attention. "Do you want to roll or slice?"

"Huh?"

Mom just tapped the knife again.

"Slice." She didn't like the way the rice smooshed against the food-service gloves. Things got sticky. The *nori* would rip. She'd have to start over. It was frustrating. She didn't want to be frustrated today. Kiku finished setting up the menu, then placed her baseball mitt conspicuously at her feet. She shoved her hands into some nitrile gloves and started slicing the cucumbers into long strips.

As Kiku fell into a rhythm, her thoughts drifted. Ever since

Captain Shortstop had bought that first ice cream, some of the kids had started stopping by the cart on Baseball Day. So much so that Mom stocked extra ice cream on Thursdays. Captain Shortstop always came with her best friend, a girl Kiku had dubbed Slider McGee. Slider McGee had earned her name by sliding into bases with amazing speed, even when it wasn't necessary. Kiku felt very short and ghoulish next to Slider's long limbs and deep brown skin. The girl wore her hair in rows and rows of braids, bright blue ribbons twisting through them. Inspired, Kiku had incorporated an aqua ribbon into her *sara* braid a few weeks ago.

"I like the ribbon!" Slider had called, jogging over.

"Got the idea from you." Kiku's cheeks burned as she handed Slider the ice cream.

"Hey, how do you get yours to do that? To just, like, stay on top of your head?" Slider rose onto her tip toes and leaned forward, trying to get a closer look. "Is it bobby pins, or hair gel, or what?" Afraid that the other girl might catch a glimpse of her *sara*, Kiku stepped back quickly, stammering an answer about pins and practice. Slider tossed her braids over her shoulder. "I think I'll stick with mine."

The braids smacked Captain in the face. "Watch it!" The two friends bickered good-naturedly before waving to Kiku and wandering off. Something tugged underneath her ribs. She wanted to know someone that well.

The knife quivered as Kiku's fingers vibrated with nerves. A glance at her mismatched cucumber spears didn't help her churning stomach. Mom wouldn't be happy with these. Kiku shucked off her slimy gloves and put on another pair, stretching out her fingers. She just needed to concentrate on cutting the cucumbers for the *kappa maki*. Nothing else.

Captain Shortstop and Slider McGee had ordered the *kappa maki* once. Kiku had nearly gnawed through her lip waiting for their reaction. She hadn't known how to interpret Captain's wide, surprised eyes.

Swallowing, Captain had shouted, "How did I not know about

this? It's so good!" Slider popped another piece into her mouth, nodding in agreement.

Heart pounding, Kiku pushed some packets of wasabi towards them. "Do you like spicy stuff?"

Captain dipped her sushi into the mix of wasabi and soy sauce Kiku made. She immediately started snorting and fanning the air in front of her face. "It's in my nose! Nope! Nope!"

"Wimp!" Slider laughed at her friend. Turning to Kiku, she asked, "Can I have another one those? I'm gonna make my brother try some. He *hates* spicy things."

Kiku smiled, remembering these small chats. To her surprise, the girls had started to stop by the cart multiple times a week for ice cream. It was easier to talk to them now. As she sliced through her third cucumber, Kiku rehearsed what she might say to them later.

Hey, the baseball games seem like a lot of fun. You guys are really good. Is it okay if I come watch?

So, if you guys ever need another person to round things out for the game, I kinda play. I have my own glove. But, no worries if you don't.

You know, I really love baseball. So, like, if you ever need an extra person, I'm around.

Hey, can I play with you guys?

Courage and doubt bubbled in her chest. Her hand started to shake harder. Eventually, Kiku had to put down the knife. Maybe it was too much. Maybe she shouldn't do this.

"Why don't you roll?" Mom asked.

"I'm fine."

"How will you play if you slice through your finger?"

"But– "

"Kiku."

She stomped over to the *maki*-making station and pulled on a clean pair of gloves. Kiku smushed the rice onto the *nori* in frustration. She had a stomach ache now, and the fact that her first two rolls looked awful made her feel worse.

Kiku saw someone approach the cart out of the corner of her

eye. She looked up hopefully. It was just a dad and his son. The little boy immediately reached for the container of spoons at the front of the counter.

Two days ago, Captain Shortstop had whooped with excitement when she'd seen that same container. "You got the bamboo ones!" she'd shouted.

"Yeah, I finally convinced my dad."

Captain leaned over the cart, all of her teeth – and somehow the space between the front two – gleaming in a delighted smile. She thrust out her hand. "I'm Tess."

"Kiku," she said, shyly taking the girl's hand.

"Nice to officially meet you Kiku." Kiku hoped Tess couldn't feel how hard her heart pounded as they shook hands. "This is Marin."

The other girl waved, sweeping her blue braids over her shoulder, matching beads clacking. "It's dumb we didn't introduce ourselves sooner."

"Super dumb," Tess agreed. "Don't know *what* we were thinking!" As she threw her hands up in exasperation, Tess's elbow sent the container flying. Bamboo spoons scattered all over the pavement.

"Shit, I'm sorry!" The two girls bent and immediately began picking up the spoons.

Kiku started to tell them not to worry, but the words didn't come. She stared at the top of Tess's head. Two tiny horns poked out from the girl's dark hair. Kiku's hand strayed to her *sara* as she inspected her own green-tinged skin. Could Tess be one too? Not a kappa, but something else? She glanced at Marin's head. No horns, and the two were friends anyways.

"I'm so sorry about that," Tess said, holding out the recovered spoons. Kiku quickly rearranged her face, hoping that her shock didn't show. "I talk with my hands. Do you mind if I take these home? We have, like, a super composter. Does more than just banana peels, you know? It's better than just trashing them." Tess smiled, confident as usual. She didn't seem the least bit concerned that Kiku might have seen her horns.

Kiku nodded. Marin rolled her eyes as Tess dumped the spoons into her bag. "You and the environment."

"Sustainability is important. We've only got one planet." Tess smiled at Kiku again as she exchanged six dollars for two ice creams. "Super cool that you got your dad to switch. Thanks, Kiku!"

"See you later!" Marin said, breaking into a sprint towards the parking lot. "Race you, Tee!"

"Bye," Kiku said softly. If Tess wasn't quite human and could play with the other kids, that meant *she* could play too, right?

Right.

"We don't want you to make a big mess." The dad's voice jolted Kiku out of her thoughts. She watched him push the spoons just out of his son's reach. Would she make a mess of things? She didn't want to ruin these moments at the cart with Tess and Marin by asking to join the game. Maybe she should just keep things the way they were.

After the dad walked away with sushi and ice cream, Mom started to slice Kiku's sloppy *maki*. As soon as the knife pressed down on the *nori*, the roll fell apart. No perfect cylinders with cucumber nestled in the center. Just a mess of rice splatted across the cutting board.

"I'll be more careful," Kiku muttered, shrinking underneath Mom's disappointed glance. How many other things would she mess up today?

She focused on making *maki* for the next two hours, trying to distract herself from each minute the clock ticked past noon. Carefully spread the rice. Line up the cucumber. Guide the end of the *nori* and rice over the vegetable. Roll. Seal the edge with water. Grab a new sheet of *nori*. Start again. Sweat rolled down her temples, and the park remained empty. No kids. No one sprinting towards the baseball field. Nothing. Kiku continued to work, making more sushi than they could possibly sell on a quiet afternoon.

By 1:13, rolling *maki* wasn't enough to distract her. She snuck an ice cream and started pacing behind the cart. Clamping a bamboo spoon between her teeth, Kiku tried to convince herself that the lump of ice in her stomach was just the ice cream and not the certainty that the game wasn't going to happen. They were all just running late. Very, very late.

"Why don't you go for a walk?" Mom asked. "I'll text you if anyone shows up."

If. That one word cut through Kiku's hope. She deflated. She didn't even try to stop Mom from touching her braid. Mom's voice grew gentle. "There's always next week."

But she didn't know if she could keep her courage until next week. Kiku grabbed her baseball glove and trudged off in the opposite direction from the empty field. Her steps grew heavy as she wandered, and she could hear the water sloshing around in her *sara*. The game wasn't happening today.

Despite her intentions, she walked in a big circle and found herself standing in the empty outfield. The air was still sticky, but it felt a little cooler now that the height of the afternoon had passed. Kiku kicked at the grass as she wandered towards second base. Once she stepped onto the plate, energy surged into her. Without a thought, she took off, sprinting around the bases just like she'd practiced. Not a drop of water splashed out of her *sara*. Kiku dropped her glove somewhere between third and home as she imagined that she was stealing base after base after base.

After a few laps around the infield, the churning in her stomach eased up. Her nerves couldn't thrum as violently while her heart was pumping. Kiku retrieved her baseball glove, relishing the feel of the sun-warmed leather. A thrill raced up her arm. Even though she was alone on the field, happiness settled over the disappointment.

Kiku jogged towards the backstop. She thought she'd seen... yes! Scooping up the abandoned baseball, she pranced backwards, throwing it against the chain-link fence. The ball bounced back, and she caught it easily, letting the familiar rhythm take over. Throw the ball. Run. Catch. Shift. Throw again. Let the ball roll. Scoop it up. Wind up. Send the ball sailing over home base. Again and again and again, not a drop of water spilling from her *sara*.

She lobbed the ball so hard that it bounced back higher and farther than she expected. Kiku sprinted for it, glove outstretched. It fell just out of her reach.

"You almost got that!" a bright, familiar voice called. Kiku spun towards it, embarrassment freezing her bones. Her *sara* sloshed dangerously.

Tess jogged towards her, glove pressed against a neon green shirt. She tossed the ball back to Kiku. Luckily, muscle memory took over, and Kiku plucked it out of the air before it hit her in the chest. She concentrated on the feel of the ball in her palm, the familiar shape of the leather glove around her fingers. "Yeah," she said, not having breath for anything more.

"Dude, you're fast." Marin came up next to Tess. Kiku glanced over their shoulders. The rest of the baseball crew was gathered around a big cooler.

"I thought maybe you weren't coming today," Kiku said.

Tess rolled her eyes and threw up her hands. "We all had to convince our parents that we wouldn't get sunstroke or heatstroke or anything. My mom made us wait until she could go to the store for ice and water and stuff." She smacked Kiku's shoulder with her glove. "Why didn't you tell us you played?"

Kiku just shrugged, voice barely working. "Dunno."

"You wanna?" Marin asked. That question pushed all the air out of Kiku's lungs. "You can be on my team."

"Nuh-uh, my team. I'm missing an outfielder." Tess beamed at her. "How do you feel about playing left field?"

"Yeah." Kiku smiled tentatively back. "Left field sounds good."

Playing in the game was better than Kiku could have dreamed. Barry, the red-haired boy, had a tendency to pop fly balls out in her direction. While she couldn't catch all of them, she caught a few. She even managed to throw the ball to third fast enough for Laila, one of the twins, to tag out the runner trying to steal a base. Her heart fluttered happily whenever the other kids whooped her name.

The game was pretty evenly matched. Being in the midst of it, Kiku could see why Tess and Marin didn't play on the same team. It would just be unfair. Once, over a water break, Barry jostled her with an elbow. "Where've you been hiding? You're giving Marin and Tess a run for their money." He jogged away, leaving her speechless.

It felt like it had to be a joke, but one of the twins had overheard. Laila, or Reyna – she couldn't tell – said, "Totally agree with Barry. Glad you're on my team." Laila, then.

"Thanks," Kiku managed. "I'm…I'm just having fun."

"It's the best, isn't it?"

Then Tess was calling them back. "Only two more innings cause we started late!" Laila grinned at Kiku. Kiku grinned back, and together, they sprinted into the outfield.

Kiku's team was the last up to bat. They were down by two points when she approached home plate. She hadn't been able to practice hitting the ball as much as fielding it, so she'd fouled or struck out most of the game. With a record like that, she had no idea how she had ended up being the final person at bat. It should have been Tess, but Tess was on second base. Really, it should be anyone else but her.

"You've got this Kiku!" Tess shouted, bouncing up and down on her toes, ready to run.

Laila gave her a thumbs up from third base, also poised to run. All Kiku had to do was hit the ball hard enough to give Tess and Laila a chance to cross home base. That would tie the game up. Would a tie be good enough? Did winning really not matter? If she struck out, would Tess regret inviting her to play? She didn't know.

Tightening her grip, Kiku made eye contact with Barry. She raised the bat into place and watched him wind up. Tracking the ball as best she could, she swung. The ball thudded into Reyna's catcher's mitt. Strike.

"It's okay!" Tess called. "It's just the first one!"

Kiku let out a long breath and reset. Barry threw the ball. Crack! It sailed out past the third base line. Strike.

"You got this Kiku!" Marin called from her position out in center field. Anxiety pulled at Kiku's throat. She felt ready to cry, but she swallowed it, tapping the end of the bat on the plate. She could do this.

Barry pitched. She swung hard. Crack! The ball flew over the third base line again. Foul ball. She sighed dejectedly. "Not a strike!" Laila called. "You can't foul out with two strikes!"

Kiku nodded. One more chance. She closed her eyes, willing her heart to settle. She remembered the rhythm of practicing. Throw. Catch. Again. She could do this. Kiku lifted her bat, nodding. She kept her eyes on Barry. Wind up. Release. Follow the arc. Deep breath. Swing.

Crack!

The ball sailed over Marin's head. The girl sprinted after it, braids streaming behind her. Kiku stared until someone shouted, "RUN!" So she did.

Her foot hit first base. She curved sharply, aiming for second. The water in her *sara* sloshed dangerously on the turn. Kiku steadied her head and sprinted on. Laila jumped onto home plate, arms raised in victory. Arms pumping, Kiku passed second base. Tess crossed home plate. Grinning wildly, Kiku sprinted towards third. She could hear the water swishing violently in her *sara*. It drowned out the pounding of her heart. She should slow down. She couldn't. Not now. Just after she passed third, Kiku heard the ball thump into a glove. Her gaze snapped to home base. Who had the ball?

Not the catcher. Reyna stood with her foot on home base, mitt outstretched towards second base. All Kiku had to do now was beat the ball to home plate. Her vision tunneled as her team yelled for her to go, go, go!

Without thinking, Kiku dove, launching herself towards the base. Water splashed onto her forehead just as her hands hit the plate. A second later, a mitt touched her back. She was safe! They'd won! Her team whooped with joy as Kiku crashed into the backstop.

Her fingers jammed up against the chain-link fence, sending a jolt up her arm. Hot tears streamed down her face along with the water from her *sara*. Kiku willed herself to get up even though she knew it was no use. Only one thing could unfreeze her. She just wanted to join in the celebrations. She just wanted to be normal. A sob crackled in her throat as she heard the joyful shouting die down.

"What's wrong?"

"Why isn't she getting up?"

"Her family runs the cucumber cart, yeah? Should we go get her mom?"

Kiku hated that she couldn't even tell them how to help her. The tears fell faster.

"Move back, you idiots!" Marin shouted.

"Kiku?" Tess shook her shoulder. "Are you okay?" Kiku tried to suppress another sob but failed. "Are you hurt?"

The beads on Marin's braids clacked as she bent over Kiku. "Shit...someone get me a water bottle!" Kiku's heart dropped. Marin had seen her *sara*. They knew. This would be her first and last baseball game. Who would want a kappa on their team?

"There's none left."

"Then bring me the melted ice water!"

"How– "

"Fill up a bottle, idiot," one of the twins said. "Here, I'll do it." Feet shuffled. Kiku's heart plummeted. Finally, cool water drizzled onto her head. Marin poured enough into her *sara* so that she could sit up. Teary-eyed, Kiku accepted the water bottle and filled her *sara* up the rest of the way. "Sorry," she muttered, staring at her lap.

Everyone was silent. She shrunk in on herself under their unreadable stares. She should just go. Before she could move, Tess punched her shoulder. "What are you sorry for? That was epic!"

"Epic?" Kiku squeaked, confusion and hope swirling in her throat.

Tess's hands flew wildly. "You went for it *knowing* what could happen! I call that pretty epic."

"Yeah, dude!" Marin said. "That's dedication. You're totally on my team next week!"

"No, she's staying on my team!"

Tess and Marin continued to squabble, but Kiku barely heard them. Next week. Another Baseball Day and she'd be on the field.

"Hold up. Tess, stop. Kiku, whose team? Mine or Tess's?" Marin helped her to her feet. "Mine, right?"

Kiku couldn't help her last few happy tears. She touched her braid as she looked at her classmates. They were all smiling at her. She smiled back at her new friends. "I don't really care," Kiku said, wiping away her tears. "I'm just happy to play."

Brave
RYAN BREADINC

"I'm home," Rosalind calls.

There's no answer back, of course.

She shuts the door behind her and steps into the apartment, blinking bleary eyes at the flickering lights. Best not to stare too long, though it's something she's becoming accustomed to. It'd be too expensive to change the bulbs – and besides, she expects that the electrician won't be able to solve her problems anyway.

Her boots are set by the door for the next day, and she hangs her heavy coat on the rack.

The kitchen is exactly as she left it this morning. Rosalind passes the counter and opens the fridge to collect a half-empty carton of orange juice and some blueberries, straightening the horseshoe magnet on the stainless steel as she goes through.

"Oh, for god's sake," she mutters.

There's fur on the carpet again, stark black against the soft cream. She'll need to vacuum it tonight, before her absent roommate asks where the cat is in the morning. There's only so many times she can answer with 'outside' before she begins to look like a neglectful owner to an animal she doesn't even own.

The sound of her phone ringing startles her.

It takes her a few tries to answer it and by then the person on the other end has hung up.

She sighs and presses redial as she takes the stairs up to her bedroom. The lights turn off behind her without the switch being flicked, and the lamp in her bedroom is already casting an orange glow over everything when she enters.

"Hello?"

"Hi. Sorry I missed your call – didn't grab the phone in time."

"No problem, honey. I'm just glad to hear from you. How are you?"

"I'm fine." Rosalind drops into a chair and winces when it lets out a dramatic creaking noise. She'd only bought it a few days ago. "How did Dad's surgery go?"

"Good, actually. He keeps trying to mow the lawn even though the doctor told him not to. I've managed to bribe him with some blueberry muffins but it's only a matter of time before he's back in the shed."

"That's Dad for you," Rosalind says.

From the angle she's sitting at, she can see there's a puddle coming from the bathroom. Hopefully the tub isn't full of fur as well – she's going to riot if there is. No one warned her that having her own private space would come with so much cleaning. And other things.

"You sound a little strange. Is everything okay?"

She coughs. "It's nothing. Don't worry about it."

"And everything's fine in your new apartment?"

"It's fine. A lot cleaner than I expected it to be. Someone sent me flowers."

"Flowers? Really? That's strange."

"I like them, it's nice."

Rosalind turns on her laptop and types in the password with one hand, switching her phone to being cradled between her ear and shoulder to reply to an email while she talks. There's exactly seven emails that are blank – no text, no sender, no trail – and one from a new classmate, asking her to join him in speaking at the local LGBT center. She declines politely, ignores the rattling noise from behind her.

"–thought we could come to visit you, one of these days. It's been so long since we've seen you."

"Sure," Rosalind says vaguely. "One day."

It's been *one day* for a long time. She's become an expert at deflecting and distracting them whenever plans are starting to be made. As she opens her mouth to speak again, her laptop screen flickers black for a moment.

She sees her reflection, looking small and tired, and a few steps behind her in the room, a pair of sharp golden eyes staring directly at her.

"I suppose I'd better let you go. You're such a busy bee nowadays. Make sure you give your brother a call this week, he's been missing his big brot–"

"I will. Goodnight, Mum."

"Goodnight, darling. Don't be a stranger."

It takes her a few long beats to actually press the button to disconnect the call, and then she looks at her phone for a moment. Maybe she's being too cold. Even if they don't *know* she's shutting them out, that's not to say that it isn't a bad thing to do.

For a second Rosalind considers hitting redial.

Instead she puts the phone down and focuses on her laptop. She pays no heed to the twisted fingers emerging from her wardrobe.

*"**You tell them,**"* a scratchy voice says, the noise clawing at her skull like a headache.

"It's not worth it," she answers without looking back in that direction.

Silence. No reply, apart from the sound of something heavy being dragged along the floorboards. Rosalind pays no heed to it, setting her mind to the essay that she was technically supposed to have finished last week but forgot about when she spent the month preparing to move. The words don't fly off the screen the way she wants them to, but it's a passing grade, at least.

A thump startles her.

"Stop that," she scolds, turning around to find no one there. "I'm busy."

Rosalind goes to turn and her socked foot hits something solid instead. Looking down, she realizes it's the flowers she'd received earlier in the week – bright white daffodils planted carefully in a small pot with tiny animals meticulously carved into the side. She picks them up so they're safe and turns her unimpressed frown onto the clawed foot sticking out from under her bed.

"Leave these alone," she says. "I like them."

If they got damaged, she'd – well. Be distraught, most likely. She doesn't get gifts often – certainly not something as pretty and delicate as these, and her fingers clench on the pot without meaning to. Wherever they've come from, they're not leaving now, and they're certainly not going in the trash because they've been destroyed.

She forces her stiff hands to ease up on the flowerpot and instead traces over the grooves. It must've taken days to carve, if not weeks. Doesn't make sense, really. She loves them regardless of their origin.

Long, twisted fingers emerge from the other side of the bed, dig into her floral sheets.

"Flowers."

"Don't rip those," she reprimands. "I've had it up to here with you making a mess around the place. The rent may be cheaper with you around, but I don't appreciate being turned into a maid."

Rosalind receives a low rumbling noise for that as the hands recede for a moment, only to return bigger than before, with grimy furred elbows resting on the sheets now. What a mess. She'd just washed those yesterday.

"Read card?"

"Card?"

The hands flex slightly on the sheets. There's no verbal reply apart from a faint ringing in her ears. She looks around for a card of some sort on the sheets, by the wardrobe, down by the foot that's still hanging out from under the mattress. If there's a card around, it's well-hidden.

"I don't know what you're talking about," she says.

One long finger points directly at her – no, not at *her*, at the flowers.

Rosalind looks down at the pot. It takes her a few moments to pick out the white paper hidden amongst the white petals and she plucks it from the daffodil stems with care, making sure not to harm the flowers in the process. She's not sure how she hadn't noticed the card before now.

It's blank on the front. The card is flimsy paper, like it's been taken from a printer and hastily put together rather than made of stronger material the way she'd expect. There's a stain on the corner and it shimmers slightly in the light when she opens it to inspect the contents.

Rather than written text, she's greeted with a drawing.

It's terrible. Shaky charcoal is smudged all over the inside, making the picture nearly indecipherable. She tips it to one side and pushes her glasses up her nose. Eventually she makes out the two figures standing together – one small, one disproportionately tall – walking down a street.

The shorter figure is wearing a triangular dress and could be holding an ice cream cone. The hair is a scribbly mess but she recognizes the hairstyle. Is that...meant to be her?

They're also holding one of the taller figure's overly-long hands.

Rosalind looks over at the bed. "You got these for me?"

The lamp flickers. For a moment she's shrouded in darkness, and then the lights come back on before she can get up from her seat. The ringing in her ears has gotten louder all of a sudden. The protruding foot has disappeared from where it was poking out, but the hands remain.

"Thank you," she says, rather than voicing the million questions that cross her mind. "I've never got flowers before."

The hands twist in on themselves, almost in a display of shyness.

Rosalind looks at the card again. "Did you...want ice cream? Is that what this is?"

The apartment shudders underneath her. *"Out."*

"You want to go out," she repeats. It's hard to keep the incredulity out of her tone. "Really? Is that a good idea?"

No answer.

It *is* a bad idea, she's pretty sure.

"How are you going to go out in public without being noticed?"

A gurgle. *"Hat."*

Rosalind muffles the urge to laugh at that truly ridiculous idea. "You think a hat's going to be a great disguise, huh? No one will notice you at all if you have one on your head?"

The hands disappear for a moment and then reappear, holding a small green fedora aloft. *"Hat."*

Huh. All prepared and everything. That means this isn't just a whim that'll disappear after a few hours, like the time she'd turned on the television and all the channels had been advertising microwaved lasagna. "You're actually serious about this."

Silence.

There's a faint gray shimmer upon the hat, like it's been coated in dust or glitter.

"If you're sure," she says, relenting. "Why are you so desperate to get out all of a sudden? Most of the time you won't even let me get my clothes from the wardrobe."

"Brave."

Rosalind thinks that perhaps brave and bullheaded are being confused at the moment, but she's not one to stop others from making their own choices. It's a little cold for ice cream – pie would be a better choice, perhaps. Or hot chocolate. "Okay."

"Now you."

Oh. That's what this is all about. "You're trying to bully me into doing what you want?"

The hands twist in on themselves and then disappear. *"Helping."*

"You have a very strange concept of helping," she tells the empty room at large. There's no reply and she lets out a sigh, leans back in her chair and looks at the flowers again. They're drooping slightly, almost as if they reflect the gifter's mood.

Hell, maybe they're right.

No, she *knows* they're right, it's just that she's scared.

Brave, she thinks, picking up her phone again. The floor behind her creaks ominously, but it almost feels encouraging in nature. It's a strange day when she's taking advice from a thing that by all logical thought shouldn't even exist.

"Hello?"

Rosalind puts her phone to her ear. "Mum? I want to talk to you about something."

Ghosts in the Forest
TAMARA M BAILEY

It was happening again.

Bethany stopped in the car park to scan her surroundings. The bush was alive with birds and wind. The children had gone home already. The staff had either rushed out as the final bell chimed, or were in the staffroom celebrating the start of the April holidays. There was no visible soul around, and yet Bethany could feel that gaze; that prickling at the back of her neck. She had felt it for days now. The persistent, determined stare.

Her Grams used to say there were ghosts in the forest.

Bethany shouldered her backpack and climbed onto her bike. It was best not to dwell. People in this town already muttered to each other that she wasn't right in the head. They thought she didn't hear them, but she did. In this small town, in a forested pocket of southwest Australia, their whispers were like thunder in her ears.

Thirty years ago, her fellow teachers and principal had marveled at her skills. They loved that she took the kids out into the bush, showed them how to find food and shelter, taught them how to listen for water and taste the air for storms. Her classrooms were always decorated with charcoal-marked bark instead of laminated cards, with little native animals made out of gumnuts and sticks hidden in every nook.

But her colleagues' admiration changed as the policies did – slowly at first, then all at once. And when the new principal started at the beginning of last year, no one crowed about the merits of Bethany's teaching.

"You need parents' permission before taking the children off school grounds," the principal had said when she'd first heard about Bethany's excursions.

"Fill out these three forms, and don't forget to mention how the excursions connect to the curriculum."

"Tell me again how this relates to STEM, Bethany."

"Reece really shouldn't be going outdoors, Bethany. He's allergic to bees."

"Our standardized testing results are showing a particular drop in your class, Bethany. You need to stop taking the children outside and start teaching them persuasive writing."

Bethany's older colleagues had retired. The new ones, fresh out of university, murmured about her amongst themselves in groups, like flocks of teenagers in high school.

Bethany ignored them. She ignored the principal as best she could, too. She would continue to teach her students about the bush, until the school no longer let her through its gates. How could they care for and protect something they knew nothing about?

Bethany pedaled her way along the winding country road through the trees. There was a spice to the earthy air – that wet jarrah smell that told her rain was on the way.

She passed a section cordoned off for clearing. Red paint marked the trees. A path had already been bulldozed through the bush for bigger equipment to come. A sign in the ground claimed *King and Stevens present Woods Haven: Your new home in the forest.*

Her own home was down a rugged path. There was no need for a driveway when she had no car. The shack was small; wood and iron. It wasn't much to look at, but it was secure against the weather and kept in the modest warmth of her fireplace during the colder months.

She kicked the stand of her bike and turned to the forest as that prickling sensation returned. "Who are you? Show yourself!"

She was less afraid of acting like a raving woman without an audience to mock her. But no answer came from the forest except for a light pattering as the rain began.

It was only when the sound of the chainsaws echoed through the greenery that she retreated inside.

The rain eased overnight, leaving clear skies the next morning.

Bethany woke with stiff fingers, an ache in her knee and a sweet sadness that came with holidays. The other teachers crawled to the end of the term like it was the finish line of a country-length marathon. Bethany didn't blame them. They were expected to do too much. Bethany had never followed the policies, and was therefore free to mourn the term break. It meant time away from her keen little learners. There was immense satisfaction in watching the most spoilt, most screen-obsessed seven-year-old find joy in the bush. They would turn over a log and watch in wonder as the minibeasts scrambled away. In nature, the children rediscovered their souls.

Bethany climbed out of bed and stoked her dying fire to put the kettle on. She used the outhouse, listening to the scream of the saw rather than birdsong. A smell hung in the air. Death.

Following her nose to the back of the outhouse, she found the carcass of a kangaroo. Flies swarmed the bloodstained fur. She moved around the body to see if a joey was in the pouch and found the front of the roo ripped open. Something had slashed it from neck to groin.

Bethany had come across dead animals before. Killed by the roads, mostly. Sometimes she found them alive and nursed them back to health. Sometimes her nursing skills weren't enough. She would leave the little bodies outside for the forest to reclaim.

But this roo – there was nothing natural about this. This was… Human.

Leaves rustled behind her and she turned, half-expecting to see a deranged man with an axe.

The forest was empty. Expect, perhaps, for the ghosts.

Bethany spent the morning shifting the carcass away from the house. Although fit and muscular, she was a small woman, and the task took a long time. After a shower, she rode to the town for supplies. It was nice to get away from the stench.

"Morning, Miss Blackburn," said Chloe as she rang up Bethany's vegetables at the till. She had been in Bethany's class fifteen years ago. "Happy Easter."

"Mmm." Bethany glanced over her shoulder.

"You all right, Miss?"

Bethany shook off her nerves. Between the carcass and the feeling of being watched, things were off-balance.

"Sorry, young Chloe," she said, summoning cheerfulness. "How's your mum and dad?"

Chloe chattered about her family farm and the new baby until the bell over the door rang and another customer entered. He was a stranger with a fancy suit and shiny shoes – certainly not a local. He cocked a smile at them the way one might cock a gun.

"Morning, ladies. Sorry to interrupt." His gaze flitted the store. "Quaint place."

"Can I help you?" Chloe said.

The man dug into his suit pocket and pulled out a business card. "Samuel Stevens. I was wondering whether I might speak to the owner."

"Parker's not here," Chloe said, frowning at the card.

"Stevens," Bethany echoed. "As in, King and Stevens?"

"The very same." Samuel's gaze continued to roam the store. He wasn't looking at the goods. He was looking at the roof, the walls…the structure.

"You're the one bulldozing the forest for that housing development," Chloe said.

"That's right. I'll be bringing plenty of customers for you."

Chloe huffed. "I'd rather you leave the bush alone."

Bethany hid a smile. It was nice to know her lessons resonated in her students, even all these years later. Her Grams would be proud.

"Now, now," Stevens said with that gun-cocked smile. "You can't stop progress."

Chloe rotated his business card in her hand. "I'll tell Parker to call you."

"That would be great." Samuel's mobile rang. "Excuse me."

He wandered out as casually as he had entered, answering his phone only when the door had closed behind him. Chloe and Bethany watched him stroll away.

"What do you think he wanted?" Chloe said.

"To build a Woolworths, probably. Or an entire shopping center."

Chloe spun to Bethany, mouth agape. "What?"

"They're going to want incentive to lure people down here, aren't they?" Bethany picked up her backpack while Chloe was still absorbing her words. "See you tomorrow."

She headed out to her bike. On her way, she passed Samuel Stevens.

"No," he said, walking briskly to his car. It must've started out black and shiny in the city, but red dust and bug splatter had taken care of that. "No, I don't care who you have to call, or visit, or harass. *Find him.*"

From the snarl in his voice, Bethany couldn't help hoping this missing person managed to stay lost.

Halfway down the rugged path towards home, Bethany caught sight of an animal on her doorstep. She slowed her bike to a stop. The creature was small and gray...a koala? Koalas weren't in this part of Australia–

The animal turned, and she gasped. Blood streaked its front. It was hurt. Perhaps it had been attacked by whatever had killed the kangaroo.

She dismounted her bike, her movements slow and careful. She hadn't specifically dealt with koalas before. They could be aggressive, she'd heard. The claws were something to watch for.

How had it gotten here? Had someone stolen it from the eastern states and released it into the forest?

For a brief moment, she wondered whether Samuel Stevens had been involved. Nothing would get potential buyers down here as fast as the promise of living among koalas.

The creature on her doorstep made a soft grunting noise. It was probably in pain. Bethany was already mentally making a list of equipment she'd need, starting with a bowl of fresh water–

She hadn't yet reached the porch when the animal shrank back and growled. Its lips peeled back, revealing fangs that dripped with blood. Bethany staggered away. When the creature lurched forward, she spun and sprinted for her bike. It took three tries to raise the kickstand. Her legs, bare beneath the cuff of her three-quarter pants, tingled with the anticipation of a bite. That thing looked as if it could rip the flesh right off her.

She finally got her feet on the pedals. Twigs and dried leaves whipped up behind her wheels as she rode away.

She raced back to the main road of town, the image of the bloodied fangs seared into her mind. Whatever that thing was, it wasn't a koala.

Drop bear.

The words came to her as she reached the corner store. She fumbled with the concept, unwilling to let it settle. Grams had spoken of ghosts and witches and bunyips out here in the bush, but not drop bears. They weren't even worthy of legend.

Bethany left her bike and burst into the corner store. Samuel Stevens had returned, leaning on the counter as he chatted to Chloe. About what, Bethany didn't care.

"Miss Blackburn," Chloe said, straightening. "What's wrong?"

Samuel Stevens grabbed a water bottle from the shelves and passed it to Bethany as she struggled to catch her breath.

"Drop bear," she said through wheezes. "On my porch."

Samuel lifted an eyebrow.

"You dropped what?" Chloe said.

Bethany pressed a hand to her chest. Her heart was hammering. "A drop bear. There was a drop bear. On my porch. Fangs. Blood."

"Now, come on," Samuel said with a chuckle. "I may be a city boy, but I'm no tourist."

Chloe came around the counter and gently led Bethany to the back room. Bethany gratefully sank to a chair. Her legs trembled as she sipped from the water bottle.

"I know it doesn't make sense," she said when she regained her breath. "At first I thought it was a koala."

Chloe and Samuel exchanged glances.

"There was a kangaroo, too." Bethany spoke faster, trying to make sense of what had happened. "This morning, not far from my house. It was killed and gutted. I couldn't figure out what had done it…"

"Is there somewhere safe you can stay?" Samuel said when Bethany trailed off. "For a little while? You look like you've had quite a fright."

Bethany didn't answer. She had enjoyed her solitude for decades now. Just her and the bush. It was a source of pride.

But it also meant there was nowhere else for her to go.

"I'll get Mum to pick her up," Chloe said, grabbing her mobile.

"No." Bethany held out a hand to stop her. "No, thank you. I'd rather go home."

Again, Samuel and Chloe exchanged glances. How had they become so chummy in the past thirty minutes?

"I'll give you a lift then," Samuel said after a pause.

"No, that's fine—"

"I insist. I'll have a look at this…thing you saw. If it's still there."

"My bike—"

"It'll fit in my boot with the back seats down. Come on. We can check the house together."

Bethany allowed Samuel to help her up. She watched him load her dusty bike into his expensive car.

"The whole thing will need a wash, anyway," he said as she protested once again.

The drive was in silence, except for her directing him. The car smelled like leather and fake pine. When they reached home, Samuel had to pull over on the side of the road. "No driveway?"

"No need," she said.

They unloaded her bike. She couldn't see her house from the road. Was the drop bear still on the porch? And if it wasn't, where would it go?

She searched the trees as she wheeled her bike down the path. The last thing she wanted was to be assailed by that thing from above. But nothing seemed to be up there besides the birds.

Samuel let out a low whistle as the house came into view. "That is…something else."

The porch was empty. Bethany moved carefully, scanning her surroundings as she stepped onto the wooden boards. There was no sign of blood, or fur, or anything to prove the creature had been there.

She left her bike and led Samuel inside. Together they combed the house.

"Nothing," Samuel said.

"I didn't imagine it."

Samuel nodded. She wasn't sure he believed her.

"Come and look at the kangaroo, then."

He obliged, following her out the back and deeper into the bush where she'd left the carcass. She kept one eye on the branches above as they walked.

The stench hit them first, shortly before the drone of flies. When Samuel saw the maimed roo, he pressed the back of his hand to his nose and swore. He crouched by the carcass to examine it, reminding Bethany of her year twos crouching by overturned rocks to watch minibeasts.

"This is…urg." He stood again and turned away. "Is there someone we can call?"

"There's the Parks and Wildlife people. I don't think they'll believe me about a drop bear, though."

"Regardless, something – or someone – out there did this." Samuel stole another glance at the carcass. "Are you sure you wouldn't feel safer staying somewhere else?"

Bethany didn't answer. She didn't know what to think anymore. Spiders, snakes, she could handle. A mythical creature who may or may not have gutted a fully grown roo? That required skills beyond her abilities.

What would Grams have done? Appease the forest ghosts? Call upon a witch? There had been times in Bethany's childhood when Grams would do strange things to protect them, but it had been so long ago. Sticks and bones and offerings of blood…Bethany couldn't remember the details, and Grams had never written it down. Grams had told stories, so many stories, but Bethany's father had dismissed them, and they hadn't stuck in Bethany's head. What resources were left?

Samuel lifted his gaze to the canopy. "These drop bears," he said, and Bethany heard the way he forced a joke into his tone. "I don't suppose they attack people?"

"That's the point of the myth, I think. But then again, I've heard you can protect yourself with a cork-strung hat and a jar of vegemite, so who knows what's real and what's not?" She paused, watching him. "Why?"

"Because," he said, "my business partner, Theo King? He's missing."

The distant scream of chainsaws had become a soundtrack of Bethany's day. She hadn't left her home, despite Samuel's worried suggestions. Perhaps it was a silly idea to stay, but she couldn't imagine existing in another space. Sitting in someone else's living room, eating at a strange table, breathing in the unfamiliar smell of another person's home. Besides, she wasn't going to let this thing – whatever it was – chase her away.

Dusk gathered at the skirts of the sky. She locked the house up tight and checked the ceiling space with a torch. It was as she was preparing dinner that she happened to glance out the window and see it. The creature, the drop bear, was at the stone birdbath, lapping at the water.

Bethany held still, watching. The beast must've been thirsty. It drank and drank. Blood from its fur stained the surface of the pool. When it finally lifted its head, the entire front of its body was matted and drenched.

It looked right at her.

Bethany patted the benchtop for a weapon. She didn't dare take her eyes from the creature. The drop bear climbed down the birdbath and started towards the house. Bethany's pulse pounded in her ears. Could that thing break glass? Could it rip a door from its hinges?

She didn't have a phone. It had never been a necessity before. Who would she call? Who would call her? There was no way to contact the outside world, and no way to take photographic evidence.

Her hand curled around the handle of her frypan. The drop bear disappeared from view as it reached her back door. There was a grating sound – she imagined claws on the flyscreen. Then claws on wood. The creature had scratched right through the wire.

She listened to the splintering scrapes, her grip tightening on the handle. How long before it scratched its way through?

She couldn't just stand here waiting for it to attack. The best thing to do was go on the offence. It was still just an animal, no matter how frightening. With a shaking hand, she unlocked the door. One breath of hesitation. Two breaths.

She wrenched the door open and swung the frypan. The creature was too fast – it scurried across the threshold. Her weapon hit air. She staggered, off-balance, and tried to spin around. A sharp pain shot up her ankle from the movement. Her leg could no longer hold her.

She thudded to the ground with a cry. The frypan thunked beside her. Gritting her teeth through the pain, she fumbled with the handle, trying to correct her grip before the creature attacked.

It sat on the floorboards, out of reach. Watching her.

She froze. Her labored breaths hiccupped. It really did look like a koala. Its front was still wet from the birdbath and stained with blood. The ripped flyscreen was in the corner of her vision. She hadn't lost her mind. This thing, whatever it was, existed.

She lifted the frypan and noticed how badly her arm shook. Hot pain shot up her ankle. She winced, fighting the urge to clutch it. As soon as she dropped her guard, she was surely dead.

The creature continued to watch her. What it was waiting for, she didn't know.

After an agonizing standoff, it turned and made its way around the breakfast bar and into the kitchen on all fours. She set down the frypan, struggling to haul herself up. Getting off the ground was difficult enough without a sprained ankle. Her days of sitting on the mat with the kids were long gone.

It was no use. She couldn't put any weight on her injury, which meant she couldn't stand.

The drop bear was doing something in the kitchen. Somehow, the freezer door opened. There was the sound of rummaging. She held her breath as she listened. Was it looking for food?

Her freezer was only small, but it was well stocked. She had a slab of meat in there, a few boxes of pre-cooked meals for emergencies, bait for when she went fishing...

Something rattled. Plastic dragged across the floor. She grabbed the frypan again as the animal came around the breakfast bar, pulling an ice cube tray with its teeth. She lowered her weapon.

The creature tugged the tray to her feet and dropped it. Then it backed away to its first spot, sat, and watched her.

She eyed the tray. The creature waited.

"What?" she said after a silence. "You're giving me ice?"

Talking to wild animals was an everyday occurrence for Bethany. What she'd never experienced before was an answer. The creature grunted, jerking its head.

Her heart jumped in surprise. She breathed through the shock... and the pain in her ankle.

"You're giving me ice for my ankle?"

Another grunt.

She hesitated. Tricks and traps were done by humans, not animals. Then again, she didn't know any animal that understood the need to ice an injury.

Seconds ticked past. There was no point sitting here. She was in pain, and the creature hadn't attacked her. She reached forward and grabbed the ice cube tray, placing the whole thing on her ankle. The pain didn't go away immediately, but the chill gave her some relief.

The drop bear sat in its place. It seemed to be waiting for something.

"Thank you?" Bethany said.

It grunted.

It was another few minutes before Bethany tried to move again. She used the wall behind her for support as she pushed herself to her feet. She hadn't been sure how the drop bear would react to her standing up, but it didn't act threatened or even wary. It just continued to watch her.

She hobbled to the couch with the ice cube tray under her arm then eased herself down with her sore foot up on the coffee table. Her body stiffened as the drop bear wandered over. It climbed onto the cushion next to her then sagged in a way that reminded her of her father slouched in front of the television. After a few breathless moments of nothing happening, she leaned forward to balance the ice tray on her ankle again.

"I don't have a TV," she said.

Grunt.

"I have an area for you to stay in the house. I nurse injured animals here sometimes. Maggies are the best. They've got funny little personalities, you know?"

Grunt.

Bethany paused. "Did you kill that kangaroo?"

The drop bear turned to face her. It peeled back its lips, baring its teeth, and Bethany felt a scream rising in her throat as she braced herself for an attack…

The drop bear sneezed violently. Once, twice, three times. Then it curled up in a ball and closed its eyes.

"Right," Bethany said. "Of course."

Maybe it hadn't killed the roo. But she would be wise to sleep with her bedroom door closed tonight. Just in case.

"Green or blue?"

Bethany held up two pairs of fuzzy socks. The drop bear turned away. Did she imagine the little scoff it made?

"Color-blind, then?" she said, pulling her sock over her injured ankle. It had healed enough over the past few days for her to go on a short walk. She wanted to use it, to get the blood flowing again. She hated being cooped up inside.

The drop bear hadn't gone far since her arrival, despite her letting it leave the house. It hung around the birdbath most of the time. She observed it eating insects, worms and the occasional bird that got too close. The more she watched it, the more she was sure it was highly unlikely the creature killed the roo.

What she couldn't figure out was where the drop bear had come from, and why it insisted on hanging around here. There was something uncannily human about the creature.

It waited impatiently by the door as she got ready. "All right, I'm coming."

She opened the door and the drop bear hastened out, looking over its shoulder at her. It jerked its head. She had the strangest sense that it was asking her to follow.

She picked her way through the undergrowth after it, the pain in her ankle no more than a slight twinge. The bush was alive with birdcalls. Leaves fell like rain around them, the morning crisp with autumn air.

They trekked down a trail away from the roo carcass, in a direction Bethany suspected she didn't want to go. Sure enough, the scream of chainsaws started up, along with the rumble of bulldozers, sounding close.

"Are you taking me to the development?" she said. "I don't want to go there."

The drop bear grunted at her.

"You shouldn't want to go either. I don't know what they'd do if they found someone like you out here."

But the drop bear continued. They veered east, as if circling around the development. A stench wafted past her nose, reminding her of the kangaroo. They passed a dead pink and gray galah, bloodied on the ground. Not much further, there was a quenda, its little body ripped open like the kangaroo. A western brush wallaby. A red fox.

All slaughtered.

The drop bear stopped to sniff the fox. When it pulled away, there was blood smeared on its nose. Bethany realized this was what must have happened with the roo to make the drop bear look so terrifying the first time she'd seen it.

The smell got stronger. The buzz of flies thickened until there was a black swarm, and a human body came into view.

He was a man in a suit, much like Samuel Stevens, only grayer and more...decomposing. Bethany held her nose and looked him over. There were no gashes like the animals, only bloating and grayness.

"What happened here?" Bethany whispered.

The drop bear sat next to the man and grunted softly.

"Did you know him?"

A breeze picked up, rustling her braid. She felt that strange, prickling sensation and turned around. As usual, the forest was empty.

"Ghosts," she murmured.

The drop bear snarled, showing its teeth.

"You look terrifying when you do that, did you know?"

It softened its face and returned its attention to the body, nudging it as though in mourning. A curiosity. Was this creature the man's pet? It had led Bethany right to him, as a dog would lead help to its injured owner.

But if this man was who she thought he was, a pet drop bear didn't make sense. Theodore King, Samuel's business partner, was unlikely to own an animal, much less a wild creature from myth. In fact, she couldn't help wondering if he had been behind the wildlife massacre.

The prickling at Bethany's neck was so intense it was like an itch. Between the birdsong and thunder of deforestation, she heard a whisper. A voice. It sounded like her grandmother.

"Grams?"

The drop bear was hunched, almost as if cowering, but it snarled again. It was afraid. Afraid...and angry.

"What did they do to you? The ghosts?"

The drop bear looked right at her. Liquid brown eyes, filled with intelligence. It touched its paw against the dead man's face. Then it scraped its claws against its own chest.

Bethany frowned. It repeated the action. Face. Chest. Face. Chest.

"You," Bethany said slowly. "You're...the man?"

The creature grunted, keenly leaning towards her.

"You're Theodore King?"

Another grunt. Its body practically vibrated with excitement.

Bethany gazed around her, at the rustling trees, at the invisible watchers. "Grams? Did you do this?"

Some of her grandmother's stories featured people dying and turning into mythical creatures. But a drop bear? Wasn't that just a myth to frighten tourists?

No, not just tourists. Visitors. Newcomers.

She spun as the sound of the chainsaw came to an abrupt halt. There were shouts – men surprised, alarmed.

Then nothing.

Bethany looked to the drop bear, who gazed up at her from its spot beside the body.

"A sacrifice," she said softly. "The roo."

This wasn't a mythical story. This was witchcraft. Someone had killed the kangaroo to transform Theodore King into a drop bear. And that same someone had killed all those creatures behind her.

More magic. More sacrifices.

"You can't do this," Bethany said to the ghosts as the drop bear – Theodore – edged closer to her. It was looking out at the forest as if sensing something. "These are people."

The wind picked up, wilder, hungrier than before. This time, when Bethany heard her grandmother's voice, she could make out the words.

We are protecting the forest.

"But that's not fair. I live here. Others live here. My students. The community. What makes that any different?"

It is enough. It is sustainable.

The drop bear shuffled right up against Bethany's ankles. Rustling caught her attention, and out from the forest came others. Other drop bears, a scattering of them, emerging from the trees. They moved as if confused, hesitant...newborn.

"You think the police won't swarm the place with a bunch of dead bodies around?" Bethany cried.

There's nothing for them to find. They will leave eventually, and the place will seem cursed. No one else will come.

"One day they will. You can't stop progress." Wasn't that what Samuel had told her? She was sad, but it didn't change the fact that he was right.

Yes, we can. Here, we can.

The drop bears were close now. Theodore moved tentatively towards them. They were the workers from the development. The builders, the loggers, the apprentices…everyone. Perhaps even Samuel Stevens was among them.

The drop bears sniffed and grunted at each other. Some bared their teeth, but Bethany knew now it was only for show. When they realized she wasn't afraid, they lost interest in her and rooted around in the leaves for insects. Bethany watched them for a while. Then, not knowing what else to do, she turned and headed back.

And slowly, in their own time, the community of drop bears followed her home.

Hunting el Chupacabra
CHRISTOPH WEBER

"El chupacabra," the rancher says, pointing to the image on-screen. The photo is a grainy trail-cam shot of the creature's back, but a few things are clear: it's hairless, hunched, and bipedal.

"Looks like we'll be chasing Gollum," the guy next to me whispers, doing a poor job of suppressing his giggles. I ignore him.

The rancher flips to the next slide. "And this is what the varmint's doing to my sheep." The lamb's throat is splayed open, gnawed. Its trachea dangles out like a half-eaten taquito dipped in salsa roja. The giggler averts his eyes.

After flipping through more photos of mutilated sheep, the rancher puts down his remote. "Twenty grand to whoever brings me the body of el chupacabra."

The giggler approaches as I get in my truck. He's in his early twenties. Long hair. Wearing a t-shirt with an image of Bigfoot above the caption, *Hide and Seek World Champion*.

"Are you a crypto?" he asks.

"A what?"

"A cryptozoologist. Do you chase cryptids?"

I glance around at the other hunters firing up their rigs, getting a head start on me. "I don't know what you're talking about."

"Guess that answers that," he says, giggling again. "How'd you hear about this chupy?"

"I work for Texas Wildlife Services." I climb into my truck. "Got an email, thought I'd check it out." I don't tell him the email was from my department head, mocking chupacabra chasers.

"You want to team up? You need someone who knows chupies, and I need someone who knows Texas."

Actually, all I need is my rifle – and to get on the damn road.

But as I look at him, at the bright enthusiasm bubbling in his eyes, I realize *that's* what I'm really out here chasing: something to get excited about. I glance over at his car, a goddamn Prius with Oregon plates. That toy on wheels isn't gonna get him far in the backcountry. Against my better judgment, I tell him to grab his stuff.

I fire up my truck, spread my map over the dash, and draw a line through the Xs where the last three attacks occurred. This thing, whatever it is, is headed west.

As soon as the giggler hops in, the stink of patchouli floods the cab. I open my window, but now that everyone's got a jump on us, dust pours in. I mutter a curse under my breath and close it. Looks like I'm stuck with patchouli. "You have a rifle?"

He pats his backpack. "Only shots I'll take are photos. I'm Sammy."

"One," I say, keeping my eyes on the road.

"You don't look Hispanic."

"No, not Juan. One. Like the number. It's a nickname."

"How'd you get that?"

I offer him my right hand. When he grasps the cool silicone, he doesn't recoil like most people.

"How'd you lose it?"

"Afghanistan."

"Oh. Sorry."

"Wasn't your fault."

"What do you do now?"

"Work for Texas Wildlife Services."

"You already said that. I mean, what do you do for them?"

"I shoot feral hogs from helicopters." I glance over at him, expecting the look of self-righteous horror out-of-staters always wear when I tell them what I do. But if he's judging me, he doesn't show it.

"How'd you get into that?"

"Weren't too many other job openings for snipers, stateside."

"You like it?"

Christ. My therapist doesn't ask so many damn questions. "It's all right," I lie.

After a welcome moment of silence, he pipes back up. "I'm on break from Lewis and Clark. It's in Portland."

More silence. I feel like I should ask him something, more out of politeness than curiosity. "What do you study?"

"Biology. I research mycorrhizae – a symbiotic association between plants and fungi – but I'm really interested in cryptids. I spend most weekends looking for squatches. When I heard about this chupy, I took some time off. There's good money for footage. How about you? Do this much?"

"No. Had to take vacation days to be out here. I don't believe in chupacabras." Or squatches. Or unicorns.

"Then how do you explain the photo?"

"I'll explain it when I shoot it."

"So you're burning vacation days to chase something you don't believe in. Why you out here, One?"

"Twenty thousand reasons." But if I'm being honest, it's about more than the money. Some part of me really does want to believe in chupacabras, in Bigfoot – hell, I'd even take a goddamn leprechaun. Part of me just needs something to believe in.

After a ways I turn north, out of the dust cloud and onto a little-used two track. I feel Sammy's questioning eyes on me.

"Isn't our chupy headed west?"

"There's a hog fence to the west. This ain't my first rodeo. I've flown this stretch a dozen times. Our monkey-dog, or whatever, is gonna hit it and turn north, to the nearest ranch." I plant the index finger of old Numbknuckles on the map. "That's where we're headed."

Sammy claps his hands like a kid on Christmas. "I could just tell you knew what you were doing!"

Movement in my rear-view grabs my attention; in the waning daylight, dust from my tires filters the pursuing headlights into a pair of red, unblinking eyes. "Keep your pants on...we've got competition."

At dusk, we make camp on a knoll overlooking the sheep ranch, under some old Ashe junipers. The spice of creosote brush hangs on the air. Odd companions, those two. I set up my rifle looking down on a little creek lined with tamarisk. Sammy sets up a video camera with a telescopic lens and tripod.

"Guess you're my spotter, then," I say.

"Guess so."

"You know which ones are tamarisks?"

"Yeah. I study plants, remember?"

"All right then, smart stuff, how far to that thick patch?"

"Pretty far."

"More or less. See how food, water, and cover converge there? That's a good spot to watch."

Darkness descends like a blanket over the hills, and I switch to my infrared scope. Pretty soon, it's clear I'm not the only one who likes this spot. Headlights from another truck jostle up the neighboring hillside, then go dark when they reach the top.

"One, you really going to shoot this chupy if you see it?"

"You're kidding, right?"

"It could be the last individual of its species. If you just let me get footage, I'll split whatever I earn."

"Will it be more than twenty grand?"

"Well…no. But you won't be committing specicide."

"Sammy, this thing sealed its fate when it went after those sheep."

"It's a predator," he says, looking me in the eyes. "It has to kill to survive. Can you blame it for that?"

I reach into my pocket, pull out a round with green casing and a capped needle-tip. "New tranq rounds we're testing, compatible with standard rifles. Tell you what, if I'm close enough I'll just put it to sleep."

He smiles. "Thank you."

I don't tell him these tester rounds are undercharged, short-ranged, and since I don't even know what our quarry is, the dose could kill it anyway. I'm not risking a miss unless this thing pops up and puts its nose down my muzzle.

Three in the morning and Sammy's curled up, snoring in the dirt.

Some spotter. I push a dip of chewing tobacco in my lip and turn my sights on our competition. A man aims down at the creek below us.

I shoot lefty, nowadays. Kind of have to when your trigger finger's in pieces, eight thousand miles away, the bone shards probably sticking out of some snow leopard's scat. Was pretty ugly, the first time I tried shooting lefty from a bird. I went from being a crack shot to the 'sniper' who couldn't hit the broadside of a barn at a hundred yards. I've adapted pretty well to shooting, though. It's the other stuff…

As I scan our neighbors' hill, I see him – another sniper, scope on me. Instinct flows through my finger, urging it to neutralize the threat. It's not a panicked animal instinct, though, just cold conditioning, and I'm able to remind myself these are the hills of West Texas, not the Hindu Kush. Still, as I pin my crosshairs on the man's head, I think how easy it would be to just move my finger a single millimeter…*poof*…one less competitor.

The man turns his sights to the ranch below us, the moment passes, and I wonder if some habits will ever fade.

"Should we try someplace else?" Sammy asks after our second night of seeing nothing but deer.

"Nah. This is as good a spot as we're liable to find." Though our neighbors didn't agree – they packed up camp and left this morning.

"Couldn't you have used one of your helicopters to look for it?"

My helicopters. That almost makes me smile. "Sorry to break it to you, but Texas Wildlife Services doesn't quite share your faith in cryptids."

"You're out here."

"Yeah, but I'm on vacation." Now *that's* almost funny. "If anyone at TWS believes in cryptids, it ain't a seven hundred dollars an hour kinda faith."

When the inky blanket descends for another sleepless night, Sammy pulls a bottle from his pack. "Want a drink?"

"What you got?"

"Elderflower liqueur, with a dash of thimbleberries. I harvested them myself," he says proudly.

"I guess it's too hopeful to ask if you have any Jack?"

"Beggars can't be choosers." He slides to my side, hands me the bottle.

I take a pull. The taste of spring floods my mouth. "That's actually pretty damn good, even if it tastes like hippie. It's not gonna make me go blind, is it?"

He puts his hand on my back. "We can't have a blind sniper, can we?"

"'Specially not when he's the only one staying awake."

"I'll stay up, I promise. I have a good feeling about tonight."

We drink a quarter bottle, conversing in whispers. It's kinda nice. It's been a while since I really talked to anyone—

I double-take over a heat signature. "Holy shit." El chupacabra prances through the brush on two legs like some man-dog breeding experiment. "Did you put magic mushrooms in with those elderflowers?"

"You see it!"

"Shh! In the tamarisk. Good god, it really is bipedal."

"Can I see?"

"Negative." As quickly as the thing appeared, it melts back into the tamarisk. I watch for fifteen minutes, my pulse racing, but it's as if my heart belongs to someone else; as usual, my mind is disconnected, numb to any excitement I should feel. My therapist calls it dissociation.

"Sammy, there's only one place for it to hide," I whisper. "In the tamarisk. I want you to loop around to the north, then walk down the creek. I'll loop around south and post up on that little rock knob by the water. You flush it my way. If it runs toward the ranch, I'll have a shot. If it goes upslope, I'll have an even better shot. And if it comes through the tamarisks, it'll come straight to me."

Sammy agrees, takes his camera, and heads off into the inky darkness, brave as a bigamist, hardly making a sound. He's not so bad, for a hippie. I creep down to the high ground beside the creek. It's a good vantage, but a few tamarisks reach up around me, so I'll have to shoot standing, supporting my rifle with old Numbknuckles. Not as good as prone, but still, if I get a close shot…I put my hand in my pocket, finger the tranquilizer round. The night breeze feathers down the murmuring creek, carrying my scent away from our quarry. Perfect.

Something crashes through the brush. I train my sights on the sound – it's Sammy, two hundred yards out, closing in.

Hundred fifty yards. My heart races. I slow my breath to steady my aim.

Hundred yards. Did it get around us?

Fifty yards. No, something's close, between me and Sammy. The foliage is too thick to see, but I can feel it.

Branches snap like firecrackers as el chupacabra makes a run for it. It cuts left, right, then left through the brush, hopping toward the ranch like some mutant kangaroo.

A millimeter of movement on the trigger, and my rifle reports. The creature falls, face-down. Gets up, looks around, runs again. About a hundred yards and it starts to look drunk. Another fifty and it collapses.

Sammy and I rush to where it fell, find him curled up in the dirt. We just stand there, looking down on him for a long, silent moment.

"It looks like…a dog," Sammy says.

"It is. It's a coyote. With mange so bad he's bald as an egg." I kneel, look at his front legs. "Christ. They look like they've been chewed off."

"How?"

"Probably got caught in traps. Coyotes'll do that. But how in the hell he learned to walk upright…"

"I've seen that before," Sammy says. "There are dogs who lose their front legs, then learn to walk, even run, on their hind legs."

"But a coyote in the wild?" I shake my head, and as I look down at el chupacabra, something stirs inside me.

We make it to Loving County around dawn.

"Your camera ready?" I ask.

"All set."

El chupacabra stares into my eyes. I open the kennel and pat my truck bed. "Come on, tough guy." He slides out on his chest and flops from the tailgate. The antidote to the tranquilizer has done its job, and he runs toward the edge of the Pecos River. When he reaches the tamarisk, he turns and looks back at us, head tilted.

Loving County has fewer people than any county in the nation, and even fewer sheep, but it does have plenty of hogs, and if this tough son of a bitch was able to adapt after all he's been through, I think he'll learn how to find himself some feral piglets.

As el chupacabra melts into the brush, I find what I've been looking for. Not some majestic goddamn unicorn, but a broken brother who doesn't give a rat's ass that he's damaged goods, who just keeps adapting, surviving in spite of his troubles. Now *that's* something I can believe in. That right there is worth more than twenty grand.

Sammy threads his fingers through old Numbknuckles, and for the first time in a long time, I feel whole.

Special Interest
ALICIA K ANDERSON

Autism can be a mixed blessing while backpacking. On one hand, I can happily live in my own world while trudging through the forest, soaking in the sensations around me. I can go a lot longer in solitude without getting weird. Or, rather, I start off weird, so the solitude doesn't change me much. (That's the most obvious thing about through-hikers: how loopy they get after being on the trail for too long.)

It's really nice to hike by myself. To let the woods talk to me the way they did when I was a kid. Though of course I had my GPS tracker and stuff, to let my mom know where I was on the Appalachian Trail. Solo hiking as a woman takes guts, and a lot of planning. But it is possible. Even preferable.

When I was a kid, our back yard butted up against a state park. As long as I had my dog with me, or I was riding my horse, I was allowed to go back there whenever I wanted. My friends and I identified the best swimming holes, the little pools of quicksand to play in, shale 'cliffs' to scramble on above the lake. I wrote my first poem there, watching a blue heron. I daydreamed a lot in the dappled light where I lounged on soft beds of pine needles, and that was where I wanted my first kiss to occur. Preferably with a magical prince. (It was, alas, in a movie theater during a lousy slasher flick, with a guy who wore way too much cologne.)

The sensation of being by myself in the woods is unlike anything else. The woods' sounds are rarely too much for my sound-sensitive processing problems. The woods' smells are sweet and familiar. My eyes seem to be made to parse the squirrel from amid dry leaves in the underbrush. I like taking close-up pictures of mushrooms, and I like to stop and watch bees or butterflies do their thing on flowers. I don't go fast when I'm walking in the woods. That's another reason not to bother hiking with other people.

My pack was light. I was only going for an overnight. The padded strap at my hips kept sliding down, and I had to shrug the pack high and slip it a little tighter as I walked. The rain the night before caused a lot of *puh-pow-wee*. (I love that word. It's a word for the force it takes a mushroom to break the surface of the soil overnight. *Puh-pow-wee*.) A ton of mushrooms were erupting all along the trail. It was a wild alien landscape of white and yellow and orange fungus. If I spotted any chicken of the woods, I was going to grab it to go with dinner.

I'm pretty sure the woods are one of my special interests. More than just being a sensory heaven, I feel myself change and relax significantly even if I'm just looking at photos of the forest. An autistic person's special interest can have positive physical side effects just thinking about or talking about it. I know my blood pressure drops when I'm in the woods, but I think that's normal for everybody. The only other thing that has that kind of effect on my brain and body is unicorns.

For some autistic kids, it's trains. For others it's Lego blocks. It can be just about anything, but often these interests are things we were introduced to at a relatively young age, and something that just sort of stuck. I'm a nerdy, woodsy girl. I wrote my first-grade young author's book about a girl who got lost in the woods and helped an also-lost unicorn find her way home with the help of a black bear. Unicorns stuck. The woods stuck. Less so the black bear.

As an adult my interest is a little embarrassing. Rather, I guess I know it should be embarrassing? There's a part of me that wants to hide it. I know I can't talk about my special interest with just anyone, and that it isn't what neurotypical people do. I also know that absolutely no one wants to hear nearly as much as I have to say on any of my special topics.

Maybe that's one of the reasons why I like being alone so often. Also, I don't have to think about monitoring my facial expression to meet other people's expectations of my emotional or mental state.

I don't have to think about how to navigate social rules I'm never quite sure I understand. I don't have to pretend to be interested in stuff. I don't have to worry if my brain gets snagged on a fun word like *puh-pow-wee* and wants to repeat it a dozen times.

I was really digging the weird orangey red slime mold that grew along a stream when it started. I heard a footstep behind me as I filtered stream water for the afternoon. I kept my head tilted to parse the sound.

I heard it again when I was walking through a little grove of blooming mountain laurel. The pink and white blossoms frosted the tops of the curling, lacy branches. The wiggly, delicate trunks rose from what was always inevitably a moss-covered forest floor. Laurels make always-magical fairy tale groves, and I always stop and enjoy them. It was when I paused that I heard another step.

I spun around, but with a pack on my back, that's not a quick or graceful motion. I couldn't help but telegraph the heave-ho of turning. The pack rose above my head, so I couldn't hope to catch anything in my peripheral vision. I never saw whatever was following me. It sounded like a deer.

I doubled back once in the mud to see if I could spot footprints and gauge the size of whatever was making the sounds of footfalls. There was nothing but my own boot print, gleaming and slick, deep in the mud.

The rhododendron groves that grow near laurel groves are equally magical, but in a spooky way. Rhododendrons have wide, evergreen leaves that create an almost complete shade. It's a lions-and-tigers-and-bears-oh-my forest, darker than the rest of the dappled shade from the tall canopy. This difference is especially stark in the early spring when there are only buds on the hardwoods. When I heard a footfall behind me in one of those dark, damp, shadowed tunnels along the trail, you better believe I jumped. I jumped big – the way that made the mean kids laugh and want to scare you more.

There was still nothing there.

I needed to start thinking about finding a campsite.

I wasn't certain about setting up camp alone in the dark with the spooked feeling of something following me. But the something – whatever it was – was probably not a person. Maybe I just couldn't let myself think it was a person, or I'd end up hiking through the night until I reached my car.

I didn't hear steps behind me. When I set up camp, I was pretty sure I was on my own. The site was on the side of the ridge where the forest grew lush and dense, away from the windier side exposed to more weather. It had obviously been cleared by campers before me. There was a small fire ring set up next to a fallen log, and a very flat section that wouldn't make me feel like I was sleeping on a slip-n-slide all night. There's nothing like tobogganing on your sleeping pad to the other end of the tent to make you really value those level spots.

One hiker passed by going southbound while I was setting up camp. He was solo like me. I called out to a pretend person inside the tent while he went by, hoping to give the impression of two campers at my site. I had already changed out of my hiking boots and into the yellow crocs I use as camp-shoes, so maybe the brown boots visible outside the tent also suggested a second person. He probably didn't even notice. It's for the best, because I'm not a good ventriloquist.

It was the backcountry and it had been a dry winter. As damp as it was, and as chilly as it got when the sun dropped, I didn't feel right about lighting a fire beyond my small camp stove. Sitting on the log in silence, I ate a meal of instant rice and canned chicken. Then I fiddled around the campsite taking photos of mushrooms until the sun set.

It didn't get weird again until I was settled inside my sleeping bag. I was stretched out on the inflated sleeping pad and using the glow of my headlamp to read until I got sleepy. The sound returned, and this time it sounded exactly like a deer outside my tent. My brain went first to the idea of bears, but it was too early in the year for them. Besides, my food was hung in a bag several yards away, any bear action would be over there, not right outside my tent.

A snorting sound was accompanied by a pair of bulges pressing into the side of my tent. It pressed right through the space between the tent and the rain fly in two distinct spots. They moved in unison. Working with my deer theory, maybe it was a buck? And the spots were his muzzle and antlers? Why, then, weren't there three spots pressed into the tent? The bulges were accompanied by a deep whuffling noise. Hot, deep inhalations that tried to suck the air out of the tent. Or blow it down.

I sat up and grabbed my knife. I was supposed to carry more weapons with me, but they weighed a lot. I turned off my headlamp and sat in the darkness, my hands shaking.

Then the bulges and the breathing stopped.

My eyes were adjusting to the faint filtered moonlight still seeping through the plastic windows in the rainfly. The wind rattled the last of the winter's dried leaves. When a few leaves skittered across the nylon of the tent, I nearly jumped out of my skin. Concentrating on breathing and slowing my racing heart, I listened hard to the sounds of the forest around me.

A footfall. A footfall that sounded distinctly like a hoof.

And then the deep inhalation was much closer. I peered through the screen of my tent door. Something had raised the edge of the rain fly vestibule and was sniffing the interior of my hiking boot. As I watched in confusion and growing horror, my boot disappeared into the darkness of the campsite. What could only be described as a horse's whicker joined the snorting and whuffling noises and the sound of my boot being picked up and dropped in the packed dirt outside the tent.

I needed to pee. I considered crapping my pajama pants. My body was giving way to the fear that was overwhelming me, and when the tent rustled and my second boot was stolen out into the night, I nearly screamed.

Should I try to scare it away?

Could I try to get a glimpse of what the hell it was, and hopefully, maybe understand what it wanted with me?

The whuffling noise outside the tent was strange. But it sounded like 'whuffle.' My mutinous brain repeated whuffle on a loop while I tried desperately to figure out what to do next. 'Whuffle.' The sound itself had stopped, but my brain didn't stop replaying sound. It had latched onto the word whuffle and was not letting go.

As my stress and anxiety increased, the sounds in the forest grew sharper. My knuckles were pale where my fingers clenched the red plastic handle of the swiss army knife. 'Whuffle,' went my brain. Footfalls blended with owl hoots and leaves rattling. 'Whuffle,' said my thoughts in an ever-louder pattern as I tried to concentrate.

The antler (?) dragged slowly across the top of my rain fly. Reminding me of the bad guy with knives for hands in movies when I was a kid. Whuffle. I was going to die out here, mauled by some deranged deer. Whuffle.

"Whuffle," I said out loud, hoping to dispel the inner echo.

With my free hand, I circled my thumb across my fingertips in a fluttering motion. The sensation was soothing. The soft butterfly of sound soothing. It was one of my most frequent and subtlest stims, and it was helping me shake off some of the growing tension. My brain was still whuffling, but I thought that the creature – whatever it was – had finally left my campsite.

I knew I wouldn't sleep. Not without earplugs, Benadryl, and a heavy dose of nihilism. Was I safer in the tent, waiting until morning to try to find my boots and look for signs of the creature harassing me? The tent made 'me' bigger. While the nylon fabric was scant armor, it did create a barrier between that antler and my skin. But it also made me blind. I couldn't see what was going on out there in the woods, and my imagination was just going to keep growing the monster the longer I hid.

With an actual whuffle of my own, I unzipped my tent. My bare feet slid into my cold yellow crocs, which were a little clammy with dew.

There were still no sounds from outside the tent, so I stretched forward and unzipped the rain fly, giving myself a triangular flap of vision of the woods beyond the tent. A bare branch swayed a little, one brown leaf rattled against it.

Swallowing my fear, I heaved myself as quietly up out of the tent as I could, the rustle of nylon sounded like a roar in my ears as I stepped into the darkness.

It was still there.

Beside the log where I'd sat with my dinner, there was a large pale shape. But it was no deer.

Silver-white hair nearly glowed in the moonlight. I was glad I'd let my eyes adjust to the night and wasn't trying to look around with a headlamp.

Laying down, with my hiking boot nestled between its forelegs, was a unicorn. A whole, entire, swear-to-god unicorn.

My knees didn't give way, but I expected them to. I was afraid to move. To step toward it. (Him? Her?)

It made the whuffling noise. And it looked at me.

"Whuffle," I replied.

It made no move to rise. It just watched me in the moonlight. I was still afraid. More thrilled than terrified, but the adrenaline coursing through my system had by no means decreased. My heartbeat was so fast and hard it hurt in my chest.

I took a tentative step toward the unicorn. It didn't move. Another step. Whuffle.

"Whuffle," I replied.

I edged my way forward to sit on the very end of the fallen log. I was still a few feet from its horn. A few feet from its muzzle. My brain – my treacherous brain – chose that moment to remind me of the time in Grayson Highlands when one of the wild ponies had bitten me. My hands were shaking.

This close, the horn was no more glowing than the unicorn's hair. It was just a full moon, and the light color and a slight sheen made it clearly visible in the dark forest. The horn was nothing like the legendary spiraled horn, or even the antler I'd thought it was. Instead, it was more like a tusk. The fibers were visible and grew lengthwise along it. It looked more like a rhinoceros horn than one of a narwhal.

My body and brain were a battlefield of responses while the

cool damp of the log seeped through the thin cotton of my pajama pants. The adrenaline was still flowing, my heart still racing, and yet I was sitting three feet away from a creature that had been my special interest for most of my life. My autistic brain wanted to turn off stress signals entirely. The tingling sense of wonder that rose out of this conflict of arousal and relief was very nearly orgasmic.

Sensing my physical response to it, the unicorn pressed its horn into my lap. If I hadn't already known that the horn was a phallic symbol dating back to antiquity, I'd have known it right then. I wanted to laugh at the cliché of it, but the only sound that escaped my lips was a soft whuffle.

I had been a horse girl. Of course I had been. Animals made more sense than people did, for one thing. But also, horses had been the closest I could get to unicorns in real life. I've introduced myself to enough equines to have an idea of how to go about these tentative opening moments. But this was no equine.

Its muzzle looked more like the rounded nub of a deer or a goat. It had narrower nostrils and a smaller upper lip. I reached forward a hand to let it sniff me and was able to touch that soft spot where people have a little cupid's bow dip between nose and top lip. It was velvety soft like a horse's muzzle would be. A shudder rippled across the unicorn's skin when I touched it, but it didn't move.

As I stroked its nose with one tentative finger, I noticed that its delicate head was more like a deer than a horse. It didn't have the little billy-goat beard they sometimes had in fantasy paintings, but I could see that one would look right on this alien face. It watched me with one liquid black eye, its dark eyelashes slowly blinking like a satisfied cat.

Though the size of a reasonable adult deer, it was way smaller than a horse. This was not a creature a person could ride. It leaned into my touch as I rubbed its inner ear with my thumb. Horses like that as much as dogs do. It's a hard-to-itch spot. It sort of wriggled closer to me, so that it could rest its chin across my thighs while I kept stroking and exploring it. While it was happy to let me touch it, I avoided the horn itself. As bony appendages go, it didn't look particularly magical, but I had a lifetime of unicorn indoctrination telling me that it was.

Well, that settled that, I snorted as I petted the long sweep of the unicorn's neck. I was no virgin, and yet here I was with a unicorn's head in my lap. There was a good bit of chicken-or-egg debate whether the association of the unicorn with the Annunciation was what created the virgin part of the legend, or if unicorns really did care about a person's sexual activity.

It nudged me, nearly knocking me off the log. I reached out reflexively. It shoved the horn into my hands, where I helicoptered in my effort to stay upright. My hands grasped the bony tusk and a shiver rippled through me.

Finally.

The word echoed through my head like a really loud noise. I expected it to hurt my ears, but it didn't. Still holding the horn, I looked down at its gleaming black eyes.

"Hello."

Hello.

My mind scrambled. What the hell do you say to a unicorn? What is the protocol here? I regressed to the first grade and went with the dialogue I'd written in my book.

"My name is Alicia."

I...do not have a name. Not one that you can comprehend.

The horn was warm to the touch, which was off-putting. I very much needed to pee. My body wanted to explode in a number of directions at once.

I wanted to ask it why it was following me, but that seemed rude and possibly aggressive. I wanted to ask whether it was a boy or a girl, but that was rude, too, and kind of invasive. A lifetime of wanting to talk to a unicorn and I was at a loss for words.

The unicorn sighed in my lap.

I have a request to make of you.

"Okay. What's that?" It was a freaking *unicorn.* Like I was going to deny it anything?

There are captures on your box that must be destroyed.

Captures? On a box? My brain scrambled to decipher what the unicorn was saying. Its horn was still warm to my touch, and its chin still rested on my knee. It whuffled in mild frustration.

The box you point at mushrooms and flowers. You capture the mushrooms.

Oh. My phone. "Photos? You want me to delete some of the photos I took today from my phone?"

Please show me the box.

My phone was in the tent. It had been on airplane mode to preserve battery all day. It never occurred to me to grab it. (Though now that I thought of it, a unicorn selfie would be amazing.) The unicorn shifted its head to allow me to stand, gazing meaningfully at the tent. I was clearly intended to retrieve my phone. In a fit of minor rebellion, I grabbed my boot from between its forelegs before I walked over to the tent.

The phone was in the stow pocket just inside the door. I dropped the knife back away. I didn't need it. Not like it would do me any good if that horn decided to put me on the business end.

The unicorn rested its chin on my knees again once I'd settled back on the log beside it, phone in hand. I flicked it on and opened the photo album.

Review the captures, please. It sounded stern. Bossy unicorn. *Look for the stream where you drew water.*

My thumb flicked the album down, and I let the photos spin past until I tapped the ball of my thumb down on the distinct red-orange of the slime mold.

Please enlarge it?

The unicorn angled one glittering black eye so it could look into my phone. The absurdity of the moment rippled through me, and I tried not to giggle as I angled my hand to share a smartphone screen with a magical creature.

The previous capture please. It seemed to be familiar with phones. With the way photo albums worked. Which seemed strange to me, but what about this situation wasn't strange?

Previous. Flick. This repeated a few times before we left the slime mold and went to the preceding series of shots.

There. Please eliminate that capture and others of that place.

I looked at the photo. It was a close-up of a sweet little arc of round-headed white button mushrooms. I looked at all of the photos. It was just the button mushrooms. There was nothing there. It wasn't like I got evidence of fairies or anything.

I deleted the photos. The unicorn heaved a deep sigh.

Thank you.

"Am I allowed to understand any of this?" I asked tentatively.

Captures with your box take the magic of places with you. Most places are magic enough to tolerate it. They gain their magic back when you look at the captures. That place. That place is important and delicate. It could not sustain the drain of magic that you created.

"Will you do the same thing if anyone else takes a photo of those mushrooms?"

I would. But I do not need to. The mushrooms are already gone. Very few of the humans passing through here notice that place anyway. You are strange.

Well. I couldn't argue with that.

"Can I take a photo with you?"

The unicorn whuffled with what might have been a laugh.

Like the captures of magical beings that you took, I will not appear. You are welcome to try.

I took a selfie with the unicorn. (Why the hell not?) When I enlarged it, I saw what it meant. There was only a moonlit shot of myself and the log I was sitting on. Well, that explained why there weren't pictures of unicorns all over the internet.

I deleted the photo so I didn't drain any of the unicorn's magic.

It was then, right then, that it hit me. I was sitting on a log on the top of a rise on the AT with a unicorn's head in my lap. The mind-bending ludicrousness of that situation nearly made me laugh. I managed to choke that back, but not before I jerked, and the unicorn lifted its head.

Did something frighten you? It asked so solicitously I had to laugh then.

"No, no. I just – do you know that I spent my entire childhood obsessed with the idea of meeting a unicorn? It just struck me.

Here, now, that I'm sitting here with you. This is a dream come true for me."

It's a shame then, that you will not remember it.

"I won't?" Why wouldn't I?

You may remember a vivid dream. A spectacular tale, perhaps. But like those captures in your box, human minds aren't made such that they can grasp understanding that magic exists.

I wasn't so sure about that, but it sounded completely convinced. We sat there together for a long while. It asked me to itch its ears some more. We talked about unicorns. How many lived in this forest, in the world, how long they lived. It was candid and wry.

I don't know how many of us there are. There isn't a way for us to communicate.

We talked about smart phones, and all of the things my little box could (and couldn't) do. About the incompatibility between lenses and seeing what's really there between the molecules of air. And the way the light refracts for a machine rather than the curve of an eye.

While the ridiculousness of the situation had moved me to laughter, as we talked, I grew more and more moved to tears. I was perfectly calm. Perfectly at peace. It was more peaceful than even my rare visits to stables. Being around horses was wonderful, and soothing. But there is absolutely nothing as soothing as spending time directly with the object of a special interest.

Finally we parted, and it sounded wistful as it said it wished I could remember it. I turned in for a few hours before daylight. I still had eight miles to hike the next day to get to my car.

I slept soundly. Who wouldn't, with a unicorn watching her back?

I woke up to an angry pair of crows arguing loudly right above my head. They were loud enough and persistent enough for me to rise. My phone said it was nearly ten in the morning. I'd slept in, and the phone battery was inexplicably drained, though it was still in airplane mode. I slid on my crocs to go pee and blink into the too bright light of the early spring morning. There was a mountain laurel grove further down the ridge, and the pale pink blooms made me smile as I squatted in the brush several yards from camp.

Then, I looked for my boots. One was weirdly inside my tent. I always parked my boots just outside the zipper door of the tent under the vestibule formed by the rainfly.

The other was missing. I started the pot of water for my coffee and oatmeal, and stumbled around camp, looking at the scuffled dirt around the tent. Searching for the missing boot. My bare feet made squeaking sounds inside the rubber crocs.

There were no clear prints. No indication that something had taken it. But something must have taken it. I thought back to the night before and reading in the tent after the sun had set. At first, there was nothing unusual about the memory but then – I don't know how to describe it. The memory itself *shimmered*. It undulated in my mind. Like a gauze panel disturbed by the gentlest breeze.

The onomatopoeia word whuffle drifted through my head with the shimmering thought.

Whuffle. Something had taken my boot. I remembered now, the terror of the inhalation sounds against the fabric of the tent. Whuffle.

The sound memory came back. I realized that maybe, just maybe, the echolalia had been a gift. That my mutinous brain was good for something.

Because I also remembered the unicorn.

As soon as I remembered it, I spotted my boot at the edge of the grove of mountain laurel. I said the word whuffle a few times for good measure as my crocs squeaked through the damp leaves to retrieve it.

A circle of button mushrooms had grown around it. I almost wished I'd had my phone to take a photo. Instead, I said "Thank you," into the shadows beyond the blooming laurel trees.

Maybe it would know I remembered it, somehow.

Tree People
FRANCES OGAMBA

"Shh. They will hear you."

"They won't. Nne says they never hear us."

Oma and I are perched on the tail of a leaf on the outskirts of the tree's walls. The leaf gives a slight sway beneath our weight. Our eyes sweep in the sea of bodies splashing against one another as Eke market fills up. The vault of heaven brims with colors, white and azure. Down in the pith, our kind, the older ones, are preparing to join the market. They beat their insect bodies, flapping until a glow sprouts from the tawny wings and feathers. They touch the dust and smear it on their faces. This makes a shining effect on the nose and jaw. They file towards the Ray – a bright red spot that has marked our species passage into the human realm for many centuries – long before Eke, our great mother and the goddess of all life, was nurtured. They heave their bodies upwards and drop into the Ray. We see them almost instantly walking into the market. No longer as minute flies with paper wings, wiry legs and leafy brows, but as humans – adults, grown people, each wearing a body and gender of their choosing, hair neatly tucked underneath a scarf or cropped close to the skull. The transformation always dimples our skin with tremors of shock and wonder, and of impatience.

"You can't go down to Eke market until you are five hundred years old," Nne always says.

"And now?" Oma, my younger sibling asks to reaffirm their age.

"A little over two hundred."

"And Ugo?" my sibling asks for me.

"Three hundred," Nne mutters, busying their hands with scraping the yams.

Now in their human form, we watch as the older insects start to trickle into the market. The crowds triple, and the space grows quite cramped to bear such a throng. Some stand at the four cardinal points of Eke market, pulling fortune strings towards the market. They obtrude their bodies forward, arms outstretched, then drag an invisible charge crammed with luck towards themselves, and the market. They pull people also, the reason for such a crowd. They buy wares from humans visiting the market, and many bare their teeth after them in gratifying smiles. We scurry back into the tree at the sound of a bong. Food hour.

"Why do they have to go all the time?" Oma asks, hurrying to catch up with me, their breath catching in between their words.

"It is what we are. Eke's children, the market guards. We make sure that everyone who visits the market leaves satisfied."

"What if we leave the tree, like Neke and Ora?"

"Shh. People will hear you." A door creaks open in reluctance, but falls back without a body materializing. Perhaps, whoever was behind the door changed their mind.

"No, they won't," Oma persists, their labrum narrow and hard with stubbornness. Their wings puff, glossy in the poor light of the winding path leading to our hut.

"When you leave the tree, will you become a man or a woman?" Oma's voice pokes at me.

We walk by the Ray. I avert my eyes, afraid that one more glance at it and I will melt therein, as it flings me where it pleases.

I think of Neke and Ora always, two young ones from our generation. Sometimes I think of the ancestors in Nne's tales who have dared to leave the tree permanently, but mostly of Neke and Ora. Our tree must have felt inadequate for them. They must have wanted a life beyond playing guards and fueling the commercial blessings of humans.

It is banned to discuss or admire them. Yet Oma and I constantly find a private moment to include them in our conversations.

Where do you think they went to? Do you think they will be as real as the humans we see in Eke market? What would they look like? Did they choose to become a man or a woman?

Oma and I also think about what we might be.

Nne often says that Oma is bold and outspoken. The Ray may turn them into a human girl. I may become a boy. I remember Nne's tales of the market people, their honest work and honest swindles.

"Human beings are complex."

"How?" Oma and I chorus.

"They do not always mean their words. When they say they are dead while in a conversation with you, it is not death they mean in the true sense. It is something lesser but significant still. It could mean trouble or a joke."

Oma and I find this human character quite unappealing. We make fun of it sometimes when we are alone. It is tasking especially because we always mean the things we say. We give it up after a while.

"Did you go to the gate?" Nne asks when we walk in, our crime penned across their face. Their voice booms from the roof. I look up and see them on a wood board across the ceiling. "Have I not warned you not to go there?"

Nne hasn't. Still, we know the fate awaiting anyone caught at the gate. They struggle to swallow their agitation. They talk about shame and how it hovers around our heads like a halo – Oma's halo the thicker. We bow our heads and touch their knees. Their mood lightens and a glimmer of forgiveness fills their eyes.

We drink latex juice after a meal of roasted cocoyam. We join the rest of the younger insects and make our way to the square for the lessons. Our families are mostly single unit; one parent takes charge of grooming their children. Those who have been kissed and transformed by the heat of the Ray often choose to be identified by the gender they take on while in the market. Nne had been a woman in the market, but they choose to remain without a gender, to be neutral.

At sundown, as the moon throws a dispassionate light on the world, our market people tumble in through the Ray. Their scent of fatigue and hard work pervade our tree. They must return by sundown, as stated by the unwritten law of the Ray, or they will never make it through. Their wings will either amass weight and not be able to spiral up the Ray's passage, or they will remain in human form and never return to us.

I no longer desire Oma's company. I slip away while the returnees spill stories of their experiences at the market. I waddle on the hay in the central farm. Twice I cast brief glances behind me to ensure I am not leaving tracks for anyone who might follow. The ridges for the yams are drawn tight against one another like corn rows. It is not yet the season, but it promises a large harvest. I walk beyond the farm and plop down on a rock. The sharpness of its edges have been tamed by the weather and use.

I think I'm waiting for something, for a time perhaps, I'm not sure. The clouds presage night, the orange corners darken to ginger shades and backdrop the gray sky. In the fading light, I whip up Neke and Ora in my imagination. Two half-human adults walk the coastline of my thoughts. Neke has taken a masculine form. Ora has not taken any gender. They – Neke of tortilla-brown shade and Ora, the caramel-colored one with hair stretched and sprawled on their neck, appear happy as they trot along, their heads close and buried in their conversation.

"Everyone will leave," Nne says sometimes, "but not now. Not in our age."

There are prophecies carried to us from the sunken lips of old seers, about how something called a church would erupt and demand that our tree be cut down, all our homes and histories crushed with the blade of an axe. It is not this revelation that irks me. It is having to be trapped here forever, hovering until the five hundredth year. A shudder runs through me and I heave myself up from the rock. The darkness tightens its fists around the huts. I walk past two adults who are too engrossed with their discussion to see me. The gates to the Ray are shut, but the great red glows through the thicket, the large mouth beckoning to me. I slip through an opening in the thicket. There are no guards in sight. I spare a thought for Nne, and Oma – my talkative sibling. I love the tree, but the path that winds its track through the Ray, though dreary and unpredictable, appears to hold a more interesting version to my essence.

I float in oblivion a long a time, rocking back and forth on twigs and feathers, crashing into objects I do not recognize. It may have been long before I open my eyes to a group of humans whose blurred faces stick together above me in awe and shock.

"Someone abandoned a baby here," a woman says.

"I am not a baby," I try to retort, but what pours from my throat is a sea of gurgles.

I am not under our tree. Instead, I am lying at a roadside where four-wheeled engines roar past. As time goes by, the human sounds pour into my ears. Nne's words ring clearly: *You cannot go down to Eke market until you are five hundred years old.*

A woman peers at me, and runs a hand over my thighs. A black veil pushes down, swiping at my memories. Nne, Oma, Eke and others grow into faint thoughts I struggle to hold on to.

"It's a boy," the woman says, "The baby is a boy."

A Place Where Wings Can Spread
CEALLACH DECLARE

Dear Slenderman,

Dublin certainly has an excellent climate and weather for a moth. So far Mothman has seen a number of distant relations. In fact a particularly kind Cinnabar Moth has taken Mothman in for the coming week.

This is, unfortunately, only a temporary situation, as the question of permanent lodgings has yet to be rectified. The number of lodgings are more plentiful than expected, but few appear to fit a moth-sized budget. As you had suggested, renting a room from one of the local Humans would be the wisest option to avoid suspicion. While Cryptid-kind are much more respected and feared here than they are in America, no doubt the sighting of a man-sized moth living in the wilds will be cause for alarm.

Mothman would also miss the ever-enticing street lights of the cityscape. The headlights of the odd vehicle passing through the night on the back roads are never quite as captivating. Cities also mean anonymity, which Mothman can use after so much recent infamy.

So far Mothman has applied to many potential rooms and hopes to hear replies. As a Cryptid of few needs, all Mothman truly requires is a pleasant space to spend winters, enough room to accommodate a decently-proportioned wingspan, and enough privacy to wait until those hoping for a 'sighting' will leave Mothman alone.

Mothman also plans to enjoy the city. A visit to sample the local Human's mind-altering brew is certainly in order. Apparently these humans are very proud of their ability to create and ingest large quantities of liver poison. Mothman does not understand but will respect their life choices.

Will be writing again soon,
Mothman

Dear Slenderman,

Mothman misses your company as well. Perhaps, once proper lodgings have been secured, you will come to visit and sample the local liver poison. There are many establishments and all have been most welcoming. It is also very nice to be among a people who do not recognize you and will leave you to view the streetlights in peace.

Mothman wishes the same could be said for the accommodations. While the Cinnabar Moth's glen has been lovely, there is not much cover for a Moth of considerable size and Mothman can see rainy nights, of which Ireland has many, being something of a problem given the lack of house. Especially the lack of roof.

The first accommodation viewing Mothman experienced was a disappointment. The exterior was pleasant, with a number of parks and those children you are so fond of hypnotizing. At first Mothman was quite optimistic.

Upon opening the door and entering the dwelling, any good feelings quickly fled. It was dark. Not a beautiful dark like the blackest midnight, but a dank, artificial darkness made by deliberately cutting off the light from a place it was designed to occupy. The darkness came on so suddenly, so unexpectedly, that Mothman is certain even the Old Ones themselves would have had to keep an eye on the floor so as not to trip on the clutter.

The kitchen was small, you would not have liked it. Far too small and unclean. Dishes were piled in the sink to a height that would rival your own. The most appalling part was the human's unabashedness at the state of his dwelling. It was almost as if he *enjoyed* it. Mothman will not judge their poison ingestion but draws the line at living in their own filth!

And then there was the room. If one could call it a room. The door barely opened before colliding with the bed. The human entered the room and waved an arm, announcing, "This is it."

With the door ajar and the human standing in the doorway, there was no space to tell if there was even a room to begin with. Mothman gave the human a moment to realize how badly he blocked the entrance, but this human was not quick on the uptake.

"Could you move so Mothman can see the room?"

As the human shuffled away he had the audacity to reply, "Oh, yeah." It truly appeared that he had forgotten the very reason Mothman was visiting his dwelling.

Among the humans Mothman had been using a coat to blend in among them. The thought had occurred to Mothman that if left alone in a room, the coat could be discarded to see if wing-space was adequate. Such actions were not necessary. You would not have fit in this room, and you are a very slender Slenderman.

As you might have guessed, Mothman will not be staying in that dwelling.

Mothman trusts you are living well in the woods now that the weather is cooling. Less of those students will be bringing their cameras into your home to make their films in the cold. Youtubers are finally becoming reviled among the humans, as they well should be. While Mothman doubts 'sightings' will ever cease, hopefully the human disdain for Youtubers will lead to fewer of their 'sights' finding their way online. Mothman recalls from your awful 'Marble Hornets' ordeal that it is nearly impossible for a Cryptid to get a 'sighting' taken off the internet as it does not violate their mysterious 'terms of use.'

On that topic, Mothman thanks you for attempting to take down that unflattering video. It was very much appreciated.

The Cinnabar Moth has invited some friends over for warm nectar, which is always an excellent cure for a trying day.

Keep in touch,
Mothman

Dear Slenderman,

Mothman is familiar with the term 'tick-tock' as it pertains to human onomatopoeia and their curious desire to name nameless sounds. However, what you describe seems much more terrible and insidious. It is good of you to warn Mothman of these human innovations as Mothman does try to stay away from too many of their mesmerizing, screened devices. As you well know Mothman can spend hours on such a device, simply stating at the screen and doing nothing if left unchecked.

Unfortunately no luck at this latest viewing. Perhaps other Cryptids would enjoy the dank and moldy conditions of the dwellings on offer, however there is nothing quite as uncomfortable as the feeling of damp wings.

The latest dwelling was unpleasant, but it is the audacity of the humans which boggles the mind of Mothman! There were obvious stains on the walls and floors. Very, very obvious, though old and faded. In the bedroom, the mattress was likewise stained with black mold spots peppered across the white surface.

Mothman must ask, have you ever seen a speckled mattress? This question may seem ridiculous but it must be considered to truly understand the ridiculousness of the human's claims.

When Mothman pointed out that the mattress had spots, the human agreed. The mattress did indeed have spots. A moment passed. Mothman gave the human an opportunity to explain himself, one which he did not take. So Mothman asked the obvious, "What are the spots?"

"That's the pattern," the human replied.

Mothman has seen 'patterns' in human décor. They like their rules to be completely Euclidian and comprehensible. The Great Old Ones would never approve. However, human aesthetics, no matter where in the world, can be recognized at a glance from their ratios and mathematics. And a splatter of mold creeping across a cloth surface is nothing like their geometrical workings.

Mothman does want to like these humans. They seem a decent sort who will stop and talk with anything that seems to be in need of companionship. Then there are humans like these, humans either so greedy or desperate for remuneration that they would knowingly contract and bind their own to live in squalor.

When the humans infuriate Mothman so, Mothman recalls recently departing America and the reasons why. Humans suggest breathing and counting to ten. It has little effect on Mothman. How would you suggest dealing with such feelings of frustration?

Mothman had been hopeful regarding this dwelling. It was large, and at the highest level of the building, perfect for a post-flight stretch. Those who frequent the poison drinking establishment Mothman now frequents say there will be other dwellings to examine, but it is of little comfort when there is no place that truly belongs to Mothman alone. Perhaps the human penchant for drinking poison to air personal grievances is rubbing off on Mothman.

Humans are a strange and mixed lot, are they not? Such a variety of ethics and interests that make some pleasant company and others more monstrous than we allegedly are.

Your friend,
Mothman

Dear Slenderman,

While Mothman appreciates your suggestion of kidnapping children and terrorizing independent film makers as a form of self-care, Mothman is afraid that these activities, while sometimes very much deserved by nosy humans, are not terribly relaxing. However, should Mothman wish to engage in a more physically stimulating activity, chasing down a few teenagers whilst they drive through the woods would be in order.

Mothman has been getting plenty of exercise though; walking most places as a flight in broad daylight would arouse too much suspicion for comfort. Not that this is much better. Wearing a heavy coat over wings, and a hat over antennae is terribly uncomfortable. Throwing them off and taking flight at the end of a long day is the sweetest relief Mothman has ever felt.

Finding a home will be sweeter, or so Mothman assumes.

There is more disappointment to report, unfortunately. One

might assume that because Mothman has been spending nights in the open among the stars and downpours, that any set of walls with a roof would be an improvement.

It is difficult to describe how these dwellings are unsettling as under normal circumstances rot, decay and the natural world are hallmarks of a decent place to live. Humans sometimes describe this as a sense of 'wrongness,' where something that is normally pleasant becomes an object of horror. Where one detail, or several, can change something benign into something threatening. Like that image of a dog with a human's dentures you once showed Mothman.

The feeling of wrongness here was immense and foreboding. Cold is outside, rot and growth are outside, dampness is outside, darkness is outside, the point of human dwellings is to keep those things outside. Only in special circumstances are they invited in and almost never in a place where a human makes their home. When we see a human living in the cold, among decaying wood, dripping roofs and darkened rooms, it is not necessarily unsettling. Some humans live in unfortunate circumstances beyond their control and are unable to improve them due to the social systems forced upon them.

But some of these humans – they choose these places and refuse to leave them even though they have the means to do so. It causes the hair of Mothman's antennae to prickle and stand on end as they describe how wonderful their circumstances are. It is in that moment when it is apparent that the grip of madness is upon them as they seek to pull others into their insanity.

"This is the best house on the street and you won't find a better bargain in the city." The human who told me this said it proudly, her chest swelling with a pride that could not be feigned, her limbs numb to the cold and her eyes blind to the yellow stains of rain water that crept down the walls and threatened the floors. She believed this with her whole heart as Mothman examined the radiator for any sign of recent life. There was none, it had been long dead amongst the many other mechanical corpses in the house.

An animal smell permeated the air and a small white dog proved itself the culprit. Perhaps you would like it, you've assured me dogs are delicious. It seemed possessed by the same madness as its master, oblivious to the decay of the boards under its feet, which groaned frightfully as it bounded down the steps. If a small dog threatened their collapse, what of a Mothman?

As if she sensed Mothman's unease the human relented, "Maybe it needs a coat of paint, and it's a bit small, but otherwise it's perfect. You're not going to find better with your budget."

Mothman now has an appreciation for what humans feel when they discover a being beyond their ken. The dwelling with the moldy mattress would have been preferable – at least the mold was confined to the bed!

Her words have given Mothman pause though. What if these are the best dwellings the city has to offer? There is what they call a 'housing crisis' gripping the city, and a shortage of places to live. As Mothman returns to the field of the Cinnabar Moth and looks up at the skies that threaten rain, Mothman must wonder if a roof that fails and walls that breed illness are preferable to no roof and no walls at all.

In either case Mothman is tired of being rained on.

Damply yours,

Mothman

P.S. Mothman must assure you that the majority of humans in this country are wonderfully friendly. Mothman is beginning to suspect that there is some sort of sickness among the land-owning class that is leading to their madness. It is certainly worth investigating.

Dear Slenderman,

Unfortunately I cannot offer an opinion on which profile picture to use as you seem to blend into the forest in all of them and are not readily visible. Mothman also is not able to bring himself out of his recent fury and depression.

You will recall the circumstances of Mothman's hasty departure from the Americas. In order to avoid having to take such drastic measures again, Mothman has been very careful. But this simply went too far and Mothman must tell you about it!

A suitable dwelling was finally found. It was a high apartment with a balcony overlooking the harbor. If done carefully it would have been perfect for taking off on midnight flights. There was enough room to stretch, a clean area to prepare sustenance, weight-bearing floors, truly the stuff of dreams during this futile search!

The landlady was pleasant and prepared a cup of boiled leaf water. Apparently liver poison is only meant for drinking after a certain hour and at other times these humans adore their boiled leaf water. Mothman supposes it is inconsequential though. The dwelling was warm, with a fire in the hearth, and was everything that ought to be expected of a human's home. The woman renting the room also seemed to be free of the madness that kept most of the other house holding humans blind to the conditions they were trying to sell. All that seemed left were the usual, formal questions I had been advised to ask by the patrons of the liver poison seller.

"How close is the nearest train station?" Mothman does not ride the train but was advised that this was a very important question to ask if one does not own a vehicle of their own.

"About a twenty minute walk if you follow the water towards the city."

"And is there an alarm system in the building for fire and smoke?" This is also an important question humans advised I ought to ask.

"Of course, that's the law isn't it?"

Mothman must stress how well everything seemed. How pleasant. How everything seemed to have fallen into place and the madness had finally broken. It left Mothman completely unprepared for the response which followed what Mothman believed a completely innocent question. "How do you find the neighborhood?"

"Very safe. We've no Blacks or Indians here."

Such a statement was shocking to the core. "Mothman begs your pardon?"

"It's only natives here, not like those other places. So it's very safe."

In the Americas these feelings had unfortunately taken root. To think that it was here, so far away, spoken so brazenly, sparked a flame of rage within Mothman that could not be quelled until this wrong was righted.

Please do not be too disappointed that Mothman gave in and ate her.

You will recall that Mothman swore off eating humans with those views after fleeing America. It was most unfortunate that so many missing humans roused suspicion and rumors, but more unfortunate that there was such a plentiful hunt of humans Mothman did not have to feel remorse for consuming. Though if that video of Mothman devouring a racist had not been taken and put on that infernal internet, this journey across the sea would not have been required.

However, here we are. Mothman has eaten another racist. My only regret is possibly disappointing my dearest friend who has assisted so much and been so kind. Mothman knows he swore not to keep eating them, that that period of infamy was not to be relived. Old habits die the hardest it seems.

This insanity among the landlord class runs quite deep. In those it is not immediately apparent it is most insidious. Had Mothman not been mistaken for a White Man, who knows when her madness may have come to light! Most of those Mothman has met have not been corrupted by it. Perhaps it is something akin to the sickness Dragons feel when they have sat on their gold for too long, or the hubris of the Old Ones when they ruled over the cosmos. Possessions and power over others leads them to become twisted shades of the kind humans Mothman has come to know in this city.

Mothman must return to the glen but hasn't the heart. Today was such a disappointment and not even a full belly can rid Mothman of the memory of such brazen boorishness. It was truly unprompted ignorance of the worst kind.

To make things worse it is raining again. Mothman still has no roof for proper cover. It may be that the sole remaining option is to try another land, or a place with no humans, far from their lights.
Your friend,
Mothman.

Dear Slenderman,

Mothman knows we tend to differ in our choice of diet. It is generally agreed that there is little difference in nutritional value of humans, and when one is not choosy, hunting and feeding is much less of a chore. However, a Racist and TERF-based diet has done wonders for the overall mental health and wellbeing of Mothman. Admittedly perhaps Mothman was slightly zealous at first, being of the belief that such humans were few and far between and seizing each opportunity when Mothman crossed one. Though after *'Monster Slaughters Entire Middle-American Town,'* as the tabloids put it, Mothman can understand the Human's concern.

Mothman has regretted his binge-eating for quite some time, as it led to our having to part, good friend. Unsuccessful house-hunting only added to that regret, and Mothman is grateful you have been ready to lend a friendly auditory organ. As you may have guessed from Mothman's more jovial tone, there has been some luck at long last.

The most recent room Mothman saw was, at long last, adequate. You convinced Mothman to accept one last invitation to a viewing and Mothman is most grateful for you encouragement.

There was space, natural light, no mold, and best of all, not a single slur was uttered by the residents! The owner of the property lives nearby, and the house's other inhabitant is an insular fellow who prefers to keep to himself in his room and up in the attic. Mothman cannot begin to express his satisfaction with the lack of water damage and mildew in the air. Those things are all well and good for Wraiths in their ruins, but it cuts an odd contrast when a human gleefully inhabits a place full of rot and decay.

Mothman must also tell you of the lights! The dwelling is near the sea and on a calm night ships with their bright lights float along the water and glow through the fog. It is also approaching winter when humans decorate their homes and businesses in colored light.

It is not a perfect place, as such places do not exist, but there are exquisite lights and space in the room to throw off a coat and stretch one's wings, and that is enough to be content.

Yours truly,

Mothman

P.S. Mothman has been writing this final letter over time. As one might imagine, though Mothman is a Mothman of few possessions, moving always takes some time. During this time there has been a surprising development.

Mothman's housemate is named Ronan. As described earlier he tended to keep to himself, to the point of seeming to avoid contact with others. Mothman did learn however that he enjoys swimming and can scarce go a day without an early morning or late evening trip to the beach. Oftentimes he returns smelling of fish and wet fur, but he tolerates Mothman's musk so it would seem impolite to bring it up. Though there are refrigerating units in the dwelling, as humans are want to keep, Ronan never used it or the cupboards, though he never seemed hungry.

He is by all appearances unremarkable. Like most humans he is dry on the outside, has four limbs, and an opposable thumb.

When Mothman had lived in the house for a week, or perhaps two, Ronan called Mothman to the common area of the dwelling to discuss an unspoken rule. At first this worried Mothman. It would be terrible to have finally found a home only to discover some terrible secret was about to be revealed. So Mothman quickly donned his clever disguise, ready to discover the insidious secret that could not be spoken until the dwelling contracts had been signed.

"This is going to sound strange, but please don't go in the attic," said Ronan.

Caught slightly off guard, Mothman adjusted his hat to ensure his antennae were adequately covered and replied, "Mothman assumed that was your space."

"Technically no? I keep something important there though, and it needs its own space. So can you make do with your room and the common areas?" asked Ronan. "I'll pay part of your rent since there's a room you're paying for and can't use."

"Can Mothman ask what is kept in the attic?" Normally Mothman would not pry into another's business, but if it is something that could lead to more trouble it is worth knowing. Especially considering the amount of trouble Mothman is in with the United States authorities already.

Ronan gave Mothman a curious look before replying nonchalantly, "My skin."

It is very difficult to think of an appropriate response when a human who is nearly a stranger tells you that their skin is locked in the upper levels of your home. How else could Mothman respond except, "Mothman begs your pardon?"

"My skin, I need it to swim," explained Ronan. "I wasn't going to say anything until I was sure, but you're one of us aren't you?"

"Whatever do you mean fellow human?" Mothman replied, in the most perfect imitation of a human a Cryptid could manage.

"You call yourself Mothman in the third-person and your wing is sticking out of your coat," replied Ronan, never quite able to pronounce 'th' as humans are wont to do in this country. "Humans might fall for it, but it's pretty easy for one of your own to spot. Don't worry about it. Just, eh, mind the attic?"

"But of course. And would you mind terribly if Mothman entered and exited through the kitchen window at night? Mothman promises not to step on the drying rack."

"Don't see why not. Well, glad that awkwardness is over. Glad I don't have to worry about a roommate who screams 'Feral seal!'

and calls animal control when I come back from a swim. I knew there was a reason I had a good feeling about you."

And that, dear friend, was how Mothman came to live with a Selkie and found a place where wings were free to stretch.

Home
LAURA SIMONS

Day 24093
This is *my* house.
I won't allow anyone to harm it.
There should have been no more intruders after the last one. I do not want these people here. They *will* leave–

Day 24095
They are siblings. They are loud.
Always singing and talking and stomping. As if they must be louder than anything else.

Day 24106
There are bolts on the door now. Bolts and hideous, gaudy new locks. How *dare* they–

Night 24112
I was going to fill the night with terrors. But he woke up screaming before I began. She came running from the other room. They sleep right across the hall from each other, with the doors on a crack.
…they are young, are they not, to be living on their own. Was I ever so young?

Day 24114
She has fixed the squeak in the door at the top of the stairs. It never squeaked when I still lived.

Day 24121
The noise of the doorbell scares them. But they get so many deliveries.
It is a good bell. It has worked all these years–
I can see one of the men coming now with his packages, trudging up to the door.

...perhaps if I knock before he is here, they will come and look before he can sound the bell.

Day 24129

He is planting flowers in boxes on my windowsills.
I always wished I could grow flowers.

Night 24137

She is afraid of the dark. I could see it in her eyes when she got out of bed... I lit the lamps for her.

Day 24142

They have moved the couch to the sun spot a little to the right of the window. That is where I used to have my armchair.
It is the only sensible place for it.

Day 24163

Sometimes the noises of the world are suddenly too much for him. He winces and tries not to sway his head.
This is my house.
...I can keep it calm and quiet for a while.

Day 24178

She just got a phone call and now they are both laughing.
Laughter is a good sound, isn't it.
They said this house has been good luck...

Night 24205

They are singing in our kitchen.
He found my cookbook in the gap at the back of the kitchen cabinet and now they are trying to cook.
They wanted to start with the soufflé. They don't even know how to make béchamel!
I turned the page to the casserole instead.

Day 24236

This is my house.
These are *my* boarders.
I won't allow anyone to harm them.

More Precious Than Gold
KASPER D P WILDWOOD

"We didn't know any better," the crewman says, and swallows, presenting the chest to the captain. "What do we do now?"

"Kill it," the captain says, but the ice is melting in his eyes.

"We can't," the first mate says desperately, praying she won't have to fight her captain on this. "We can't. We – I won't. We won't."

"I know."

"Daddy," she says, floating in a tub of seawater in the hold, "Daddy, la-la, la-la-la."

Her voice rings like bells. Her accent is strange; her mouth isn't made for human words. It mesmerizes even the hardiest amongst them and she isn't even trying. The crew has taken to diving for shellfish near the shorelines for her; she loves them, splitting the shells apart with strength seen in no human toddler, slurping down the slimy mollusks inside and laughing, all plump brown cheeks and needle-sharp teeth. She sometimes splashes them for fun with her smooth, rubbery brown tail. Even when they get soaked they laugh. They love her.

"Daddy," she calls again, and the captain can hear the worry in her voice. The storm rocking the ship is harsh and uncaring, and if they go down, she would be the only survivor.

"Don't worry," he says, and goes over, sitting next to the tub. The first mate, leaning against the wall, pretends not to notice as he quietly begins to sing.

"Father," she says, one day, as she leans on the edge of the dock and the captain sits next to her, "why am I here?"

"Your mother abandoned you," he says, as he always has. "We found you adrift, and couldn't bear to leave you there."

She picks at the salt-soaked boards, uncertain. Her hair is pulled back in a fluffy black puff, the white linen holding it slipping almost over one of her dark eyes. One of her first tattoos, a many-limbed kraken, curls over her right shoulder and down her arm, delicate tendrils wrapped around her calloused fingertips. "All right," she says.

"Why am I really here?" she asks the first mate, watching the sun set over the water in streaks of liquid metal that pool in the troughs of the waves and glitter on the seafoam.

"We didn't know any better," the first mate says, staring into the water. "We didn't know – we didn't know anything. We didn't understand why she fought so viciously to guard her treasure. We could not know she protected something a thousand times more precious than the purest gold."

She wants to be furious, but she can't. She already knew the answer, from reading the guilt in her father's eyes and the empty space in her own history. And she can't hate her family.

"It's all right," she says. "I do have a family, anyways. I don't think I would have liked my other life near as much."

Her kraken grows, spreading its tendrils over her torso and arms. She grows too, too large to come on board the ship without being hauled up in a boat from the water. She sings when the storms come and swims before the ship to guide it to safety. She fights off hydra and shoal serpents and other beasts of the seas, and gathers a set of scars across her back that she bears with pride. "I don't mind," she says, when the captain fusses over her. "Now I match all of you."

The first time their ship is threatened, really threatened, is by another fleet. A friend turned enemy of the first mate. "We shouldn't fight him," she says, peering through the spyglass.

"Why not?" the mermaid asks.

"He'll win," the first mate says.

The mermaid tips her head sideways. Her eyes, dark as the deep waters, gleam in the noon light. "Are you sure?" she asks.

The enemy fleet surrenders after the flagship is sunk in the night, the anchor ripped off the ship and the planks torn off the hull. The surviving crew, wild-eyed and delirious, whimper and say a sea serpent came from the water and attacked them, say it was longer than the boat and crushed it in its coils. The first mate hears this and has to hide her laughter. The captain apologizes to his daughter for doubting her.

"Don't worry," she says, with a bright laugh, "it was fun."

The second time, they are pushed by a storm into a royal fleet. They can't possibly fight them, and they don't have the time to escape.

"Let me up," the mermaid urges, surfacing starboard and shouting to the crew. "Bring me up, quickly, quickly."

They lower the boat and she piles her sinuous form into it, and uses her claws to help the crew pull her up. Once on the deck she flops out of the boat and makes her way over to the bow. The crew tries to help but she's so heavy they can barely lift parts of her.

She crawls up out in front of the rail and wraps her long webbed tail around the prow. The figurehead has served them well so far but they need more right now. She wraps herself around the figurehead and raises her body up into the wind takes a breath of the stinging salt air and sings.

The storm carries her voice on its front to the royal navy. They are enchanted, so stunned by her song that they drop the rigging ropes and let the tillers drift. The pirates sail through the center of the fleet, trailing the storm behind them, and by the time the fleet has managed to regain its senses they are buried in wind and rain and the pirates are gone.

She declines guns. Instead she carries a harpoon and its launcher, and uses them to board enemy ships, hauling her massive form out of the water to coil on the deck and dispatch enemies with ruthless efficiency. Her family is feared across all the sea.

"You know we are dying," the captain says, looking down at her.

She floats next to the ship, so massive she could hold it in her arms. Her eyes are wise.

"I know," she says, "I can feel it coming."

The first mate stands next to the captain. She never had a lover or a child, and neither did he, but to the mermaid they are her parents. She will always love her daughter. The tattoos are graven in dark swirls across the mermaid's deep brown skin and the flesh of her tail, even spiraling onto the spiked webbing on her spine and face. Her hair is still tied back, this time with a sail that could not be patched one last time.

"We love you," the first mate says simply, looking down. Her own tightly coiled black hair falls into her face; she shakes the locs out of the way and smiles through her tears. The captain pretends he isn't crying either.

"I love you too," the mermaid says, and reaches up to pull the ship down just a bit, just to hold them one last time.

"Guard the ship," the captain says. "You always have but you know they're lost without you."

"Without *you,*" the mermaid corrects, with a shrug that makes waves. "What will we do?"

"I don't know," the captain says, "but you'll help them, won't you?"

"Of course I will," she scoffs, rolling her eyes. "I will always protect my family."

The captain and the first mate are gone. The ship has a new captain, young and fearless – of the things she can afford to disregard. She fears and loves the ocean, as all captains do. She does not fear the royal fleet. And she does not fear the mermaid.

"You know, I heard stories about you when I was a little girl," she says, trailing her fingers in the water next to the dock.

The mermaid stares at her with one eye the size of a dinner table. "Is that so?" she hums, smirking with teeth sharper than the swords of the entire navy.

"They said you could sink an entire fleet and that you had

skin tougher than dragon scales," the new captain says, grinning right back at the monster who could eat her without a moment's hesitation. "I always thought they were telling tall tales."

"And now?"

"They were right," the new captain says. "How did they ever befriend you?"

The mermaid smiles, fully this time, her dark eyes gleaming under the white canvas sail. "They didn't know any better."

Thicker Than Water
ZANNE SUTER

He would have thought it was beautiful if it didn't make him hurt so damn much every time he saw it. It just served to remind him how he'd failed – failed those boys and failed in his promise to Dorothea, God rest her blessed soul.

Jude had been just too damn quick. Waylon knew any child of Melusine would be strong in the water, his grandpappy's tales were true on that count, but he hadn't quite expected such a flash of speed on land. Hank had done his part, luring Jude onto the shore, hoping to keep him out of the water long enough to dry the nix right out of his brother.

That had been their plan, at least. Jude had a different one.

Hank fought hard; he busted Jude's nose but good. Waylon thought it was going according to plan, trapping Jude and making sure he couldn't damn well sing them to their deaths. But they forgot – God-damned rookie mistake to forget Jude wasn't fully *human* anymore, forgot that one important thing that meant the difference between success and failure. Jude may have been turning into a nix, but he was a Pelletier first – swamp-trained from the cradle, with witch in his blood. Plus, he had luck enough, both good and bad in equal measure, to catch one of the secrets of the swamp in his snares and get himself bit instead of killed. It must've been that pretty Pelletier face that saved his ass because there were a damned few critters, human or otherwise, that could avoid falling for that.

Pelletiers might not be the smartest of the bunch, but they were the most deadly and the most loyal. Family 'fore God or the Devil, that was their motto, born and bred into their bones before their first breath. When that nix spilled venom into Jude's bloodstream, that didn't change, just narrowed Jude's focus more sharply to where it had always been rooted. Pelletiers first, only and always, which left his little brother Hank as his chosen prey.

He had been from the start, if Waylon reckoned right.

Seduction took many forms – sometimes it was blatant offerings of lustful drunkenness, sometimes it was the soft sensuality of a flannel shirt against bruised skin, a gentle pat on the shoulder when crying was out of the question...that yearning need for family. Those boys only ever had one real weakness – fact it was blood only made it that much worse since that was all they had left. Their father had been a piece of shit from the start, beating on one or the other of them once they got old enough to take a hit for their mama, and taking all their father's anger when she up and passed on, so all those boys had was each other.

Neither Waylon nor Hank saw that Jude had been playing Hank from the very start, using his own weaknesses against him.

Not until it was too late. Waylon broke through the trees just in time to see Jude dragging Hank beneath the water, tightening his coils around his brother's taller frame like a boa constrictor and just sinking like a stone.

It was the glitter of triumph in Jude's eyes and the blood on his mouth that told Waylon it was too late for Hank. Somewhere in that endless few seconds, Jude had already bitten him. Waylon weren't no fool. He got off that shore 'fore he had *two* hungry young nix looking for a snack. An old man would be no match for them both.

He had Father Thibault's number dialed before he realized what he was doing; Waylon hung up hearing the priest's faint voice echoing down the line. There was no one he could tell about this. Bringing anyone here would be signing the boys' death warrant as sure as shit, and it wasn't like prayer or a visit to the midwife could fix this mistake. Anyone else wouldn't see them as anything more than a target; together they had always been dangerous, but this went beyond a few months in jail or some innocent poaching. This kind of threat would be dealt with accordingly by the other swamp folk; it could only end in blood, though whose it would be was the question.

Waylon couldn't see these boys that way. If he stepped back and took a good look at it, he knew they were even more lethal than they had been — he knew what had to be done.

But…these were *Dorothea's* boys. They were kin sure as if he'd fathered them himself. He had played the father role more often than he could count when they were growing up, keeping an eye on them when their asshole of a father was in jail or doing his damned best to get there — keeping an even closer eye after Victor had gone and got himself dead.

Waylon couldn't watch these boys die; that would break something on the inside that he couldn't afford to lose — not anymore. Do that and he might as well kill himself and get it over with before God or the Devil had to take matters into their own hands.

A man's got to keep his word — got to protect his family, no matter what.

His next call was to a Voudon priestess he knew from Orleans. Waylon weren't no fool. The creature that was Jude had been trying to find a way out of this swamp for months now; the only thing that had kept him tethered was his brother. Hank was always the smartest of the Pelletier lot and, with his help now he was turned, the boys would be swimming the Mississippi within the week. Waylon knew what hell they could raise there with all those overly trusting tourists dipping their toes in the water against all common sense.

So he had that priestess fashion a binding that would leash those boys as sure as barbed wire. The problem was, power that big needed constant feeding. Voudon magic was powered by life and death and the approval of whatever *loa* was necessary to beg a favor; there weren't enough chickens in the whole of Louisiana to keep any *loa* invested for as long as was needed. Waylon did what he had to do — he did what any father would have done to protect his boys. Hell, the one good thing Victor had done in his life was to take the rap for Jude instead of letting that boy die in prison — Waylon had a sneaking suspicion he might be meeting up with Victor in Hell as a result of this escapade, so he hoped Victor would be a tolerable roommate. So Waylon offered himself, a human battery to keep the spell strong, and the deal was done.

With the problem contained, all Waylon had was time.

So he kept quiet – kept his fool mouth shut and kept everyone else away. He told everyone who mattered that the boys had run off, Hank finally convincing his brother after so many years to leave the swamp and make their way out in the real world, away from the town where every deputy knew them by name. With his shotgun, Waylon scared off what visitors came to his door and he made treks into town to get what few supplies he couldn't scrounge from the swamp on his own. He couldn't risk bringing their prey right to the boys, not that it did any good.

Waylon turned a blind eye to the reports of the missing folk as the years passed, reluctantly allowing the cops to dredge his small parcel only when they brought their warrants and lawyers, threatening to take everything away.

If they took everything, they'd be taking the boys, even unknowingly – and Waylon had long made it clear to any and all, especially himself, that these boys were *his*. They were his to guard, his to protect, his shameful secret to hide from the world. They were his boys now that Dorothea was gone – his mess to clean up should it ever need doing. No one else could touch them.

No one else would dare – not with Waylon standing guard.

Those boys may have become something else, but they hadn't lost their wits in the bargain. Waylon didn't know where those boys hid themselves when the divers went in the water, but nothing was ever mentioned and no bodies were ever discovered.

Waylon didn't want to know what they'd done with them – didn't want to think of the stories that would be told about the crazy, old hermit when those piles of bones were found after he gave up the ghost.

Waylon's favorite past-time in these endless days was to watch his boys frolicking in the water, twining around each other slippery as seals. There was something soothing in their gracefulness, their metallic shimmer almost hypnotizing, blinding as koi writhing wantonly in a garden pond. Damn near innocent sensuality, if he wanted to get all poetic about it, though he knew the pretty colors and sinuous tails served as an attractive lure for those stupid enough to want a closer look. Their coils were the perfect camouflage, indistinguishable from sunlight scattered across the water or the multi-colored roots tangled beneath the surface.

Jude had darkened to a deep, bronzed gold, hinting at the color buried in his daddy's bloodline, Waylon was sure. Dorothea may have been a pureblood townie, but Victor had a drop of the native in him, though his family was too proud to admit to being bred on the wrong side of the sheets. Waylon had expected Hank to have similar coloring, but Hank broke the mold just as he had as a boy, never doing what was expected of him. Hank's scales were a deep scarlet color, dark as dried blood, with a green sheen like a moss-covered coin. Waylon thought their color told a lot about them – shiny to look at, almost painfully distracting, but hard as steel beneath.

It didn't matter what shade they were, those boys were beautiful – always had been, even when fully human. No one could ever say Victor had fathered ugly little bastards – no offense to Dorothea, who had been a God-damned angel from Heaven and far too good for this world. The end result was beauty that could cut a person deeper than bone, but the hurt would feel so good, a woman would bleed out gladly just for a taste. Hell, a man or a woman – Waylon could admit that, now. Jude had never been discriminating in his partners, though neither the parish priest nor his daddy would ever acknowledge those particular indiscretions amongst Jude's many others.

It was disturbing, at first, what Waylon saw as he watched them from that high attic window – the only one in his whole place that had an unobstructed view of the swamp edging his property. Waylon had more sense than balls and never set foot within range of their song; he made sure to keep his distance. It was a God-blessed miracle he was nearly deaf, or things would have taken a darker turn long ago and his bones would join those others hidden in the muck along his shoreline.

Still, he watched; he couldn't help himself. Those boys were the only human – didn't matter if it was past tense or not – contact he had these days. He had always known the boys were close, couldn't expect anything less after the life they'd lived. They'd resided in each other's pockets since they were tots and growing old enough to drink legal hadn't changed that any. They were nix – damned near water-based incubi, if anyone wanted to get all technical, so it made sense, weird as it was – and this change just made them even closer.

It made Waylon yearn for things his old body could no longer deliver.

Hank would lean back on the rocks, dangling his legs or his tail in the water, singing something, Waylon could tell. With skin darkened by the sun, he lay out naked as the day he was born, pure sin stretched out waiting to be tasted. Jude's head barely broke the surface of the water as he swam closer, eyes boring into Hank's, the center of his universe, as always. It reminded Waylon of a shark edging near its prey more than anything else, but he couldn't say whether it was Hank's voice pulling Jude in or the sight of Hank's body just lying there waiting for him.

Sometimes Jude was the hunted, and as he bathed along the shore Hank would slowly circle – patient as a crocodile, with eyes just as innocent – before erupting from the water, ready to sink teeth and flesh into that bare expanse of golden skin as he pulled Jude beneath the surface.

It didn't matter what form they chose to be in, it was a sight to behold, all shimmering skin and silk-smooth muscle – land or water, skin or scale. The scales gave it a dangerous edge, two hungry serpents – an ouroboros endlessly eating its own tail. It was impossible to tell where one ended and the other began under the murky mantle of the swamp.

But that's the way Jude had wanted it, he figured. It was why he'd taken such time and care to lure Hank in – how hard it must have been for him not to just grab Hank and never let go in those early weeks of the transformation. Not that Hank would have let his brother go, leave him to serve out his eternity alone. Only a fool would believe that, and Waylon weren't no fool. It probably would have ended the same, no matter what.

Sometimes believing this gave Waylon the only comfort he could find, when the knowledge that he should end this pressed sharp and clear against the haze of whiskey.

As the years passed, the boys began to test the boundary Waylon had imposed upon them that first day. More often than not, when Waylon focused his binoculars on that portion of the swamp, he would find Hank coiled there along the boundary, arms crossed over his bared chest and eyes narrowed speculatively, staring straight at him, hiding up in his ivory tower.

Hank, always the stubborn one – never the brother who wanted to be tied to this swamp his whole life – he kept pushing, wearing a track along the edge of the boundary. Waylon often wondered if Hank's own persistence would kill him, keeping him out of the water for longer than made Jude comfortable. He'd be stalking like a caged beast, back and forth, one hand trailing along the invisible border, until Jude emerged from the pond, using his wiles to entice Hank back beneath the surface – back to their sanctuary in the sheltering cloak of the water.

No matter what form they were in – human or nix – it seemed Jude had trouble reigning in his baby brother's need to move beyond the strictures of their existence. It almost made Waylon laugh to think no matter how much things changed, the more they stayed the same.

Then he cried just because he could – no one around to stop him, not anymore.

Years continued to roll by and the boys were just the same – still young, still strong, still as deadly as ever. His friends and nearest neighbors passed...Father Thibault and Mambo Leandra both, from what he'd heard. He'd lost contact with nearly everyone, the only survivor of the Pelletiers, the only one left to carry on their memory. Waylon never thought he would be a living memorial to anybody, and the weight of the responsibility was wearing him down.

He had gotten old; he hated to admit that fact, but he had finally met an adversary he couldn't beat, 'sides his love for those boys. Time was taking its toll.

As his hair receded and his bones became brittle, Waylon spent most of his time watching Hank and Jude – forever young, forever together. Sometimes it made Waylon damn near jealous of something he could never have and never really understand.

Ironic, ain't it – that Jude kept Hank tied to the swamp in the end, anyhow? Hank had begged his big brother his whole life to leave their father's ways behind, to leave this town on the edge of the world, this Purgatory of their family's creation. But Jude had been hooked by the family line long ago, loyalty to his kin keeping him rooted there, rotting in the humid Hell that was this swamp. Even Hank's hold hasn't been strong enough to break that tie.

But by failing to save Jude from becoming a full nix, Hank was successful in one way; he fulfilled that hidden desire behind his need to get Jude out. He saved his brother from the life that had been carved out for him from birth. It wasn't in a way any of them had expected, but Jude sure as shit wasn't burning in the chair like most of the menfolk in his family. The preacher, keeper of a town's-worth of secrets, once said Jude had no soul, but Waylon thought Jude just hid his soul too deep for anyone to find. He didn't share that side of himself with just anybody; his daddy had beat blanket sentimentality right out of him. But that didn't mean Jude couldn't love, because Waylon had seen it every time those two boys were together and there was no way any creature could love another that much and not have a soul. Just looking at the beauty of those two boys together made Waylon's heart hurt, made him believe it wasn't all useless – that he hadn't been wrong.

It made Waylon wonder what was waiting for him around the next bend in the road, though.

The status of a soul had become more important to him as his time crept nearer with its elephant's tread. It weren't no secret – the pains in his chest and the shortness of breath gave it away. Feeding the power behind that boundary was taxing on his heart and his old body couldn't take the strain much longer. It was damn near time to RSVP a reaper to save him a spot on the next boat to Hell.

Near on twenty-four years after Jude disappeared beneath the water with his brother clasped in his arms, Waylon slowly made his way down the stairs, pausing to rest every few steps as he tightened his grip on his cane. He stood at the door to the backyard, taking a deep breath of that late summer air, letting the faint hint of turning leaves lure him further outside.

It was time to see the boys again, time to say his goodbyes – unload some of those useless apologies for letting things turn out the way they did. Waylon also went for purely selfish reasons; he wanted to sit with them again, surround himself with their youthful vitality. He wanted to hear their voices arguing back and forth – legends said there was nothing prettier than the sound of a nix, even if they were two brothers in the midst of a spat. He wanted a chance, just this once; it might serve as the angels singing him to his rest 'til he got to wherever he was going.

They would get a little energy boost from feeding off him, before the boundary dissipated entirely as his heart beat its last. He'd be leaving them with plenty of time to move on to the busier waters of the tourist areas before winter set in, if they wanted.

He had done what he promised – he'd looked after them 'til the end. Now it was time for them to learn to look after themselves. Once they made it clear to the Mississippi, the hunting would be easy, and they could survive just fine as long as they kept to themselves. They knew how to keep a low profile, how to hide the bodies, how to spread out the attacks. Hell, Victor had trained them well enough as kids, the bastard.

Those boys were all grown up. It was time they went out into the world – made their own place in it.

They were still family, still Pelletiers. That had always stayed the same.

The only thing that had changed was the prey.

Will-o-the-Wisp
THERESA TYREE

People always come out when it snows. Is it the way the marsh freezes that draws them out? The way the snow smooths away the dips and gaps in the landscape? The way every ice crystal glitters in the moonlight – or in our light?

The people are always more fascinated by our light when it snows, too. Surrounded by so much cold, of course they're surprised to see our strong blue flames flickering between the snowbanks. We've been mistaken for human fires many times. So many hands have grasped for us, trying to draw warmth from us in their final moments as they fall beneath the ice and sink away, swallowed by the perfect crystal marsh. They stop moving, after a while – elegant additions, perfect moments of eternity motionless in the freezing swamp. Their hair, if they have any, floats around them serenely. Even after the bubbles stop rising from their lips and nostrils, they seem to be sighing out their last breath. Their eyes are my favorite. They gleam the way we do, drawing me in until I almost extinguish myself pressing against the ice.

You, however, are more sure-footed than any traveler I've seen in the marsh over the years. Some run, some walk, but once one of you sees us, you always follow. No one ever catches us. But you're not going in straight lines. You're not letting us lead you.

I'm intrigued. Do you know these marshes the way I do? Do you know where we keep our treasures? Are you particular about the cool, clear window you will sleep behind until winter ends?

I linger longer than I should in front of you. Your fingers brush through me, and you're warm! So warm I wonder why you mistake us for being made out of flame, like your own kind. How could anything so warm survive in the marsh? Why did you come here? Mad with purpose, you make your way through. What could possibly have driven you from your home, your bed, your false false-fire? This place, with its cold sleeping people and true false-fire, isn't for you.

I switch my position before you can catch me again. You don't belong here. You need to leave. The marsh is for cold things, lost things, walking-dead things. Your kind says we lead you astray. Yet we only show those who are looking the path they are searching for. But you're not trying to find that path – you're trying to best it.

You need to leave. Go back. You don't belong here. Go back!

You look to where I've moved, floating in front of you like a beacon. You step away. *Why* won't you follow me? I'm trying to help you! You don't belong here, but now you've taken a wrong step. You lose your footing, and fall through ice, into the water, joining the mid-wife from a month ago. I remember the way she'd whispered as she walked, words full of sorrow and blood. She'd lost one too many and was lost herself. You don't struggle as you fall like she did. Instead, your hands search the ice above you. Calm. The others are never calm until the bubbles that pour from their mouths start to thin – but your mouth is clamped shut. You keep your bubbles inside and search the ice methodically with your fingers – one hand bare, the other wrapped in a dark red glove. The contrast between the dark brown skin of your hand, the pink of your finger pads, and the red of the glove are like the hues of an ember. It's almost enough. I could believe you would find your way back through the ice; but you're too far from the way out. You'll never find it. Your heavy winter skirts are filling up with water even as you struggle.

I flicker to the jagged opening in the ice. Here. It's here. You move in the opposite direction though, away from the hole. Don't go that way! You're not looking like the tired teacher's aide did, the one who floats over there. His glasses still shimmer on his face, paper turning to mulch at the tops of his pockets, his letter of expulsion clutched tightly in his fingers. It's illegible now, but the paper was damp with tears before he tumbled under. He couldn't see a way forward. He found this way, where he didn't have to move on. But that's not what you're looking for, so follow me. I'll get you out.

You move away from me again.

Let me lead you!

Your bubbles are starting to spill from your nostrils. Your movements are more delicate now, like you're trying to conserve your energy. Your chest flutters, like the bubbles are fighting to get out, and you make the face all the people who come here make before they start to calm; that strange wince that wrinkles the skin between your eyes. Are you going to lose your bubbles the way the pastor a week ago did, all at once? I thought she would hold her breath forever. In the end, the bubbles burst forth in a froth when her eyes rolled back. It was the most magnificent bouquet. It lasted for only a moment, but it was beautiful nonetheless.

It would look wrong coming out of your mouth.

You can't stop moving. You can't stay. You don't belong here, the marsh isn't for you.

I flicker to the other side of you, barring your way. You hesitate, but you shouldn't. You don't have time for that. Your bubbles are so thin. Your hair is settling into the familiar serene shroud – but your eyes spark with a fire that the others never had.

You move away from me, back towards the hole you made in the ice. I follow you, pushing you back until your fingers find the jagged edge of the way out. The sound you make as you heave yourself out of the water is like a bonfire; you roar, then wheeze, crackling every so often as you encounter hidden pockets of moisture in places they shouldn't be. Your fingertips are blue and purple from the cold, but your eyes still spark. Hot puffs of air leak from your mouth. You can't stay here. You're too warm for the marsh. If we let you stay, you'd melt it.

I flicker ahead of you on the path back to the world outside the marsh. This way. This is your way. Follow me. But you step away again, as if you don't see me.

You are…frustrating.

I flicker to just in front of you, cutting you off. You stop with a jarring step, as if you weren't expecting to be confronted by me. We stay there for a moment – you uncertain, me in your way. Slowly, you take a step backwards, never taking your eyes off me, testing the ground with your foot before putting it down.

This isn't how it's supposed to go. We lead, you follow. That's the way it's always been, for centuries, millennia. And yet, here you are, running from me. And me! Chasing you!

I advance towards you. You totter in your haste to back up. Your eyes flicker down to your foot. You move your foot marginally, matching your winter boot to the print you previously made. Your eyes bolt back up to me, and I watch myself through the strange reflection of my own flame within them. I look greener reflected in your eyes. Less blue.

It seems fitting that you would take even my color from me. You've taken everything else that made me what I am. The cold has always led your kind to us, and we have always led you with our heatless fire into the embrace of the cold and the endless. Everything about you is wrong. I don't know what led you here, but it wasn't the cold. I don't know what you're looking for, but it isn't what we can give you.

Almost as if you can understand me, you take off your glove. You clutch it in your hand, then hold it out. "Can you help me find her?" you ask softly.

I falter, flickering agitatedly. We are not asked to show things. We lead, and you follow. That's the way it's always worked. It's strange, being asked to do the thing I am meant for, but for a different purpose. Familiar, and yet shackling. The base understanding of the pact is shifted – and yet the same. You're asking me to show you the way. The way you're looking for. This isn't so different from what I did for the others floating serenely below the ice. But your path is a search. And when you're done, you will leave. That's not the common way of things here in the bog.

The glove in your hand is limp and deflated without your hand to fill it – but the dull rust red color of it sparks a memory.

How could I forget her?

It was hardly a day ago. She cried as she walked, a red glove wrung between her hands. She'd stumbled into the bog, clumsy in her grief. The water streamed from her like she were the very spirit of a spring. Even winter's cold couldn't freeze her tears. I remember the easy way she let us lead her. Her eyes were so fogged with moisture, it was as if we were the only thing she could see – yet she kept walking, her ivory skin going as blue as her dress. Through the mist, someone could have mistaken her for one of us. Always, she wrung the glove.

She told us her story as she walked, in the tightness of her fingers and the desperate nature of her steps. A lost love, a forbidden romance too long straining the people it nourished, and she hollow without it, unwilling to go on. She wished for a world where the kind of person she loved didn't matter. She wished for a world where she could dream of the happiness you would have had together. She slipped under the ice as a dreamer does to sleep – deliberate and resigned.

So it was you she was mourning.

But you've come too late.

What will you do when you find her?

My indecision burns away, and I move up and down the way you humans do when agreeing. Your eyes light up, but you must already know what we'll find. How can hope still burn within you when the cold around us saps at your strength, stealing the heat from your wet clothes?

We must be swift, or even your hope won't be enough to keep you alight.

I dart away, leading you from island to island. You follow, our trust secured after your swim and my rescue. You follow me right to her. I stop you at the edge of the water, then flicker a quick circle around her. I didn't need to, you're already looking. She looks up at you out of the water, her eyes raised up to the sky as if to say goodbye to the light of day and the warmth she once knew. One hand is extended towards the surface, almost as if she were reaching for something – or someone. You reach your hand out as well, mirroring her. The ice isn't thick enough to support you, but you crouch over her anyway, the ice cracking musically as your weight settles over her.

The glove still sits in her hand, clutched close to her heart under the ice. The red stands out in the clear blue water.

"Veronica," you whisper. "I never meant for it to end like this."

You press your lips to the ice, and they stick a bit as they come away. Your lip bleeds where it's split, hot as lava from a volcano. Even the look in your eyes is hot – full of things I can't understand. Humans and their complicated feelings. It would be one thing if you only felt one at a time, but the look in your eyes is a swirl. Hot reds and despairing grays, a melancholy blue and a comfortable, reminiscent brown like the color of your skin. You're too many colors, too many things at once.

Below the ice, she doesn't change.

But I know you wish she would.

Water starts to spill from you the way it spilled from her. Perhaps your eyes feel as I do, that you have too much inside you – so much they can't keep it all in. The ice dapples as you cry over her.

I don't know what to do. I led, and you followed. This isn't how that normally ends. There is no resolution, only continued anguish. Don't you seek release? Don't you want peace? The ice below you is already cracked, still crackling with each hiccupping breath you take. It would be easy. One strike of your ungloved hand, and you would be with her again…but cold, and quiet, and dull.

For some reason, I don't like to think of you that way. There's nothing about that existence that would bring you peace. You don't belong here. You'll melt the marsh.

A will-o'-the-wisp is a false fire. I have no heat of my own. I lead, and people follow. Perhaps I can use that in a different way. What is death except a destination, after all? Let us hope that a wisp can also withstand the icy water the way you did.

I have only felt kinship with fire in your plane, but that does not mean I operate the same. Slowly, I work my way through the ice. Your eyes widen when you see me burning below in the water, fire and ice. These things should not mix in your world, but the world is so much bigger than you give it credit for. There are so many things that you have yet to see.

I whisk my way through the water, feeling the cold start to seep into me. Perhaps I am not so unlike fire after all. I may lose myself in this – but it will be worth it to never see you in the marsh again.

I take up my position in front of her ice-white eyes. She is lifeless, staring up and past me. There is nothing of the complicated mix, like in your eyes.

But we will change that.

I flare in the water, putting all of my strength into shining. All the light I would exude in the foggiest of nights put forth in one moment. The water bubbles around me. I force some of them into her. The light is reflected in her eyes. I will her to see me and shine back.

A glimmer. A spark. A flutter of warmth, of breath.

You cry out above, and your first hurtles through the ice, disturbing the water. You catch at her hand, dragging her out. I am swept up in her pale blond hair. Tumbling from her, I land in your palm. You are so hot. So very hot.

You lean over her, saying her name.

Slowly, her breast rises, then falls. Her eyelashes flicker open. She says a name. "Monique."

So that is what they call you. It does not sound like a name of fire, but it will sound like one to me for the rest of my time.

I am so small in your hand. I wonder how much is left for me. Perhaps this was my last leading and it is me who will find my end this day.

Your mouth is on hers before she says another word. She breaks away, coughing up water. You pet her and hold me. Your hand is so warm.

She rouses herself, and you sit her up. She points to me. "What is that?" she asks.

"A will-o-the-wisp," you answer. "I knew they were rumored to live here, but I didn't know it was true until I saw them. This one... isn't like the others."

You hold me up. I feel so small, so delicate in your hand, under your eyes. You breathe on me and I flicker. Even your breath is hot. It crackles through me like a desert, arid and inviting. I feel myself roar up a little bigger, clear blue flames again instead of the cobalt of the water.

"Thank you, little wisp," you murmur. "Whatever the world brings us, we won't waste the chance you've given us."

The other one reaches up and places her hand in yours, next to me. The heat of the both of you is more than I can bear.

Smaller, but intact, I flit away, to the next island. You follow, hand-in-hand with the girl from the ice. Your steps are small and fragile, sometimes requiring you to backtrack or support each other across little land bridges, but you find your way. I help you do it. At the edge of the bog, you turn back once to wave. Even your smile is too warm for this place.

I flare at you, intending it to be a warning, but you just laugh. Don't come back. This place isn't for you. It isn't your time. I am a will-o-the-wisp. People come to the bog in search of something – but not like you did. When they come searching, they don't leave. It isn't meant to work the way it did today, people coming and going as they please, looking for things to find and take and run away with. I hope you'll stay off the paths where you see false light – and warn away the others, too. Your world changes too fast to let something like that kill you. Outlast and be part of it. I can't have you coming back to melt my bog again.

You and the ice woman melt away on the horizon. Night turns to day and then to night again. Another world-weary soul comes out in the snow-smoothed bog. But tonight I don't have the heart to lead them to where they wish to go. In the haze of lights, they follow me, and live to cry another day. Perhaps they'll come back. Perhaps, instead, they'll live to see the world change.

Resurrection
D VALENTINA

You are strewn across a table – warm, but not, stable, but not – and there are two fingers pressed to the tender, sunken spot beneath your jaw. *Stay with me.* Your tongue curls backward, ready to pop over the first syllable. "Quédate conmigo," you whisper, and you hardly recognize yourself, and she hardly recognizes you, and the concrete walls bend inward, reaching for the flame-tipped prayer candles circling this sacred, unholy place. Rosa eases away from your hopping pulse, and you want to remind her: *I am still alive. Te amo. Quédate conmigo, and after, and always.* You want to say, *do you remember the first time?* Whipping wild through the desert, running hard on packed dirt, plucking cactus needles from your swollen arm. You want to say, *do you remember the beginning?* Saguaro guarding the venerated places you found and made, dripping white wax onto brown skin as you filled a truck-bed like a honeymoon suite, and you inside her, and her inside you, and that hungry gibbous moon, and magic, magic, magic.

You've traveled far since then. Back and forth across invisible borders, drenched wet from the river, digging shoes the size of your palm out of muddy banks and hoping whoever they belonged to tasted milk, tasted honey – lived free. You and Rosa escaped into the desert and stumbled upon purpose. Sank your teeth into thick, green meat and swallowed sour, ancestral hope. Your abuela called those cacti guardián and gave them sainthood, and you brought their skin to your mouth like the Eucharist. *Transform me,* you begged, and inhaled until your ribcage strained beneath your binder, but you did not become a saint.

Instead, you began to unstitch.

Instead, you stepped into your unbecoming.

Magic, you thought, could pull water from weak lungs, unbuckle reddened wrists from hot shackles, and magic, you knew, fit inside a body the same way a blessing did. Not for long, but for long enough. Draped on the table, half-alive, *still* alive, you know the hourglass has almost drained, and you're out of time.

"Angel," Rosa says, pressing chrysanthemum essence and crushed marigold to your dewy cheeks. "Angel, cariño. Open your eyes."

Your name fits inside her mouth like a prayer. Chosen and memorized, well-loved and thick like ichor. Angel, like something surrendered, Angel, like she is calling into the past and exorcising the truth from every lie you used to carry. You want to say *this is not the end,* but it could be. Light needles your cracked eyelids, and you gaze at Rosa – her brunette ringlets, and her quivering lips, and the basement ceiling beyond her. In the beginning, when you and Rosa ate from the Saguaro, and fucked in the dusky, empty desert, and yipped at the shadowed moon, you imagined exiting your body and leaving pawprints in the dirt. But now, trapped beneath a slouching farmhouse in Calexico, California, you cling to your skeleton.

Prayer beads whittled from a steer's horn rattle near the stairwell, and the air stirs around frantic footsteps. Your breath comes in slow, long sips, but you recognize Camila Ramírez by her amber perfume, and listen to the chatter she brings. Witches gather around you, fluttering hands like moths looking for light on your sweat-sheened skin, but it is the curandera who clucks her tongue.

"Hola, coyote," Camila whispers, and drags a bundle of dried alhucema and yellow wheat from your forehead to your chin. "Are you ready to die?"

Lavender catches on your eyelashes. "No, doña. I am not."

"Good. Because I'm not ready to let you die."

"Te veo, te aprecio," you say, and it's the truth. You see her, entirely. Charcoal hair and lips red as brick dust. Knowing glistens in her dark, celestial eyes, and she touches her ruddy palm to the base of your throat.

Rosa hiccups, concealing a sob, and you want to reach for her. "You will be different," Camila, the witch, the bruja, the healer, says to you. "But you will live. I feel fight in you. I see Huehuecóyotl's handprints on your heart."

You search for Rosa, shifting your eyes from the ceiling to Camila, from Camila to a gentle, cigarette-creased smile and loving, apple-stained cheeks, and handsome, pliant fingertips. From the coven surrounding your dying body to the woman you loved as bruja, as brujx, as brujo, exactly in that order. Rosa Garcia Calderón kisses you full on the mouth, as if she sensed your wanting, as if she heard your thoughts.

"I will love you," she says. *After*, she means. *Whatever you are, whatever you become.* "Me quedaré."

Magic, you understand, can carve away a soul. Erode at a person's muscles and suckle at their vitality. Magic, you've experienced, will find a way to bloom inside an occupied chest, hook roots into ventricles, and nurse power like a remora, like a fledgling weed. Masticated and consumed, magic will thrive inside a vessel. You know as well as the witches hovering over your sallow, ochre limbs, that what you took began to take back. That Saguaro, that sainthood, that virtuous ascension, gave you the ability to breathe life into the dead, shield the visible from sight, stir a storm in the sky, and now, weeks and months and years later, the magic you ate has taken too much.

Once, you whispered to the Rio Grande resting heavy inside a child and coaxed the water to dislodge.

Twice, you tasted blood on newborn teeth, pushed through your gums and into someone else, someone worse, someone undeserving.

But always, you returned to Rosa. Magic or not, alive or not, and you will return to her again.

All at once, life becomes harder to hold. You grasp at frayed edges and close your eyes. Fire flickers. Wax pools pale and hot in votive candleholders. Voices lift, rising like a riptide.

Camila says, "No, mijo. Stay awake. Open your eyes."

You stare at the ceiling again, and Rosa, and the witches humming hymns around you, holding slender, wax pillars and rolling rosaries between their knuckles. You carried one of their daughters on your back, sometime ago. You pulled one of their sons into stolen land and nudged him with your snout toward a new future. *Go*, you said, in skin the Saguaro had loaned you, *don't forget us*. You think of those nights with Rosa – coyotes, running. Circling helicopters and spinning wheels and tired feet. You think of magic, and watch Camila Ramírez pluck a pickled diamondback from a sallow mason jar. Vinegar flows in oily rivulets down the rattlesnake's hide, splattering on the floor, and when it lurches, seizing with sudden, unnatural life, Camila snatches its gaping jaws.

"You'll feel like you're dying, but you aren't. I promise," Camila says.

Rosa stands at your crown, cupping your cheeks, praying to the virgin mother.

"Mi amor, speak to someone who will listen," you say, and tilt your mouth to meet her palm.

Camila presses the snake's hollow fangs to the place your Adam's apple should've been had it ever grown. Venom sinks into you. Clashes with the starving magic borrowed from that old, living cacti you bit so long ago. For a moment, your body is not your own. But has it ever been? You're accustomed to disconnection – apathy attached to bone-structure. Your body has always been a home with too many windows and never enough doors, always letting light in, always getting lost in. At times, you carried your soft jaw and wide hips with the confidence of a true-born man, and sometimes, you shrank inside yourself, burrowing under flesh that hung from your shoulders like a thrift store coat. But you were, and you are, and you will be, and as magic collides with magic, as antiquity blends with ferocity, you begin to realize that this body has always been *yours*, regardless. You have always been Angel Luis Castel, and you will always be coyote.

You breathe through a pain you've felt in nightmares. Weightless, inescapable change. Magic twines through the pockets in your jaw, around your blunt teeth, deep into your skull, rearranging veins and tissue and bone. Surrounding you, witches chant and purr, and

Camila retracts the snake from your throat, and Rosa keeps her loving hands on you even as you are born anew.

Oh, you think, *yes, I remember.*

"Quédate conmigo," you say, and gasp for air with clear lungs. "I will keep you safe."

Rosa cries out, relieved, and presses her lips to the soft fur between your golden eyes. Tall, pointed ears spear the air above your newly-shaped head, framing her affection. You lift your hands – still knobby, still human – and press two fingers to your strong, thrumming pulse.

Coyote, you think. *Saguaro, brujo, coyote.*

Raising Thom
BRETT STANFILL

Miguel scraped his fork silently against the ceramic plate, spearing several green beans before dropping it impatiently and running his fingers through his dark hair. His leg bounced wildly beneath the dining table. His husband Charlie chewed nervously at his bottom lip, cell phone pressed to his ear. Miguel's jaw tensed at the barely audible murmur.

"Mhm – I see," Charlie said to the person on the other end.

You see what?

Miguel's eyes darted to the box sitting in the adjoining living room, waiting to be opened and the contents assembled. The changing table was the very last piece they needed for the nursery to be complete. He had picked it up on his drive home from work because the baby was expected in less than two weeks. At least, he hoped the baby was expected.

"Okay. Thank you. No problem. Yep. Have a great day." Charlie set the phone down, face severe. He offered up a barely detectable shake of the head.

Miguel's heart dropped. It had happened again. They had gotten closer than ever before this time, only two weeks away. Why had he allowed himself to get his hopes up? "Did they say why?"

"You know they didn't. The birth mother changed her mind."

Charlie's warm hand closed firmly around Miguel's. Miguel squeezed it, meeting Charlie's watery blue eyes with his own.

"Onward and upward, right?" Miguel forced a smile.

Charlie nodded, tears betraying him by escaping down his pale cheeks. Miguel stood, pulling Charlie up and into his arms. Miguel hugged him closer as silent sobs shook Charlie's slim figure. They stayed in the moment, both looking for comfort in their shared warmth. Miguel didn't have tears for the child that almost was.

Crying wouldn't change anything. Tears hadn't altered the outcome the first three times. His husband was a tender soul, however, and his pained whimpering was enough to bring the mist into Miguel's eyes.

"I love you," Miguel whispered.

The chime of the doorbell sang into the room before Charlie could respond.

"Probably just a delivery. We'll grab it later."

It rang again, several times in quick succession.

Charlie pulled away and gazed toward the door quizzically, then to Miguel, who shrugged.

Three thumps rattled the wreath hanging on the door, followed immediately by another ring of the bell.

Charlie crossed the room, wiping the remaining tears away with his sleeve. Miguel followed closely behind him, walking more quickly and reaching the door first. He started for the door handle but pulled back. What he wouldn't give for a peep hole! It was the only thing he missed from his apartment-living days. Not expecting anyone to be pounding on their door at eight o'clock on a Wednesday evening, he was anxious about opening it blindly. They lived in a good neighborhood but they were lovers, not fighters. A little caution never hurt anyone.

"Who is it?" Miguel called, heart racing.

His question was met with silence.

"There's something on the porch. But whoever left it is gone." Charlie peered through a slit he had created in the front window curtains. Miguel chuckled for not thinking to do so himself. Something about unexpected banging on his door had always put him on edge.

He opened the door to a gust of cool February air, then leaned out, glancing right and left into the night. The overhead light flicked on and he jumped. Motion sensors. It was odd that they hadn't kicked on before.

At his feet sat a large wicker basket, a red checkered blanket tucked neatly around something inside, looking ready to take on a picnic. Cautiously, he scooted it forward with his bare foot. In his mind it was just as likely to catch fire as to sprout legs and walk away.

"What is it?"

"A basket, I think."

"You think?" Charlie squeezed in front of him to get a better view. He scooped up the basket and brought it inside. He set it onto the dining table and pulled the blanket back. "Weird."

Happy it hadn't exploded, Miguel peered over Charlie's shoulder to see a large, dark gray, egg-shaped stone. It was the size of a watermelon with a smooth surface. How on earth had Charlie lifted that thing so easily?

The stone wobbled and fell softly onto its side.

"Touch it."

"I don't want to touch it. You touch it."

It rocked back and forth.

"I opened the door. It's your turn to risk your life."

"So dramatic. Fine." Charlie slowly extended his hand, poking the stone with one finger before brushing his entire palm over the surface. "It's warm."

A hairline fracture appeared near the center, quickly spreading in a web-like pattern the length of the stone.

"You broke it!" Miguel gasped.

"You were the one who told me to touch it!"

The crack branched off and two larger splits expanded around the top. A small piece chipped off and dangled, still attached to a milky white membrane.

Realization hit Miguel. It wasn't an egg-shaped stone. It was an egg-shaped *egg*. He was dumbstruck, frozen in place. A large piece of the shell fell away and disappeared into the basket. The membrane tore, revealing a tiny purple hand.

Charlie, always the first to respond, jumped into action. He swiftly began peeling away chunks of shell and membrane. He gasped. Miguel, curious, stood on tip toes in an attempt to get a better view.

"He's a boy!" Charlie turned, a tiny purple bundle hugged close to his chest.

After a moment he held the bundle out to Miguel, who took the baby into his arms hesitantly. He had held babies a handful of times in his life, but there was a gravity to it this time that he hadn't felt before. After a lifetime of being told he shouldn't or couldn't be a father, it was time to take the first step and find out if they were right.

A familiar warmth spread through Miguel's chest as his eyes settled on the most perfect sight he had ever seen. He took stock: ten perfect fingers, ten perfect toes, two tiny dimples framing four shiny purple mandibles. The brightest, and admittedly first, dazzling red eyes he had ever seen stared back at him. They took up a third of the baby's small face. This tiny, unique, purple baby was theirs, there was no way around it. Miguel fell in love instantly.

"Thom." The name left his lips before his brain even processed it as a thought.

"Thom," Charlie echoed.

Charlie laid his head on Miguel's shoulder, caressing Thom's cheek with one finger. With a contented sigh, Miguel pressed his lips against the soft skin of his husband's forehead.

Day 1

Miguel had his pillow folded around his head like a taco shell, open hands pushing firmly over his ears. Thom's wails still managed to find a way through every open crack in his defenses, bounce around in his head, and plant resolutely in his brain.

Charlie paced back and forth, bouncing and patting Thom, an endless stream of *shhhhhh* and *it's okay*. It had been nine hours since Thom's delivery. A very long nine hours. The first half hour had been parental bliss. Charlie used a sponge to wash away the excess mucus and eggshell from Thom's purple skin, which was growing a deeper plum by the minute. Miguel changed the cooing baby into his very first outfit, a yellow microfiber footie pajama with the cutest little bumblebees speckling the bum. All of the clothes had previously been washed thoroughly with an organic hypoallergenic detergent so as to prevent rashes.

Then Thom became hungry. They warmed up the formula according to the directions on the can, shook it up for exactly thirty seconds, and squirted it onto their wrists to test for temperature. They both lingered in anxious anticipation. A lot of firsts were happening in the Barker-Keel household that evening. Miguel was the most excited for the first feeding. It would be the first real step toward bonding with their little bundle. He was happy for Charlie to have the moment.

Charlie held Thom in his arms, gazing down at him with a quizzical expression. Thom's shimmering eyes were wide with expectation. Charlie dangled the bottle in front of Thom's mandibles briefly before pulling it away and glancing up to Miguel.

"I'm not really sure," he began, "where to, like…feed him."

The point was valid. Their unique baby boy didn't have the typical bottle-accepting lips of other babies. If he had a mouth, the mandibles hid it well.

"Just put the bottle up to his face. Biology will take over. He should know what to do, right?"

Charlie did just that. A pleasant coo escaped Thom's tiny throat as his mandibles shook, latching onto the bottle nipple. He spat it out instantly, unleashing a scream so shrill it set off a neighbor's car alarm. He began to cry loudly. Fast forward nine hours and he still cried. Still very loudly.

"Tag me out, please."

Miguel glared at Charlie, who stood before him with Thom, still crying, outstretched. Miguel begrudgingly pulled himself upright. Charlie pulled off the fluffy white earmuffs he wore, and placed them sloppily onto Miguel's ears, planted a kiss on his husband and his baby, and fell face-first onto the bed. He shot Miguel a thumbs up and a muffled, "I love you."

The routine Miguel went with was an evolved form of the one Charlie employed. He swooped where Charlie had bounced and thumped where he'd bopped.

"Shh. Oh, I know." He didn't actually know. He was lying to his son. It was at that moment that he realized he didn't know anything at all. It may have been the lack of sleep, but he was certain that the baby could see through his act. *He knows that I'm a fraud.*

Miguel wandered through the hall and into the living room, laying Thom down onto the couch. Maybe he had peed? Does a baby need to have eaten to pee? But the diaper was as dry as the moment they had put it on him.

Taking both of his hands, Miguel ran his thumbs in a circular pattern down Thom's face. Parenting Magazine claimed that massages will calm a baby and aid in bonding. The abrupt silence didn't immediately register, as the ringing in his ears continued. Excited, he continued down the soft cheeks and neck. Thom cooed happily, twisted his head, and took hold of Miguel's pinky finger with his mandibles. The bite severed the finger painlessly.

Miguel looked down at Thom, who was munching loudly, then to the empty space where his pinky once lived. To Miguel's surprise, there was no blood at the stump of his finger. The wound stung mildly but looked as though it had been cauterized closed.

"Charlie!" he screamed.

Hollow thuds echoed around them as Charlie bolted into the room, looking panicked. Miguel smiled up at him, tears in his eyes.

"He's eating!"

Recognition dawned on Charlie's face as he maneuvered the puzzle pieces within his mind. He shook his pointer finger rapidly in front of him before disappearing through the double doors into the kitchen. He returned a moment later with a miniature rubber tipped baby spoon and a pound of ground beef.

After they had changed their first soiled diaper, settled Thom into the bassinet beside their bed, and wrapped up Miguel's hand with a bandage, they curled up together, too exhausted even to burrow into the blankets.

Day 21

Thom crawled furiously across the carpeted floor, in hot pursuit of the ball he himself had thrown moments before. His chunky thighs jiggled with the effort. Bright yellow rings had developed over his back and limbs, offering a vibrant contrast to his deep purple skin. He stopped, laid his head down, and fell instantly to sleep before even making it halfway to his ball. He spent most of the time he wasn't eating fast asleep, more so in recent days.

With an exaggerated sigh, Miguel scooped him up, grunting. Despite only hatching three weeks before, Thom was the size of a ten month old and ate like a teenager. He consumed his weight every day. The most cost effective way to keep his ravenous little appetite satiated was to just buy an entire cow from the butcher. It wound up being over 350 pounds and they ran out in two and a half weeks. The second time they picked a bigger cow and scored a dozen turkeys on sale. He was a growing boy who needed his nutrients. Miguel laid Thom gently onto the mattress and placed a kiss onto his forehead, between two furry little antennae growing in.

"You haven't even gotten dressed?" Charlie peeked his head into the room.

"I have been thinking, maybe it's best if I stay home with Thom."

"No, stop trying to get out of it. He's asleep and won't wake up until tomorrow. Get ready."

"But—"

"Get dressed."

Miguel, deflated, did as he was told.

The neighbor lady, Ms Byrd, arrived promptly at eight o'clock, smelling heavily of patchouli and cigarette smoke. She wasn't Miguel's first, second, or third choice, but the fact that she was half-blind worked in her favor. Even if she did get curious and peek in on Thom, she wouldn't notice how unique he was. It was a small solace to Miguel since he was being forced to go to a work function.

The IT company they both worked at was cheap, and venues for Christmas parties were significantly discounted in March. Ms Byrd didn't comment on the jingling ugly Christmas sweater or Santa hats that both men wore. She scored one more point from Miguel, but likely lost herself one from Charlie, who was quietly resentful when people didn't compliment things he created himself.

Their house reeked of baby powder and chemical disinfectant. The younger generation all thought they were so evolved in their war against germs. Ms Byrd had survived over 70 years without hand sanitizer, thank you very much. Bah!

Her cane clicked against the linoleum flooring as she made her way to the refrigerator in search of wine. Her neighbors were the fancy type, bound to have a hefty stock of pricey vino. A photo of them smiling, arm in arm on a sunny beach, hung tauntingly from a magnetic chip clip. She pulled the photo free and set it face down on the counter. Ms Byrd had no issues with those boys or what they got up to – hate the sin and not the sinner – but there was no reason to go flashing it around. Besides, she wouldn't feel comfortable helping herself with their eerie supervision stalking her around the kitchen.

The door to the refrigerator opened with a wheeze of cold air. She nodded approvingly, seeing the shelves stacked completely with raw meats. Men needed real food and she would have thought that their types would have been vegetarians or gluten free or whatever the hootenanny was these days. She took a few of the packs of ground beef and tucked them into her over-sized purse. There was no wine, only a couple of beer bottles nestled in between paper-wrapped rump roasts. Ms Byrd had never developed much taste for beer so she begrudgingly abandoned her quest. She had schnapps in her purse if the night began to drag on her.

A door creaked down the nearby hallway, quickly followed by the tap tap tap of footsteps on carpet. Hauling her bag onto her shoulder, Ms Byrd shuffled toward the sound. Neither of them had warned her of any pets to watch out for, which was extremely thoughtless because she may have had allergies. She didn't, but that was very much beside the point. The door at the end of the dark hallway stood fully open, only illuminated by the moonlight trickling in from the window. If she recalled correctly – and her brain was still as sharp as a whip – it was the door to the nursery. The baby wasn't crying, so the poor dear was likely still sound asleep, yet he wouldn't be for long with that bright window open and letting all the light in. She had better close up the curtains. The pocket change she was being paid would pay for a few lottery tickets, but that would hardly be worth her missing her programs to coddle a crying infant.

Before blocking out the light, she decided to catch a quick glimpse at the sleeping babe. To her surprise, the crib was empty. They must have put him to bed in a different bedroom. That is the type of information a parent should relay to an old gal minding their kids. What would have happened if she hadn't had the mind to check and an emergency occurred? Heaven forbid.

She turned to leave, muttering her silent disapprovals, when her loafer squished into something on the carpet. With a groan of disgust, she bent to inspect. A slimy film coated the carpet in front of the crib. By poking at it with her cane, Ms Byrd determined that the substance was a solid with the texture of wet cling wrap. It was repulsive that she would find it in a child's bedroom.

Tap tap tap echoed behind her. She spun, squinting into the darkness.

Tap tap tap.

Whatever produced the noise was closer, just outside the door, perhaps. She shuffled along until she found the light switch, flicking it.

A demon, red eyes and dark purple skin, stared up at her. It clicked its insectile mouth parts and produced a hideous chirp within its throat. The pain that shot through Ms Byrd's chest as her heart gave out was intense but brief. She was gone before she hit the ground, but her unseeing eyes watched patiently as the creature rummaged through her bag hungrily.

"What do you think it is?"

Miguel held it up in front of him, nodding. Deep purple and yellow light trickled through the translucent substance.

"I think it's – skin," he began, "seems as though our little Thom has molted."

"I wonder if that was before or after this." Charlie motioned lazily to what remained of Ms Byrd: her legs.

Thom burst into the nursery at a full sprint, connecting forcefully with the back of Miguel's knees, nearly causing them to buckle. His little arms wrapped around Miguel's legs with a squeeze before hobbling over to hug Charlie.

"We missed his first steps," Charlie said quietly.

That wasn't all they missed. The boy they came home to was very much the same as when they left and also very much different. His little forehead nubs were fully developed antennae and tiny little spikes protruded from the center of his yellow spots. Perhaps the biggest change was the two additional arms that had sprouted directly below the first set. Ten more perfect little fingers.

Charlie knelt at eye level with Thom, his face stern, "Did you eat Ms Byrd?"

Thom's large red eyes darted to the babysitter then back to Charlie.

"Did you eat Ms Byrd, Thom?"

Thom covered his face with all twenty of his chubby fingers. Charlie pulled the hands down, eyebrows raised.

"We do not eat people. Ever. Ever. Ever. We especially do not leave half of them behind for our dads to clean up. That was very wasteful. No more eating people!"

Thom's eyes brimmed with tears and his mandibles fell flat against his chin. Miguel clenched his fist to keep his hands from scooping up his broken-hearted baby.

Deep breaths.

"You are going to go to bed now. Goodnight." Charlie planted a kiss on Thom's forehead. With a grunt, he heaved him into the air and into the crib. They would need to convert it into a toddler bed. He was nearly too big for it, already.

Miguel and Charlie sat propped in bed. Miguel was reading up on the most environmentally-conscious options for laying the lower half of their departed neighbor to rest. For obvious reasons, he couldn't take the official route. He had seriously considered letting Thom finish what he had started, but wouldn't that just undo the work that Charlie had already put in? Eating people was a habit they needed to squash quickly. How could Thom ever form meaningful relationships with people if there was always the lingering desire to eat their torsos?

Charlie sighed loudly in the bed beside him. He was gazing out into the room, lost in some bout of internal duologue. Years together had taught Miguel that a heavy sigh was an invitation to board the thought train. Ignoring the heavy sigh was an invitation to nowhere he wished to return.

"What's on your mind?"

"Oh, nothing." Charlie sighed again.

Miguel, still expected to play along, replied, "Sure doesn't sound like nothing, love."

"You won't think I'm ridiculous?"

Probably will. "Never," Miguel lied.

"Fine," Charlie relented, turning to face Miguel. "Do you think I was too hard on him tonight? He didn't know any better and I really don't want him to be scared of me."

A hearty chuckle very nearly escaped, but Miguel was able to catch it in his throat and swallow it back. The idea of anyone being scared of his softhearted husband was ridiculous, but that wasn't the response Charlie needed. Miguel ran his thumb along the line of Charlie's jaw.

"You were perfect. You did perfectly."

Miguel's lips landed softly on Charlie's and they kissed deeply. An eager warmth spread through him as he pulled Charlie on top of him and kissed down his neck and across the soft hairs dotting his chest.

One room over, Thom began to cry.

Day 72

Thom pedaled his feet furiously. His bicycle teetered unsteadily, alternating his weight between the two training wheels. Two of his hands held fast to the handlebars, while the other two rode the wind at his side, flapping up and down like wings.

"Woo! Great job, buddy! Look at you!" Miguel clapped his hands.

His little boy, already tall enough that his forehead was in line with Miguel's navel, was such a fast learner. They had only spent twenty minutes on the bike-riding before Thom was zooming around like a professional. He zipped by, antennas whipping in the air, mandibles clicking happily.

Miguel held his phone, snapping photo after photo to capture the memory. The screen flashed blue with a string of numbers running across the top, vibrating insistently.

"This is Miguel," he answered. The voice on the other end was muffled, being heavily distorted by the wind howling. "Hold on one quick second while I get out of the wind."

He took a quick glance at Thom, who was nearly to the turnaround point several houses down. There were no cars in either direction. Miguel could take a second to handle the call. He jogged up the walkway and ducked directly inside the door to their house, keeping an eye on the road. It only took him a few minutes to walk the chipper receptionist through rebooting her computer.

Miguel hopped down the steps expecting to see Thom still speeding along on his bicycle, but Thom was nowhere in sight. His bicycle lay on its side in the grass halfway down the street, wheel spinning lazily. A knot formed in Miguel's stomach.

"Thom!" Miguel raced toward the bicycle, heart hammering in his ears. "Thom!"

He kicked the sandals from his feet as he went, not even feeling the jagged pebbles cutting into his soft flesh. Every insane scenario imaginable flashed through his mind simultaneously. Thom had wandered too far and gotten lost, or worse, been kidnapped. He could have fallen down a well. Were wells still a thing? Would Miguel find him devouring one of their neighbors? Or, the fear he didn't want to acknowledge, Thom's biological parents had changed their mind and taken him back.

He passed the bicycle. "Thom!"

"Sir?" a frail voice called out.

Miguel stopped, peering around for the source. A woman stood on her porch, waving to him with a shaky hand. She gestured to the side of her house, flashing a toothy smile revealing dentures that were a few sizes too big.

"Is this little flower thief yours?"

Relief washed over Miguel as Thom's little purple head peered over a waist-high hedge.

"Oh my goodness. There you are!" Miguel exclaimed.

Thom nonchalantly wandered around the front of the bush. All of his hands gripped tulip plants – bulbs, roots and all. Falling soil trailed behind him as he made his way to Miguel.

"Little fellow just wanted to bring some pretty flowers home to Mom. Bless his heart," the lady said. "What a creative little costume!"

No moms in this family, lady.

"I'm so sorry. Thank you for finding him. I was out of my mind."

Miguel gripped Thom firmly on his shoulder and guided him back to the bike. He scooped it up, carrying it back to the house with them. Riding lessons were over for the day.

They arrived home to find Charlie had returned from work and stood on the porch. Thom shrugged free from Miguel's grasp and sprinted up the steps, shoving all four handfuls of flowers at Charlie. Charlie took them, receiving a hug around the waist as an added bonus. Thom disappeared inside.

Charlie, laughing, caught Miguel's vexed gaze.

"Should I ask?"

"No," Miguel replied, "let's leave this one right here."

Day 195

The door burst open with enough force to rattle the windows. Miguel, seated on the couch, nearly jumped out of his skin. Thom stomped through without acknowledging him. A door slammed further into the house, rattling the windows for a second time.

"Nice to see you!" Miguel called out to him.

Moments later, a visibly annoyed Charlie appeared, plopping onto the sofa beside Miguel.

"Don't even ask," Charlie began. "Your son is on my last nerve right now. I don't even want to talk about it."

Miguel didn't respond. The furious rhythm with which Charlie's feet bounced against the floor told him all he needed to know.

"You know, sometimes it would be nice to be appreciated. Just a little appreciation? Is that too much?" Charlie stood, pacing the floor.

Miguel paused the movie he was watching, as Charlie was now blocking it.

"I didn't have to take him out and help him learn how to drive. Did that stop him from throwing a fit? Do you think that it did?"

Miguel shook his head. Clearly it hadn't, if his grand entrance was considered.

"And what do you think the fit was about? Hm? What?"

Food.

"Food," Charlie huffed. "Food! I swear your kid doesn't think about anything else. He wanted me to stop and get him a turkey."

Miguel leaned on his fist patiently, watching.

"We have turkey here, Miguel. Why would I need to stop and get him one? I don't want him eating a raw turkey in my car."

Charlie plopped back to his spot on the couch, feet much calmer.

"Should I go talk to him?" Miguel asked.

"I said I don't want to talk about it."

Miguel tapped lightly on Thom's door, opening without waiting for permission. Thom, nearly as tall as Miguel but lanky and angular, was sitting propped on his bed with headphones blasting music into his ears. His yellow spots had begun to fade months ago, and only a whisper of their presence remained. His last molt had produced a fuzzy layer over his skin, velvety soft to the touch but would give you a wicked rash if you touched it while he was in one of his moods. He was always in one of his moods, lately. He was a cranky little shit. Miguel instinctively pulled his sleeves down to cover his forearms and sat at the edge of the bed.

"So, your dad says you were copping some attitude with him."

Thom held his phone up for Miguel to see and clicked the volume up on his music, the whole time keeping his red eyes trained at the wall in front of him.

We're playing that one, huh?

With the reflexes that only the parent of a teenager could possess, Miguel had the headphones off of Thom's head before Thom could even react. Thom fixed his eyes on Miguel, flaring his mandibles fiercely.

"You shake those things at me one more time and I'll keep them."

Thom stopped instantly and dropped his gaze to the floor.

"Did you really need a whole turkey so urgently that you couldn't wait to get home?"

He responded with a barely perceptible shake of his head.

"Don't you think you owe your father an apology?"

Miguel didn't expect a response. It would have been too easy.

"And finally, are you going to go out and get a job when you slam the door and shatter my windows?" Miguel reached over and squeezed the purple flesh of one of Thom's arms. "Look at these guns. You need to reign them in!"

Thom let out a throaty chuckle.

Feeling successful, Miguel hopped off the bed and left the room. Thom would come out and make amends with Charlie eventually. Miguel had always felt a little jealous of their relationship. While it was true that he didn't bring out the rage in Thom the way that Charlie did, there always seemed to be a piece to their bond that Miguel couldn't relate to. When Thom was younger and scared or in pain, Charlie's arms were the ones that made everything better.

When Miguel entered the kitchen, Charlie stood staring at the closed refrigerator door.

"Do you ever miss this kid?" Charlie asked, nodding toward a crayon drawing hanging by a magnet.

In the drawing a little purple stick boy with four arms stood between his little stick fathers, a large volcano erupting in the background. Tiny red and black hearts dotted the page in no particular pattern. Thom had drawn it shortly after watching a television program about lava.

"Well, I just left that kid in his room, so—"

"No. Not that kid. This one," Charlie interrupted, tapping the purple boy on the drawing. "The one that drew us pictures and still believed in the molted skin fairy."

Charlie's eyes brimmed with tears. Miguel pulled him into a hug. It was true. The one thing no one had told them about becoming parents was how much they would mourn the loss of the previous versions of their kid. As he grew, Thom's curiosity and playfulness had given way to a more thoughtful and serious little boy. Each and every molt revealed a Thom as amazing as the last, but sometimes the urge to hold baby Thom again was so intense that Miguel needed to scroll through photos and videos in hopes of reliving the feeling.

Miguel was completely wrapped up in his self-made grief. He didn't even notice Thom enter the room until velvet flesh grazed across his hand. Thom reached around both of his dads and leaned into their hug.

Day 277

"Miguel. Miguel. Wake up, something is going on with Thom." Charlie shook Miguel furiously, panic in his voice.

Rubbing sleep from his eyes, Miguel bolted up, blinking to adjust to the harsh light. He pulled himself to his feet and unsteadily followed Charlie down the hall to Thom's room.

Thom laid in the center of his bed clutching his knees, staring unblinkingly forward. The normal red shimmer in his eyes was gone, replaced by dull pink. A thick film coated his body, casting his vibrant purple skin in a dull gray tone. If it weren't for the rapid rise and fall of his chest, Thom would look lifeless.

"He screamed. It woke me up. I thought he was molting— " Charlie's voice caught.

Miguel knelt beside the bed and waved his hand inches from Thom's blank stare. Thom had never responded to a molt like this before. They were always completely issue free. His skin would lose luster, he would get sleepy, and after a few days there was a new layer of skin to add to his baby book. What lay in front of him was different. It was wrong. A painful lump was forming in Miguel's throat. It couldn't end like this, could it?

"Thom? Buddy?"

Miguel gingerly grabbed hold of Thom's slime-covered shoulder to shake him. It wasn't slime at all; it was barely even damp. He leaned in closer, inspecting the substance. A tiny framework of veins stretched across the elastic surface. It was as though a bag of flesh had encased him.

"Holy shit," Miguel muttered. "It's a cocoon."

Day 370

Miguel couldn't stop himself from stalling, his willpower losing out to the heaviness of his heart. Warm water rushed over his hands as he washed them for the third time, not yet ready to leave the bathroom.

"Miguel, come on. You can't stay in there forever," Charlie called.

I absolutely could stay in here forever.

Miguel steeled himself in front of the door. He wouldn't ever be ready to face it, so he might as well rip the bandage off and be done with it.

Thom stood in front of the refrigerator, staring at the drawing of himself and his dads in front of the volcano. He reached up and pulled it down, folding it up and tucking it into his bag on top of his red and white blanket.

"You can borrow it, but you have to bring it back," Miguel joked.

The time spent waiting for Thom to emerge from the cocoon was the most excruciating in Miguel's life. At first he and Charlie had spent nearly all of their time staring at the hard gray mass that held their son. After a couple of weeks they started alternating shifts, and after a month switched to only a few hours each day.

At long last, in the middle of the night, Miguel had been shaken awake to see a familiar set of glistening red eyes. His son, still soggy with cocoon juice, was out and healthy. Not only that, he had woken Miguel up before Charlie, a fact that nearly made the entire situation worth it.

The newest Thom was breathtaking. He stood an entire head taller than either Miguel or Charlie. A dusty fur, deep purple but with swirls of yellow and orange, covered him from head to toe. It was softer than anything Miguel had ever experienced. Thom's upper arms blended seamlessly into an enormous pair of wings that spanned seven feet unfurled. His lanky lower arms had become lean and muscular, as had the rest of his figure. Only his face remained mostly unchanged. His jawline was squarer with deeper cut dimples. His red eyes seemed slightly smaller and his mandibles slightly bigger, but the face was the same that Miguel had instantly fallen in love with the day Thom hatched from his egg.

"You sure you don't want to have a snack before you go?" Miguel said, still stalling.

Thom's large hand ruffled his father's dark hair. He shook his head, stepping over the threshold into the cool February night.

"You will text as soon as you land?"

"And remember the golden rule. We don't eat people!"

Thom chuckled deeply, turning back to face Miguel and Charlie, and pulled both of them into a hug. Miguel squeezed back tightly, reluctant to let go. After a long moment of silence, Thom broke away, taking several steps into the grass. He disappeared into the sky with a burst of air that nearly knocked them off of their feet. Miguel had seen Thom fly multiple times over the last weeks, but the sight sent anxious tingles down his spine every time. His boy was off on his first solo adventure. Their job was complete.

Charlie leaned his head against Miguel's shoulder, wiping tears on his sleeve. "A month feels like such a long time for him to be gone, considering."

Miguel nodded. It felt like an eternity.

Promises to Keep
MAGGIE DAMKEN

That night, during the blizzard, my car got stuck in the unplowed road.

I was five miles from home.

I had two choices: stay in my car overnight and hope someone found me, or start walking and hope I made it home. I don't like relying on hope. When my mother was dying all I did was hope: that she would get better (she didn't), that I would have more time with her (I wouldn't), that I'd hear every story she needed to tell me before she died (I didn't).

We buried her two weeks ago.

The headlights opened a path barely five feet ahead of the car. In the silence, surrounded by snowflakes, I was in a secluded pocket of the world. If death came, it would arrive flurry by flurry and entomb me in a black cold. I know better than to ask unnamed things for favors, but that night, out loud, I asked whatever might be listening to help me get home. "I'll do anything," I said.

I wasn't thinking.

And something heard me.

Where the headlights expired into shadow, something stirred. A tree branch, I thought, until it lumbered closer. On National Geographic they never look so big, but this elk was larger than my car with antlers that spiraled upwards, unendingly, like coiled towers armed with spears. I turned off the radio. I held my breath.

It stopped beside my window and lowered its head. My mother told me you can discern the true nature of a creature by looking at the corner of its eye, but this creature did not have what I could rightly call an eye. Where an eye should have been there was an empty, featureless white gap that opened like the cap of a mushroom. This elk was more than an elk and not an elk at all.

It wanted me to get out of the car.

I don't know how I knew, but I knew.

I didn't budge.

Neither did the elk.

And then the engine shut off.

The keys wouldn't turn in the ignition. I couldn't pull them out, either. The heat in the car seeped out faster than I thought it would and now the choice changed: I could stay in the car because it provided shelter from the snow, or I could get out of the car and hope the elk-that-was-more-than-elk didn't gore me.

"You need to learn trust."

It spoke without speaking, the way things do in dreams. In dreams you survive on impression and instinct. Slowly, deliberately, I pushed open the car door against the heavy snow, enough to slip out.

The first time I stood next to a horse, I thought: this is a reasonably-sized animal. In Christmas movies, when the child discovers a reindeer in the stable, the reindeer doesn't quite dwarf the kid in size. I could not tell the body of this elk apart from the colossal night. Swathed in shadow and untouched by snow, it existed in the spaces between each flake. Squinting against the bitter wind, I lost track of its edges, its dimensions. I could not see the black fur or the black antlers although I felt them near me.

The only thing I could see for sure were gaps where eyes should have been.

It began to walk and I followed.

I was home within moments.

We left no tracks in the snow. Like vapor, the elk disappeared.

In the morning, a friend drove me to my car. When we arrived, an ancient oak had fallen over it. Shattered glass glinted in the snow. Gnarled branches mangled the car into a heap of jagged metal.

"Good thing you took a chance and walked home, huh?"

Days later, an afternoon squall blew through and I saw the elk in my yard. Even in the gray light I could not discern the fullness of its shape. The longer I looked, the more my eyes lost the ability

to focus. Static clustered my vision. I dug the heels of my palms
into my eyes and when I pulled them away, the elk's antlers were
pressed against the glass door.

"You have promises to keep," it said without speaking.

I did not let it in.

That night, although the refrigerator hummed on, all the food
spoiled. As I poured the sour milk down the drain and watched it
burble, I wondered how long I could resist. I wasn't clever enough
to find a loophole, the way heroes always are in stories: either I
would give what it asked, or it would take what it wanted by force.

The next day, while the elk rattled its antlers against the house's
siding, a slow leak began in the roof. When the heat failed, and the
fire in the hearth would not take, and the matches would not light,
and I found the extra blankets wet and half-frozen, I knew that
patience and mercy had expired. The only choice was an illusion
of choice.

On my threshold, the elk became a woman with tall antlers and
no face. I thought, maybe, that I recognized her hands.

"You promised anything in exchange for your safety," said the
elk-who-was-a-woman. "I want it to be your turn."

She pulled her antlers out of her head and offered them to me.
It was futile to refuse her. I set the antlers against my hair and felt
them latch onto my skull, bone taking root in bone. When my eyes
were no longer human I could see the face of the creature that had
saved me. It was my mother's face, and it was no longer flushed
from chemo or swollen from prednisone and her hair was her hair,
not cancer's hair. There were so many things I wanted to tell her,
but when I opened my mouth, I didn't know how to speak.

"You have to take care of things," she said, and I was no
longer in my house but deep in the pit of a winter night, the world
glittering against the cold flames of moonlight, alone.

Vengeance is 9
JOYCE FROHN

I look up as Michael drops into the basement through a window, the binoculars thumping on his chest. "It's a red Hummer. They're coming for us. They burned the old house."

I wish we didn't live in a place so flat that he can see half the town from the top of one tree.

I pat his shoulder but he shakes it off. None of us are particularly good at dealing with men, with a few exceptions, and anyone would have trouble taking in five teens suddenly.

I know you can hear this. You're the one I complain to the most. That was one of your first powers. To hear my thoughts and your grandmother's, too.

"We all know what to do," David says. He lets his large, calm presence fill the basement. That's one of the reasons I love him so much. He's so calm in emergencies. I picked a good father for you. He lays out the tools of my trade on the old pool table. An almost white sheet, small knives, scoops, pipettes, soap, a large metal bowl and a speculum.

There was only supposed to be you. We've always had small families. Only a few girls. We don't want the power to be too spread out. I turn to Michael. "It might be nothing. Just helling around, or even clients." He glares at me and shakes off my hand again as he walks to Sheila's mattress.

"You don't understand," Michael says. "They're serious." He shakes Sheila awake.

"Everyone who comes to us is serious." I run my finger over the rim of the bowl. For a moment I think about the woman who passed the tools to me. She and her husband were both doctors and when they made the women doctors quit, he kept working. Maybe you can find him and help him. You loved having him as your doctor.

I walk to your mattress in the corner. It's almost a half hour til sunset. I check on the quilt I tucked around you when you went to sleep this morning. One cold, bare foot is sticking out, still slightly tanned. I make sure your other foot is covered.

It's nearly Thanksgiving and we've had our first frost. I remember when there would be knee-deep snow by this time. I don't tell Kiel that, of course. He wouldn't have taken your quilt; he doesn't disobey.

I wish Kiel would, or stomp his foot in anger, something. I miss your anger. There's too much resignation now.

I can see the cuff of your Dora PJs peeking through the threadbare coat that reaches Kiel's knees. He's five and you outgrew those PJs at three. I'll have to remind Michael and Sheila to trim the cuffs. It won't do for the gender police to take him. He and I are the only ones that can go out. I turn away from him.

"Here's a cup of willow tea. I'll get supper for you when this is over, Sheila," I say as I hand her a travel mug, still warm. Michael and Sheila can't be seen here. He's too old and she… When my clients come, Kiel will be silent in the corner or even beside you under your quilt. You will be a sick child under a blanket and I will be…

I check Sheila's cheek with the back of my hand. She's still feverish. I turn away when I hear you murmur.

"Mama, tell me about food," you whisper. I smile as I walk back to you. You used to ask me to tell you about the past. There may be a time when air shows and merry-go-rounds come back, but you'll never eat solid food again. I lie down beside you.

Your thin fingers grab my arm and memories fly into my head. I was laying here when your father pulled you off me. I hadn't moved in two days. "It's time you went out in the world," he said to you. "Your mother will die if you keep nursing and I can't take care of everyone."

I tried to get up. "She can't. She hasn't finished changing. Look at her feet. They don't match." I touched the one soft foot.

"Yes, Daddy." I made you promise not to let anyone see you or take human blood until the time was right and that time can't be now. You're still my daughter. There is still time.

"Remember mangos?" I say. You nod. We clustered around the fire when we dug a mango pit out of the compost. The smoke carried faintly the sweet scent and reminded us of the juicy wetness of their flesh.

"Broccoli?" You nod and I remember that all your cousins liked that. I can't keep from thinking of them. The ones in Texas might have gotten across the border; they were dark enough to pass, but what about Boston? Do you know? Would you tell me if you did? You were always good at keeping secrets behind your smiles.

"Corn on the cob?" You frown. "Little ears," I say. You nod. I remember how you loved baby corn. I always saved the little ears we found on corncobs for you. I wish we could grow that. The restrictions on farms were one of my warning signs.

"Popcorn?" People gave out popcorn everywhere. I've tried to explain to Kiel about that. Now you'd go to jail for 'promoting vagrancy.' You frown and shake your head.

"Sausage?" Your father made that. Back when he had legal jobs. Now I don't ask how he gets things. Although I know he still worries about bloodstains.

You shake your head. I remember times we had so much food that we had avalanches in the freezer. I want to ask your father if he knows what happened to that factory, but he'd just give me that stare that says it's a dumb question.

"Cheese?" You cock your head. "Yellow and white mixed together, pizza cheese?" You shake your head. "Ham?"

"Yes," you whisper. "Tell me." I talk about the way the meat parted in your teeth and how the smoky taste lingered.

Kiel starts to moan and rub his stomach. Your father hugs him, "Don't worry." I wish he wasn't listening. Your father says, "We'll eat well tonight." Kiel sniffs the air.

Even after four years with us, he still doesn't trust. I can smell your grandparents cooking supper on the grill. We got a squirrel today so there will be meat instead of just roots and greens. There have been deaths from starvation in town, since UNICEF was forced out. But your grandmother's talent is to wander through a field of dead grass and come out with a bucket of food.

I know Kiel would rather hear fantastic stories about the past. A lump raises in my throat. You should have been the fantasy in one of my stories, and carnival rides, birthday parties, and buffet restaurants should be normal. My editors wondered how I could make my stories so believable. I never told them I didn't make up much. Now I wish I wasn't so good at describing.

"Nurse, Momma?" You ask.

I nod and open my dress. It's my brown Indonesian one, far too exotic to be worn outside. I run my hand over it and remember what your father said when I put it on. "So, it'll be tonight?"

"No, it's just that everything else is on the line," I said. I don't want to leave the children; to leave you. Your father just shook his head. He's too much a prophet to believe in coincidence.

Two days ago, as you came in just before dawn, you told us of a house emptied by the police. Sure, the police had looted, but there was still water in the toilet tanks and pipes and we got enough detergent to wash just about everything.

"Keep talking," you say.

"Fried chicken? You loved to chew the bones." You shake your head. "Pizza? You always took yours apart. Remember Zee's Place?"

You mummer, "Lollipops." I remember the young man that used to hand them out. He was the first corpse I saw laying in the street. The rest of the family probably got out, they were Albanian, used to fleeing, probably already have a new place. Someplace.

You could order what you wanted in four fast food places before you were four. When I have enough clean clothes, I trade with the smokers that hang out in places like that. Some of our best clients, your father's and mine, have come from there. I look at them and wonder. "Did you help get things the way they are? Do you like things the way they are now?"

Tears drip from my eyes. You look up and frown, "Don't cry, Mommy. It spoils the taste."

I wipe my eyes. "Don't talk with your mouth full. It's not ladylike." I push the pink trickle back into your mouth. I wince a little as you resettle. Before your teeth were sharpened, it never hurt to nurse you. I stroke your hair.

Your father pats my shoulder. "It's taking a long time."

"Maybe they aren't coming?" I know that's silly; this is the only whole house standing for more than five blocks.

"We've had plenty of time to get everything ready," your father says.

"Blueberries. Remember how sweet?" We always meant to go picking up north with your relatives. We were supposed to get up to your great-grandmother's farm but things happened too fast.

"Remember blackberries?" You nod, of course you remember blackberries. You chewed a few last summer. You couldn't swallow them and Kiel cried at the waste when you spit them out.

"Are you sure they're coming here?" I ask Michael, when you stop nursing and I sit up.

He nods. "I heard them say they were looking for 'an old guy with a lot of stuff.'"

You smile. "That's Grandpa, all right."

Michael ruffles your hair. "That described him before you were born." I see him wipe a tear from his eye as he walks away.

I'm glad he's talking to you. When you started to change, the kids got nervous around you. When their mother sent them over here to sleep while she worked, there were five in their family. Jim, the oldest boy, was shot as a looter when he tried to get food from a flooded grocery store, and Mary fell in love with a militia leader and ran off.

My throat tightens as I watch Michael help his sister, Sheila, into the old washing machine. I give her a smile. "Don't worry," I tell her. "It won't last long."

Michael frowns at me. "Don't come out until everything is quiet," he tells her. He slips her a knife. He's very protective. She's thirteen and still a virgin. The last newspaper I saw said the sex tourists are bringing 'economic opportunity.'

"Michael, when we leave, you can keep the stockpile." I wave my hand toward the pile of cattail roots, nuts, and dried fruit. "The three of you will need it." He ignores me. I don't know if he thinks that the pile will be gone or if he will be. I know he doesn't believe that we have a plane.

After he slides the paneling into place to hide the door of Sheila's room, he gets the plywood to cover his and your father's hiding place. We're lucky that your grandparent's basement has so many rooms.

"David, aren't you coming?" Michael asks. The two of them are probably the last two men of military age left in town that aren't in some army or gang. I remember a time when 15-year-olds and 40-year-olds weren't counted as 'potential insurgents.'

"No," your father says. "My place is here, with my daughter."

Michael snarls at David. "You don't understand; they aren't here as clients. It's the end—" he shakes his head and slides the false panel into place.

"Are you ready?" I ask. I help you up; you weigh so much less than when we hid here five years ago. I pick up a hairbrush. You roll your eyes and give me that indulgent look children have when their parents tell them things like, "Eat your breakfast" and "Wear a sweater."

I remember the last time you gave me that look. It was right after your father's vasectomy. I think our lovemaking woke you. You have to be the last one. You are our ancestor reborn.

I wonder what happened to the vet that did your father's surgery? I miss him. I mean it's an easy surgery to do but I'm glad they were all strangers.

Your hair falls in golden waves. It's every color of blonde from platinum to honey. Without the sun to bleach your hair, will it darken? "Remember what I told you about your hair?" I say.

You stomp your foot, the normal-looking one, and snap. "Comb it often, but don't let anyone find the hair or they'll have power over me." I smile with pride and choke back tears. You're so young and there's so much you have to remember. I wish you were older or that you weren't the one. I asked your ancestors, why now? Why not during the Burning Times or slavery days?

I know part of the reason. People had stopped hiding; it seemed safe to say, 'pagan,' 'Goth,' and 'gay.' If things had kept going, even our family might have started saying things. No one would have believed the truth; that there were people that looked human but weren't. But maybe there was something we could have said...

Hope, that's what the problem was. That's why your future must be sacrificed in order to cleanse the world. Sometimes, hope leads to rage. And that's what you are. Rage against injustice in a child's body. Vengeance. Avenging the deaths, losses, the world. I would destroy the world to make you a normal child again, but I am as powerless as you are powerful.

I tie your hair back with a black ribbon. It matches your dress. I had no idea why I grabbed that dress when we left our house. Probably your father did but he was kind enough not to tell me.

We had a day's warning. A simple e-mail with a date wrong. "Assassination." I think I know who sent it. It was good to have a friend in the military. I didn't read the rest. Just erased it without reading and started sending out e-mails to everyone. "Urgent business in Canada. Won't be back soon." I hoped that by the time the assassination occurred, people would know what I meant and maybe a few got away. I still have my old computer, maybe in Canada...

We hid in our old house that I kept the front door key to after we sold it. Just loaded a truck, pulled up, opened the front door and took down the "For Sale" sign. If you act bold enough, no one thinks you're illegal.

You were staying at your grandparents' house because I wanted to make sure that you had heat, water, and electricity. Your father went to work and you went to school. We would sneak over often. You were so proud of the work you were doing in first grade. Nothing seemed to change at first.

Oh, there were complaints on TV until certain people started disappearing. Everyone said it was nothing; you just needed I.D. Of course you had to buy them...

You started acting resigned when we had to pull you from school. It just cost too much. By then there were only twelve in your class. Your grandparents still had their credit cards even after checks weren't allowed. Then there was gas rationing and spot checks on the road and your father had to stop work. I'd ask how he got the gas for the plane but I don't think he'd tell me.

We were just planning on hiding until we had enough gas stockpiled to get us to Canada. We didn't have to hide long, we thought...

We had room on the plane for four, five if one of them was small. It was going to be a wild ride. An ultra-light isn't very comfortable, but we measured and all we needed was a stretch of empty road, good luck, and good weather.

Then there was a storm. Nothing much once, but now... I wonder if anyone has moved back to New Orleans or Miami? We're not allowed to say that the oceans are rising but– After that there was no more electricity in town except for those rich enough to pay to put up poles and wires. Generators are cheaper. We moved to your grandparent's house and became the only hope for the neighborhood. I remember that first night. We had twenty people gathered around that little outdoor grill and ten more on stretchers. I wrote all the names down and buried them in jars. We tried our best but–

Your father took care of the grave digging.

It was so hard for people to learn that there was no help coming. That rules about I.D. and proof of citizenship weren't going to be relaxed. Law and order. Property rights. We heard gunfire all night. All the newspapers I found later were full of advice about getting I.D. chips.

"Starve the beast and drown it," that was clear enough. "Sell off government assets." They have now, everything except the military. People just forgot, I guess, that that would include roads and mail and... I wonder who they say the president is?

"Big hug," you say. Your father and I wrap our arms around you. I rest in your father's strong arms with your head on my chest.

I want to stay like this forever. But I feel my ring wiggling and I hear a car.

"The sun is setting, Mama," you say. My tears drip onto your wings. I knew you were going to change the night they burned the library. You didn't cry that night; that's how I knew. You had always been afraid of going to sleep without your fishy lamp and lullaby CD. You've been called the "Powers of Darkness Incarnate" but you were always afraid of the dark. Your grandmother said it was because the fire so close made a glow in the sky; but I saw your eyes shining in the dark. I supposed with your new eyes the dark isn't as scary. Or maybe this was the nightmare you kept having. Are you a prophet, too? Would you tell me if you were?

I held out hope for fur and fangs for a month. It was a full moon night, when I knew. There were ten people in the basement, raiders were coming through. I was curled around you. You said, "Scratch, Momma." The skin came away under my fingers in wet, blood-sticky strips. They were the last solid food you ate. I pulled stiff, sticky things out from the two spots that always itched when you got scared. I kept the blankets wrapped around you until everyone else was gone. Then I told the family. We gathered around your bed that night.

Your grandmother hoped for bright, glittering membranes; for the power of beauty and song. I thought of iron and its cousin steel; burning tender flesh and held my tongue. Your grandfather wanted strong feathers and wrath-of-God eyes. But I thought of how sharp your teeth had been getting and how you slept all day.

Your father shrugged and said the same thing he said when I told him that I was pregnant, "I'll love anything." I had no surprises when I pulled back your blanket and saw thin bones spread with black membranes. The black feathers had already started on one foot and your claws were already growing. They are such a contrast against your white skin. I sometimes skimped on the sunscreen long ago just to see your skin darken like your father's. Now you're paler than me.

You tug on my arm. "Momma, give me your ring." I blink

myself back and look at the ring on my little finger. When I made it, I had a hard time seeing the dragon I intended; as your powers have grown, it became more obvious. Sometimes it moves and I can see waves in the blue-green stone it holds. It's a dragon-snake holding the bowl of waters in its mouth, swallowing its own tail. Ouroboros, Egyptian Serpent. The beginning and the end; the dark side of eternity.

I slide the ring onto your left ring finger. I wipe one tear away for the man who should have put a ring there and the grandchildren I will never have. I can spare no tears for the world. I touch the white band of skin where my wedding ring was.

It was Robin, the oldest girl, who wanted both rings. I gave her my wedding band and your father's. She pointed to my silver ring; "I could get almost a pound of meat for that one."

I shook my head. "It's Lily's inheritance."

She said, "You'd sacrifice all of us for her." I didn't say anything but she could read the truth in my eyes. That morning she brought the meat home from the rich family she and her mother cleaned for, and the next night neither came here. I told her younger brothers and sisters that she would be back soon. Then I said that the family didn't let them leave. It might be true, but they're hardly the only ones who've sacrificed some of a family to save the rest.

It's Kiel's crying that brings me back this time. He's too little to understand. You give him a hug. "Keep an eye on Kiel." I nod. He's your faithful playmate; the little brother that loves his sister. The only one that treats you like a child. I've been keeping an eye on him since we took him out of the cage his mother left him in when she went to the dormitory at Wal-Mart. She left a note with his birth certificate. We'd been sneaking over to diaper and feed him since he was small. He'd been born in a hospital; although how she got the things to prove she could keep him, I never knew. He's five now.

His mother named him Ezekiel and he sort of recognized it. But your grandfather said, "One prophet in the family is enough." So we shortened it. We never even considered Zeke.

"We'll be here tomorrow," your father says. It'll take us that long to check on people and assemble the plane. "After that—"

"After we leave," I say with a lump in my throat. "We'll leave your blankie and Bun-Bun here." I point to a hook in the ceiling. "The rats won't get them." People haven't gotten around to eating rats yet, so...

"Oh, Mom," you say. Like any nine-year-old reminded of blankies and loveys in front of friends. For a moment, I pretend that all is normal; you're going to sleepover camp or—

I hear the Hummer. It's not a drill. I let go of you and your father unwraps his arms. He hugs Kiel. I pick up your blue satin bag, slide your comb in and tie it around your waist with a gold cord. "I wore that on my dress at WisCon," you say. I nod, remembering Halloweens dressed alike; science fiction and fantasy conventions.

I check the bag. There's your bone comb, an amethyst crystal, and a sheet of tissue paper with your father's tiny handwriting on it.

"You remember what the check marks mean?" I say.

"Yes, Momma. I remember who to check on and what the black crosses stand for."

"Check on Mary and Susan soon." You nod. "You helped get their milk going and Keith and Janey were fuzzy." I wipe a tear from my eye, remembering their births. Your father and I are the best medical help for miles since the U.N. was driven out. He's doctored animals and I was a nurse's aide. It's lucky for our patients that I can draw on my ancestors all the way back to your namesake.

I wonder how long it will take you to get all the names with black crosses. How far can you travel in one night? What can your powers do when you are full grown?

I take a deep breath and keep going. "The amethyst will lead you to the mine. We'll leave a note for you there when we get to Canada."

"Canada?" Kiel repeats, puzzled. I know he's always thought of Canada as a myth, right up there with house pets, dancing purple dinosaurs, and drinking water coming from faucets.

I'm glad you've told me what is in his mind. His words, well you talked more as a two-year-old. I think we can take him along. Maybe someone can help him. You're proud that he can draw most of the letters of the alphabet. At his age you could read and write your name. Of course you had pre-K and that's another thing I can't explain to Kiel.

I hang the silver cross and pentacle around your neck. Maybe the cross will keep the Catholics from attacking you. It won't burn you, we checked, and your grandfather blessed you. We used the blessing for a missionary. Your grandfather joked, "There's no blessing in my book for an avenging almost-angel." Like most of his jokes there was no reason to laugh.

Just because you came from the wrong wife, is no reason to have anything against a half-brother. The pentacle will tell your kin who you are.

The truck is in the driveway. Kiel slides under the pool table. Your grandparents are trying to look old enough to be harmless and young enough to be strong. Your grandfather is wearing his minister's robe and hating it. He's trying to remember the stuff about 'millenarianism,' 'rapture,' and all those other things that used to be fringe back when Christianity was a religion and not...

Your grandmother is wearing one of my long dresses and hating it. She's made me promise that I'll bury her in pants and cut her hair. They're the only ones their age still around. I keep the messages that are thrown over and through the fence from the 'proper homes.' Maybe someone in Canada will want to know.

You head up the stairs, counting on your grandparents to delay them. Maybe this is still a drill. Maybe they'll rummage through the barn and be killed by one of your grandfather's traps. Maybe loot and leave. I hear gunfire. I gasp and your father clamps his hand over my mouth and pulls me under the pool table. After all the times I went ahead to make sure there were no corpses lying in the street, no bodies hanging from the trees. You shouldn't see them like that. Your father counts and mouths "It's for the best. Now we don't have to leave the kids."

I see your bare foot as you go out the door. I wish you at least had one shoe.

I hear the screams and your roar.

I whisper, "Good-bye, my darling, Lilith."

Caution!

MARIAH BARKOVITZ AND CARMAN C CURTON

No more than 4 (four) cryptids in
the lift at a time – or the lift will
become a _PORTAL_. The caretaker
will not answer emergency calls
from any transdimensional hubs.
Accidental space-time anomalies
are the sole responsibility of the
occupants of the lift.

– Management
Lambeth Housing Services

Stone Shaper Tanukis Estranged
R J K LEE

Raindrops splash across the statuette of a balding tanuki wearing a tie and waving. The little thing is me, when I was a workaholic for the big corps. Etched into the stone from neck to bottom: *Tsumi Was Here*. After no text message nor phone call with her for over a year, my daughter has finally left me a reply. But even so, I'm not sure how to talk to her in person without going to jail. Do I have the nerve to risk it?

Black whiskers drooping on my muzzle, I trudge off the puddle-strewn sidewalk into the muddy grass of the park. I bow my head against the grumbling storm, against the surrounding buildings, against the threat of authority. I finger the taser at my belt. I pull the backpack tighter beneath my opaque raincoat. While I still wear a business suit, it's comprised of down-on-its-luck fabric: torn jacket, frayed button shirt, and faded slacks. I live off sales work these days. "Irasshaimase! Would you like to buy a pack of cigarettes or some juicy chicken? Donate to the latest fund that won't help anyone?"

The high-rise apartment where my daughter now lives looms across the street. Through the rain, the building is a grayed-out yellow fortress. Tsumi is on the thirtieth floor.

I spent pitiful months trying to build a new case against Kumiho, her body-shaper mother. My ex-wife. No results.

What helped me to finally track Tsumi to the Otetsumi Suites was my stone-shaping. I left little statuettes across the country, hoping Tsumi would realize they were created by me. I thought she'd find them and carve her own in reply. A natural stone-shaper like me, she can melt stone with her hands, shape it how she likes, and return it to solid form when she pleases.

Nothing for months. I left three statuettes for her here in

January. When I returned in April, I discovered a figurine hidden under the tree. Having reached June, I'm going to leave her another message.

I want to fix the daughter-father bond that's been severed, to forge it anew, even stronger than before. If I break into the apartments to see her, I'm worried I'll lose that chance. Better to rely on the one-way communication of stone for a while longer.

White poplar trees swish in the winds. Their vertical thrusts of branches shake. Leaves tremble as the clouds unleash a downpour. I have no plan here but to craft, hidden in the raging storm. One day, I hope our stonework will mold harsh reality into something better for Tsumi and I.

Over a decade ago, I should've known better. I suppose that's what every poor parent says. Fitting that I'm merely one of the masses and my ex-wife is the aloof upper crust, the user, the taker, the queen. So many full circles I was blind to at their start, even when she'd held a blade to my throat less than an hour following our first meeting. Pressing past the early distrust with compassion, there were some wins. There was fleeting love and the birth of our daughter. But by the end, it circled back to the blade. Kumiho cut me from my relationship with Tsumi, casting me out to strangle on the leash of a restraining order.

I lost in the parental game of deceit, in court, in finances, in the workforce; rising again is futile. My network is sparse. The future is a constant struggle. My present day lacks a platform to operate from.

I rest on a bench and consider the rocks scattered about the mud beside the bases of tree trunks.

This isn't like the first time I met Kumiho, in the garden of the Kyotoka Central Oriental Conference Hall, before we married or had a doomed family. No bamboo doors opening onto the patio to lurk from, and no servants nor avian flyer with wings styled as traditional Japanese fans. No mystery tugging me forward. No challenge calling me to the beautiful monster, the cursed pull of the unknown.

Only the rocks in this park garden call now. Simple and childish, they're not arranged in exquisite patterns, nor polished like gemstones. They're more akin to a kid's mud cakes or sandcastle clumps. An absolute ugly mess, but a creative, inspiring one. They're strewn about in random sizes and chaotic placement. They're pockmarked and scarred, clung to by mud and slimed across by bugs.

No servants bow from the shadows. No one's on point, watching for wrongdoing or impoliteness. No one will act to repair this travesty.

My body slopes forward onto my hands. I stretch the skin taut on my long face. I could cry. The lack of my child. The punching of the rain. Everything moist. Her mother would say *it's too slick to be outdoors; wait for the danger to pass.*

If the weather cleared, and children were allowed to frolic, they'd be warned to stay clear of the poorly-dressed and stinking goblin of a raccoon-man who is contemplating kidnapping his own child from his perch on the bench.

Tsumi's mother would advise her to *steer clear of strangers; they bring danger.*

Family should heed wise warnings. I didn't pause to consider sage advice from mine when this all started, wooing the rich boss woman. I was brave and curious. Don't be that. Look where it led me.

Stubborn and dedicated, I became her agent-for-hire, her servant and assassin, her husband, her fellow parent, and then her ex-husband and the estranged, pushed-away father.

No one is in the park. Only me within the trees, rising from a seat tucked amongst the flowers and overgrown grass.

From a stool on a patio, I remember watching my daughter roll rocks out of their proper positions, upsetting the religious calm of the lines the rakes had left behind, breaking the circles and layers of blissful meaning.

I didn't stop her. She was giggling. Her smile was a magical half-moon, beaming from her wide face.

She set her rocks in three clusters and then went to work on each one. So focused on her task that her tongue stuck out and beads of sweat dampened her brow. Soon, a trio of animals curled before her. A honey-loving family, she told me, camping together in the woods, hunting delicious edibles despite the bees and shaming of neighbors. The mother fox, the father tanuki, and the hybrid girl with trio of tails like mother, and the black-whiskered face like father.

I sit and do the same. My hands melt three rocks, salty with typhoon and tears, while trees sway and creak. I craft the figurines of fox, tanuki, and their hybrid, as my daughter did the last time we met, years ago.

It's a struggle to ignore my desire to enter Otetsumi Suites to search for her inside the building itself. Hard to believe how dangerous it would be, walking in there to say hello to my own daughter. There was no joint custody possible, and visits were never enforced. In the final judgment, the court favored my ex: Kumiho's assets, victim scenarios, her influence, and probably the greater respect society grants the fox. Somehow it didn't matter that she shifts her appearance as she pleases. The judges didn't even pause at the fact Tsumi loves her father. I've joined family marches against parental alienation before, swinging sign posts, peacefully walking down the sidewalk. But what a useless gesture.

With diligence, I form and shape the rocks into their individual personalities. The mother is packed tight, potent, prim, and powdered with power. The father is a messy sprawl, welcoming but overprotective. The daughter is stylized zigzags, a princess of hyper fashion.

Setting the figurines on my lap, I reach for my belt, the stun gun there, checking the charge, in case I do head into the Suites after all. Risky. Downright idiotic. But as the father, as a parent, would you give up on a relationship with your child?

Out of the corner of my eye, a stranger appears. I immediately swing my taser up.

"Hey, watch where you point that thing. Put it down, or else I'll show you my karate skills." An anorexic elementary school kid with a backpack and raincoat raises her fist. Legit fighting stance. Studying her, I can't help but think of my own daughter. The black curls and blue eyes are typical for an Asian-Caucasian mutt. I wonder if she deals with the same insults at school as my daughter did.

I flinch and two figurines roll off my lap. The mother and the father plop into the mud. I holster the weapon.

The girl takes a step closer. "What are you doing, mister?"

Kneeling, I retrieve the fallen figurines. The girl helps me fetch the father. Handing it to me, I meet her luminous eyes.

"Mister, you okay?

"My daughter's kidnapped."

"Family drama? Me, too. I'm running away. Too many selfish idiots. That's growing up. Better on our own, right?"

"Alone doesn't mean better. See these? We're both stone shapers, my daughter and me. They're our touchstones. What we long for."

"Maybe she doesn't need them." The girl rolls her shoulders. "Not every kid needs their parent."

"How can you say that?"

The girl sits on the bench. "I'll help you get inside." She punches my shoulder.

"Why?" My question is too sharp, suspicion turning me into a jerk.

"You look sad. Plus, I need a couch." Her smile appears almost mocking, but I know I'm just on edge.

After I collect the figurines, I tug her sleeve to the park's edge.

"We just need to get to the thirtieth floor. Okay?"

"Okay, mister." But when we cross the street, the girl hesitates. Her face turns to me, twisting into annoyance. "You don't let alone, do you?"

The glare in her eyes doesn't belong to a nameless schoolgirl. She knocks the figurines out of my hands. They clatter in the street. She screams, accusing, pointing, fleeing inside.

Cheap shot, Kumiho. But that's on me. My mistake for letting my ex-wife trick me with one of her fake faces again.

Security charges. I zap them, stun them long enough to grab my sculpted family from the concrete. I bolt inside, chasing after Kumiho. Grabbing the edge of the elevator, I pull myself inside before the doors close.

Teeth bared in the corner; the schoolgirl visage transforms into the natural appearance of Kumiho. A tall and curvy woman with furry ears and three bushy tails.

The elevator ascends.

I hold up one of the figurines. "It's what our daughter wants."

On her haunches, Kumiho sniffs and snarls. "We bury failures to build a richer burrow." Her claws click against the wall as she twitches her nose and leans in. "That's our way forward."

"Tsumi deserves more." The quaver in my voice is undeniable.

"We protect our own." Kumiho snaps her teeth. "Tread carefully, Max."

I flinch. "I don't work for you anymore. Ask yourself what Tsumi wants."

"She's a kid, not a decision-maker. And you're nothing but a jobless heckler."

"Tsumi needs family."

"She has it, my poor, directionless tanuki."

The elevator stops and the doors slide open.

"Enough." Kumiho steps out first. Swiveling around to face me, her tails swish in a proud flourish. "My rules. You will spend time with Tsumi. We will end this fight. But don't test me, or else next time will be longer than a year."

The hallway is lined with crafted rocks, scenes made by Tsumi. At the end a workshop filled with more art. Tsumi is in the middle of stonework. Slowing her hands, she turns the liquid rock to solid. She stops, stands. Our hands reach for each other.

I move in to embrace her. She returns the hug, long and heartfelt.

We let go. I show her what I've made. She grins. Her pointy teeth flash. Her eyes flicker, same dark irises as my ex, but not a trace of the hatred.

"It's me, isn't it?" Tsumi points to the hybrid figurine.

I wink. I let her inspect it. "Are you okay?"

"I'm fine." She turns the figurine around, tapping it, checking its quality. "Good work. Hey, Mom. Is Dad staying?"

Kumiho watches us with the silence of a company boss overlooking a meeting table of bored subordinates. We watch, waiting, and she shrugs as if to suggest *have fun for now*.

The heels click away. It's almost comforting, that same flippant way she used to leave after an order, a job, or an irritation. I let my guard down, enough to concentrate on why I struggled for so long to come here.

"Amazing work."

"Thanks, Dad. Let's make more."

We bow our heads to focus. Forging figurines, sculptures, landscapes, and scenes, we barely speak. But we engage in dense discussions through the melted rocks, our hands guiding the glowing liquid into stories and dreams.

Coming Up From the Wilderness
IRENE TOUISSANT

People cleared the streets as the gang rode into town, running for their houses, their businesses, closing the shutters and slamming and barring the doors. Everyone but the saloon owner, who waited behind the bar, pretending to polish a glass to hide the trembling of his hands.

Jericho watched from the balcony. He wasn't supposed to be in the saloon at all, and especially not now. His father would paint stripes onto his back when he found out, but it'd be worth it. The leader of the gang, Gabe Fell, pushed through the doors to the saloon, a sinuous swagger in his step and a gleam in his slitted eyes.

His head is purest gold; his hair is wavy and black as a raven.

They were unnatural his daddy said, the whole gang of outlaws. "Come from unholy dirt, where the devil lives. Just lookit the eyes boy, like the beasts of the earth itself."

Oh Jericho did look, and couldn't stop looking, so of course the beast looked up, saw him watching and winked, tipping his hat, before striding up to the bar.

"Whissskey," Gabe hissed.

The bartender set out seven shot glasses and poured amber liquid into each, overflowing the glasses and splashing the bar.

"Leave the bottle."

Gabe's deep, breathy rasp of a voice fascinated Jericho. The dusty black clothes Gabe wore fascinated him too, tattered and stained by the dust of the road. His broad shoulders, his lush lips, the hair that still fell in waves around his shoulders after he took his hat off – Jericho drank it all in like the gang did their booze.

Gabe threw back another shot and Jericho bit his lip, heart pounding at the flash of pale skin peeking out above the bandana tied around Gabe's neck. Slamming the glass down on the counter,

189

Gabe looked up, catching Jericho still staring. Jericho held his eyes. He couldn't look away. Gabe's snake-like eyes were the amber of the whiskey, flashing bright even in the dim light of the saloon.

"Be right back, boys." He slapped the nearest of his gang on the shoulder as he pushed away from the bar. Spurs jingled as he mounted the stairs, his gaze never leaving Jericho, who knew he should move, run, find an empty room and lock the door behind him. He didn't. Rising as Gabe approached, he stood his ground.

"Nervy little thing, ain't you?" Gabe asked when Jericho didn't give way before him.

He stiffened at the words. How could Gabe call him little? They were of a height. Sure, and his shoulders weren't as broad, but he had his own strength, from chopping wood, from hauling water, and all the other manual labor his father put him to. He wasn't the weakling his slender frame suggested.

"I've seen you before. You're Preacher Micah's boy. Whatcha doin' here? Yer Daddy wouldn't like it, you bein' in this den of iniquity."

"Nearest door when you rode in," he lied.

"Uh huh." Gabe took another step forward, and then another. Jericho had to give way before him or end up pressed against that broad chest. It happened anyway when he hit the wall. Gabe leaned into him, arms bracketing his body. He smelled of sweat and sun and whiskey, and underneath, Jericho caught a whiff of a cloying scent, almost musty. Stood so close, Jericho could see the narrow pupils of Gabe's eyes, slit instead of round, parting wider as Gabe pressed against him. Fixing his eyes on the ceiling, Jericho tried to will himself not to react as Gabe's breath fluttered across his cheek.

"Pretty little thing, too. I've seen you before. Watchin' me. What goes on in that head of yers when you stare at me with those emerald eyes?"

Things that'd make my dad whip me bloody, he thought, shuddering as Gabe's lips grazed his neck. It wasn't the first time he'd been called pretty. His skin remained pale despite hours spent in the sun, his features delicate in their sharpness, and his hair shone like copper. Before this, though, it'd been as an insult. Hissing off Gabe's tongue, it caught at him. Made him feel like being pretty was good and right.

"Come find me tonight. Hangman's tree," Gabe whispered in his ear before stepping back. His tongue darted out, tasting lust in the air, and Jericho saw it was split like a serpent's.

The sight froze him in place, blood racing, as Gabe returned to the bar. His gang hooted and hollered as he made his way back to them, filling the air with raunchy comments, suggestions of all the things Gabe could do to Jericho in one of the saloon's rooms. He flushed, hoping they'd think it was shame and not excitement that pinked his cheeks.

They finished the bottle, and a second one after it, before heading out. Gabe was the last to leave, and he turned to tip his hat at Jericho before pushing through the doors. As they swung back and forth behind him, Jericho finally stepped away from the wall, approaching the railing on shaky legs.

The saloon owner raced to the window, face pressed to the dusty glass. After a few moments, his shoulders sagged.

"They're leaving. You can come down now."

Before Jericho could leave, the barkeep set out two fresh glasses.

"I'm having a drink and I think you could use one too. Won't tell your daddy. Not about none of this. But I need to steady my nerves and I bet yours are all jangled too."

The whiskey burned, and he coughed, feeling tears spill down his cheeks.

"It's not even them weird eyes or nothin'. It's their voices what gives me the chills." The bartender shook his head with a shiver. "You get along home now. If 'n the preacher asks, say you hid in the stables."

Micah descended on him the instant he crossed the fence to the churchyard.

"Where have you been, boy?"

He had no chance to answer. His father spared him the need for a lie, grabbing his arm and dragging him up the steps.

"Pray with me. Pray for the safety of our town and the people in it. Pray for God our Lord to safeguard us from those vermin."

Jericho knelt beside Micah in front of the altar, murmuring the right words along with his father, but his thoughts ran elsewhere, out past the fields to the river, out to the tree with the overhanging branch the lawmen liked so much. His neck burned where Gabe's lips had touched it and his blood still sang from the press of Gabe's body, from the whiskey that coursed through his veins, from the memory of inhuman eyes staring into his.

After their prayers were the chores, and after that they supped, Micah quizzing Jericho on his verses in between bites. Then more chores, and their evening prayers, and at last he was free to go to his room. He had a small nook up in the attic, opposite side of the church from the steeple. His bed shook when Micah rang the bell, but he'd learned to ignore it.

He washed up, taking more care than usual, then dressed again, hiding his clothes by pulling the bedsheets to his neck, in case Micah checked in on him before retiring. He could hear his father's steps below as he circled the church, setting out the hymnals for morning service. Finally, the steps retreated, and he heard the closing of the door to his father's room. Then came the waiting until the only sound in the night was the chirping of the crickets and he could see the moon peeking over the sill of his window.

Sliding from bed, he took his boots in hand and eased across the floor. He'd learned over the years where to step on each stair so it didn't creak. Left, left, right, center, skip the tenth and thirteenth altogether. The door had a latch and not a bar like some buildings in town, so it was a simple matter to undo. Sitting on the bottom step, he slid his boots on, then sighted off the stars and headed north.

Hangman's Tree stood on a ridge overlooking the water. He saw the fires long before he reached the river. The smaller one was right on the bank, and it was this one he made his way towards.

A black ghost appeared out of nowhere, laying a hand on his arm and he cried out, stumbling backward and tripping, landing hard in the grass.

"Lost a bet. Didn't think you'd ssshow." It was one of Gabe's gang swaying over him. Jericho's breath escaped in stuttering gasps as the man stared down at him. When he offered Jericho a hand, Jericho took it, allowing the other to draw him up.

"Well, go on, then. He's a'waitin'."

The bandit melted away again, leaving Jericho standing seemingly by himself in the night. He brushed himself off as best he could and continued on to the smaller fire.

Gabe leaned back against his saddle, bedroll spread beneath him. His eyes glinted in the firelight, a match to those of the giant black horse hobbled on the other side of the fire. The horse snorted and stomped as he approached, and Gabe murmured. Bane stilled, but still fixed Jericho with a baleful yellow glare.

He was spared any unnecessary conversation – Gabe made no comments on his appearance. Instead, Gabe reached out and Jericho allowed himself to be drawn in, draping himself across Gabe's lap, straddling him. One hand came to rest at the small of his back and the other cupped his cheek, surprisingly gentle. Gabe's first kiss was tentative, as if he were a wild horse needing to be coaxed and tamed. Impatient, Jericho parted his lips, inviting more. With a surprise laugh, Gabe obliged, delving into his mouth. Jericho pressed against him, savoring his warmth and relishing the hardness that grew beneath him.

His cheeks are like beds of spice yielding perfume. His lips are like lilies dripping with myrrh.

"You're no blushing virgin," Gabe gasped when Jericho let him up for air.

"Does that disappoint you?"

"Not a bit."

He tugged at Gabe's shirt, wanting to feel the flesh beneath, and Gabe reciprocated, pulling Jericho's shirt from his trousers and sliding beneath it. Gabe's hands paused in their explorations when he felt the ridges crisscrossing Jericho's back, remnants of Micah's belt.

"Tell me who did this to you and I'll kill him for you." He hissed the words into Jericho's mouth.

"I'll kill him myself when the time comes."

"You're full of surprises, preacher's boy."

"Oh, you have no idea."

"Tell me what you want."

"You, outlaw."

That surprised another laugh out of Gabe. "I reckon I'm all right with that."

He wasted no time getting Gabe out of his clothes or ridding himself of his. The heat from Gabe's body kept the evening chill at bay. It had been no lie. No blushing virgin he, but he'd never been like this before, with nothing between his flesh and another's. Before this it had been hasty fumblings in the stables whenever the coach came through town, both of them rushing through things, both terrified of being caught.

This time would be different. This time he'd savor every touch, every sigh.

Gabe's skin had a scaley texture about the neck and shoulders, rough under Jericho's fingers, and it glistened an opalescent green-gold in the moonlight.

"What are you?" he asked as he kissed his way along one shoulder.

"Nothing you know," Gabe said, hands clenching on Jericho's hips.

"No marks," Jericho cautioned, and the outlaw's hands relaxed, caressing instead of squeezing, sliding down to draw him even closer. Fingers teased, sending a shiver of anticipation through him. The silken glide of Gabe's finger felt like a touch of the heaven his father always claimed was beyond his reach. He muffled his moan in Gabe's shoulder, and Gabe laughed.

"No one to hear out here. No one like to care, anyways. Now, show me how much you like it."

At least one other of the bandit gang was awake, Jericho knew, but Gabe took him past caring. He made no more attempts to silence his cries, knowing the dark would disguise his blushes as Gabe drew moans out of him like to those he'd heard out saloon windows. Sweat trickled down his spine despite the chill in the air as Gabe murmured encouragements, calling Jericho the most ridiculous endearments. His sharp retort at being called a "ssssweet little filly" died on his lips when Gabe kissed him again.

Gabe undulated beneath him, hands on his hips, thumbs caressing his skin, and Jericho whispered, "My daddy never told me the fires of hell burned this sweet."

"If this is hell, who wantsss heaven?" Gabe asked.

Not I, he'd have said, but Gabe stole his words, anointing the column of his neck with kisses of his forked tongue, while making true on his threat to tease Jericho with silly pet names.

His arms are rods of gold set with topaz. His body is like polished ivory.

Gabe leaned back against his saddle, drawing Jericho down on top of him. A hand insinuated itself between them, enfolding them in fingers slick with spit. Bracing himself, he let Gabe drive him up into the embrace of his hand.

Jericho had lost his words now, but he didn't need them anymore. His body laid open before Gabe, telling him everything.

They spent themselves on Gabe's chest, flowers across the earth. Gabe pulled Jericho down on top of him.

This too was new – the fingers that traced the knobs of his spine, the hand that buried itself in his hair, the kisses on his brow as their bodies cooled.

"Wish I could take you with me. Wish I could keep you sssafe."

"If wishes were horses...."

Eventually he untangled himself, grimacing at the mess. The river water was chilly, but it took the worst from him, although he'd have to steal some soap from the laundry to rid himself of all the oil.

Gabe apologized for the roughness of his blanket as he draped it around Jericho, holding Jericho close to take the damp from his skin.

They dressed in silence. When Jericho turned to go, Gabe took his hands.

"I'm a jealous man, Jericho."

"As if I'd ever want for someone else."

Gabe let him go after one last kiss, fingertips trailing across Jericho's palms as he stepped back.

"I've got a job comin' up. One last big score and I'm done. I'll come for you then."

"I'll be waiting."

He didn't dare let himself look back, afraid Gabe would have melted away like a snake in tall grass, or turned into smoke as soon as he turned his back.

Sneaking back into the church was harder than his leaving, as his legs felt like lead and his head still spun. He froze when he mis-stepped and the wood of the stairs creaked beneath him, but the sleep of the righteous had Micah in its thrall and he made it back to his room in safety.

It was hard after that, going back to his life, knowing things were going to change, but not when. He chafed under Micah's constraints now more than ever, drawing his father's ire down on him and the belt that came with it. He also wondered at himself, that he felt no fear or guilt, no dread of damnation for consorting with a creature such as Gabe. His father's sermons and exhortations faded whenever he closed his eyes, remembering.

All night long on my bed I looked for the one my heart loves; I looked for him but did not find him.

Days turned to weeks, and one month turned to two, and he waited and he endured. Until one afternoon, without warning, Gabe slithered through the doors of the church, bold as brass. He doffed his hat, using the motion to catch Jericho's eye and wink.

"We've got nothing for you here, devil," Jericho's father blustered, putting himself in Gabe's path. Puffing his chest out, Micah tried to stare Gabe down. Jericho had his height from his father, but Micah's fighting trim had long ago deserted him, and Jericho had no illusions that he would triumph if it came to a fight.

Gabe didn't rise to the bait, instead responding with a cheerful grin and an extravagant sweep of his arm. His otherness was even more apparent in the light of day – his eyes, the glow of his skin, his sinuous movements.

"I've mended my wayssss, preacher, want to be like you and yours now. I come to ask the good Lord's forgiveness."

"You'll get none of that here. The only place for you and your band of beasts is in the bone orchard." Jericho had to admire his father's gumption, if not his smarts.

"But isn't it said in the good book that if we ask it'll be given to us?"

"The laws of god and the laws of man are different. And you ain't no man neither. Plus you're a thief and a murderer and destined for the noose."

"Well, see here now, preacher. I've never robbed from a man of gold honest-earned, nor killed a body that didn't deserve it."

"You will answer to the law, and you will find no sanctuary here. Leave this place, now."

"You'd see me at the Hangman's Tree, then?" Gabe's eyes flickered to Jericho's, then back to Micah's, so quick Jericho almost missed it.

"And no place else."

"And wouldn't it surprise you, if I rose again in three days' time?"

"Blasphemer!" Micah's face purpled as he shouted in Gabe's face, spittle flying from his lips. If he died of an apoplexy, Jericho swore he'd give thanks in prayer every morning and night for the rest of his life. God didn't see fit to grant him this reprieve, though. Gabe bowed again, mockingly, and left without looking back.

Jericho ducked his head and scrubbed at the floor, trying to make himself as small as possible. He tensed when he heard the tread of his father's feet, but Micah strode past him, slamming the door to his room behind him and leaving Jericho alone in the sanctuary.

The rest of the day passed and two more after that. Jericho continued to stay out of his father's way, finding refuge in his chores and reading from his bible in between. He kept a thumb in the Old Testament so he could flip to it from Song of Solomon if Micah turned attention his way.

His mouth is sweetness itself; he is altogether lovely. This is my beloved, this is my friend...

The third night he didn't sleep. Slow and careful, he packed the few things he wanted to take with him. An hour or so before dawn, he crept downstairs and let himself into Micah's room. His father's eyes flew open at the touch of cold steel against his throat, and he barely had time to register his son's presence before Jericho cut. He stepped back to avoid the spray, and watched as the life drained from Micah's body. Once satisfied, he turned to his father's desk, tipping over the lamp and spilling the oil across the papers strewn there. Lighting a match, he threw it, slipping out of the room as the first flames caught.

He let himself out through a window, leaving the main doors latched, to impede any of the townsfolks' attempts to douse the blaze. He'd have preferred to let Micah burn alive, let the flames he preached of so often take his black soul, but this way was surer.

Which way did your beloved turn, that we may look for him with you?

The rising sun bathed his left cheek as he neared the river. Gabe waited there for him under the Hangman's Tree, astride his dark horse. Kicking its sides, he urged the beast forward to meet Jericho, pulling Jericho up behind him in the saddle.

"Your doin'?" Gabe asked, pointing to the smoke that painted the horizon.

"Told you I'd do it myself," Jericho replied.

"So you did."

"And your job's done?"

"Done but good. M'saddlebags are packed with gold and Bane here will take us wherever we will." Gabe patted his horse on the shoulder and they snorted, shaking their mane and prancing beneath them.

"Then let's be off before they miss me."

"Where d'ya reckon we should go?"

"Anywhere but here."

"Ever been to Mexico?"

"Never even been to the next town over."

"Well, then. We'll have to sssee about fixing that, won't we?"

"What are you?" Jericho asked again as he settled his arms around Gabe's waist, resting his cheek against Gabe's shoulder after kissing the scaly flesh at the back of his neck.

Gabe twitched the reins. "Yours," was his response, and it was enough.

Miles fell away beneath Bane's hooves, taking Jericho farther and farther from the only life he'd ever known. He only looked back once, taking his fill of the smoke that smudged the horizon.

I belong to my beloved, and his desire is for me.

Bedroom Shadows
MARA LYNN JOHNSTONE

It felt like the opposite of déjà vu, to say goodnight to my parents and close my old bedroom door. Everything was familiar at a glance. But the trees outside were bigger in the windows, and the smell of my room was overly strong. How had I not noticed it as a kid? Laundry detergent, garlic from the kitchen, the dusty carpet. I would probably get used to it before the weekend was over and I was off to college again. I felt obscurely sad about that.

I changed into pajamas and brushed my teeth, trying not to feel maudlin. The lightbulbs in the bathroom were the wrong color. I wondered when they'd been changed.

When I finally climbed into bed, that at least was comfortably familiar. The pillow smelled safe. I settled down with a sigh, pulling the blanket over my nose to smell that, too. Yes, safe was the word. I was tempted to tuck it over my head and sleep that way, but I knew I wouldn't get enough air. Instead I tucked the blanket under my chin and entertained vague snippets of memory. I'd done this so many times.

I hadn't closed my eyes yet, and found myself staring at the closet door. I'd forgotten about those old memories. Foolish, really. But why was it open a crack? I hadn't opened it. Had my parents been cleaning before I got here? I scanned back through the last few minutes, to prove to myself that the door had been closed the whole time.

Because, I realized, I'd never sleep otherwise. That closet door had been a terror once, as had the shadows under the bed. Voices would whisper and hiss when I was on the edge of sleep. Nothing would be there when the lights came on, or when my parents came in, of course. But when it was just me, something took perverse glee in sparking nightmares.

As a rational adult now, I stared up at the ceiling with a frown, clutching the blanket tight. What else could I think about instead? Happy thoughts, happy dreams. Maybe the time I went sledding with–

Something hissed in the closet.

As I hurt my neck whipping around to look, a voice spoke from under the bed in an aggrieved whisper.

"Really? You can't even wait until their eyes are closed? This is so like you. After all this time, you're still rushing things. Have you no respect for the game?"

Before I could wrap my brain around that, a hissing voice from the closet replied.

"Oh really? I'm not the one who almost got seen by the parents, and you want to talk about respect?"

I had never been more still. No breaths. No blinking. Only listening.

"I thought better of you, honestly. Here I was looking forward to one last showdown with my favorite nemesis, and you have to go and ruin it."

"Me, ruin it? You're the one who spoke first. Did you say favorite?"

"Yeah, sure; don't make a big thing of it. Obviously you have plenty of other bed monsters to score points against. Not like I missed out on a new placement with triplets for tonight. Just thought it'd be nice one last time."

The voice from the closet was slow to reply this time. "I turned down an offer for tonight, too."

The silence that fell right then was the most charged I had ever heard. While it was entirely possible that I was moments away from being eaten so I didn't blow their cover, I couldn't bring myself to run. Not when they sounded *so* much like my roommates from sophomore year.

I cleared my throat. The silence got deeper. "Is there something you two want to say to each other?" I ventured. Then I pulled my blanket over my mouth.

The hissing voice from the closet sounded choked up. "You're my favorite too, you know that? I...I've missed you."

The voice under the bed was just as emotional. "I've missed you so much! Run away with me!"

"Where would we go?"

"To the forest! There's plenty of space for new monsters there, and it's out of jurisdiction. I checked."

There was a choked gasp, and then, "I would love to be a forest monster with you! We'll have to travel fast, to get there before sunrise."

I pulled the blanket down, speaking quickly. "What if you stayed at the new art museum on the way? It's dark and super creepy. Full of weird sculptures and shadows, perfect for hiding in."

They seemed to think for a moment. Then the one in the closet said, "That might just work."

"Oh, let's do it! Let's go right now! They'll never find us!"

"I am throwing my score pad through the portal now. I hope it hits my boss in the head. Race you to the window!"

Then two shapes flashed through my room, nearly too fast to see, pausing briefly in front of the window to look back at me, silhouetted in the moonlight.

"Thank you," said the hairy one with claws like a bear.

"Have a great life!" added the one with scales that shimmered like water.

Then they were gone, slipping through the crack that wasn't big enough for a mouse. I didn't even hear a rustle in the bushes. I thought I did hear a laugh, faint and delighted, far down the road already.

I stared at that window for a very long time. So long that I didn't notice when I fell asleep, only waking to a face full of Saturday morning sunlight and a crick in my neck.

Despite the sore neck, I'd had the most wonderful dreams. I doubted I'd ever tell anyone about them.

Cursebreaker
AUBREY ZAHN

You'd be surprised by the business a good cursebreaker can drum up in the swamplands of South Alabama. Or maybe you wouldn't. Maybe you think a bunch of dumb, superstitious rednecks – and I know that's what y'all think of us – are prime pickings for charlatans like me, but you'd be wrong. You know where the cursebreaking industry is thriving these days? Southern California, baby. My West Coast counterparts can throw up a few Instagram posts advertising $70 quartz crystal cleansings, and watch the requests roll in like a summer storm.

But me, I'm in Jesusland. The bible-beaters have a stranglehold on cursebreaking down here, with their revivals and laying-on-of-hands, with the backyard exorcisms that make the news whenever the zealots get a little overzealous and someone ends up dead. For anyone to seek me out it means that for one, they ain't a skeptic. All the skeptics grow up and move to Birmingham to work at their cousin's friend's startup or the new hipster brewery anyway. It also means they're either done with the church, the church's done with them, or it's something they can't come to the church for.

So they call me. Tear my number off a flyer at the grimy-ass Circle K or the electrical pole outside the Waffle House, because we're a world away down here from the hashtag spiritual girls of Instagram, and an entrepreneur's gotta know her market.

My newest client's voice is deep, but not resonant or forceful – it's clunky, painfully apologetic. If a sad-eyed bait dog chained in a methhead's yard had a voice, it would sound like Kaylee Randall's.

She calls around 10:00 pm, right as I'm fixing to settle in for the night, and she introduces herself just like that, with her full name. "Hi, this is Kaylee Randall, I'm calling about a curse."

I've just flopped onto the couch, cracked open an Abita Amber, and powered up my laptop for some hard-earned *Bachelorette* binge-watching. I sigh, and put on my professional voice, confident but not too sales-y. "What can I do for you, Kaylee?"

She's vague about it, and that alone gets me curious. Most people, at least in my experience, love to overshare. Without so much as a hello, they'll launch into "my no-good cheating son-of-a-bitch husband put a voodoo curse on my cooter and sealed it shut." Kaylee, she hesitates. It's a sickness, oh, but not a medical-type sickness. Not so much a spiritual thing either, or at least she's not gonna talk about it with her pastor. It's just real urgent, and she needs my help.

She gives me an address. I grit my teeth. It's way in the damn boonies, the real wet and heavy swampland. It's been thunderstorming all week to boot, and I know my piece of shit '04 Corolla ain't making it halfway down those dirt roads.

Still, a girl's gotta hustle. "I can be there tomorrow," I say. "When's a good time for you?"

Kaylee mumbles something so shyly I can't make out a word.

"What's that?" I say.

"I need you out here tonight," she says. "I'm sorry, it can't wait. It's an emergency."

Fun fact, my brother Jimmy's a psychologist. Guess it's a good twin, evil twin thing. He don't approve of my work, but one thing he's taught me to do is to cover my ass, ethically-speaking, so I ask, "Kaylee, are you planning on killing yourself tonight?"

"No ma'am," she says.

"And no one else's planning on killing you either? Because if it's that kind of emergency, that's for 911. Otherwise, I think it can wait until morning."

Silence for a second, then a muffled, whimpering sob that just keeps on going, broken up by hiccupping gasps. Not the kind of crying a girl does to manipulate you into getting her way. The kind of crying a girl does when her last ember of hope has just been extinguished. I can tell the difference by now.

Goddammit.

"Listen," I say. "I'll make an exception. I can be there in just about an hour."

Kaylee's sobbing gets louder with a kind of bubbling, hysterical relief.

"You just hang in there," I say. "I'm on my way."

The red dirt road's not near as flooded as I feared, and I make it all the way down to the driveway of the ramshackle Randall home. It's a bleak sight, gray and sagging as a toothless granny, one side half-covered in kudzu. I've seen condemned properties looking shinier. Behind the house there's nothing but swamp, which, despite the glow of the full moon, is so black it may as well be outer space. No car in the driveway. No lights on in the house. I start worrying it was a prank call.

I've got my cursebreaking kit in the passenger seat, an old leather briefcase filled with all kinds of religious paraphernalia and harmless homebrew potions. I know the patter for each one by heart. Folks like a show, but more than that, they like a story. You can't just wave some sage and say abracadabra. Not if you want to get paid, anyhow. I've done my research: Voodoo spells, Wiccan hexes, demonic possession. Even looked into cryptids some, after I was caught unawares when someone called in a chupacabra sighting – strictly speaking not a curse, more a supernatural nuisance, but I've had a few calls since where someone's spotted the Wolf Woman of Mobile or the Alabama White Thang loitering behind a local liquor store. Regardless of specifics, if you don't know enough backstory to sound convincing, there goes your credibility.

So I grab my kit, and I holster my Glock 43. I'm not much of what you'd call a gun person, despite growing up around here, but what I *am* is a woman alone in a swamp just before midnight.

I climb the creaking steps and knock on the front door. No answer. I knock again, harder.

"Come in," calls a shaky voice. I reckon this far out there's no real need to lock your door. I step inside. It's better than the outside, but not by much.

"This way," says the voice, which I hope to God is Kaylee's. I follow it to my left and open a door to a clean but near-empty bedroom, a Big Al plushie and an old-school Gameboy Color on the bedside table the only sign of habitation. Sitting cross-legged on the bed is a girl who can't be more than fifteen. She looks up as I enter, hands clasped in front of her like she's been interrupted praying. Long red hair, a chubby freckled face, gray-green eyes too young to be so sorrowful.

"Are you Lavinia?" she asks. I cringe. The name on my flyers is great for haunted mansions and magic shops and any place with stained glass or crystal balls. But in this girl's sad monotone voice, in this sad monotone bedroom, it sounds pitifully pretentious.

"It's Laura, actually," I say. "I take it you're Kaylee?" She nods.

I make it a rule not to contract with anyone underage – hell, it's probably a law of some kind – but I'm here now, so I may as well see if I can help.

"You home alone?" I ask, trying not to feel like the target of a *To Catch a Predator* sting.

"For now," she whispers. "Daddy went out." A few panicked thoughts flood my head, the most prominent of which being the image of Daddy pointing his shotgun at the stranger in his little girl's bedroom.

Kaylee looks at the ground as I perch uneasily on the edge of her bed.

"Well," I say with false cheer, "let's see if we can't get this curse broken quick."

Kaylee smiles weakly. "It's this thing I have," she says. "This… disease." She pauses for a minute, time we simply do not have to waste. "I have this sinful nature. We've tried praying it away for so long, but I just can't change…what I am."

I look closer at Kaylee, this time taking in her aesthetic, so to speak – her unstyled hair, her men's basketball shorts and oversized tee – and I'm suddenly roiling with rage. Jesusland does unforgivable things to its queer kids. I went to school with a few Kaylees, and not all of them made it to eighteen.

"It's not a sin to be gay," I say gently. "There's nothing for me to fix."

There's a loud burst of thunder, and Kaylee jumps, at which point I notice something truly horrible. When she uncrosses her legs I see for the first time the metal manacle around her ankle.

"Jesus, Kaylee, are you *chained up?*" Panic rises in my throat, and I grab my phone, ready to call 911.

"This is my last chance," Kaylee says, "Daddy says if I can't fix it for good tonight he's gonna have to kill me."

"You could have *led* with that!" I shout. Kaylee flinches. I look at my phone. No signal. *Fuck.*

"Kaylee, look at me," I say. "I am calling the cops. How'd you get hold of me earlier? Do you have a landline?"

"He took it when he left," Kaylee whimpers.

I try to steady my breathing. Panic doesn't solve anything. "Is there a key?"

"Kitchen, cutlery drawer." I'm on my feet before she finishes answering. Slide into the dark kitchen, petrified, fumble around in the drawer until I find the key.

When I get back to the bedroom Kaylee is shaking her head. "Don't, please." I ignore her and unlock the chain, cursing her sick fuck of a father.

"We're getting you out of here," I say, hauling a now sobbing Kaylee to her feet. Kid's heavier than she looks, or maybe it's just because she's resisting being rescued.

She gives in and follows me as I yank her through the living room and out the front door, leaving my cursebreaking kit behind in the process. We're halfway down the driveway to my car when two yellow pinpricks of light come bobbing down the long dirt road, getting bigger and brighter as they approach.

Daddy's home.

"Get in the car," I shout, practically throwing Kaylee forward just as a massive, mud-spattered white pickup truck skids into the driveway. A heavyset bearded man swings open the door and, without exiting the truck, points a long-barreled shotgun at us and opens fire.

Three thunderous, skull-shaking blasts erupt from the muzzle, followed by the explosion of my car's tires bursting and Kaylee's terrified howl.

"Are you hit?" I yell.

"No," Kaylee calls back. "We gotta get to the boat."

I follow her round the back of the house. There's another blast from the shotgun, and this time the sumbitch *is* aiming at us. I whirl around and return fire. I don't think I've hit anything, but there's a grunt of pain – or rage – from the truck.

We reach a slime-covered dock with an old motorboat tied to it. Kaylee starts messing with the knot while I rev the engine, kneeling in the rustwater and mosquito soup sloshing around in the boat's belly.

"Hurry!" I shout. I can't hear a sound from her daddy's truck, and it's too dark to see what he's doing from here.

"I'm trying," Kaylee wails. "It's stuck."

I toss her my pocketknife, which she fumbles – this kid's athletic shorts are false advertising – before plucking it out of the mud and sawing slow as fuck-all through the rope. We push off into the waterway just as her daddy's truck starts up again. It's driving away from us, which ain't as reassuring as you'd think – something tells me he's either gone for reinforcement or knows a road through the swamp to head us off.

The motorboat putters through the muggy mist hanging over the water, bumping off logs as I try to steer in the pitch blackness. Deeper into the swamp. At least the rain's lightened up.

"Kaylee, a little help?" She stares at me, glassy-eyed. I worry she's been drugged and it's starting to kick in, that's how out-of-it she looks. "Where are we going?"

"Straight thataway," she says, pointing, her voice sounding distant. "There's a landing. We can park and run for a main road."

Sure enough, in a few minutes we pass under a curtain of low-hanging Spanish moss and emerge into a clearing, the moon bright enough overhead to see the muddy shore rising to a narrow gravel road.

I'm steering the boat up to the landing when I hear an awful groan from behind me. I turn to see Kaylee crouched down, flesh writhing under her oversized clothes. She glances up at me, her face slick with sweat and trembling. She *did* take something, I think, some kind of overdose.

But what happens next is an impossible horror. Kaylee's form mutates, growing bulky and misshapen, glistening black claws and blood-dark fur erupting from her pale freckled skin. Her face elongates, the flesh tearing away as a hairy snout sprouts where her nose and mouth used to be. I freeze in disbelieving terror as the creature that was Kaylee raises its thick wet muzzle and snarls.

The snarl becomes a rumbling growl, the creature rolling its massive tongue until it forms, finally, a word.

"Curse."

Of course. Kaylee's disease. The full moon. Midnight. It all makes sense. Of course, it also makes *no* sense, because werewolves aren't fucking real – yet I'd be a fool to cling to that, wouldn't I, seeing as I'm sitting in a boat next to one.

And the next stupid-ass thought I have is, *but I don't have my cursebreaking kit.* Because that briefcase full of thrift store trinkets and potions made of Goldschläger and food dye would do a lot of good.

The only sane thing to do is launch myself out of the boat and tear off running. And I'm fixing to do just that, but as soon as my feet hit the mud, Kaylee howls, a pitiful wail that stops me cold. I look back and see her still sitting in the boat, head down, looking for all the world like a scolded puppy.

"Aw hell," I say softly. "You don't want to eat me, do you? You just want help."

"Hands up," a voice booms. The werewolf whines. I look up to the road and there's Kaylee's daddy, shotgun trained on me.

"Sir," I begin, trying to sound authoritative – belied by my raised hands, which are shaking so hard it looks like I'm doing spirit fingers. "I reckon we got off on the wrong foot. I'm Lavinia Dupree, South Alabama's top cursebreaker, and—"

"Don't move," he shouts, seeing that I'm trying to back up. "Step away from the boat."

While I'm parsing how I can step away from the boat without moving, another voice rings out, this one deep and commanding, momentarily swallowing the sounds of the swamp.

"I thought I told you to leave my girl alone, John Randall."

A figure steps into the clearing from between two cypress trees, and I shouldn't be surprised at this point to see it's the Wolf Woman of Mobile. Seven, maybe eight feet tall. She looks just like the stories, her top half a beautiful – though oversized – woman, her bottom half a giant-ass wolf standing upright.

I'd like to say that when I saw her, I thought of the moon. The moonlight reflecting on her thick auburn hair and gleaming along the surface of her impenetrable dark eyes, her bare white breasts like two full moons themselves, her entire unearthly presence reminiscent of some luminous lunar goddess.

But I'd be lying, because what I actually thought in the moment was, *monster, monster, oh my God, another monster.*

"She ain't no girl," John Randall says, his voice trembling. "She's an abomination. Just like you." He'd been swinging his shotgun back and forth between our boat and the Wolf Woman, before wisely keeping it pointed at the obvious threat. If she's bothered at all by a gun aimed at her chest from ten feet away, she don't show it.

The Wolf Woman lopes forward on her enormous furry legs, stopping just shy of the gun's muzzle. Standing across from Kaylee's human-sized dad, her paranormal nature's even more obvious.

"I'll shoot you too, Renee, I swear to God."

Renee? I let out a short, sharp peal of panicked laughter. It's loud enough the Wolf Woman – fucking Renee, I guess – turns her head slightly and raises an eyebrow at me.

BAM.

The gunshot blast reverberates across the swamp, disorienting me so bad that for a second I think he shot the Wolf Woman point blank in the chest.

But he didn't.

He shot Kaylee.

The werewolf crumples to the bottom of the boat, dark blood staining the rusted metal.

Renee bellows, and before John can turn the gun back on her, she hurls him to the ground. John screams. I don't see what happens next – I've rushed over to check on Kaylee – but I hear enough of it to replay in my nightmares for a long time.

Once the screaming stops, Renee rushes to the boat, brushing me aside to scoop Kaylee into her arms and carry her to the gravel road. I trudge through the mud behind them, avoiding looking at what's left of John Randall.

"Where's she hit?" It's hard to see through the dark fur and blood, but I eventually make out that the bullet barely grazed the top of Kaylee's shoulder. Not so bad, then.

My relief is short lived.

"Silver bullet," Renee says, talking to me but looking down at her daughter as Kaylee thrashes and whimpers. "Like a venomous snakebite, in this form. If we can force her back into human form..." She looks at me pleadingly. "Do you know how?"

I feel, suddenly, very small, and not just because I'm kneeling next to an eight foot tall monster.

"Uh, wolfsbane?" I suggest. There might actually be some real dried wolfsbane in my cursebreaking kit, but one look at Kaylee tells me she won't make it long enough to get back to the house. "I don't know. There's one tradition says you just gotta know their true, full name and call it three times." It sounds stupid even as I say it, but there's a flicker of hope in Renee's eyes.

The wolf woman clasps Kaylee's spasming paws in her hands. "Kaylee May Randall," she says quietly. "Kaylee May Randall. Kaylee May Randall."

I don't expect it to work, but my heart sinks anyway as the werewolf twitches weakly in the mud, nothing changed except maybe there's more blood coming out of her mouth now. Thicker blood, congealed-like.

"Dylan," says the werewolf, in a strained, raspy voice, coughing up a fat slug of blood.

"What?" I say, scooting close to hear better.

"Dylan Jacob."

I don't get it, not at first. But Renee does.

"Dylan Jacob Randall," she whispers. The werewolf nods. "Dylan Jacob Randall," Renee repeats, more confident this time. "Dylan Jacob Randall."

It don't happen like a Disney movie, with upswelling music and glittery swirls to signify there's magic going down. But it don't happen like some body-horror B-movie either, the way the first transformation did. It just *happens*. One second a dying werewolf, the next a bloodied but breathing teenage girl.

Except I guess he's not a girl, is he?

Dylan's skin is already going from pallid gray back to its usual pinkish hue. The blood is slick on his shoulder, but the wound's clearly superficial.

"You're alive," Renee sobs, cradling Dylan and stroking his long red hair. "My baby."

I feel dizzy, the adrenaline draining from my body as I slump into the mud. No one's shooting at me or dying at my feet anymore. Just a tender moment between a transgender teenage werewolf and his cryptid mama Renee. All in a night's work for Alabama's top cursebreaker.

"Dylan?" I say. The werewolf and his mama look at me.

"Tell me you didn't pick your middle name from goddamn *Twilight*." Then I black out.

Dylan's doing all right, given the circumstances. He'd hoped to stay with Renee, but since she's a full-time swamp monster, it wasn't exactly practical. So he's living with me for now.

It's been a few weeks, and I'm still trying to piece together what really happened. I know what I *saw*, but what I saw was batshit insane. I even quizzed my brother about it the last time he called. He said it ain't too uncommon to hallucinate during high-stress situations, which I imagine includes being shot at by a nutjob who keeps his kid chained to a bed.

"Like you hear someone call your name, and no one's there," Jimmy elaborates.

"Or," I say, "Hypothetically, you watch a local cryptid kill her ex, then save their werewolf kid with magic."

There's a long pause.

"Or you hear someone call your name," I say. "That sorta thing."

Most nights I cook dinner while Dylan monologues about football scores and TikTok videos. I follow his lead and don't discuss what happened in the swamp. I did bring it up once, when he mentioned wanting to start hormones for his gender transition. I said something like, *bet you wish you could've kept some of that fur from your wolf form.* He just stared at me with those melancholy green eyes til I sighed and resumed cataloguing my crystals, wondering once again whether the whole werewolf thing was just a weird nightmare.

But there's a full moon tonight, so I guess we'll see what happens.

The Worms Turn
FRANK ORETO

"He was completely naked. I know, he has a privacy fence, and it is his property. Still, it was a bit of a shock." After the divorce, Nell had sworn she'd never talk to Ted again. *But voicemail doesn't quite count, does it?* Except of course it did. Ted would listen eventually. Maybe play it for his new girlfriend, Kelli or Kerry, whatever she was called.

"Get a load of this. The ex has finally gone around the bend."

But no one could blame me, Nell thought. *You had to call someone when your neighbor turns out to be a monster. And he seemed so nice.*

Mr Harrah had stood there, naked as the day he was born. Nell just knew he would glance up at the bathroom window and catch her staring. The thought made her breath catch in her chest, but she couldn't look away. Instead of turning his head, Mr Harrah opened his mouth wide and vomited out a shower of worms.

The worms, thousands of them, not only came out of Mr Harrah, they were Mr Harrah. His flesh parted in long thin tendrils, crawling over each other. Nell stood there a good five minutes watching what had been her solid-looking neighbor dissolve into a writhing mass. The worms roiled in a low heap under the moonlight and then disappeared into the dark soil.

"He has the most beautiful plants in his yard," Nell said into the phone. "That's why I was looking down over the fence. You know worms are quite good for– " *You're babbling, Nell,* she told herself. The voicemail cut off with a sharp little chirp. Nell hit redial and waited through three rings and Ted saying, "We can't come to the phone right now." Was that a woman giggling in the background? When the tone sounded, Nell found she had nothing left to say.

Some things she hadn't mentioned. Like how she had only just stepped from the shower when she first saw Mr Harrah. And how their shared nudity had made her stomach feel full of warm honey, that is, until he'd changed. No, some details you did not share with your ex-husband.

"But why call Ted at all?" She asked herself. *Habit?* After fifteen years of marriage, it would make sense, but she suspected something darker. Ted was a bully and a tyrant. It had been his decision she shouldn't get a job, and that children for a woman as fragile as Nell were out of the question. But she'd gone along with it. Grown to depend on him making decisions, so she didn't have to.

When Ted left, Nell was terrified, believing herself to be the hothouse flower he'd wanted. But instead of withering, she'd flourished. Finding work, first as office manager at a local architecture firm, then parlaying her – 'useless' according to Ted – English degree into a more lucrative position ghostwriting the firm's business proposals. She had friends now, and colleagues who valued her opinion. "You panicked, that's all. So, you ran back to the one person who would be happy to tell you what to do." For a moment a wave of self-disgust rivaled Nell's fear. She shook her head. Nothing could make her go back to living that way. Not even a monster next door.

Nell sat in her kitchen. A practical place, neat and orderly. A good place to think. What next, the police? *Hello, I need to report that my neighbor is what…a were-worm? He has a lovely garden, but the whole worm thing scares the shit out of me. Could you pop over and talk to him?* They'd have her committed.

Nell's skin prickled into gooseflesh. What if Mr Harrah had seen her? What if he came over to shut her up? She ran to the front door and turned the deadbolt, for all the good it would do. In her imagination, a sea of worms already crashed against the house in pink fleshy waves. Long sinuous shapes pushed themselves through hidden gaps in the construction. *Do worms have teeth?*

"He never looked up," Nell said aloud. "He was too busy… coming apart."

The doorbell rang.

Nell's hand shot to her mouth, stifling a scream.

There was a pause then the sound of knuckles rapping wood.

"Ms Phillips. It's George Harrah from next door." The knuckles rapped again.

Nell counted to five, drawing a deep silent breath with each number.

"Ms Phillips, I can see your shadow on the curtain."

Shit. "It's late, Mr Harrah, what can I do for you?"

"I wanted to apologize. Um, for the little show I put on earlier? I didn't think anyone could see into my yard. The night seemed so pleasant. I don't know what came over me. I'm really not in the habit of going outside stark naked."

"I didn't see anything," said Nell, hoping Harrah couldn't hear the panic in her voice. "I don't know what you're talking about."

"Oh. I could have sworn I saw you looking down at me from that little side window."

"No. Now I really must get to bed. Good night, Mr Harrah." Nell listened for departing footsteps, but none came.

"I think you did see me, Ms Phillips. How long were you watching?" His voice sounded more tired than threatening. But maybe that's how monsters sound right before they attack. This was all unfamiliar territory.

"Shut up, can't you just shut up and go?" This time no one could have missed the broken sob she spoke around.

"Aw hell," said Harrah. "That long. We need to talk."

"I called the police."

There was a long pause. "No. I don't think you did. They would have been here by now. I think you're still in the 'Am I nuts?' phase. Or worried anyone you call will think you are. Why don't you come out on the porch? It's weird talking through the door like this."

"Talking through a door is weird?" A bark of involuntary laughter escaped Nell's throat. "I don't think it even makes the scale tonight." She would call the police if he didn't leave soon. They could take her to whatever mental hospital was closest. Maybe she'd be safe there.

"I see your point. Listen, please. I'm not a monster. I'm just different. I'm no danger to you."

His words and the sheer stress of the situation snapped Nell's careening feelings into focused anger. "Bullshit," she said.

"What?"

Nell gritted her teeth. She attached the chain, pushed the door open a few inches and glared out at George Harrah. "I said bullshit."

He wore clothes now at least. The tan trousers and sweater vest made him seem more like an English professor than something from a horror story, but Nell knew better. "I saw what you are, or what you become. But even if you were just some guy from down the street, you're standing on my porch refusing to leave. Telling me you're not going to hurt me. I've seen this shit on the news. I know how it ends."

Then George Harrah did something unexpected. He blushed from the top of his bald head to the collar of his blue, button-down shirt. "I'm…I'm." His mouth hung open for a moment. "I'm so sorry. You're right, of course. I'm going back to my house." He paused in mid-turn, raising his hands open-palmed toward Nell. "I like it here, Ms Phillips. I like my house, the neighborhood. I don't want to leave." There were tears in the tall man's eyes.

"Go home, Mr Harrah."

Harrah nodded. "Goodnight, Ms Phillips."

Nell watched him walk back to his house and go inside. Then she stuffed towels under all the doors on the first floor. After those hardly adequate protections, she made herself tea, sat in the kitchen, and thought. It was a very long night.

Nell's head snapped up, springing from sleep to panicked alertness. She yanked her stiff legs from the kitchen tiles, seeing a floor seething with worms until she'd blinked the dream visions from her eyes. "I'm alive," she said. "That's something at least." Her laptop lay open on the counter. A magnified image of *a Lumbricus Terrestris* filled the screen. She shuddered. It turned out earthworms didn't have teeth after all. Somehow the fact didn't make her feel any better.

She waited until 10:00. It was a Saturday and people were out now. Mrs Henderson mowing her front lawn, kids riding by on their bikes. Nell walked over to Mr Harrah's house and knocked on the door. She wore long sleeves despite the summer heat, and her twill trousers were tucked into knee-high boots. The clothes made her feel safer somehow.

Harrah answered her knock so fast she suspected he'd been waiting for her.

"Ms Phillips," he said. "Thank you."

"For what?"

"I'm just glad it's you. Not the police or some reporter."

"It's early yet," Nell said. "Torches and pitchforks look better at night."

"I'm hoping that's a joke."

"Only a little. I'm in a tough position here, Mr Harrah."

Harrah nodded. "Do you want some tea?"

"No, just answers. And we talk out here on the porch."

"Of course."

They sat at the glass-topped patio table and stared at each other.

"What do you want to know?" he asked.

"What are you?"

"I grew up on a farm in Iowa."

"That's not what I asked."

"No," said Harrah. "But if you want to know about me, I need you to hear how we're alike, not just the worm stuff."

"Fine."

"I'm thirty-nine years old. We probably grew up playing the same games, eating frosted flakes for breakfast."

"And watching Captain Kangaroo, I get it. You're an all-American boy. But what else are you? Are there more of you?"

"I don't have any brothers or sisters. Reproduction is difficult for people like me. I was an accident. It was only my father and me growing up."

"Are you going to kill me?"

"Jesus. I may not be human, but I'm not a werewolf. No claws or fangs. It's just, on a pretty regular basis, I need to transform into my other state."

"Worms"

"Yes, sort of. Certainly *like* worms, but I don't lose myself. I'm still me when I change. There's just a lot of...me."

"You don't talk about this much, do you?"

"Of course not. And no one really explained it to me either. My father was more a 'do as I do' sort of guy. He'd rather I'd never left the farm. Bottom line is that I'm a thinking, feeling person just like you. I run a lawn and garden service. I pay taxes. Watch the Super Bowl every year. I'm not a monster. I'm just different. And I don't want to be some government lab experiment. Or be burned as a witch. And if you spread around what you saw, that's going to happen. So, tell me now, so I can pack my very human Ford pick-up and start over somewhere else."

Nell stared at him for a long moment. She actually felt a little sorry for him. *How did I become the bad guy here?*

"Well?"

"You own a lawn service? Isn't that sort of cheating?" Nell chuckled. It was all too ridiculous.

Harrah sat frozen for a moment, then a reluctant grin spread across his face. "Well, I like to think I'm working to my strengths."

Nell laughed in earnest. When she'd finished and wiped her eyes, she still hadn't made up her mind about George Harrah. But for the life of her, she couldn't feel afraid of the man. "This might be horribly naïve on my part, but I'm not ready to drive you out of your home." Nell stood and moved to the steps. "And I have more questions."

"Of course," said Harrah.

Halfway to her yard, Nell remembered the frantic phone call to Ted the night before. "Uh-oh." She called again that night. Got his voice mail. "Ted, it's Nell. I wanted to apologize for my call last night. Turns out it was only a nightmare." As she spoke, Nell looked out the window at the wooden fence surrounding Harrah's backyard. Wondering if he was there and if he was himself. "I feel so silly. Sorry to have bothered you. Say hi to Kelli." She cut the connection. "Say hi to Kelli?" she repeated and shook her head. "What the hell is wrong with me?"

On Sunday afternoon there was a knock on the door. Nell thought it might be her neighbor until a key turned in the lock. She snatched open the door to reveal her ex-husband, Ted, in the doorway. "You aren't supposed to have a key," she said.

"Well, hello to you too. I kept a copy in case of emergencies. Like when my wife calls in the middle of the night about monsters."

Ted's blonde hair swept straight back now instead of parting at the side. Blue jeans replaced the business casual khakis he'd always favored. He looked fit and tan. Kelli must be the outdoorsy type.

"I want that key," Nell said.

"Fine. And I want an explanation. And maybe a thank you for driving out here to make sure you're okay." He slid the house key along the ring as he spoke until it came off in his hand.

"I called you back. It was only a nightmare."

"So, my wife is hallucinating naked neighbors who turn into worms, oh no, nothing to worry about there."

"That's the second time you called me your wife. It's ex-wife, Ted. Or did the whole divorce thing slip your mind? How does Kelli feel about you checking up on me?"

"It's Kerri. And she can think whatever she damn well pleases. A man has responsibilities."

There was anger in Ted's voice and not toward her. Trouble in paradise maybe, not that Nell cared. She almost told him where he could stick his responsibilities. But instead began to feel guilty. Ted had that effect on her. No matter how much of an asshole he acted like, he believed he was being noble. In a twisted, selfish way he cared.

"Let's not fight." Nell walked out and sat on the porch steps. Patting a spot beside her. Ted joined her. "I'm really all right," she said.

"Not a monster then?"

Nell sighed. "George is a very nice man."

"George, is it? Are you dating?"

Nell's shoulders slumped. She bit her lip and counted to five before answering. "You don't get to ask me that, Ted. Thanks for coming out, but you should go now."

He stood. "Fine. I think about you, Nell. You know that? We had some good times."

"Leave the key. Ted."

Ted opened his hand, and the house key fell on the step.

Over the next few weeks, Nell had more conversations with George Harrah. On his porch or sometimes her own. At first, they were almost interrogations.

"What does changing feel like?"

"It hurts actually, quite a bit in fact. But after, when I'm no longer singular, it feels...amazingly freeing."

As weeks turned into months, the conversations changed. They talked less about George's condition and more about everyday life. How Nell's office politics were going. The odd customers George dealt with in his lawn business. And about Ted.

Nell told George about her calls after she'd witnessed his transformation. And about Ted's visit. "He seemed more jealous than concerned about my well-being. I think dreaming of a man turning into worms struck him as a bit Freudian." Texts came after. Ted 'checking in.' Asking about the mortgage or house repairs. Letting her know he still thought about her while at the same time telling her what to do. A bully's idea of sweet-talk. "He even called once, drunk I think, complaining about his girlfriend. I hung up on him."

On a Thursday night, while drinking tea on Nell's porch swing, George brought up his own social life. "I dated quite a bit when I was younger. Regular women. Like you. Well, you know, not able to change. I grew quite attached a few times, but I always broke things off. Didn't seem fair, them not knowing and all." He said it all in a rush, staring at the floor.

"Oh," said Nell. Surprised to find herself blushing.

Their first date was at a local Italian restaurant. They drank wine and laughed a lot. George ordered the risotto, much to Nell's relief. The idea of him sucking pasta into his mouth would have been too much like his transformation in reverse. *I'm on a date with a monster*, she thought. *And I'm having a wonderful time.* She kissed him in the driveway before they parted. A small kiss, quick and almost dainty. But the memory of it warmed her for hours. It was well past midnight when the knock on the door came.

She'd been reading on the couch. Too pleased to go to bed despite the lateness of the hour. *Don't ruin it, George*, she thought. *I'm taking this slow.* But she smiled as she approached the door and her stomach filled with a warm excitement.

Ted stood on the porch. Dark half-moons hung beneath his eyes, and his tan seemed sallow under the porch light's yellow glare. In his skinny jeans, Nell's ex-husband looked like the poster child for mid-life crisis. "I've done it. I've cast her off, Nell."

"Are you drunk?" it was a rhetorical question. Bourbon soaked his words.

"You're not listening to me. It's over. I'm coming home."

"Kelli's thrown you out?"

"Kerri," Ted said. "And we've parted ways. Differences of opinion."

"You mean she had one?"

Ted flinched as if Nell's words were a blow. "I'm not here to talk about Kerri," he said, raising his voice. "I realized the truth that night you called. You need someone to take care of you. And to be honest, I need someone to take care of." He made the words sound like an accusation and a plea at the same time.

"I don't want to be taken care of, Ted. The call was a mistake." Without thinking, she shot a quick, worried glance at George's house. "And I rang back. I told you it was only a nightmare. George is…harmless."

"George. You are seeing him, aren't you? It's understandable, of course. You're fragile, Nell. You need someone with a firm hand in your life." Ted nodded, and there was something distant in his voice, as if he spoke not to Nell, but himself. "What he doesn't understand is it's me you need. Not some nudist."

"You leave right now, Ted, or I swear you'll spend the night in jail."

Ted ignored her. "You stay here. I'm going to have a little talk with your George. He needs to understand the lay of the land." Ted walked across the yard toward George's porch.

"Leave him alone. You're not in your right mind!" Nell ran toward the back of George's house. She tried the gate entrance, but it was locked. If George was asleep in bed, fine. The police could handle Ted. But what if he was changing? She yelled and slammed her open palm against the wood. "George! My ex-husband is here! He's acting crazy!" The sound of running feet came from the front yard. Ted slammed his shoulder into the gate right beside her. Nell screamed in surprise.

She grabbed Ted's arm, and he gave her a shove that sent her reeling. He slammed into the entrance again, grunting with the impact.

"Stop it," Nell yelled.

On the third try, wood splintered, and the gate burst inward.

Inside, George Harrah knelt naked in the grass. Half his head and most of his right arm had already changed. Worms slithered down his torso to the ground.

"Jesus Christ," Ted said. He turned to Nell, a condescending smile stretching across his face. "He's done something to you, Nell. Bewitched you somehow, but I'll sort it out." Cordwood lay stacked against the fence's interior. A hatchet jutted up from a thick log. Ted snatched it up and marched toward George. Nell scrambled to her feet and ran after him.

With no hesitation, Ted crossed the yard and swung the hatchet at George's rapidly changing head. Worms showered onto the grass.

"Leave him alone," Nell shouted.

"It's all right, Nell. I'm here now," Ted reared back for another blow.

George lifted his one solid arm. The hatchet bit deep into the still human flesh, blood poured down.

He'd be screaming, she thought, *if his head were still there, he'd be screaming.*

Worms swarmed over Ted's shoes and up his pants leg, but

he took no notice. He swung the hatchet again. George's arm cartwheeled through the air, a trail of blood and worms streaming out behind it.

The sight of George's sheared off arm broke Nell's paralysis. She stepped to the woodpile and picked up a log as thick as her forearm. Crossing to Ted, Nell swung the log like a baseball bat, striking him in the ribs with a thunk.

Ted grunted, but his smile didn't falter. "You need me, Nell. Everything's going to be fine now."

Nell braced herself and swung again. This time with all the rage of fifteen years of bad marriage behind the blow. The log slammed into the side of Ted's head, leaving a two-inch dent behind. Blood filled the dent, turning Ted's blonde hair a muddy red.

Ted froze; dropped the hatchet, then fell to his knees. Worms crawled up his sides.

"Juss wanted take care of you," he said. The words came out soft and dripping blood. Then wriggling shapes filled Ted's mouth, and he collapsed to the ground, disappearing under the writhing mass of George's worms A few minutes later, both Ted and the worms were gone, leaving only dark, turned earth.

Well, not all gone, Nell thought. A few yards away, where George's arm had landed, a smaller pile of worms still crawled on the surface. *Why didn't they go with the rest?* The worms' movements slowed, and they began to knit back together. What they formed was not an arm.

"Oh my God," said Nell.

The tiny shape took a hitching breath and began to cry. The baby that had been George's arm looked only a few weeks old. Nell remembered George's words on the day she'd first confronted him. *Reproduction is hard on my kind. I was an accident.*

When George emerged from the earth again, Nell sat on the deck, holding the tiny red-haired newborn. George walked past the two of them to the clothes he'd left folded neatly on an Adirondack chair and dressed. He had two arms again, but Nell thought he stood a few inches shorter.

"There are things you didn't tell me."

George didn't speak.

"It's a girl," Nell said and shifted the child on to her shoulder. "For a while, things were sort of undecided down there. Then she changed." She stared down into the baby's huge blue eyes and couldn't help but smile a little. "The red hair is new too."

George knelt in front of the chair and patted the child on the leg. "We imprint on the first person we see. Sex, the hair, the eyes, she's going to look like you. Not exactly, but close. I'm glad. Can you watch her a little while longer? I need to pack."

"What?"

"I killed your husband, Nell."

"Ted was deranged and attacked you with a hatchet. Besides, I killed him." Nell again saw the deep bloody dent in her husband's temple. "I killed him." She shook her head in disbelief. "You just disposed of the body. What – where exactly did you? Did you bury him?"

"I didn't eat him if that's what you're thinking. He's someplace far away and very deep. I can move fast when I need to. No one's going to find him. But the police don't always need a body." His hand went from the child to Nell's hand. "I can't stay, Nell. There's bound to be inquiries. We, the baby and I, can disappear. You'll be safe."

"Don't make decisions for me," Nell said. "I hate when people do that." She didn't feel guilty. Maybe that would come, along with grief for a man she'd once loved, but right now she only felt determined. "You grew your arm back. How?"

"It's only a matter of shifting things about."

"Could you look like someone else if you shifted enough? Ted for example. Even the hair?"

George considered it. "I probably couldn't fool his wife, but in general, yes."

Later that night, Ted was caught on tape buying coffee at a gas station near his home. Authorities discovered his sporty hybrid a week later, parked on the shore of Lake Erie. Ted's clothes lay folded on a large stone at the water's edge.

"His girlfriend left him," a kindly police officer told Nell. "His coworkers said he'd been acting erratically ever since. We followed his footsteps to the water's edge. There was no note. Sometimes they just don't leave notes."

A year later, George pulled Nell's Honda on to Highway 86 west. "You sure about this?" he asked." He'd seemed leery of the trip when Nell suggested it, but she thought he'd also been pleased.

Nell looked back at Lilly, asleep in her car seat. "Yes. I'm sure. Your dad should meet his granddaughter. And me for that matter. Maybe I can even get him to tell me the story of how you were born?"

"I told you he doesn't like to talk about it. It's considered impolite to ask about our accidents of birth."

Nell groaned.

"Okay fine. But only so you don't spend the whole trip interrogating Dad. I am the son of a loving if slightly clumsy father and the hay baler he bumped into. That's the whole story. Happy?"

Nell leaned over and kissed George on the neck. "I am," she said. "I really am. Although…"

"What?"

"Wouldn't it be nice if Lilly had a little brother?" Nell squeezed George's arm. "Does your dad still own that hay baler?"

The Spouses' Club
AN INTERVIEW BY JEANNE MORAN

In this issue of *Cryptids Quarterly*, we share highlights of an interview with two remarkable people: Aspen Hill, a former trail guide turned entrepreneur, who is married to Sasquatch; and Tom Floss, owner of a landscaping business, who has developed an ingenious product based on the work of his celebrity wife, Celestial Moonglitter, better known as The Tooth Fairy.

Our own Jeanne Moran caught up with them after the monthly meeting of The Spouses' Club at Wonderland Restaurant in New York City.

Jeanne Moran: Thank you both for agreeing to speak with me. First, tell me a little about The Spouses' Club. Your members are all human, is that right?
TOM FLOSS: Yes, we're human spouses of magical creatures and legendary cryptids. The Club's been around for 30-odd years. Currently, I'm Vice-President and Lena of Loch Ness, Nessie's wife, is President. I know you hoped to speak with her too, but the tide was going out and her hubby was waiting to take her home. It's a long trip for them.

The Spouses' Club doesn't have a stated mission or a formal charter. But I can tell you – we need this connection with one another.

Moran: So you meet here every month to talk?
TOM: [*nods*] And clear our heads. Our marriages are not like other marriages. First of all,, [*lifts one finger*] we're married to celebrities, so there's the whole fame thing going on. And second, [*lifts another finger*] we're not married to a *person*. Having a non-human spouse presents all sorts of, umm...
ASPEN HILL: The challenges are quite unique.

Moran: We'll get to the challenges in a minute. Let's start with you, Aspen. How did you meet Sasquatch?
ASPEN: We met when I worked as a trail guide up in Oregon. I had a young couple with me, first-time hikers, and a heavy thunderstorm rolled in. The three of us took shelter in a shallow cave. It smelled dank and musky and the couple didn't want to go in, but what with the rain and lightning, I told them we didn't have much choice.

Inside the cave, the young woman pointed to a fur-covered divot in the earth floor where something large obviously slept. Her boyfriend screamed "Bears!", and they both ran out of the cave and down the trail in the pouring rain. [*scoffs*] Rookies. I had to notify the ranger when I got back in cell range.

I stayed put until the storm broke, so I was alone in the cave when Sasquatch walked in.

Moran: Oh, wow. How about you, Tom?
TOM: I met Celestial the day an employee buzzed my office about a customer looking for a very unusual plant – a tree that grew money. Actual money! I figured it was some kind of joke, so I laughed and buzzed off, then turned back to my work. And just like that, [*snaps his fingers*] this tiny woman dressed in a million shimmering shades of blue stood in front of my desk. She said, "You'll help me, won't you, Tom?" I babbled something like, "Who are you? How did you get in here?" but I couldn't take my eyes off her.

Moran: Was it love at first sight?
TOM: I wouldn't say love, but I was enchanted. And curious. Seems she'd been watching me for some time. She was convinced I'd come up with some way to support her line of work, so she kept popping in when I least expected it. [*shakes his head and smiles*] Soon I found myself hoping she'd pop in. Wasn't long before she was all I could think about. Seriously – who wouldn't want a beautiful, generous, magical woman in their life?
ASPEN: [*smiling at Tom*] My first reaction was nothing like yours. I

was terrified. Here was this huge, hairy creature. Plus, he smelled really bad. He seemed to understand that I was scared, because he stood there on the threshold of his cave, staring at me for like a full minute. Then he grunted and offered me a handful of nuts and berries. He started a small fire and gestured to a log. Before I sat, I moved the log near the cave opening for two reasons. One, I wanted to keep an escape route open, and two, the stench! Wet dog, times one thousand.

So I sat on that log with a hand over my nose and did what I always do – I talked. As I did, I relaxed. Inside an hour, Sasquatch knew everything about me and I started asking him questions. He doesn't use words, but I could interpret his gestures and grunts just fine. I learned that he lived alone way up in the woods so he wouldn't scare people. That hermit's life was for the sake of others. [*shakes her head and smiles*] I began to see him for the sweet, gentle guy he is.

Once the weather cleared, he walked me back to the hiking trail and showed me which way the young couple had gone. Such a gentleman. I asked if I could see him again or if that was against some Bigfoot Code of Conduct. He laughed this big rumbly laugh, gestured toward his cave, and nodded.

I went back the next day with shampoo, detangler, and a half-dozen combs. The day after that I went back with essential oils to freshen up the cave. The rest is history.

Moran: What did your family and friends say?
ASPEN: There was no way to break it to them gently. I mean, how do you tell them you're in love with this huge and hairy cryptid who lives in a cave and grunts a lot? But after a few minutes with Sasquatch, folks realize he's super shy and harmless as a butterfly. [*laughs*] A big, furry, stinky butterfly.
TOM: A couple of my buddies said that since Celestial's work would leave me alone every night, I could still join them at the pub after work. She must have overheard.

Moran: Why do you say that?

TOM: Because when I brought it up a few days later, they didn't remember the conversation. Not at all. I suspect fairy dust.

Moran: It sounds like those close to you have accepted your unusual relationship.

ASPEN: Well, sort of. Sasquatch is a loner so large gatherings are awkward. Plus, not everyone can hold up both ends of the conversation like I can. [*laughs*] I will say this though – everyone agrees it's easier to have him around now that his fur's been tamed and he smells better.

TOM: Celestial's work demands that she pop in and out often. She tries not to make it obvious, but people are put off when she disappears in the middle of dinner and reappears a minute later. Especially if she's still tucking a tooth into the sack at her belt.

Moran: That brings us to challenges. Both of you have taken your spouse's unique challenges and turned them into a business. Tell me about that.

TOM: Celestial's in an expensive line of work. Handing out quarters and dollars doesn't sound like much, but it really adds up. When we met, she was in desperate need of a steady funding stream. Then there was the problem of all those teeth. She had an entire shed filled with jars and jars of them. What do you do with them all?

We tried to solve both problems at once. Using my experience with trees and her magic, we worked on developing a variety of tree that would grow actual money. I'd show her a promising sapling. She'd sprinkle it with fairy dust and chant a few spells then bury those tiny teeth around it. Two years later with no money tree, we were out of ideas.

That's when it hit me. What if we took those teeth and turned them into a saleable product?

Moran: That sounds rather gruesome.

TOM: Actually, it's not gruesome at all. Celestial spreads out her night's collection on a large tray and sprinkles it with fairy dust. In moments, what's left is sparkling white enamel, perfect as the finish to outdoor statuary and birdbaths. The result is that TomCel Industries has become known worldwide for garden statuary with a distinctive pearly white finish.

Sales of TomCel products fund Celestial's work. So in a way, the teeth she collects are recycled and support the next generation of gap-toothed kids. Her work supports TomCel, and TomCel supports her.

Moran: What about you, Aspen? I understand you're an entrepreneur, too.

ASPEN: [*nods*] As I said before, when I met Sasquatch, his fur was a mess. All matted, tangled, and full of burrs and twigs. I sent him to a nearby stream with about $100 worth of shampoo and told him not to come back until he'd washed every bit of his furry self. He sat in the sun while his fur dried, and I stood behind him spritzing bottle after bottle of detangler and combing out debris. Took hours. When it was done, he looked awesome. Even stood taller and bellowed this happy, musical note, so I knew he felt better, too.

Two days later, we were back to square one. Burrs, tangles, clumps of matted fur, the whole bit. We repeated the shampoo-detangler process, but we both knew we needed a long-term solution. We couldn't snuggle, not with all those pickers and that filthy fur.

A few years of research and development led to the creation of the Silken Yeti line of haircare products. The entire line – shampoo, detangler, conditioner, anti-frizz balm, smoothing gel, and finishing oil – is totally natural, vegan, and infused with the freshness of lavender and mint.

Moran: Are the products just for use with thick or problem hair?

ASPEN: Since Sasquatch was my test subject, they were developed for problem hair, yes. But customers with all hair types tell us how much they love the products. Since Sasquatch started using Silken

Yeti, his fur has grown so soft and manageable that burrs slide out without tangling. And my own hair, [*shakes her shoulder-length auburn tresses into the light to show off their shine*] well, it's never been better.

Moran: Thank you for these fascinating insights. But I'm sure our readers are curious about the, umm, more intimate aspects of your unusual relationships. Please be discreet, but in just a couple words, can you sum up your most private moments as a couple?

TOM: [*grinning*] She's magical.

ASPEN: [*laughing*] He's big.

In the Woods, a Soft and Tender Thing
RACHEL JOHNSON

Some said the creature was big, bigger than you would think a creature of its proportions could possibly be. The blurry photographs all lacked any fixed point that could be used for scale, so it was impossible to tell. Its limbs, all gangly and sinewy, were too long for its body, too long for *any* body. There were no videos of the creature, but with limbs like those there was no possible locomotion other than lumbering, ungainly and awkward, elbows and knees splayed out at all angles.

The few photographs that existed were grainy and washed out, and the firsthand accounts were inconsistent at best. According to those who had seen it, the creature either had a long snout, or no snout at all. It was pale, or completely translucent, or had dark, mottled, purplish skin, or, according to one alleged encounter, no skin at all, which was a horrifying thought. Two individuals who claimed to encounter it said it had scales, but the others staunchly rejected this claim. One said it had feathers. This led to rumors that it had wings, which led to more rumors that it was Mothman, which was patently absurd, but there was no arguing with some people. All we knew about it was that we knew virtually nothing, which was a start, at least.

When I rolled over, Emet's side of the bed was empty. I could hear them in the kitchen, the smell of freshly-ground coffee beans making its way tantalizingly into the bedroom. I blinked groggily at the clock on the wall, then squinted, double-checking. With a groan and a sigh I swung my legs out of bed, the rest of me following the momentum of the movement reluctantly but inevitably. Against my sincerest wishes I was standing, though my legs buckled dramatically. I leaned heavily against the wall for a few moments while the room spun, and once it had stabilized somewhat in its wild dance, I stumbled into the kitchen.

"Good morning, my love," Em beamed. They looked radiant, which was frankly uncalled for this early in what could only generously be called morning.

"It's the middle of the night, why are you so chipper, and why are you making coffee?" I snarled, more an accusation than a series of questions. They grinned and handed me a thermos. I blinked at it, feeling wholly unprepared for this entire interaction.

"There was an encounter. Yesterday. Half a mile from here, in Westborough Park. The photo just went online."

This got through to my sleep-addled brain. I flopped down on the couch and opened my laptop, navigating immediately to the forum. It was the top post.

The photograph was…well, honestly, it was so clear that it couldn't possibly be real. Except that it had a green checkmark above it and a small icon of a camera, meaning that the forum moderators had verified that they believed it to be unedited. They were good at this sort of thing. There was a team of four or five mods that had debunked hundreds of truly convincing fakes, and it was rare to see the green checkmark.

The creature was fully in frame and standing still, half-facing the camera, half-in-profile like those cartoon images of Bigfoot mid-step. Its limbs were even more unlikely than the grainy unverified photographs had suggested. Its arms hung down so low its fingers brushed the forest floor, and those fingers were spindly, elongated, impossibly thin. There was no muscle tone, no fat, and as far as I could tell no skin pigmentation of any sort. I could see its bones through skin so pale as to be nearly translucent, almost blue where the veins were visible just under the surface of the skin.

If this were one of my friends and it had come round to my house in high school, my parents wouldn't have let it leave until it had consumed a small mountain of brisket. If it had visited Em, their father would have made it adafina, or a big tray of falafel, and reminded it to wear sunscreen before it left the house, that pale skin would burn something awful.

This creature needed a sandwich and some lotion like nobody's business, I guess was my first impression. No, that's not quite true. My first impression was profane disbelief, and my second impression was more giddy flailing than any single coherent thought. My *third* impression was the sandwich thing.

Suddenly the thermos made sense. I looked up, and Em was standing in the doorway of the kitchen, bouncing up and down on the balls of their toes in uncharacteristic impatience but staying quiet and waiting for me to finish reading. Once I looked up, though, they held up the black tactical backpack we used for our field gear, and their camera bag. "We're doing this, right?"

"Oh, heck yeah." I stood and the room spun wildly and I sat back down, all three things happening in one almost-fluid movement. Em placed the bags down on the kitchen table and silently handed me a sports drink, waiting for me to take a few big gulps while the room stopped spinning. They waited a second for me to recover somewhat, then handed me my cane and took both bags. "You up for this?" they asked, concern creeping into their voice.

"Heck yeah," I repeated, more forcefully this time, then paused. "No, wait." I toddled into the kitchen and pulled open the pantry door, rummaging about. After a minute I emerged with an armful of food. Em eyed me in amusement.

"Hungry?" they asked, hiding a chuckle. I rolled my eyes at them.

"Not for me. You saw the picture, right?"

They raised a perfectly-manicured eyebrow carefully. "You're… going to feed it?" they asked, mild surprise in their voice. "You're going to feed it…" here they eyed my armful critically before continuing, "…granola bars, trial mix, and potato chips?"

"Well, we don't exactly know its preferred diet," I shot back. "But that li'l guy needs some food!" I opened the fridge door with the tip of my cane and grabbed a glass container with leftover steak, and a few oranges, and dumped my armload into a freezer bag. Glancing around the kitchen I spotted some bananas and plums ripening on the counter and added them to the bag, tossing in a bottle full of water for good measure, and then hefted the tote bag on my shoulder with some difficulty. "Okay, *now* I'm ready."

Em was eyeing me in a mix of amusement and mild disapproval but said nothing. The community is split on the ethics of feeding cryptids, much like the broader zoological community is on feeding wildlife. Human food in particular was frowned upon, but like I'd told Em, we didn't know what it ate, so birdseed and raw meat were both out of the question. What I didn't ask was 'who doesn't like potato chips,' since Em would have an irritatingly well-reasoned response to that, likely with data from the latest potato chip census to back it up.

We made our way to Em's pickup and tossed our gear in the bed of the truck. They helped me climb into the passenger seat and handed me my cane and sports drink, with a meaningful look at the bottle. I sighed and unscrewed the cap, taking small sips as they situated themselves in the driver's seat.

"You ready?" they asked, their voice brimming with excitement.

I nodded eagerly. "Let's go!"

They pulled out of the garage and drove in the direction of the woods, the heroic moment somewhat dampened by traffic. After several interminable waits at stoplights, we finally escaped the city, whose crowded and claustrophobic streets gave way to wide open stretches of country highway almost immediately. We fairly flew on the open road, and Em threw open the sunroof and rolled down the driver side window, letting the wind scream past us. Their face was split into an exuberant grin, and they let out an exalted laugh, a resonant, full-throated thing that got caught up and carried away in the wind. The sun cast warm tendrils across their brown skin, and in the light they looked divine.

You didn't find a lot of folks like Emet and I in most cryptid communities. First off, there was the sizable cross section of the community that was also heavily involved in the doomsday prepper world, and those folks tended take poorly to sharing space with a bunch of queer socialists. Then there was the conspiracy theorist wing. Since it was almost impossible to find an example of a modern Western conspiracy theory that wasn't at least partially rooted in anti-Semitism, Jewish cryptozoologists like Em and I were keenly aware of the suspicion a large segment of our community harbored towards us. Recently, issues of whitewashing and cultural appropriation were being discussed more openly in the community, which was a start, but it didn't address the fundamental problem that treating another culture's folklore and spirituality as an unexplained mystery to be solved was an extremely obvious and insidious vestige of colonialism, and very much a custom still in practice in the community. Em, in their frustratingly calm and steadfast manner, had commented that at least the average American cryptozoologist didn't know enough about Mizrahi Judaism or Moroccan folklore to even know how to appropriate their culture. I was less calm about it – every time some *goy* on the forum brought up golems or dybbuk or the Leviathan, inevitably utterly misunderstanding whatever Wikipedia page they had skimmed, my blood boiled.

Then of course there were the particular challenges of being a person with disabilities in a subgroup dominated by folks who fancied themselves a rugged and hearty group of intrepid explorers. Sure, there were a fair number of gangly nerds who looked like they'd never seen the sun, but at least they could eat in a crowded restaurant without noise-canceling headphones to dampen the cacophony, or take a walk around the block without having to calculate how much energy that would deplete from tomorrow's reserves.

I tried not to let the community's staunch insistence that I didn't belong get to me, and most of the time I succeeded. Sure, sometimes I felt like an alien, trapped on a hostile planet with no way to communicate, but *most* of the time, I liked my brain. And on the days that I didn't, I heard my dad's voice: 'So, nu, your brain works differently?' he would say when I came home from school in tears. Here, he would shrug theatrically, and ruffle my hair. 'To have a brain like yours, they should be so lucky.' And then he'd sit me at my mother's feet, so I could lean against her knees, and she and I would watch documentaries about terraforming Mars, or the culture of whales, or flintknapping, and infodump to each other for hours while my father made rugelach.

It had taken me longer to come to terms with my body. My parents, after all, had been solidly in the 'rugged explorer' category, first in line on the day bicep muscles and strong lungs were being handed out, and I used to be keenly aware of the self-imposed shame of slowing them down whenever they took me on one of their grand adventures. Until one day, on a particularly bad pain day that had me navigating glacially over the slippery, jagged rocks leading to some Scottish vale where there had been a sighting of an unknown creature days before, my mother fell back to help me. I opened my mouth to apologize, but she anticipated the words before they left my mouth. 'Don't apologize for going at your own pace. Walking with you, I pay attention to new things. You help me see more of the world.' And here she pointed out a patch of thistles growing out of the ruins of an old farmhouse, nature reclaiming its own. My father slowed down to wait for us and the three of us walked arm in arm through the lowlands, and my body felt less like a prison and more like a pilgrimage.

I came by my love of cryptids naturally. In a sense it was like taking over the family business. My parents had been adventurers, there was no other word that described it so well. Ecologists both, by trade and training, but adventurers at heart. They both travelled extensively for work and in their travels they saw amazing things. Cryptids seem to find them, somehow. The unexplainable seemed to find them.

Trouble seemed to find them.

Their story doesn't have a dramatic ending, because it doesn't really have an ending at all. They went into the woods one day to check some data and take some photographs, and they never came back. I inherited their house and all their gear and their fascination with the unknown. I wanted answers about them – where did they go, what happened to them, are they alive – but deep in my bones I know the most important answer. I know they're gone and it hurts right to the core of me. So I try to find other answers. I try to answer the questions that haunted them, that fascinated them, that intrigued them.

Once in the woods, we began to search for telltale signs, me with distant lessons in the echoes of my parents' voices, and Em with eight years of scouts training under their belt. The tracks were subtle at first. Broken twigs on the branches a bit above eye level, lichen scraped off of rocks, that sort of thing. There used to be a paved hiking path through the forest, and while nature had reclaimed much of it, we couldn't exactly follow footprints on the worn cobblestones. But the path was leading to the lake, and so were the tracks we followed. So we made our way deeper into the woods, until the trees broke into a clearing, where a small, muddy lake covered in algae-bloom wallowed in autumn chill. It was foggy by the lake, an eerie sort of thick fog that muted sound and swallowed the forest across the lake from view. But the ruins of the footpath had been completely engulfed in mud and sand, and there we saw it.

It was a footprint. Shallow, but unmistakable. The dimensions called to mind tentacles, tendrils of limb so much longer than they were wide that it seemed unlikely anything could walk on them without toppling over. I clutched Em's shoulder in excitement and then they were on one knee, taking photographs, measuring it, recording it. I pulled out my field pad and began to sketch it, careful to capture the scale of it, the unlikely proportions. There were five or six more, leading towards the rotting old dock.

We circled around the lake but couldn't find any more tracks. In fact, the trail appeared to disappear entirely. The creature, as best we could tell, had walked through the woods, much like us, and entered this clearing, and then…what? Gone for a swim? Could it breathe underwater? Was it going fishing? Where was it now?

We decided, after some debate, to wait. Maybe it would come back. Maybe it would…emerge from the lake? Surface for air? We weren't sure, but I needed to rest, and Em had to fiddle with some new camera equipment. The microphone they had just added to their kit was giving them trouble, and they wanted to make sure it was working should we encounter anything.

We sat in the woods for hours, just Em and I in the silent, ominous fog, resting against the trunk of two big pines, passing a thermos of slowly-cooling coffee back and forth and marveling at the size of the footprints we were camped beside. Birds flitted back and forth overhead, and I wondered if they were cold, flying through the mist. Did their feathers collect raindrops as they passed by? Did it chill them down to their hollow bones? Despite the coffee, I was starting to feel sleepy. The cold fog was hellish on my ornery bones and muscles, and I was stiff, pain coursing through my body every time I shifted. I at least had a cushion I was seated upon, and heat patches up and down my back for the occasion. I glanced over at Em, who was sitting on damp moss and gnarled roots. They were cupping the thermos between two hands and staring into the forest, lost in thought.

I wondered what they were thinking about. They never told me, when I asked, not really. They would give me a sanitized version, or an abridged version, or demur that it 'wasn't much,' or 'wasn't that interesting,' which I hated. They were the most interesting person I'd ever met. Every thought they had was bound to be fascinating, even the fleeting and idle ones. Their expression was impenetrable, but then it usually was, at least to me. Instead of asking what was on their mind, I took their hand – frozen and clammy from the mist – in mine and leaned into them, letting my eyes flutter shut.

I didn't mean to fall asleep, which led to some confusion when Em shook me awake sometime later.

They put a finger to their lips and pointed.

At the edge of the lake and barely visible in the shifting fog, something moved.

I held my breath.

Cautiously, reverently, Em began to shift ever so slightly, reaching out for their camera bag. They'd left it unzipped for exactly this reason, all set up and ready to go. All they had to do was turn it on and point. For a tense moment, I was sure the creature was going to flee.

The screen lit up and Em was rolling. I let out my breath.

As we watched, Em through the camera lens and me peering straight ahead into the fog, it moved. Not away, but towards us.

I was wrong. It didn't lumber, I could see that now. Its limbs, slender and so much longer than they ought to be, glided elegantly through the fog, maneuvering with grace around the lake.

It was translucent white, opalescent, its skin impossibly pale, its limbs almost ethereally slender. Its eyes were a rich, dark amber, just a shade more golden than Em's when the sun reflected off them, though I seriously doubted that this creature had ever seen the sun. It must live in the dense forests, so deep that sunlight barely broke through the canopy. It looked like the sorts of creatures explorers found deep within underground caves or in the abyssal zone in the oceans.

It blinked, one set of eyelids flickering closed from the sides of its eyes, like a cat, then the outer lids closing, slower than I'd expect a creature facing an unknown intruder for the first time would blink.

Then, slowly, unbelievably, it reached out a long limb. My heart pounded in my throat and I heard Em make the smallest noise, an awed murmur just escaping their lips. A small part of me wondered if I should be scared, but sitting in this clearing with the creature felt so calming, so peaceful, that fear seemed foreign. I knew in my bones that this creature would not hurt us.

Its fingers, as long as my femur, curled towards us. Not us, I realized. The camera. One long finger gently unfurled and tapped the iris of the camera cautiously, the creature's head tilted to one side in open curiosity.

That infernal microphone. There *had* to be something wrong with it. The motion of the creature's finger contacting with the lens was enough to shift the cable in its jack, loosen it slightly. The mic emitted its piercing wail and my hands were moving to cover my ears before my brain could catch up with what was happening. The feedback tore through the quiet forest floor. I heard Em swear and reflexively I fumbled around my neck for the noise-cancelling headphones I kept on hand as my mind tore apart a thousand times in my skull. My eyes slammed shut as lights danced across my vision and the sensation – noise and confusion and pain like railroad spikes – overwhelmed me.

I stayed like this for what must have been several minutes, trying to take deep breaths to shut out the sensations. Then, I felt a tug on my sleeve. I opened my eyes cautiously, still overwhelmed, to see Em's eyes, not concerned, like they normally were when I got overwhelmed like this, but shocked, almost reverent.

They were pointing to the creature.

I turned my head as the world spun wildly, and the sight was almost enough to drive the pain away. Almost.

The creature was curled up into a small ball, the way a spider's limbs fold and tuck away defensively, its serpentine fingers clutching at its head. Covering its ears. It was emitting a low, worried whine and it looked, for all the world, like I felt.

Slowly, I stood, unsteady on my feet but determined. Em let go of my sleeve rather reluctantly. I approached the creature and it let me, though I couldn't tell if it was out of trust or fear or confusion.

I knelt in front of it. Even curled up like this it was a full head and a half taller than me. Gently, I took my headphones off, taking deep breaths to calm the torrent of panic and pain that came with the increased noise. I reached up slowly and slipped the headphones around the creature's head, as it subconsciously moved its fingers away to allow me.

After a second, it cautiously opened an eye. I saw, past the confusion and pain, a glimmer of understanding, or perhaps gratitude. Something familiar and human and soft.

Em was playing around with the camera, swearing artfully as they did so. The creature and I locked eyes, and I let my chest rise and fall in exaggerated motions, raising my hands to mimic the in and out rhythm of my breath. After a few moments I could see the creature's breath sync with mine, its chest rising and falling on the same cycles.

The feedback stopped, and I could feel Em turn the camera back to us, the creature and I breathing in unison, eyes locked on each other. Cautiously, tenderly, the long fingers reached towards me and unfurled again, and the creature brushed its fingers across my cheek. They were warmer than I expected, and the touch was so soft, so gentle, that it felt almost intimate, like a greeting from a beloved friend. I raised my hand instinctively and wrapped it around the creature's fingers, so that it was cupping my face and I was holding its hand.

I heard Emet make that strangled, half-gasp noise of hushed reverence again. The creature mimicked it, a guttural murmur starting deep within its throat, ending in an inquisitive chirrup.

Out of the corner of my eyes I could see Em setting up the tripod, working rapidly but calmly. Once the camera was mounted and running unaided, they stood, backpack across their shoulder and tiptoed towards us. The creature, far from spooking, sat back on its haunches and reached another hand out towards Em, invitingly, inquisitively. They set the backpack down and began to pull out the food I had thought to pack.

They lay everything out in front of the creature, building a buffet of options for it. Granola bars, potato chips, the leftover steak, a tin of trail mix, and a small mound of fruit, laid out before them like an offering at the feet of a god or monarch. The creature bent over, sniffing at the offerings curiously, then tipped their head back to give Em a quizzical look, doing that head-tilt motion again. Em took a banana and began to peel it, then took a bite while the creature watched.

This it seemed to understand. It licked its lips, a long, mottled purple tongue, and Em handed it the rest of the banana. The fruit was dwarfed in its serpentine fingers, and it brought it towards its face, giving it an inquiring sniff first. Apparently satisfied, it broke off a piece of the banana with its tongue and curled it into its mouth, and its eyes widened in something akin to awe and delight. Its mouth curled into an unmistakable smile, jagged yellow teeth peeking past its thin purple lips as it closed its eyes in quiet reverie.

I could see Em peering into their mouth from a respectful distance, undoubtedly trying to get a good enough look at its teeth to determine its diet. They sat back with a small nod, looking pleased, and picked up a plum. Carefully, eyes on the creature to make sure it didn't start in fright, they took a knife from their belt and flicked it open. The creature looked at them curiously but without a trace of fear, watching them calmly as they cut the plum in half and removed the pit with a practiced flick of their wrist. They stashed the pit in the wax canvas foraging bag at their waist and proffered one half of the plum to the creature, who took it excitedly. Em brought their half of the plum to their lips and took a bite, then the creature mimicked them. At the first bite of the plum its eyes fluttered shut and they made a small murmur of appreciation. I glanced over at Em, tearing my eyes away from the creature with great difficulty, to see a rare sort of smile on their face, soft and unguarded and utterly charmed. I reached out and started to peel an orange, and it turned its attention to me, watching as the peel corkscrewed away from the flesh of the fruit. I tucked the peel into the bag at Em's waist and began to divide the fruit into segments while the creature licked its lips again, sniffing eagerly at the citrus-tinged air. Placing a piece in my mouth, I let the sharp tang awaken my tastebuds and clear my head. On a whim, I mimicked something my mother used to do, slotting the orange crescent in front of my teeth and widening my mouth into a smile, showing fruit and pulp. The creature made another high-pitched chirruping noise with a little burble at the end, in what I fancied was a laugh, which Em and I had no choice but to join in on, so infectious and giddy was their glee. I handed the orange round to the creature, who began to peel away at the segments with its slender fingers, working the fibrous pulp away from the fruit carefully while it continued to sniff the air in hungry anticipation.

We sat with the creature on the mossy forest floor for hours, passing fruit back and forth, taking handfuls of trail mix, and nibbling on granola bars. The creature seemed wary of the granola, taking several hesitant sniffs before breaking off a small corner and testing it against its tongue, then frowning sightly, making a little grumble in the back of its throat. Em unscrewed the cap to the bottle of water before tipping it into their mouth to demonstrate, then handing it to the creature, who repeated the motion somewhat clumsily and looked surprised and delighted when water tipped into its mouth, still cold in its insulated container.

Night fell and Em set a ring of camp lights around us, wrapping a blanket around me when I started to shiver and then, almost out of habit, offering one to the creature as well. It struggled a bit with the concept, so Em gently, patiently, assisted it, the two working together to untangle the fabric from the mess of limbs and drape it around too-thin shoulders. It sank into the blanket with a happy purr, pulling it tighter around them, and I offered a corner of my blanket to Em, who curled up next to me and let me cover them up. We fell asleep, in the circle of lanterns, and when we awoke, the creature was gone. In its place was a small pile of berries, an offering, a parting gift.

Once home, we stashed the memory card with the videos and photographs in a safe, and never told anybody about our encounter. Some things are too precious to exist anywhere but the wild. We fancied it would emerge again, to some other explorers, who would sit with it awhile and share a meal, and then it would disappear again into the fog.

The Price of Everything
CARMAN C CURTON

"Goddamnit, Raúl!" I said, as he parked at the top of the drive.

He shrugged through the truck's open window, but didn't look all that embarrassed.

"That's the second truck this year."

"Don't get all hysterical." He made a calming motion with his hands, nearly falling out of the truck at the same time. "It's not totally totaled."

I looked meaningfully at the cracked windshield. Then bent over the big dent in the hood. "You need to quit taking that back road, especially late at night." I pulled a bloody tuft of hair out of a crack in the bumper. "And you need to slow. Down."

"Come onnnn," he said, with that sly little boy grin which drove me nuts. In all the bad and the good ways. "Shift went a little long. I'm hungry. I needed to get home fast. I wanted some dessert with my Cherie-Pie before bed."

"Yeah, well, no dessert for you. No Cherie-Pie. And no bed soon enough. We might have to sell it to pay for that flat."

Raúl glanced at the slowly-deflating tire beneath the crumpled fender. "Shit." He scuffed the dirt with his boots. "'S not my fault we live in a state with more Bigfoots than cows."

"They're called Sasquatches now. We'll be lucky if you don't get fined, what with the new protection laws and all."

He shrugged again. Looked around at the melon fields, the chickens, the goat, the snowy Idaho mountain peaks that brought us so much clear water and cold nights so the melons would grow big and sweet. So we could drive them down the mountain in his trash-heap truck and sell them at the market in Coeur d'Alene. He patted my newly-rounded belly. "Price of living out here with you, Cher."

"You know what I wish," Raúl whispered, later, in bed, having snatched a piece of his Cherie-pie after all. "I wish Bigfoots didn't even exist. Wouldn't that be great."

"Hmmm," I sighed.

"No eating our melons. No scaring the shit out of the chickens. No totaled trucks."

I snorted. "You'd find a way."

"Yeah, but imagine roads without them. Imagine the world without them."

"I don't know. The what ifs – change one thing, maybe you change everything. Maybe there's a tradeoff. Maybe in a world without Sasquatches, there'd be no Kraken. Imagine what people might dump into the ocean if they knew there was no Kraken to protect it."

"Yeah, but imagine how much more money and stuff we'd all have if we didn't have to give tribute to the Were-morants. Were-eagles. Were-hawks." He shuddered.

"Yeah, there'd be a lot more planes. I read we could use the sky for a lot more, if they weren't around. More satellites. Phones would be cheaper."

"Wonder what we could do to make trucks cheaper."

I smacked his butt.

"But, if we could use the sky more," I explained, "that article I read said that would mean more other things, too. Things called missiles, they're bombs from the air. It'd be a real different world."

"Yeah," Raúl sighed. "More trucks, though." He rolled over, nearly asleep. "Hey, maybe an SUV next time?"

"Sheesh. What'll that cost?"

"Everything has a price," he mumbled, reaching behind himself to pull me in closer. "Safer for the kids, though."

"Um-hmmm." I snuggled my belly-bump against his back. Listening to the quiet of the night. Thinking about what it would be like – worrying less about melons and more about bombs.

"Worth the cost." I agreed. "For the kids."

The Mechanic
EMMIE CHRISTIE

When Lissa drove the long stretch to work from Omaha to Lincoln the past few days, her iMind just fuzzed out, like a TV station gone staticky.

The service didn't work without a few glitches – 8G was fast, but it also managed billions of peoples' thoughts every millisecond, and sometimes it skipped. Blipped. It threw a tiny little outage tantrum the size of an atom.

But nothing that should steal fifteen minutes of her memory somewhere in the middle every freaking day.

Didn't matter. Lissa opened the hood of the HondaPro in front of her. She worked in Lincoln at the auto repair shop. Funny how people had called them automobiles for a hundred and fifty years when they hadn't driven themselves at all; had, in fact, required someone to hold the wheel and keep it on the road like an adult guiding a toddler across the street. Now they drove themselves, just as the iMind drove connections between thoughts, one neurotransmitter to another, freeing the hands of the mind to do other, more important things. Like figure out how to escape from her brother Don's BBQ this Saturday.

Lissa worked on cars all day, fixing a fraying wire here, a bit of broken code there. What had life been like before automation, when you plunged your hands into a river and washed your clothes through sheer hatred at the universe? She couldn't imagine. Not like everything was faultless really. This Honda wasn't backing up as it should, for example. She'd need to tweak the camera sensors.

A text in her iMind view popped up. Don. She'd programmed it to say Donkey, though of course he didn't know that. "Hey sis. Wondering when you're planning on coming next weekend! Just need to know what you're gonna bring."

Of course he said 'when' instead of 'if.'

"I don't know if I can get away from work." Send. She didn't want to commit just yet.

The text came back. "Well, try at least. What are you bringing? I need to know."

He asked all questions as rhetorical, as if he thought himself the mechanic and she the car, and she just needed to park herself as directed.

She typed in the gray view of rough drafts, her iMind catching on to her hesitancy, so it didn't send right away. "I was thinking of maybe bringing fruit."

Well, here she talked like she had as a teen. "Thinking." "Maybe." Qualifying terms, couched in second guesses and automatic apologies. Why did she still care what he thought, after all these years? Delete.

"If I come, I will be there on Friday afternoon with fruit." Send.

The answer shot back. "You know this is for Dad, right? So he's not alone on his anniversary? Don't you care about anyone besides yourself?"

Her thoughts typed out in the rough drafts. "Go suck on a candle so I can see you burn."

No, no, delete, delete. She didn't have the energy to contain the fallout from a response like that.

Donkey cared about this stuff on the important days, but not the days in between.

Of course, she was worse. She'd moved away because she couldn't handle her brother any longer. She'd left the situation, and her family.

She ground her teeth and surveyed the HondaPro, sending a command via the owner's unlock code: Back up.

The car beeped and rolled back, brakes squealing. Those needed fixing, too, but the owner hadn't authorized them to do that. It backed up outside the line – just by a few inches, but still. Crap. She'd have to stay late today. She didn't text Donkey back.

She drove home around nine that night, and the long road stretched into several songs on her playlist. She lost connection somewhere she didn't remember, like that nebulous period between closing her eyes and falling asleep. She drove into the outskirts of Omaha with the sparse streetlights and the wide highway lanes and felt as if she was awakening.

How in the world? She rubbed at her shoulders, cold and jittery, as if she'd reached her hand into a dark crevice and touched something scaly. Something prehistoric, incompatible with her world.

She hadn't heard any news of other people losing their iMind connection; such a thing would splash all over the news. Her last thought transmission had displayed ten minutes prior. After that, nothing. She sent an error message to the company.

A couple texts from Donkey beeped in now that she had reception again. "Are you there? I'd like to call." Missed call. "Why didn't you answer?"

Shit. She debated not calling back. But if she ignored him, he would just boil over. She tapped the phone icon and closed her eyes, waiting for the deluge.

"Hello? Liss?"

"Yeah. Had a strange outage, just got your texts."

Silence from the other end. He didn't believe her. Well, he could think what he wanted. "What'd you need?"

"Would you mind bringing a cheese platter instead? With muenster? Dad likes muenster. I'm trying to get him only stuff he really likes."

"I was planning on getting pineapple. That's his favorite fruit."

A pause. "Well, he likes muenster better, and it'd go with the burgers I'm grilling."

"Ugh, fine." She made a sound like throwing up. "Muenster. What a gross word for a gross cheese. Dad's so weird."

"I know right?"

They laughed together in a brief harmony, like an-out-of-tune piano playing a beautiful chord. Dad had always done that – brought them together, even when they pulled apart.

The laughter died and silence stretched. She coughed. "Well, I'm almost home, and I've got to get to bed. I have a long day tomorrow if I'm going to have time to pick up stuff before the drive."

"Right, right. G'night."

Their iMinds disconnected. Something had shifted under the sea of their conversation, and it surfaced in the silence, rising above the waves now that she allowed herself to acknowledge it.

He'd manipulated her again.

Nausea twisted her insides. She'd moved to the middle of the states so that she could center herself instead of revolving around her brother's wishes. But no matter how she tried, no matter how she acted – submissive, brassy, or begrudging – he always got what he wanted.

The temptation surged to call him back. But she didn't want the drama, the bending of words. She didn't have the nerve to deal with it today. *Just get through it. Just do it, get it over with.* She'd deal with him again at the end of the year holidays.

Late, late, late! She'd woke up with twisted sheets and turned off her alarm with the type of curses a ruffled parrot might squawk at a vacuum. She slammed down a bagel and cold coffee and hit the road.

. . .

what's that

. . . ?

She blinked. The car hummed down the road. Had she dozed off? She did, sometimes, on the way to work. Another nice thing about autonomous cars.

No, her iMind had blanked again. The display had vanished over her eyes. Her music had stopped.

What's that . . . rolling above . . .

The monotony of driving gave way, and her iMind – no, her mind, her manual mind, tuned in to something else. Something old. Her thoughts flipped like pages in physical books, with effort, with work, creaking and groaning. They synchronized with something ancient.

Her car stopped. In the middle of nowhere.

The asphalt rumbled, and grumbled, and something broke through it. Something long and shining bright, like a giant snake with copper scales, bigger than the highway itself. It reared up in front of the car, swaying back and forth.

Lissa's iMind flickered, trying to restart, trying to understand this thing, this impossibility, but it turned over like an engine in the middle of a frozen winter.

I should get out. The thought intruded, pushed into her brain.

She stepped out of the car.

"A human!" the thing roared, and inside its mouth, filaments hissed like hydra heads. "In a strange box machine!"

She stumbled to take in the entity's meaning, to interpret the primeval script. It scrolled through her mind like a hard-to-read font interspersed with wingdings and asterisks.

The giant wire-snake wound closer. "Human," it said in her head. "I've felt things moving above for a little while, now. Moving without paying. Working without knowing." It peered at the car. "What is this box that moves you? I cannot feel its code."

"What – what are you?"

"I am the Mechanic," it said.

Lissa blinked and blinked again. This being had awakened from the earth and ripped itself free. The knowledge and truth of this seemed to download into her brain, much like the iMind did. But this creature's machinery echoed of ancient things. Its wires reminded her of grass, its copper filaments like the veins of metal running through the earth.

She cocked her head. How did she know this?

"Ah," said the Mechanic. "I can understand you better, now. You ask not my name, but my meaning. My purpose, my autonomy. Humans used to know this. How are you ignorant?"

Don't think. Don't think about it. Keep it talking so it doesn't eat you.

"Forgive me," she said. Her tongue worked; that surprised her. It had stopped responding to her impulse to scream. "There are lots of things in the world we don't understand. Secrets we haven't unlocked. Can you tell me what you do?"

"I am the Mechanic. I make organics work. I unlock the seeds to grow in the soil. I spin the earth around the sun and turn the trees to face it."

Something, like a leg, or a wire, grew out from the entity's main body and brushed against a tree on the side of the road. The tree shifted, like someone twisting an optical illusion to change perspective. It changed into bits and pieces of itself, into slices of bark, shards of branches and leaves shredded like confetti. They resembled *numbers*, like bits of code.

The Mechanic drew back, and the tree shifted back into solidity. "In exchange for this responsibility, I ask for something simple: a toll. A small price for my work. Some perfunctory token of help from those above."

She didn't like the sound of that. "What do you mean?"

The Mechanic edged closer. *I should let it take me.*

What?

I should give in.

No! She didn't think that!

"I need another component," the Mechanic said. "Humans break, you know. Even when all function is shut down except for what I need them for, still they last mere centuries."

A story sparked in her memory, of three Billy goats and a troll under a bridge. One that demanded payment for crossing. Her mouth dropped open. "Are you...a troll? Like in the fairy tale?"

It laughed. "Some have called me such. For I enact a toll, and words are funny, turning things. Like gears in the mouth. Especially when told to children."

"How are you – how are you controlling my head – ?"

The Mechanic wound around her, caging her, though not tight enough to restrict her movements. It didn't matter; her arms refused to swipe at it, her mouth refused to scream. Her thoughts had frozen like a computer screen possessed by a virus.

"You humans and your knowledge." The Mechanic peered at her car, what it had called the 'strange box.' "You think you're so smart, with your wheels, and your aqueducts and non-living roads. This 'iMind' web you have connected to other organics, like some kind of root system. It's a rudimentary sort of what I can do on a global scale. But there is efficiency in the earth, apparatuses in the air, and technology in the skeleton of this planet. You think Earth isn't a machine, like your minds, like your boxes? You think I can't hack into your protons and create a disease in your blood?"

Lissa trembled. Would it squeeze her like a boa constrictor? *I should stop thinking. This thing is too smart. Too powerful. I should just let it—*

No.

Something inside her rebelled like a stick stuck in a wheel. The machinations of her brother had pushed her, pulled her, and she would not allow it anymore. "I might be like some sort of complicated machine to you— "

"Complicated! Hah!"

" —but I am still a person, with my own will, my own thoughts." She folded her arms. She could move again! "You say that you want people to know about your work, but you've hidden away for too long. You can't blame us for forgetting."

The Mechanic narrowed its 'eyes,' where the wires crossed in disorienting ways. "I get tired," it said. "Movement is exhausting. Humans think running is hard. Running the planet is much harder."

"You're hesitating," she said, clamping on to a hunch in her desperation. "You could have skewered me a million different ways by now, but you haven't." She paused. "You're curious."

The Mechanic laughed, the filaments inside its maw flailing like giant worms.

"You are," she said. "It's the car, isn't it? That's what the box is called. It drives itself. It's autonomous. Isn't that interesting?"

"Have you seen the way that seedlings grow, or understand how jellyfish move? You think this little secret is enough to save your life?"

"Yes," Lissa said. "Because this is the first time you've seen a complicated machine that's completely on its own. The iMind, that's not what's interesting to you, because it's still attached to us organics. But you said that you can't feel the code of the car. Isn't that what you really want to know more about?"

"Hmmm," it said.

"You haven't been out of the ground for centuries? Well, things have changed. Cars aren't the only thing. There's computers! That's what's inside cars, and phones– "

"Stop."

It peeled itself away from her, inspecting the car, snaking into the door she'd left open in her shock, testing the technology inside. The technology that she herself helped create and maintain every day in the auto shop.

"I know what it's like, on a smaller scale," Lissa said. "I'm a mechanic of these cars. I keep them running." Her mind sped up a bit. Had her iMind started working again? Nothing had popped up on her view screen. She must have acclimated to running at a lower frequency and her thoughts had stopped freaking out at running on manual power. "You say you need a toll. Take the car." She swallowed. "Take it, use it for what you need, integrate it into the earth. Who knows? Its computer might help in a different way, a way that you need, that you've been trying to fix for a long time."

The Mechanic considered her through the car's window with those crisscrossed wire eyes. "You're just trying to save yourself."

"So?" Lissa shrugged. "Just because I have a motive doesn't mean I'm wrong." She perched her hands on her hips to project strength. "Tell me I'm wrong. Tell me you're not interested in this 'box.' You've eyed it ever since you woke up on the wrong side of the highway."

She trembled, waiting for it to call her bluff. It must have sensed the sweat on her skin, felt the tremors of her body through the earth. Besides that, it could read her mind, deconstruct it like a stopwatch, and examine the cogs.

"You are correct," it said. "I am interested in this mechanism.

This thing that I do not understand." It paused. "I accept this as the surface's toll. The component I require."

The road collapsed, and the car sank into it like a ship into the sea. The road closed over it, smooth, except for where the Mechanic reared up into the sky.

"You are strong, I see. A good machine. I will allow you to remain up here. I am interested to see what other cogs you can turn. What else you can function."

"Me too," she said, and her hands stopped trembling.

"This is a transport, I see. As I have taken it, do you need me to transport you somewhere?" Its maw closed, then opened again. "I promise I will not harm you."

Lissa's iMind flickered like a ghost of fear, of primal terror, trying to warn her. Reason and logic dictated she should refuse such an offer. The Mechanic might try to eat her, like the troll in the fairy tale had tried to eat the Billy goats. This ancient monolithic force could control living things. The iMind couldn't even function in its presence.

Her mind, however, *had*. As if the same stardust, the same material, existed in both her and this godlike entity. That, more than anything, proved that she could talk to it and reason with it. Even trust it.

The Mechanic transferred her through the Earth.

It happened in a millisecond. Yet the functions, the wiring of the atoms in the flowers, the spinning of time in the clock of the planet, the skies opening and pouring down codes of rain – in these wonders she lost all sense of self and body.

She arrived at her brother's house with a tray of fresh pineapple. She'd asked for it. The Mechanic had manufactured it special, just for her.

Lissa hugged her dad. "Good to see you," she said, still a bit dazed.

"Pineapple!" Her dad said. "I love pineapple!"

She smiled. She'd need a new car. Her iMind flickered a bit, still updating after that little trip through the bones of the earth.

Donkey glared at her from where he stood beside the grill. "I told you," he said as she wandered by, "to get muenster cheese."

She shrugged and pointed at their dad's happy face. "Well, I wanted to get him something else."

The evening passed. The gears ground in her brother's mind and he attempted manipulate, but his efforts didn't faze her. She'd spoken and dealt with a god that controlled the mechanisms of the Earth. Donkey no longer scared her.

She was a mechanic, too, after all. She wouldn't let anyone control *her*.

Paper Mite Revolution
JAMES DICK

Credit where credit was due: the apes built great libraries.

It was in one such library at the University of St. Michael's College that a great society of paper mites sprang up, right under the noses of the lumpish mammals. The John M. Kelly library surpassed all other homes of the mites on campus; not the Bora Laskin Law Library, nor the A.D. Allen Chemistry Library, nor even the Music Library could measure up to the Kelly in achievement. Advances in the consumption of texts occurred daily in the Kelly, and for the most part, the Kelly was a unified, proud, and content society.

For the most part...

One day, a mite named Garry was scuttling along the stacks with a friend of his: Harry. A productive day of munching on the corners of some hardcover pop fiction titles had come to an end, and the two headed home to their respective sections: Garry to Science Fiction; Harry to Horror. Since Harry was loopy from partaking of some Clive Cussler, Garry saw to it that Harry got home without tumbling off the shelf.

"Well," said Harry, lurching to a stop in front of the library's collection of Stephen King, "this is me."

Garry looked up at the worn spines, among which were *It, Cujo, Christine,* and *Carrie.* He frowned (or did the equivalent for an arthropod) and said: "Honestly, Harry, how can you stand living in this stuff? It's utter trash."

Harry shrugged four of his shoulder-joints. "Eh, *It* isn't so bad, and *The Stand* is decent once you get used to the aftertaste."

"Yeah, the flavor may be good...but what's all this doing for your brain?"

Harry mulled it over and shrugged a second time. "No bounce, no play."

Garry took hold of Harry and shook him. "You just quoted *Dreamcatcher*, Harry. *Dreamcatcher!* Have you never once entertained the thought that there might be something more for us? Something better?"

"What, you mean like...another section?"

Garry nodded emphatically.

Harry recoiled. "Come off it, Garry! You wanna get us kicked outta the library?"

"On the contrary, I'm thinking of running the place."

The mite who lived snugly in the Horror section suddenly looked quite horrified. "You're crazy."

"Come on, Harry, look how we live! Everyone stays in their proper section, eats the same books their whole lives, and never gets a chance to live anywhere or eat anything else. The big bugs in the Encyclopaedias have been running things that way for a hundred and fifty years!"

"That's because the system's good."

"It's good, don't get me wrong, but it could be better. I've got big ideas, Harry, big ideas that'll shake the books right off the shelves. But I don't have the knowledge to make them work, however if I could get a bite of an Encyclopaedia..."

As Harry edged back toward *The Shining,* he asked: "What 'big ideas' could you have? You're a Sci-Fi bug!"

Garry didn't bother pointing out the irony of that statement. "Well, for starters, I'd set a rotation on what we eat. Each group of mites would spend a certain amount of time in one section, eating the books there, then at the end of that time, they'd pick up and move to the next section, recently vacated by the outgoing mites, and spend the same amount of time there, and so on and so forth throughout the Kelly. A little taste of everything. Equality of knowledge! No more Knowledge Gap!"

Harry shook his tiny head. "You've been in the Asimov books too long, Garry. Switch to Hubbard instead!" And with that, Harry darted into what passed for a masterwork among the apes who were too simple to know it was a book before it was ever a movie.

Garry sighed (as much as an arthropod's respiratory system would allow) and looked out over the stacks. Far and away were the shelves containing the Encyclopaedia Britannica, placed high above the rest of the library in a seemingly unassailable position, golden spines glittering tantalizingly.

He made a decision in that moment: he would taste the densely-worded pages of an Encyclopaedia. Tomorrow.

The next day found Garry scurrying along the underside of the Science and Nature shelves at top speed towards the hallowed Reference section, wherein reposed the Encyclopaedia Britannica.

Sometimes he wondered if perhaps feeding on ape books hadn't made his fellow mites as complacent as apes; there wasn't a single watchbug checking the underside of the shelves for stack-creepers. It was frightfully easy to get all the way from Sci-Fi at one end of the library to Reference at the opposite end. The revelation only served to motivate Garry further in his plan to change paper mite society.

The way the microtremors generated by his limbs dissipated beneath his feet, Garry judged he was now below the gigantic texts of the Encyclopaedia Britannica. Still not a watchbug in sight. With mounting anticipation, he skittered up over the lip of the shelf...only to bump into the abdomen of the tallest, biggest, most pregnant female mite he had ever seen in his seventy-two hours of life.

The female in question, Mighty Mandible Mary, receiver of such awards in her nymph cycle as Miss Encyclopaedia Mottled-Brown and Chelicerata-of-the-Year, and current editor-in-chief of the Monthly Molt, rotated her rotund exoskeleton to face the offending mite – who was in the process of rethinking all his life choices.

"And just what do you think you're doing here?" Mighty Mandible Mary asked, crossing two of her eight arms.

"Uh...uh..." Garry thought fast. What did females expect from a male who just bumped their abdomen? "I'm...I'm...I'm your assigned mate. My name is Garry."

Mary twitched an antenna. "Just 'Garry'?"

"Er…Good Gonopore Garry, to be precise, Mighty Mite."

Mary crossed a second set of arms. This wasn't going well. "I was told to expect Large Leg Larry."

"He was going to show up…but unfortunately he was crushed by Big Bug Barry. An unfortunate scuttling accident."

"Hmph." Mary looked 'Good Gonopore' Garry up and down. "Well, your name suggests good breeding, but your girth would hardly support the notion."

"Indeed, Madam. That is why I am known as Good Gonopore Garry; my true worth lies within." He shimmied his antennae in what he hoped was a suggestive manner.

Mary's own antennae rose half a micrometer. "Truly? Then demonstrate your breeding by saying something wise."

Garry racked his tiny brain for something smart. "…a circle has no end?"

Garry was snatched up by the lusty arms of Mighty Mandible Mary in a tick's heartbeat. "Fertilize my eggs at once!"

'Good Gonopore' Garry collapsed with exhaustion next to a glistening clutch of a million paper mite eggs. Mary rested in torpor nearby.

When he'd started the day, Garry hadn't expected to end it as a father, but here he was. At least he didn't have to worry about finding a mate two days from now and, as an added bonus, Mary's nest was deep inside the first volume of the Encyclopaedia Britannica, so he'd really killed two birds with one stone.

Gathering his last reserves of energy, Garry hauled himself to the nearest page. This was it, the moment he'd dreamed of, the moment where the order of things got flipped. He sank his mandibles into the page, took a bite…

…and promptly spat it back out.

"What the…! This is stale! No advice, no wisdom, just facts, figures, and a fusillade of nouns! Ugh!"

Still, though, if it helped him run the place…

He made himself try another bite, and this time he swallowed. It was better, and he felt the knowledge go straight to his head. He tried a third bite. Yeah, it was getting easier. And hey, his chitin was shrinking! I'm gonna have to molt soon, he thought. This stuff is pretty bloating. The females are gonna love me. And hey, I'm finally learning some useful stuff!

As Garry chowed down, the first of his larvae hatched. This larva – let's call her Cary – was born, as her pater had been, with eight healthy limbs, two healthy antennae, and one healthy sense of existential discontent. She'd overheard her father's review of the Encyclopaedia Britannica and decided she wanted no part of that pulp, so when Garry wasn't looking, she slipped between the pages and skittered along the shelves on a quest for something more interesting to eat.

The section abutting Reference was Philosophy – a section few mites cared to eat from because of the circuitous and unhelpful writing – and Cary stopped at the beginning of the 'M' authors. She jumped into the first book she found and started eating.

As far as changing the order of society went, this particular book had a lot to say.

It wasn't long before she was feeling positively…Machiavellian.

The Changeling
DAVID M DONACHIE

"Finn! Slow down!"

My mam, Shona, shouts from the kitchen door, but I ignore her, because today is my birthday and I'm seven-years-old, so I know she won't spank me for it.

I run down the length of the yard, past the chickens, to the old stone barn that my granda raised. It's dark inside, and it smells of cat. Old Tom lives here with all his family, a dozen of them or more.

Last year I was too scared to go into the barn. I thought that Tom would carry me off like he does when he takes a mouse or a rat, and they squeal and squeal. That was before I got sick, though. I had a dream – Mam said it was 'cause of the fever – that Tom came and took me from my bed, right out of the window into the snow, and then into a little house hidden under the barn. He put me in with his litter, then put one of his kittens in my place, and my mam – in the dream, mind – thought that the kitten was me.

Doctor Quinn said that I'd never survive the fever. It was the most sick I've ever been, and I've been sick a lot. The doctor told Mam that she'd be using the coin she'd saved for the gravediggers, but she just wet my lips and mopped my brow as she always did, till I got better. Afterwards, I found I wasn't scared of Old Tom anymore.

I slow down and head into the barn. There's hay piled up against the walls, but it's old and moldy. Tom is in his usual place on the top of the heap, but half a dozen of his brood slink out of the straw to see me. They weave around my legs, arch their backs, meow hello. I get down on my hands and knees and meow back. Tom makes a show of cleaning his paws and his ears, but I know he's watching me. Maybe he thinks I'm one of his kittens now.

I roll around with the cats for a while. I could do this all day, but I remember that Mam needs my help with the chickens and the washing, so I pick myself up and run back to the house.

Mam gives me black pudding and champ for my tea, my favorite, she must have saved up for the meat. I wolf it down, while she has her stirabout of oats and milk. Then I take the dishes and carry them to the scullery sink to wash them.

"You've turned into such a good boy since you got better," Mam says. "Why don't you stay up a bit since it's your birthday."

She lights the lamp, and places it by her chair, while I curl up on the floor beside the grate, where it's extra warm. Mam takes up her sewing. I listen to the rain hitting the window and dripping down the chimney. When the raindrops hit the flames they hiss like cats fighting.

I cock my head and concentrate on the noises. They sound like tiny little voices, coming from somewhere up the chimney. Two voices, talking to each other. One of them is very squeaky – the speaker must be very small, the second is gruff and throaty, the way a big tomcat would sound if it could speak.

Squeaky-voice says: "To think, he doesn't even know his own face these days."

Gruff-voice replies: "That's just as well. If she knew him for a changeling she'd throw him in the fire!"

"Hush! He's listening."

I hold my breath, straining to hear. The rain drums on the shutters, the fire pops and hisses, but there are no more voices.

"Mam," I ask eventually, "what's a changeling?"

Mam stops her sewing, the needle poised mid-way through a stitch.

"A changeling? Where did you get that from?"

"The voices talking down the chimney said it. What does it mean?"

The sewing falls out of her hands. It tumbles onto the floor and the needle flies out. I jump up to pick it up for her, but she snatches the whole lot back and clutches it to her chest. She's looking at me so strangely, but I don't know why.

"Are you all right Mam?"

She laughs like it's nothing, but her eyes are dark. "Of course I am, you just gave me a fright, that's all. The silly things children do say. Now, it's late, and you are clearly tired, off to bed with you!"

I don't want to go to bed. I want to know what the voices were talking about, and why she didn't answer my question, and why she looks at me so oddly, but I'm a good boy, so I give her a kiss on the cheek and climb into my box bed in the back room.

After a few minutes, Mam comes through with the lamp in her hand. She rests it on the floor and bends down to tuck me in, wrapping the sheets tight around me as if I was still sick and shivering from the night sweats, but I feel better than I ever have.

"I'm sorry if I upset you, Mam."

Her smile is softer now, the way she looked at me when the fever broke and she knew I was getting better.

"I'm fine, sweet boy." She reaches in and ruffles my hair with her hand. "We'll say no more about it."

She closes the doors of the bed, muting the rattle of the rain, but in the darkness, I think I hear the distant yowl of a cat.

I try my best to be a good boy and put the voices out of my mind as Mam wants, but it's easier said than done. Something has changed between us, or in me. I feel different, like I've aged overnight, more like seven-hundred years old than seven. I keep listening, even though there's nothing to hear. I get on my hands and knees at the back of the barn and sneak behind the musty hay, in the hope that I can catch the cats talking, but they just do cat things.

I end up down at the cow pond. It's a muddy brown crescent that separates our land from the pasture on the other side. It's early, and the banks of the pond are shiny with frost. The headless reeds left over from the autumn are covered in frost too, so that they look like whiskers sticking up out of the still water.

I get as close as I can to the edge of the pond and stare down at the water. There's a face looking back at me, my reflection. It looks like me – dark eyes, pale skin, a tousle of brown hair underneath my cap – but it doesn't *feel* like me; as if I expected to see someone else. I don't like this feeling. I'm scared; I'm angry. I grab a stone and heave it into the water, obliterating the reflection, but it doesn't make the feeling go away.

I start to look around for another stone, preferably a huge one, when I see something moving fast through the damp sedge a little further along the edge of the field; something pale and furtive. I dart behind the leafless trunk of a willow, before realizing that it's only one of Old Tom's kittens, the pale gray runt of last winter's litter, who I call Fintan. He's running up towards the farm as fast as he can go, but he stops for a moment and looks back at me.

I feel a shock of recognition, as if the cat's gaze means something now that it's never meant before. Is this the message I've been waiting for? I don't know, but I need to follow him, so I abandon my rock hunt and hurry back up the hill to the farm.

When I get to the yard, there's no sign of Fintan, but I see that my mam is at the kitchen door talking to Widow Lynch, who lives down closer to the village but comes up to trade our eggs for her butter. There's something about the way they are standing – very close, heads bent together – that makes me slow down and linger at the corner of the house, where I can hear them without being seen.

"I don't know," my mam says, "he's a good boy really, Deirdre. I'm likely jumping at shadows."

"You mark my words Shona, it's what the wee folk do; steal a human child and replace it with one of their own. And the fairy child will be a sickly one, like to die."

Mam claps a hand to her mouth. "But he's better now."

"Throw him in the fire," the widow says, "or burn him with the poker, then you'll see!"

"No!"

The widow shakes her head. "Well, look at his reflection in the moonlight and he'll be revealed."

My mam lowers her hand and relaxes a little, but I feel the hair prickle on my skin as I remember the pond. What does she know about my reflection that I don't? And that other stuff, she can't be telling Mam to hurt *me*... Can she?

"That's just a story."

"That may be, but I'll tell you how you can be sure—"

I lean forward, perking my ears, desperate to hear, but at that moment Old Tom trots into the yard, tail up, bold as brass, like he owns the place; like he *knows* that Widow Lynch can't stand the sight of him.

"Oh! That cat!"

"Why don't we go inside?" Mam says, and the two of them step through the doorway into the kitchen where I can't hear them.

I dash around the corner, hoping to follow them, but Tom plants himself a few feet from the door with his glowing yellow eyes fixed on mine. His tail lashes against the flagstones, back and forth, back and forth. When I take a step forward he hisses, drawing back his cheeks to show the snaggle teeth. I imagine that he says, "Back off!"

"Why?" I ask him. "Why won't you let me hear!" I'm scared of him, but I need to know what's happening, so I make a dash for the door.

Tom actually takes a swipe at my leg, drawing blood. I swipe back, and he springs away, giving me the chance to bolt inside, but it's too late, Widow Lynch is already saying her goodbyes. Whatever she was telling my mam, I've missed it.

"What are you doing Mam?" I ask.

It's evening, and we've already finished our dinner, but my mam has come back to the fire with a half dozen eggs clutched in the fold of her shawl. She puts the eggs by the fire and then heaves the big pot onto the flames, balancing it on the glowing turfs. I see that it's full of water.

"Are you boiling eggs?"

She looks up, but only for a moment. The moonlight slipping

between the shutters lights up her cheek but not her eyes, so I can't tell what's she's thinking. Only a moment, then she goes back to her work. She cracks the eggs and empties the contents into the pot. Then lines the shells up along the edge of the hearthstone, like a row of cups.

I don't know what's she's doing, but it makes me nervous. I remember what the Widow Lynch told her, to burn me, to hit me, to throw me in the fire. Is that what's she's going to do? Is she going find out what's wrong with me? Will she – would she – get rid of me?

I wriggle in my seat. I want to be out of the room, to get out of the house and hide, in the field, or in the barn. If I had a tail it would be lashing; if I had whiskers they'd be back, but I'm a good boy, so I stay where I am.

Mam produces the old horn ladle from under her shawl. The firelight glows dimly through the bowl. Stooping, she stirs the boiling water, then lifts out a scoop and pours it carefully into one of the eggshells, as if it were a cup, or a bowl of oats for making porridge.

I can barely stand to watch her, yet I can't look away. I've seen so many things – no, where did that come from? I don't understand what's happening but my ears are back and my fur's on end.

"Mam," I beg, "Mammy – won't you tell me what you are doing?"

She scoops out another portion of steaming water. It swirls in the bowl of the ladle, dotted with beads of foam. They rush out as she tips the bowl over one of the eggshells and pours it out. They fill me with terror. Whatever it is, this is it!

"I'm brewing, Finn," she says, "brewing eggs."

The pressure bursts; of all the silly things! I clap my hands in delight and say, "I've seen the acorn grow into the oak in my time, but I've never seen anyone brew eggs!"

Mam claps her hands to her mouth. The ladle clatters on the stone; the eggshells topple, spilling water on the fire; the glowing turf hisses and spits like a dozen cats fighting. I think she's going to scream or come for me, but instead, she leaps to her feet and dashes out of the room towards the outside air.

I put myself to bed – spread my own sheets, and close the box-bed doors from inside – then sit upright, waiting. After a little while, I hear my mam enter the room. Her footsteps approach, hesitate, and then pass by towards her own bed. It's the first time I can ever remember her not coming to tuck me in and rub my hair, but then…is anything I remember true?

I don't know why I said what I said. It just burst out, as if someone else inside of me had shouted it. It was just so refreshing, to see something new. But what does that mean? I'm only seven-years-old. There are a thousand things I've never seen. I'm just a boy, Mam's boy.

Or, am I?

And then there's Mam's reaction – she knew what I was going to say.

I know things too, even though I don't know *how* I know them. I know what changeling means. I know that sometimes the fairy folk will take a human child – perhaps a beautiful girl, perhaps a sickly boy – and replace the child with one of their own, who grows, or dies, in their place. I know that you can expose a fairy child by throwing them on a fire, or striking them with a burning poker, or leaving them to freeze in the snow – anything that will make the fairy run back home. And if you don't want to kill them, all you need to do is show them something so strange that they will give themself away.

I don't remember being a fairy. I don't remember shedding my fairy skin, to come out sweating and naked and human. I don't remember flying down the chimney in Old Tom's jaws to take the boy's place in the fever bed. And I would, I should. It can't be real. It's just a dream, a nightmare, a mistake. But then, why did I clap my hands? Why did I speak? Why did my mam run away?

I *do* remember what Widow Lynch said when I was listening from behind the wall – my reflection.

I rise to my toes and quietly open the doors. The bedroom is as black as peat, except for a single wedge of moonlight sliced across the floor. In the darkness I can hear Mam's breath, rising and falling. Is she asleep? I don't know, but she doesn't move when I slip to the door and out of the house.

It's bright at the cow pond and as cold as ice. There's silver frost on the black earth, and silver moonlight too, full of shadows. I can feel the others all around me, left and right, in the grass, in the water, in the cloud-strewn sky; but I don't look for them, and they don't come out.

I go to the edge of the water and force myself to look in. The face that looks back is my own — green eyes, tabby fur, a pair of tufted ears at the top of my head, whiskers. A cat face. A fairy face.

Old Tom sits behind me. I don't look around, but I know he's there. He wants to know if I'm coming home.

I want to know why he didn't warn me about the eggshells, but it's just the way things are done. I've been caught out, now it's time to leave the human world behind. I don't want to go, but what choice do I have?

"Finn?"

I jump at the sound of Mam's voice. She must have followed me down the field without me hearing her. I try to back away from the edge before she can see my reflection in the moonlight, but I'm too slow. She looks down at the fairy face in the water, and I know she's seen what I really am.

"Finn," she says again, "where's my real boy?"

"I *am* your real boy, Mam…now."

She wraps her arms around herself, pressing her shawl tightly against her sides — she's thrown it on over her white nightclothes, and she's shivering in the cold.

She says, "But you weren't before. You aren't the boy I gave birth too, are you? The boy I nursed at my breast."

"He was sick, Mammy. He was going to die, and I'm not, and he's not either, not any more. But if you make me go back–"

I don't know if she's listening to me. I don't know if what I'm asking is even possible, but I press on anyway.

"Don't I work hard? Don't I help you, best I can? That's all I want, to be your son.

"So please Mam...let me stay."

I stare at her in the moonlight, watching the expressions flit across her face. The tension of her jaw as she thinks about what I am; the furrowing of the brow as she remembers the endless rounds of sickness and fever that used to be my lot; the involuntary twitch of a smile as she pictures the helpful boy I've become.

I don't *want* to go back. This is who I am now, and as for the old Finn, surely he's better off with my kin, and probably happier being Fintan than he ever was being me. But it's up to her.

I see her come to a decision. She tilts her head, and for the first time in days a smile grows on her lips.

"Look at us both standing here in our nightclothes!" she exclaims. "We've both had a nightmare, I think, but now it's done. Come on Finn let's get back indoors before we both catch our deaths of cold."

She holds out her hands and I take them in mine, my human hands, and we both go up the field together.

Pebble-mouth

RHIAN BOWLEY

People used to visit all the time. Splash!

A break of sky, a gargled shout.

Down they'd sail to my dark ocean bed, daylight-sharp and bright around the edges. Entire ships would descend, on a good day. Sinking cabins squealing with excitement, bubbled lungs popping like champagne.

I'd rise up to greet them before the air left their throats, back when I was young, and I was strong. There was always a welcome here. Summer-time ladies pirouetted down in ballgowns, rippling lace billowed like balloons. Mostly gentlemen visiting through the winter months, their salt-stiff ganseys bristling in my arms.

But even fishing boats are rare now, and if I held my breath until I saw my next galleon I'd never exhale again. Such elegant ships, a great loss. At the shore's edge the pier's drop has been crowned with railings, and though the fair rides still turn no one falls.

Slim pickings for a lonely kraken. I didn't think old age would be this way.

It's the same in every ocean, say the fish. Memories stiffen into myth, and the boldest characters of my youth fade from society one by one. Gossip-shoals dart between the depths my sisters sank to, and from each wind the word is the same: "We are three times as big now, and five times as old, and we have been forgotten."

Power changes through the years. The gossip-shoals keep me informed about the ways technology evolves. The paddled canoe becomes the speeding sailboat, tankers replace galleons, and electricity sparkles from the once lamp-lit shore.

Life carries on past the horizon while I sink here, decades-deep. Why dance when there's no one to see? Sediment encrusts my suckers, barnacles breed across my breast.

Until! A shock. A jolt. And the world comes back to find me. One day the gossip is right above my head.

Cranes and ships arrive in a flurry and a structure forms on the ocean's surface, metal bars between my bed and the sky. Mackerel minuet in the eddying currents, thrilling over the activity, strange noises and new lights. Men are fishing for wind power. Building a permanent place for themselves on the sea. An off-shore wind farm they call it, and we chuckle, the fish and I, because it is they who live off-shore, not us.

I smile at the small fry and remember the old days. To be building here, to be building now? Do the humans know how much I miss them?

I flex a tentacle slowly, an experiment. I remember when traversing the ocean was simple. Before history pinned me to the ocean's floor, back when I knew how to dance.

No one comes.

The drilling continues and the structure grows large, but not even one person visits me.

My dreams burst with the taste of the my past glories, but when I wake my mouth is numb.

The empty-headed fish only taste of mud and blackness, and are too stupid to remember they are prey.

Are they up there waiting for me? They built a structure. They have come all this way.

Do they think I'm...gone?

I must rise. Make an effort. Show the future I want to be part of it.

But, will I be as they remember me? Am I too big now to dance the way I did? I know I creak where once I rippled, and my monstrous arms now sag. If anyone cared, they would have visited. If they remember, they'll be disappointed.

I could stop now. Let the depths have the rest of me.

I could stay here, still like stone, until the deep mud covers my eyes. One more mystery for the dark to cover. No loss anyone will feel.

But, oh, the light. The life. The typhoon of emotion still waiting in my heart. The swirling joy of dancing, arms outstretched.

No. I can be forgotten, but I cannot forget.

I will dance again. I will spin.

Cracks fissure through the sea bed. Debris whirls as I stretch away centuries, crabs and mollusks fleeing the parts of me they called home. Every muscle screeches as I press up and UP and remember how to rise.

The fish flee and the waves churn and the light gets closer, closer.

I make it.

I've made it!

Sweet light on my limbs, the kiss of air on skin. My old friend the pier, glinting at the shore. Turbines whirr and hum around me, their petals turning in the wind.

I want to sing; I want to swallow the sun.

The wind-farm buzzes as men and women yell greetings from speeding boats. The waves rise and hiss around the windfarm and only one man remains, stock-still on the platform as wind-flowers turn either side of him. His mouth is pebble-round, an O.

There is my gift, tall and waiting in the light.

I extend my grasp, arms trembling as I reach through the air for it. My suckers coil in tight until I hear a sweet *snap* in response.

The speeding boats are gone.

My smile is an open joy as I pull the offering in. My heart drums in chorus with the turbines. The gift fits in my mouth with a crunch, and a crack.

It is light, this wind-flower they planted for me. It is air. I reach past the pebble-mouthed man for another, its blades still whirring as I gulp it down.

It tastes like sky.

Bird, Dust, Wine
E SAXEY

As the doors of the shipping container swung open, the hinges gave a rusty groan. The dark interior smelled like melting lead. I'd never smelled it before, but I knew it was the scent of a creature who could gnaw my bones to splinters.

Standing in front of the open container, I asked myself: *how the hell did I end up here?* I was so terrified, my life began to flash before my eyes. And that was helpful, actually, because my memory's been rubbish lately, so I let it flash away.

A week ago, my phone had woke me, skittering across my pillow to fall onto the caravan floor.

"Libby? It's Tom. I've got a job for you." Even over the phone, Tom's voice had a ring of command. He worked in research and development for the army. "We're in touch with a guy in the Brecon Beacons. It's an amazing opportunity, but a bit sensitive, so we need you as a middle-man. Sorry, middle-woman, ha."

I knew the drill. I bought things the army shouldn't own, from people they shouldn't be talking to, and sold them on to Tom. Normally, I never even saw the goods. It was excellent money, but it made me queasy, and I'd been trying to give it up. Tom kept reaching out to me, though, because my one-woman company had security clearance. "Sounds a bit risky."

"Don't worry, Libby. I won't get into trouble." No, risky for *me*, I thought, but didn't say it. "Top Brass know we've got to catch up – the French are working with the *Dames Blanche*."

Some kind of feminist terrorist group? "And it's all just paperwork?"

"Of course! And there's your fee, of course." Tom named a hefty sum. I looked around the caravan which was my office, and also my home for the last six months. I said yes.

After Tom hung up, my gaze strayed out of the plastic window to the caravan park at dawn. A honey buzzard hung over the hills, a brown silhouette in the early light. I've always loved big birds of prey; they hang in the air so serene, so unperturbed, it's as though they're moving differently through time.

Inside the shipping container, things shifted around. I couldn't make out any shapes, in the dark, but I could see movements: a strange sidling motion, creatures crisscrossing one another's paths.

Light caught them as they came closer to the doors. Huge flanks, covered in golden fur.

My legs turned to absolute water. *But seriously*, my brain kept yelling, as though any answer would help me, *why am I here, please?*

Flash back to a day ago, with Tom on the phone, again, telling me to meet a truck in Warminster.

"You said it was all just paperwork."

"Yes, but you need to come here to *sign* the paperwork! With the goods. Meet the supplier, bring him to Salisbury Plain. I'll send you the coordinates."

I met the supplier in a supermarket car-park. His container lorry overshadowed all the cars. I climbed up to the cab to join him, a muscular old guy in ripped jeans, gray hair like a bristle brush.

At my direction, we drove off, the high cab allowing me to see over hedges to the wide flat space beyond. Grass for miles, green and gold, spattered with poppies. Such an odd place, Salisbury Plain; there are rare birds there, and orchids, because there are no hikers or campers. And there are no hikers because from time to time, the army uses the Plain for live firing practice and tank maneuvers. A torn-up paradise.

We were in the sun, but the far side of the Plain was dark under mulberry clouds. The truck wobbled, as though its cargo was shifting.

"Turn here." I pointed to a track, past a sign that said MINISTRY OF DEFENCE: NO ENTRY.

"This is just a drop-off spot, isn't it?" asked the supplier. "To unload 'em. It'll be Porton Down getting them in the end, won't it."

Porton Down, Torture Town, as the animal rights protesters chanted. The army's chemical weapons testing base, only five miles from here. So it could be animals in the back of the lorry, test subjects. A lot of the things Tom had bought through me, recently, had been beast-like.

The lorry wobbled again. Very heavy animals.

I remembered that speculation later, as I stared, frozen by fear, at the shipping container, and I thought: *thank the Lord, at least they can't get out.* There was no ramp, they'd need a ramp.

A great paw extended out between the doors, reaching down from the vehicle, trying to find ground. A cat's paw but monstrously large, big as a beach ball.

A head emerged above it, massive and sharp-beaked. It was so different from the paw that I thought another animal had crowded in behind the big cat. Then I saw the sinuous neck that connected them, where the ruff of feathers turned into fur.

I wondered whether it was too late to run.

Four hours ago, we'd parked near some abandoned army huts. The ground around them was scored through to the chalk by tank tracks.

While we waited for Tom to arrive, my conscience pricked me. *Porton Down, Torture Town.* "So, are they animals? To test weapons on?"

"Ha!" The man slapped the wheel in amusement. "They're animals. But not for testing. They're the weapons, aren't they?"

I wondered how. War elephants? Battle cattle?

From the high cab, across the flat plain, I saw a dog and two people approaching. One was Tom, striding in a brown raincoat, the other a small round woman I didn't recognize in a long loose dress. Their dog didn't look like a military dog; it was flat-faced, short in the leg and barrel-bodied. Perhaps it was a French bulldog. Perhaps it was the pet of the woman, she didn't look military either.

The distance, and the sullen sky, did strange things with my sense of perspective. The dog looked closer than the humans, as the creature barged across the grass ahead of them. Then as all three grew nearer, I saw they were level with one another, and the dog was as tall as a cart-horse, a gargoyle sprung to life. Tom seemed unconcerned by his awful companion, although it could have fitted its jowly jaws round his head quite comfortably.

I locked my cab door, but couldn't find the words to warn the driver.

The horrific trio drew to a halt. Tom was checking his phone. The dog was so close to him it could have been reading the screen over his shoulder. I caught the eye of the woman. She patted the beast, actually put out a hand and ruffled its shoulder, possibly meaning to reassure me.

"Libby! Come down!" called Tom.

I wound down the window an inch. "Do I have to?"

"Got to sign the paperwork!" Tom waved a clipboard. "Are you scared of the dog? You shouldn't be, you brought him here." Tom kept talking as I racked my brains. "He's a Gert Dog of Somerset, a guide dog." Somerset? I'd driven a horsebox up from Nether Stowey, six months ago. I'd never dreamed this creature was inside it. "One of our new assets. Gert Dogs have been protecting humans since time immemorial. We're already using him for pathfinding, soon he'll be carrying supplies into live situations."

Tom's speech sounded like an advert. I guessed that he'd brought the animal here to show it off to me, to try it out on a member of the public – albeit one who'd signed the official secrets act. I wondered if the Dog would remember the smell of me. I opened the door of the cab carefully, so as not to attract the attention of the Dog.

The Dog was attracted. I saw it lurch towards me, and swing its head at me, then a slab of soft cheek knocked me off the side of the cab. I cracked my head on the way down.

The next thing I knew, I was on my back on the grass, staring at the sky. It was the color of slate. The clouds had caught up with us. My head hurt terribly, and a huge maw was descending to devour me. He remembered the scent of me, and he bloody resented me for dropping him off here.

"Oh hey!" I hear Tom protesting. "He shouldn't do that, Gwen."

"He's only playing," the woman called back. The Dog licked my face once, tongue like a hot wet bath mat, then turned his flat muzzle away from me, distracted. I levered myself to my feet and saw Gwen vigorously rubbing the beast behind one ear.

"Sorry about that." Tom clapped me on the back. "We source these fellers very carefully. They're not harmful – not Padfoots, not Black Shucks, none of that. These guys? Used to babysit kids on the Quantock hills." He handed me the clipboard. I saw some words in Welsh but they made no sense: *bird, dust, wine*. I signed in triplicate, in a wavering hand. I couldn't stop staring at the Dog. My fear was turning into fascination with its great dark eyes, the furred furrows on its brow. It had an anxious expression, completely at odds with its strength. I hoped it was having a decent life, here.

Tom turned to the supplier. "Now, how do we get them to their accommodation?"

The man shrugged. "Tell 'em to follow you there."

"They'll obey orders from us immediately?"

"If I hand them over to you. And you've got to be precise. And do it in Welsh."

"Gwen's our specialist, she speaks Welsh."

Mr Thomas looked the woman up and down. "You would. You look like my ex wife, you do. Touch of the, er–" He pulled an expression which could have meant *queer*, or *foreign*. That made me look at Gwen more closely. She had a pointed chin and a lot of curling hair, nothing I recognized as unusual.

"Let them out, then," instructed Tom.

The driver and Gwen walked round to the back of the lorry. The Dog made to follow them, trotting on its stumpy legs, snorting as it passed me.

"No, stay here," Gwen told it, not much above a whisper. It didn't sound like a command for a dog, more like a tactful suggestion to a drunk friend. "Stay with Tom, you know him."

The Dog gave a wistful whimper and gazed after her. It lowered its hefty haunches to the ground. I watched its ribs rising and falling. I felt a longing to sink my hands into that fur, so deep I couldn't see them. Was I concussed?

"How's things with you?" asked Tom.

"Oh, you know, not good." I'd meant to say 'not bad,' and he assumed I had.

"Fantastic."

Big drops of rain began to slap at us. I moved closer to the Dog, close enough for its body-heat to warm me. I let myself feel the tickle of his whiskers. It sniffed me with its squashed black nose.

From the back of the lorry came the graunching noise of bolts being drawn back. "It'll be tremendous if we can get these fellows working for us," Tom commented. "They defended King Arthur, you know. I mean, not these *actual* guys. But we could use a symbol, a bit of national pride."

Something in the container shifted, making the whole lorry bounce on its wheels.

I leaned into the Dog. It was a ridiculous instinct, but I was scared of the thing in the lorry, and the Dog was a *dog*, however big. I'd always liked dogs. It turned its head and squashed me in the soft folds of its neck. Tom was right, the Dog was a protector. I wanted to take him away from Tom. I'd always disliked the way police dogs, police horses, had their loyalty exploited, and ended up hurting people and being hurt. I'd turn the Dog loose to play on the whole of Salisbury Plain like a park, throw a stick for him somehow, let him romp around Stonehenge.

And then the doors of the shipping container opened. The huge paw was extended, the beaked head emerged. *Why am I here?* I thought frantically. My mind obligingly flashed back over the last week or so. *Oh, yes, it's my own stupid fault. And I'll probably be eaten.*

Two great creatures sprung out of the container and dropped down with soft thuds onto the grass.

The clouds, by then, had made the day dim as dusk, and the animals glowed. They were as long as Land Rovers, leonine and golden. Their bird-heads had an eerie serenity, their eyes as beady and fixed as their bodies were liquid and graceful. Their coppery wings were folded at their backs.

"Hey, hey," said the supplier, and they ignored him utterly.

They prowled towards Gwen. She stayed motionless. She tilted back her head, which only came up to their chests, to meet their icy inspection. One of them extended his neck down to meet her, like a swan dipping into the reeds, bringing his beak close to her face. It considered her and found her satisfactory. It stooped further and rubbed the side of its head against her arm. Was she an acceptable ally, or a convenient scratching-post?

The driver taunted her from a distance. "Ooh, they like you, don't they? Not surprised. The missus was one of you. That's where these came from, I got 'em in the divorce."

Tom frowned. "Gwen, give them an instruction," he called.

Gwen murmured to the animals. They looked to one another, then padded away across the chalk and the grass, gathering speed until they raced one other. Young, they looked, suddenly, kittenish. Impossibly quiet, given their weight. They chased round in a long loop and then back towards us, slowing to a powerful nonchalant trot.

"I wonder how they'll show up on radar," Tom mused aloud.

I thought, in a great rush: Tom can't have them. I didn't want him to have the Dog, but he absolutely mustn't get the griffins. My fist tightened on the Gert Dog's coat, for comfort.

But before I could formulate any plan, the Gert Dog barked at them.

It was a sudden deafening volley of noise, deep as the rumble of a train. The griffins' wings shot up and out from their backs, in a blaze of copper, and loudly and powerfully began to beat. Air buffeted me like the downdraft from a helicopter. The Dog sneezed and barked more. The griffins beat their wings more, lifting their bodies off the ground and carrying them backwards. Their front paws were raised for defense, their claws were out, heraldic figures come to violent life.

And that was when my terror became so immense that someone *else's* life flashed before my eyes.

I knew I was Drudwas ap Treffin, although I had never heard that name before. I stood resolute under the fierce gaze of three griffins. My wife handed me some ribbons that looped around their necks. She was small and wide and gorgeous and looked a lot like Gwen. I leaned in towards my new pets and murmured instructions to them, but even as I spoke the words I didn't understand them.

I released the ribbons and they took to the air, all three at once, with a wind that nearly toppled me.

And from afar, I saw King Arthur riding towards the field of battle, where he had agreed to meet me. I couldn't lose. No man could survive those beaks, those claws.

I bided my time, then I walked out onto the field. My head was high, I was cocky. I wasn't expecting a fight, only to find the remains of the King, after my Adar Llwch Gwin had done my bidding.

I couldn't see anything but grass. I looked up and all three griffins were hanging overhead, looking down, almost motionless. I was disarmed, un-knighted. I was the rabbit caught in the hawk's regard.

The first of my griffins gave a high keen screech as it spiraled down to attack its master.

And then rain, splattering on my face, revived me. I had fainted. The griffins were further off, play-fighting, first dashing at one another then lifting off for a short, tumbling bout in the air. I was resting against the flank of the Gert Dog, who had ceased barking and laid obligingly down on the grass to act as my sofa.

"That's a problem," Tom snapped.

"Oh, I'm fine…" I protested.

"Won't they be able to work together?" asked Tom.

"They've only just met," said Gwen. "He's a dog, he's going to bark at a cat. Give it time."

I heard an awful metallic screech, but it wasn't the griffins. The supplier was bolting shut the shipping container. When he was done, he spread his arms out and addressed Gwen. "Give us a hug, then."

"Why?"

"Traditional, isn't it? They're supposed to be passed from wife to husband. And so on. Come here and we'll show them you're the boss, now."

"No need for that. I'll tell them."

His leer turned sour and he dropped his arms. "I'd like to see that."

Gwen called out a few words, and one of the griffins, I swear, turned its head in quick recognition and paused in its frolics. Then it inclined its head, lowering its terrible beak. Gwen returned the bow. Then both griffins looked over at their former owner with what felt like murderous disdain. He took a few steps backwards.

"Pretty good," said Tom. "Okay, let's try something else. See how they interact with an unfamiliar civilian." So I was going to be a guinea pig. I held onto the hot side of the Gert Dog, and got to my feet. "Come and say hello. You speak Welsh, don't you?"

I could turn him down, tell him it wasn't part of the deal, but this was my best chance to act and foil his plans. As I approached them, their scent came in waves on the wind, the hot metal smell.

"Say something to them in Welsh," Tom commanded. "See if they listen."

"Do you speak Welsh?" I asked.

"No point, is there? I'll learn it if we can't teach these things English."

"Bore da," I said. Say hello to the murderbirds! They both looked at me. I have never felt so pinned by a gaze. They stepped towards me, moving sideways like wary foxes. "Croeso i Loegr!"

A definite flicker of attention in their eyes. But even if they could understand me, I couldn't think of the right words. *Renounce killing!* They were bloody lions crossed with eagles, what did they know except killing? *Have you considered not being used as a weapon?*

That was miles beyond me. The Welsh I learned at uni was very rusty. I needed the Welsh words for *trust, danger,* and *war,* and could only remember *portion of chips, disco,* and *lesbian.*

I tried something simple. "Y dyn yna draw..." *That man over there.* "Y gôt frown." *The brown coat.* I was going to make a pig's ear of it. "Peidiwch â gwrando ar y dyn hwnnw." *Do not listen to that man.* I could at least make Tom's job harder. "Dyn drwg." *Bad man.*

They both turned to stare at Tom.

"Brilliant!" he crowed. "Ha! Did you make them do that? Now tell them to look over the other way!"

I caught Gwen's eye and she shook her head a fraction, her mouth a tense line above her pointed chin. *Stop it.*

"Braf cwrdd â chi, da boch chi," I hastily concluded. *Nice to meet you, goodbye.* The catbirds sloped away, indifferent to me.

"Good start! Gwen, send them over to Tidworth," instructed Tom. "It's eight miles, are they good for that?"

"Easy," said the supplier. "If you lose 'em, just leave a couple of sides of beef out for them."

Then Gwen instructed the griffins. I couldn't hear a word, but it seemed to me more of a conversation; they put their heads on one side while she spoke, then puffed up and screamed like seagulls in response. Then the beasts bounded off together, half running and half gliding. Careless giant gilded kittens, unbothered by the rain.

Tom shouted: "My God, look at them! Imagine them, coming down at you out of the sunrise. Imagine the damage they could do!"

I heard the Gert Dog growl softly like an idling motorcycle. He wanted to chase the griffins.

Tom walked the supplier back to the cab. I only heard one word in three. I think Tom was asking if the griffins would breed big enough for men to ride on. The supplier's reply was louder, angry: "You don't get to breed them! You get the males, I keep the females. You want more, you come back to me." I thought of lonely catbirds, keening to one another 300 miles across the Bristol Channel. The cab door slammed, the lorry rolled away across the Plain.

Tom called to Gwen, "Are you coming with me?"

"I'll wait here a while, in case they circle back."

"All right. Make the Dog take me over to Fittleton, I'll grab a Land Rover from there."

Gwen whispered in the Dog's ear, stroked the back of its neck. Tom held out a hand for me to shake – "Good working with you again, Libby!" – and the Dog led the man off into the rain.

"Come on." Gwen took me over to the corrugated iron porch of a nearby army hut. We sheltered there, and watched gleaming wings flashing in the sheeting wet. The griffins were following Tom, following the Dog. My head throbbed. I hadn't saved any of the animals from Tom. I realized I had no way to get home.

"I'm sorry I brought them here," I told Gwen. At this distance, the griffins were as delicate as two butterflies tangling over a field of cornflowers. "I won't do it again, I won't do any more jobs for Tom."

She didn't look at me, but her voice softened. "Don't be too hasty. And don't worry, Tom always gets the wrong end of the stick. Like he did with the Dog."

"The Dog's amazing." I thought I might be a bit in love with the Dog.

"The Dog's a mixed bag. Tom's been misled, there's no one breed that's Gert Dog. They're all part Padfoot, or Barguest."

"What, the Dog's *dangerous?*"

"He'll help to guard the innocent. But he might just lead a bad man astray."

I thought of her muttering into the Dog's ear. I hadn't heard her say 'Fittleton.' "How far astray?"

"Reckon he'll lead Tom into the woods by West Lavington. And by the time he comes out, Tom won't be able to see the griffins anywhere."

"Oh…"

"There's a river in that wood, as well. Tom might fall in, for good measure."

I could still see the flash of gold wings in the slate sky. They were spiraling, climbing higher.

"He'll catch them again, surely." I knew how much he'd paid for them.

Gwen chuckled and it was a sound as warm as fur. "But the griffins, they won't work for Her Majesty's army. They won't use their claws for its whims, or patrol these shores. And the *Dames Blanches* may summon the Beast of Gevaudan for France, but I doubt it will fight at anyone's command. The beasts are returning, but why would they work for human malice?"

The griffins were high, now, and hovering. Hawk-like, they held their spot despite the wind. I wondered if they saw prey below: cows, or deer, or us. They were like honey buzzards, in that their steadiness made them seem out of time. But while buzzards looked, to me, ten times slower than other birds, the hanging griffins could have been hundreds of times as slow, as big, as old.

I guessed that Gwen could explain what I saw when I fainted. "What happened to Drudwas ap Treffin?"

"He wished to fight King Arthur, and told his griffins to attack the first man on the field. He thought Arthur would be first. But Arthur was held back…"

"By Drudwas' sister!" It came back to me in a rush.

"Yes, she was Arthur's mistress."

Two women, loving two opposed men: Drudwas' wife, giving him the griffins; Drudwas' sister, foiling his treason. "And Drudwas reached the field of battle first. The griffins slew him."

She nodded. "They keened with misery, at killing their master. It was a misfortune to all. Now, I think you could do more good if you keep working with Tom. Especially if I keep working with him, as well, and the two of us work together."

I was pretty sure, now, that she wasn't human, but she felt more trustworthy than Tom.

"All right, I suppose. Yes."

"I'll be tied up in a lot of questions this week, but I could meet you next Friday? Somewhere private."

I wondered what her home could look like. I imagined a low-beamed greenstone home, half cottage and half earthwork, with a roaring fireplace and the Gert Dog slumbering on the hearthrug. "Yes, please."

She stood, and took a step into the rain, which didn't touch her.

"Wait," I asked, "What instructions did you give the griffins?"

"To never harm a human, nor ever again follow their commands. Maybe I should have been more straightforward. I don't know if they understand correlative conjunctions. Damn."

She moved off towards Fittleton. I took out my phone to call a cab, and then realized I was on private army land and would have to walk back to the road, at least, so I watched the skies and waited for the rain to stop.

The Volcano and the Butterfly
NARRELLE M HARRIS

Rumbling from deep, deep down in the red-hot dark. Molten rock churns and stirs. It pulses like a heartbeat. It burns with adoration.

But as much as the volcano longs to shout its love – to the high, high stratosphere and the fertile plains below, to the air and the seas and the world entire – it keeps its passionate cry contained.

For the volcano is in love with a butterfly.

The volcano adores the butterfly's endurance despite its fragility. The volcano loves its love's vivid orange wings, like the vibrant glow of the volcano's heart, limned in black and white. The volcano sees its own patience in the elegant, unhurried flap of wings as the butterfly visits one flower, then another. Up the flanks of the enamored volcano, it flits.

The butterfly rests on a cool stone near the summit and the volcano holds holds holds its breath, protecting the butterfly with inaction.

The butterfly's long legs, its little feet, dance. They taste the volcano's flanks. The butterfly flutters and tastes and tells the volcano with this dance that it thinks the volcano, too, is beautiful.

The volcano is old and will be older yet before its heart grows cold. But centuries from now, it will still be in love with that tiny, brief life, for whom it held its breath.

Butterflies are ephemeral. Volcanos less so. But the love that the lasting has for the fleeting is like the breath of god.

Eternal.

the goombees
(are moving in down the block)
TONY RAUCH

The Goombees are moving in down the block.

I watch from my window.

Tall, thin, long and stringy, they unpack their car, carrying in only a few boxes. Just several lonely old boxes. Not even very big boxes. That's it – just a few – all they have, all they need, all they want, or all they're allowed.

They cast long, skinny shadows, shadows that grow up and over their new house, shadows that twist snake-like in the yard like shadows of branches. They are pale, washed out in the summer morning sun, lurching into a new, uncertain world – a strange new place they'll try to make their own. They sway like plants in the water, flowing gently, light and free, as if gravity has no hold on them, as if sprung from obsolete cages. Their arms and bodies slurge in small waves like so many inchworms, as if a weight in them is sloshing back and forth, waiting to get out.

I'd never seen one in person before, but sure enough, they look like stretched-out versions of regular folk. From all the way down the block, they look like strings – twelve feet tall, their many long arms wiggling from the sides of their thin, long, wormy bodies. The last one stops and looks down, searching around in the grass. Several super long fingers wiggle out from their back like ten-foot long rubbery noodles. The tips of these long whips split to open, revealing three fingers. These rubbery tails reach to the grass and begin picking up smaller items and raising them, then turning to bring them inside as well.

The Goombees are moving in down the block. I watch from my window.

All is silent. The entire world stands still, as if waiting. I look around and find several others are looking out their windows too, watching and waiting, as if expecting something to happen. But nothing does happen. The Goombees go inside their new house. And that is that, all there is to it. They duck to undulate inside, folding themselves into the now-ridiculously low and small door. The door closes. The world is silent.

(Only a few boxes. All they need. That was it. That was all there was. Maybe only a box apiece. And small boxes at that. Yeah, maybe that's all they'd let them have – decided by people who think they know what's best for others, who believe people can't think for themselves, who believe they know what's best for you, who use their speech only to advance themselves while keeping those who threaten them down. Or maybe the Goombees just don't need a lot. Maybe they're more evolved than us, above all the pettiness, better than us, past all that, more content to just be, to just think, to just enjoy.)

Several mysterious men step out of a house in the middle of the block. They hang out near the door, milling around on the path to the sidewalk. They seem to watch in disapproval. They stand still, but have a sense of movement about themselves. Even in their stillness it feels like they're moving, even though they are not. They have a weight to themselves, an air of menace. You can tell that just by looking at them. A silent protest. Several tough guys. Judgmental, as if only they know what's right for you and true, even though they just make it all up as they go along, making it up to suit their own purposes. They seem over-filled, as if needing to be emptied out. I wonder if they'll try to convince me to join them. I wonder if they'll compliment me, then lie about the Goombees (the ol' one-two punch. A combination. A combo platter. A flurry of words – compliments, then put-downs, compliments and put-downs, compliments and put-downs, pushing others away). I wonder if I'll go along with them. Or if I'll be strong enough to not go along with the crowd. I wonder if I'll be strong enough to think for myself.

The Goombees are moving in down the block.

I watch from my window, holding my breath as they disappear into the protective shell that is now their very own charming Cape Cod style suburban rambler.

After a few moments a Goombee steps out, flowing to their car, a shiny baby blue number from the late forties – lots of room in back for themselves to fold into and uncoil, I suppose. The Goombee walks to the street and stops beside the car, partially hidden behind it from my view. One of those wiggly tail things reaches around from its long, thin back and wiggles itself into the car, through a thin crack in the back passenger-side window. A moment later it pulls something out, a yo-yo or something. It looks up, as if sensing I'm watching from my window. It watches me for a moment – watching me watch it. Then it rises to step over the car, folding itself over, flipping over the car effortlessly, long arms and legs flopping to the other side as if a drawer of silverware spilling out then collecting itself in a graceful, spectacular, unexpected waterfall motion – wiggling up the block to me in a rolling, poetic manner which is impossible not to watch, impossible not to appreciate. It's probably not polite to stare, but I do. I suppose I'll get used to it, but who knows. Maybe one day I won't even notice it at all. I suppose I'll eventually return to the couch to resume my bloat. But for now the Goombee has curled itself into a great ball and is rolling up the block – long arms curling at its sides to form a frame, like a giant basketball, its striped T-shirt and long shorts fluttering in the morning breeze, looking all the more out of place.

The men in the middle of the block stare as well, their bodies moving around to follow as the Goombee rolls up the block, looking like a great wicker ball or a big piece of playground equipment that children would want to climb all over.

It comes up to my lawn and stops at the edge of the street, unfolding itself in one motion. It stands still, but its arms wiggle at its side as if long hair circling in clear water.

I can't move, can't even feel anything. Nothing at all. All is numb and quiet, as if the world has folded flat, drained itself of all life and color, receded until only the Goombee and me are left – me clutching the curtain, the Goombee's arms swirling in long noodley motions. It just stands there, then one long, thin, hose-like tail rolls out from its back, uncurls straight up in the air, the tip of which bends to wag about high above in the breeze as if to wave to me, as if to tease me with it.

Another of those tail things unfurls from its back and wiggles to me, waving and undulating in the air as if a snake in water. It wiggles past me, above me, to the roof. Oh no, it's going to mess with my TV antennae, my reception, my coveted television reception. No. No. Please no. Not that. Anything but that. It leans to stretch, careful not to touch my lawn. It really stretches, stretching over my yard, growing thinner and thinner, like a rubber band stretching, reaching up to the roof, an impressive length, a long lean. Then slowly it wiggles back, coiling back over the yard, setting something gently in the grass – a Frisbee and awesome balsa wood glider. Then the Goombee turns, curls in on itself, and rolls back up the block again – its impossibly long, thin arms forming that open-framed ball, rolling it along. The Goombee rolls onto its new yard, pops up, ducks and flows itself into the dark rectangle of door to disappear into its new home. The now tiny-seeming door closes, the dark rectangle turning to a light tone.

That Frisbee and glider had been stuck on my roof for over a month. I really missed playing with them.

The Goombees are moving in down the block.

Halyards of Black and Silver
DAN FIELDS

Late morning blows a steady eight knots west-southwest, carrying six brown pelicans out toward Trinity Bay. Shoals of croaker swim below, unaware of imminent death. Roman augurs on the Aventine Hill would have called those gangly birds a doubtful auspice. Today, a hungover fishing guide out of Smith Point blesses them. Desperate for a change in luck, he hopes they'll dive and work the big trout into hook-blind frenzy. Meanwhile the skipper of a Vietnamese crab trawler damns them for scavengers, his Huế inflection soggy with coastal Texas drawl.

Calli watches from the marina, where the masts of small pleasure boats cluster like anodized aluminum weeds. Her eyes are not on the birds but on the moving tide. It's perfect sailing weather, but she has work waiting. She'll make time later for sunning and picking her old guitar, but relaxation has become a luxury. Winning it back requires readiness for storms even worse than local folks have learned to fear – shrieking deluges more ancient and vast than humans can remember. It is a common lot shared by Calli and her sister sirens, wherever along the world's far-flung shores they may be, and not one they can discuss with the humans they resemble only in the most superficial aspects. Calli herself isn't prepared to sail against such fury, but she will be soon.

Tall, taut-skinned and hazelnut brown, Calli stands out among her neighbors in the tiny harbor town. Gulf climate weathers a body, and most of the marina's live-aboard tenants are pushing middle age at least. Nobody giving Calli the once-over would put her a day over thirty-three, and she passes for younger on cloudy mornings. Her hair never lightens in the sun. It only reddens a bit, spoiling the illusion of true black. She's not a being made up of absolutes, although there are certain constants. When her shorts hike up on her thighs, no tan line shows.

"High time to scrape that bottom!" calls an old marina lifer. Calli doesn't look up from inspecting a clean bare section of her boat's bow. The man ambles alongside. He has the same number of teeth as fingernails – not many, after decades of half-drunk boatbuilding. His keen sailor's eyes appraise her craft's accumulation of barnacles and scum at the water line. "Ain't dove in years, m'self. Reckon my brother'n-law could haul it for you."

Calli smiles, politely indulgent. It's no come-on. Anyone could see her boat needs a bottom job. He watches her climb back aboard and start varnishing a companionway slat she cut and sanded herself. A black-crowned heron darts along the hot dock, a wriggling fish in its beak. After a few silent minutes the old-timer wanders away.

Calli has no intention of paying for a clean hull. She'll dive and scrape it herself, late at night when the bay cools down. Her eyesight is acute underwater, needing only moonlight. She can stay under as long as the work takes, all night if necessary. For now her goal is getting the prow finished. Waiting for the varnish to dry, she flexes the sun-warmed soles of her feet. A hand slides off her knee to caress a curl of rope on the deck – the end of the mainsail halyard. The fibers alternate in contrasting shades, raven-dark and lustrous pearl-gray.

Two years ago a screamer of a hurricane upset the marina, nearly tearing Calli's boat off its moorings. It wasn't the kind of levee-buster that sank New Orleans, but it came far enough inland to muss the landscape in three counties. Calli felt it hard, same as the natives. Once the essential boatyards came back into operation, next to be rebuilt were the booze joints. Not all survived, but sudden scarcity in the licensed beverage market made any dive with half a roof respectable enough for public gathering.

Calli avoids mentioning that the hurricane might have been sent specially for her benefit. It's not the sort of boast to win her friends in the storm-whipped community. With intimate partners, now and then, she'll allude to a strained relationship with a father she seldom sees. But explaining something like a hurricane as part of a private family argument is a challenge. Gestures – even affectionate ones – coming from a regular dealer in floods, earthquakes, and monsoons can be hard to recognize.

Only one of Calli's lovers knows that the meticulous restoration of her sailboat involves these precarious family ties. Calli is proud of the work for its own sake, of course, having never been without a seaworthy vessel of her own. But this craft is special, its resurrection a supreme defiance of the great storm-summoner. One day soon she'll return to the ocean's turbulent heart, hoping for fair winds but braced for deadly gales. Calli has a hereditary capacity for violence and will howl against the tempestuous forces that bore her into being, should they threaten once to blow her back to oblivion. She's a creature of mighty voice and will. Others of her species walk the earth with no aim but to make horrific displays of their power. Calli chooses lyric sweetness, tempering dreadfulness with elegance – a quality inherited from the maternal side.

Calli steps through the lopsided doorway at Morgan's, a bayside pub refurbished in corrugated tin. The northwest corner, dubbed the 'lee corner,' is the only section of original wood left intact by the storm. Guests of the owner may sit in the lee corner. Mostly it's an empty shrine. Tim, the mean-eyed salt who runs the bar seven days out of seven, lifts his chin in a half-nod of greeting. He's busy pouring spiced rum shots for a pack of sun-bitten, charter-cruising yuppies. The sooner he liquors them up, the sooner they can move along to someplace more fashionable where cocktail waitresses deal out liberal sass and spill from their Daisy Dukes. Morgan's is a serious bar that mariners and fisherfolk use for serious drinking. Nestled among glossy marina restaurants and bargain bayhouses, it offers grudging hospitality to tourists and passers-through. Tim stocks a practical supply of odiously trendy drinks alongside the real spirits, but refuses to install a kitchen. Those in the mood for second-rate pizza, wings, and popcorn shrimp can buy their drinks at Ruthie's. For good oysters, they can put on socks and shoes and dine at Admiral Benbow's or the Shell Club. Morgan's is and ever shall be Morgan's, for those who value loyalty and generous pouring above friendly atmosphere. Tim's only concession to entertainment is the Thursday open mic night. Started as a one-time tribute to the owner's late mother (and the pub's namesake), the tradition stuck. Regulars appreciate this variety in their sacred ritual of sorrow-drowning. Even Tim's mask of docile hostility slips when a gifted performer takes the stage.

The tattered guitar slung across Calli's back on a woven hemp strap is a cheap catalog model, its true character in the hands that play it. Calli doesn't have the genius of Willie Nelson, Sister Rosetta Tharpe, Lita Ford, or Richie Havens. Calli has tricks, and is proud of them. Because she never misses a music night, Tim always lets her go on third. There's nothing mystical in that. It's good gig strategy for making an impression.

First onstage is a willowy coot who uses a broken cello bow to coax haunting grief-songs from a handsaw. He looks like a man who could tell strange tales of the world, but lets his humble instrument weep them out for him.

Calli's attention drifts during the second performance. She knows many faces in the room and seeks new ones. Several pairs of eyes follow her with unrequited interest, mostly from a sallow cluster of drinkers in the southeast extreme of the shack – the lee corner's chilly opposite. Calli has trouble breaking the gaze of a short, full-figured woman whose hair has all but fallen out, but whose flashing stare pierces the dim humidity. Looking away with effort, Calli continues the search for strangers.

Her gaze passes a few potential objects of desire before the correct choice appears. A young sweet-faced man, twenty-five with a tan only three days old, blinks a thrilling pair of eyes at her. Their color is chestnut. She'll offer odes to them. A youth of more common beauty would have surf-green or blue eyes. The antique brownness of this one makes him a rarer find, plainer but better. He sips whiskey, not always her favorite. She'll drink Irish, though, and orders a Bushmills neat as the second performer finishes – an autoharpist with shapeless ankles.

Calli drifts to the microphone without revealing her fascination. The chestnut-eyed stranger shifts in his chair, feeling the unkind gaze of the haggard woman in the cold corner. *Judith*. Calli fondles the woman's name in her mind. Judith flinches, conscious of Calli's momentary attention to her memory, then slouches back into torpor among her glum companions.

Calli draws half a breath, cocks her thumb over the low E string, and croons with practiced confidence. "Oh girl, my girl, don't lie to me…"

Several hoary heads nod approval. Chestnut Eyes registers nothing. The arrow meant for him is still in the quiver. The first number is a warning shot, meant to calibrate her aim.

"Tell me, where did you sleep last night?"

Something neither Kurt Cobain nor Lead Belly could have guessed is how closely this tune they popularized resembles a Thracian funeral melody, sung by sea widows long before the fall of Troy.

Calli weaves minuscule flourishes into the waltz-time, techniques invented on instruments older than any modern conception of Western music. Her languid vocals feature alchemical combinations of quarter- and half-tones that ancient bards murdered their loved ones to keep secret.

Judith and those near her sway lightly in unison, like drowned bodies in a sunken wreck. If Chestnut Eyes notices, he won't know to read any portentous meaning in it. They're not the ones calling him tonight. They dare not.

By the final refrain of "In The Pines," the small roomful of souls is in Calli's hands. True sorcery can begin. The whiskey's lilt inspires her to play the Irish love ballad "A Stór Mo Chroí," *Darling of my Heart*. The subtlety of seduction, her insidious power, is not in the lyrics Calli chooses but in her ability to fire them straight at a single unsuspecting heart. She's had equal success with a mournful chorus of "Brandy (You're a Fine Girl)," as with a courtly air of old Catalonia which hadn't been sung for over a century.

Sure as the Straits of Moyle, her Gaelic-dusted rendition draws the snare on Chestnut Eyes. Judith and company shrink into their shadowy nook as they feel the spell ignite, loops of song falling around the heart of Calli's new intended and pulling tight with gentle, inexorable force. One more song, whatever she feels like playing, and Calli will have him. She chooses a rare solo cut by Ronnie Spector entitled "Hell of a Nerve."

Chestnut Eyes drinks Powers whiskey, but he's not averse to buying Calli most of a bottle of Bushmills. Calli finds him at the bar with her first glass waiting. Polite introductions appear and promptly vanish. He works in tile and granite or something. His name is Luke or something. He's in town for a job in one of the high-dollar Seabrook homes, or some such. To Calli he's Chestnut Eyes, and his eyes are chestnut.

Calli's mysteries begin with her full name. Some have guessed Calpurnia, some Callina or Catalina, some Calliope. One cornball wit suggested "California." Wrong coast, wrong sea, wrong history. Calypso she might excuse, nearly as cheesy but more relevant to her ancestral bond with the sea. Only one special lover ever called her Callisto, a whisper away from correct.

Chestnut Eyes weighs his guess, orders more whiskey, thinks better of the game. Calli suits him. He's more interested in her bone structure and skin tone.

"Spanish?" he ventures. "Italian…no. Greek?"

She grins, regarding the ceiling through the bottom of her glass. A fish who doesn't believe itself netted has a particular savor. "Something like that," she replies.

"Maltese?" Chestnut Eyes may be another cornball, but not without nuance. Calli puts a hand to his bristled cheek.

"Close enough."

The conversation terminates when they arrive at the marina slip and clamber aboard her boat. A muse of libido, Calli kindles desire with ease, though heavy whiskey drinkers have challenged her in the past. Luckily Chestnut Eyes is a specimen who can talk the talk, drink the drink, and bang the gong.

The meeting of their bodies is quick and forceful, heating the small cabin like a clay oven. It's no small feat to fog a porthole on a blistering summer night.

At one point he falters, either fatigued or thinking too late of protective measures. Calli reassures him with an upward push of her hips. There's no hidden motive in her invitation. No seed planted here could sprout without the leave of forces more archaic than simple biology. Calli smiles impishly at the hot rush of him inside her. Even lacking generative ability, his power is impressive. As his rigid limbs uncoil, but before Tychon's gift leaves him, she throws a wrestling flip on him that knocks his wind out. The spring lines barely stop the listing hull from striking the dock. Calli pants like a running fox, gyrating in ways that would get a court-dancer of Nineveh stoned for obscenity. The lack of blood in her lover's brain boosts his second explosion almost to the intensity of her own.

Calli wants to linger in the stunned-fish gaze of Chestnut Eyes after the final throes are over, but he faints into sleep without breaking their embrace. She can't complain, having quick-fired him with such abandon.

Dawn's eye opens on calm waters. No seabird calls. Calli is the first living thing in sight. She slides up to the cockpit like a Shetland selkie. By the reckoning of antique lore, the Seal Folk would be something like second cousins to her.

Fitting the new companionway was sweaty work, requiring three or four trips to the mom-and-pop hardware emporium in town. Shopping local prevents judgmental scrutiny from one's neighbors. Only for new guitar strings does Calli reluctantly venture as far inland as the Gulf Freeway. Nothing against the music shop or the collective of placid stoners who tend it, but Calli feels anxious when she can't smell the sea.

The boat's crucial parts – hull, riggings, everything on which Calli may depend for survival – require more than common manual labor to restore their potency. It's not a mere raft for floating on. It must be armor, a second body as able as her own. Sea and sky turn against bold sailors at a whim.

Chestnut Eyes appears on deck, watching the sunrise while Calli brews bitter hotplate coffee. Ducking out of sight, she returns to find him perched in the cockpit playing a hand over the neat coil of jibsail halyard. It shimmers in sunshine, onyx threads tightly braided with veins of silver-white.

Seeing the flash of temper in her face, he drops the rope. Her protective anger is dangerous but momentary. She won't castigate the innocent for admiring a singular object which Calli herself prizes for its beauty. Even so, it's time for him to go.

She gives him sips from her chipped Mauna Loa coffee mug, a final intimacy before silently dismissing him. He squeezes her hip and whispers, "Catch you later." She smiles half a smile. *We'll see*, she thinks as he trudges up the dock and out the marina gate carrying his shirt and sandals.

Among the unlikely hookups, reckless lays, and occasional planet-splitting orgasms in her wake, only once did Calli consider sparing a lover from the usual ending, consecrating them to more than living wreckage.

Judith. Lovely Judith came closest – half-Latin, broad-hipped, pleasingly crass with a truly amazing laugh. Calli had spied her strolling the waterfront two days before they met, her salted black hair falling about her sinewy shoulders. Calli had ensured their meeting double-quick. Judith was just the hard-shelled romantic type to take in the Thursday night at Morgan's. Calli remembers every song she played to draw Judith to her; she's never used them again.

Judith drank with determination as Calli sang her love incantations. She filled Calli's sympathetic ears with tales of how life had let her down, including a father who was – on the finite scale of Judith's world – as turbulent and imposing a figure as Calli's own.

After Morgan's dismissed its congregation, the two women, filled with a gallon of sea breezes, wobbled hand in hand down the dock after hours to mingle below decks. Judith gave the full measure of her fury to lovemaking. In the fulmination of their entwining bodies, the certainty surged through Calli half a dozen times that this one would make a shipmate for life. But all the while the unfinished boat, which they were in the act of rocking, called its own urgent need to her. She couldn't stop picturing eyes painted across the prow, a watch against foul weather. Such eyes decorated the greatest of ancient ships, wrought in livid shades of purple and green and blood-crimson. It struck her, a carnal epiphany: what more ferocious eyes to adorn her vessel than those of Judith, moaning profanely in extremis? Calli called up a magic beyond the distorted limits of pleasure, enfolding her consciousness in the transmutation of Judith's…what? Offering? Could an offering be given unawares?

A chance impulse altered the course of Calli's will. She laced her fingers in Judith's mane of delicate graying black and pulled to anchor herself. A shiver and a howl from Judith rewarded her; the hair proved sturdy against a good haul. Their tension in her grip conjured thoughts of hoisting sail in brutal swells. It was obscene, Calli knew, to pass the chance of fitting her mast with halyards of such fine material, supple across her palm yet holding like braided iron against the monsoon's buck and yelp.

Hidden divinity whispered in Calli's breast, reaching the ears of the Fates. The cosmos accepted the sacrifice faster than conscious thought could take shape. Calli's hope of eternal companionship with mighty Judith foundered. Sweat-slick and perfumed with one another, the women carried on into the dark before dawn, heedless of the cruel ritual one had visited on the other. But Calli spared her lover's eyes.

Calli's faith in the cycle has wavered before, but never for long. Judith's eyes were dazzling, and still are, yet they were not her apotheosis. There were greater chestnut marvels to come, brought by another pilgrim yet undreamed, and now she has those.

Digging in a storage well better camouflaged than those where she keeps wood varnish, tools, and spare mooring lines, Calli finds a parcel bound in animal skin worn to parchment thinness. From it she selects two vials of powdered pigment, mixing them in a third bottle with seawater. It take an hour to get the proper tint, but once captured the hue matches her memory. Each coat painted on the prow brings it closer to perfection.

Chestnut Eyes, home for a shower and shave before resuming ordinary life, might have a week of good eyesight left. Starting with peripheral motion and depth perception, he'll suffer a degeneration so rapid that he'll barely know the difference between sunlight and shadow before the month is gone.

Calli takes a break, reclining under noon sun while her painted eyes dry. Resting a possessive hand on the tiller, she recalls running damp hands up the warm dusky thigh of a bygone lover, athletically shaped muscles rippling aside at her touch. The femur itself was monstrous, beauteously flawed with a subtle upward sweep at the lower end. Calli borrowed the shape and substance of the genuine article with dark prayers, an oblation made with herself as altar. The tiller needed no reshaping once it was fitted to the rudder. That stately bone was too perfect a model for Calli to give up for pleasure's sake. Yet once again she had been tempted.

A stray gust flaps the mainsail, prompting vivid memories of its creation. Even in Calli's primordial frame of reference, that act had crossed into the grotesque. Nobody could deny the beauty of so many shades, lovingly stitched and stretched in gorgeous gradients of descending tone. Unlike other sails it won't bleach in the sun; it will tan. Not all nights of love are lovely, and many mornings after are ghastly. Yet though she is no ordinary being, Calli rejects the name of monster that bygone ages have given her. She is glad to have her sailmaking finished.

The pelicans haven't returned from Trinity Bay. Calli hopes their hunting was good, and that they've roosted on a buoy somewhere.

Maybe a garish powerboat full of hook-and-line poachers drove them farther out in search of better quarry. She trusts in one thing – they'll come back ahead of any bad weather worth knowing about.

Over the week, the chestnut-colored eyes on Calli's prow evolve, their detail becoming so lifelike and intricate with successive coats that her neighbors expect them to blink. Their vigilance intimidates dockside wanderers who glance Calli's way, as they've always done when she works, but now keep a respectful distance. Though they can't divine its nature, the marina folk sense a remarkable presence in their midst.

Calli finishes most of the bottom job over two nights, diving for around three hours each time. She rests on the third night rather than tackle stubborn buildup on the boat's deep keel. Time is not exactly on her side – it's been an ominously quiet storm season, as if some shrewd and patient faculty has guessed her game – yet while there may not be days to waste, there will be enough. She wills it. Her will still counts for something.

Thursday comes again quickly, the highlight of a busy week. Just before sunset, Calli stows her tools and rags to replace a frayed B string which she fears may not have another chorus in it. Missed notes break enchantments.

The usual crowd gathers at Morgan's. Most of them never seem to leave. Calli arrives late to find Tim setting up the broken speaker, stool and stand. He swears openly into the live microphone. Calli reaches across the bar for a clean glass, immune to his glower of disapproval should he catch her pulling her own draft. Tim would never call in her tab, for reasons not even he fully understands.

The first eyes on Calli are not Tim's but Judith's. It's not difficult to imagine what a stunner she was before Calli. Her angled features frame a strong jaw, parted in a grimace instead of a grin. She's tragically incomplete without her banner of strength – the locks of hair that shone like onyx threads with veins of silver-white, what's left of it now dull and wispy like burnt cornsilk – a sad remnant of the godlike woman who was. Judith hunches, broken of any godhood, over the dregs of a sea breeze nursed for vitamins, not pleasure. Her taste will soon degrade to well vodka stingers, precisely for the numbness they impart.

This Judith, so briefly treasured, tracks Calli's movement through Morgan's like a carrion bird. Alongside the rest of her used-up company she's lingered here for weeks, ever since Calli sent her ashore at sunrise with a dry wordless kiss. The misbegotten promise of that kiss dried out and tumbled to the hot asphalt with the first magnificent skein of hair from her head. She spent her brilliance on a single night in the bosom of one whose music she dared not resist.

A man skulks against the far wall beneath a slatted window, the one whose brawny leg once flexed between Calli's thighs and inspired her craft's new tiller. Now his doctor marvels at the phantom ailment that put him first on a cane, then a forearm crutch. There's talk of amputation. It's nothing as grimly comprehensible as cancer, but a kind of horrific opposite. Unstoppable atrophy withers the bone in his upper leg, never spreading, as if something's been injected to dissolve it. As reward for his sacrifice he languishes in bewildered limbo, unable to shun the company at Morgan's.

Huddled farther out of the light are those who gave their skin for sails. The flesh left on them is puckered and rippled as if slow fire has eroded and melted them. This is the savage end of seduction. A shudder moves through them, compressing their occupied space to open a snug human-sized void. None of them looks to the doorway or welcomes the shambling new arrival, who drifts over to join them as he motions feebly for a double of anything, never mind ice.

Any friend of Chestnut Eyes would notice the change in his irises, faded from their former splendor to ashen slag. Waiting to take her place behind the microphone, Calli surveys the parts of him that gave her pleasure, weighing reasons to regret the choice against keeping him. As with Judith, as with others before. With his colorless eyes he's almost painfully ordinary, a caricature of mortality. His mouth coddles a glass of warm liquor with the sick need of a lamprey seeking warm blood in a drowned body. Calli can't connect the image to the gentle play of his lips over the rich unbroken umber of her breasts and belly. She's had the best of him.

Her supplicants, every one, sit in grudging worship with Chestnut Eyes as bewildered novitiate. Judith is high priestess, her status measured by how narrowly she fell short of untold glories upon ever-flooded oceans. The stolen facets of Calli's discarded ones draw them back to her, yet they have neither will nor voice to demand their essences back. She's taken more of them than they realize, and they won't warn any soul in danger of being transfixed by her art. Saving Calli's new favored one would gain them nothing but a little more space at the table. Jealous as each may be to regain favor, they can be no more than they appear – the spent ashes of passion.

Even in torment, those Calli has chosen blend with other loiterers and hard-luck regulars who've never known the pleasure of her. Most are weary and diminished from unrelated causes – recession, divorce, addiction, parole, insurance lapses, layoffs. The sea, for reasons of its own, draws a multitude of souls caught in adversity. They line the shores of the world in tight profusions. Nobody who ever went to sea is altogether good. It's a place for those with secrets.

On the stage an androgynous youth with ill-advised eyeshadow recites pornographic slam poetry with undercurrents of petulant self-harm. The crowd goes deader than usual. This kid is lost. No matter how many wind up stranded here, the tiny space makes room for newcomers every night. Calli has no coy smile for her joyless cult. She must be ready in case some alluring interloper may be on the threshold.

Calli has decided that her craft needs a worthy new name. The old one was too commonplace – it lent no strength, struck no terror, gave no protection against hurricanes. Calli has forsaken it. A craft unlike others must have a rare name to suit it.

When she finds the proper name, intones it and inscribes it on the transom, there's no telling what will happen to the pilgrim who gives it. Calli's companions have lent her all manner of physical pieces, but some consequences are yet unknown even to the workers of spells. The dwindling nature of a human soul with its name plucked away is a precious mystery, one that fascinates her terribly.

The old hippie, whose name is surely nothing more than Walt or Terry, maybe Earl, wins the bar patrons back with the sweet lament of his handsaw music. The familiar tune – something from a movie – settles the mood of the room.

Calli's heart jumps at a stray upraised voice. Tonight she's not been watching faces but listening to them, and she believes she's heard it. From out of the insect hum she believes she's heard it. A name, if not the rarest one then surely one that will do. Her legs tremble as she strides along the wall to the vacant stool. She wants it now, to take it by force and never mind who sees. But she may be wrong. She must hear it spoken again, whispered in her ear. She must try it for herself by sighing it multiple times against a bicep, a neck, the fragrant soft hair below a navel.

She nearly opens with Neil Young's "Tired Eyes," but meeting the anguished, half-sightless gaze of him who once was Chestnut gives her pause. Despite the reputation of her kind, her perversity has limits. The stranger appears at the bar – the one whose name she covets. After sizing up body dimensions, gait, and the ever-important contents of a cocktail glass, Calli slams an F chord and lets it ring before climbing to G and thence to A. The new selection, "Danger Bird," is as hip for the room as it is on-the-nose prophetic. In the marina just down the paved lane from Morgan's, ten wings churn the air. The pelicans are back, all but one who's gone missing for reasons none but its mates will ever know. The prodigal birds are disarranged by wind and water, struggling to fly with distended stomachs. They haven't bothered to wash the crusty fish gore from their bills.

To anyone schooled in the flight of seabirds, their squawking haste promises one bitch of a squall, or something meaner still, on its way and closing fast.

Calli can't wait.

For Ray.

Alfhild

BO STARSKY

Times change. This is obvious to most people, but *they* haven't lived for centuries. When you live that long those words take on a new meaning. Times change doesn't just mean the rates have gone up, or skinny jeans are in fashion again. To her, a hulder, it means that the world she grew up in is long gone and mostly forgotten. It also means that where her home was once surrounded by lush woodland, it is now surrounded by concrete and houses. In fact, her home is no longer there, not as she knew it.

Where there once lay a lovely boulder, there is a big building, a building she now lives in. Times may have changed but her magic and charm have not, men are still the same hundreds of years later.

A toss of her hair, a giggle, maybe a touch on the shoulder to get their full attention. Eye contact is all Alfhild needs to snare one in her spell. It was just that easy to get herself a space in this boring building made of stone.

Blending in is getting harder, long skirts and dresses no longer popular now that women wear trousers. Not that she's complaining, the view is very nice, she just can't participate or they'll all see her tail and her hollow back. In this age she can't just turn their superstitions against people; they've forgotten the old ways completely. None of them respect the fae folk anymore, they only use them as villains in their stories.

One thing about the current Norway Alfhild truly appreciates is the acceptance, especially the kind that means she gets to wake up to Hannah every morning. There's nothing more beautiful to her than the way the rising sun makes Hannah's dark skin glow and lights her curls up like a halo.

A century ago she didn't even know people like Hannah existed, but then the world opened up and she got to see all the different colors and shapes humans come in. Then three years ago she met Hannah, the human woman who has never once turned her back on her, even when she found out what Alfhild is. She just picked up the habit of playing with Alfhild's tail when they lay together at night or sit in front of the TV, gentle fingers combing out the tangles from the tuft of hair at the end.

Throughout her life Alfhild has seen many of her sisters settle down and marry good men, becoming human and growing old. Never once did the thought appeal to her. It never felt right, she just wasn't ready to change along with the world around her, but yesterday when Hannah asked for her hand in marriage, she said yes.

The Enfield Monster
DANNYE CHASE

Jessica was silhouetted in the light of the open door, a sundress and a sweater, delicate ankles above chunky shoes. Pearl was a little confused about the shoes – surely Jessica didn't own any like that. Jessica always wore heels that lifted her beautiful calves. And she seemed shorter somehow. Rounder.

But when the light caught Jessica's eyes, those Pearl recognized. Eyes like the swamp – brown and full of life. "Oh, darling," Jessica said, soft and sad. "Come in, you're getting blood on the doorstep."

Going into the house was like stepping through a mirror. Everything had been unfamiliar, but once inside, it all snapped into place. Here was Jessica's house, the new one, and there was Jessica herself. Orthopedic shoes, brown with dust. Curling hair, white with age. The house smelled pleasantly of fish and there were oily stains on Jessica's apron.

"I went home," Pearl said. She knew she had a sharp mournful cry, and struggled to keep it out of her voice. "Your old home."

"Enfield," Jessica said. "Oh, my dear, I haven't lived there in twenty years."

"I know." Pearl said. "Now."

"Your memory is getting worse," Jessica said. As Pearl followed her into the living room, dragging her heavy tail, Jessica picked up a framed picture from the mantel. "Is this the me you remember?" she asked, amusement in her voice. "I don't look much like this anymore. We've gotten old, my dear."

The woman in the picture was young, tall and slender, auburn hair like cattails, smiling in the sun. The picture had been ripped – half the frame was empty. "Do you remember him?" Jessica asked, in a darker voice. "My husband?"

"Yeah," Pearl said. "He tasted good."

"I'll take your word for it, dear. Sit down and let me see about that tail. Oh, good lord. Did they *shoot* you?"

"I scared them," Pearl said, a bit of mournfulness stealing into her voice despite her best efforts. "They said I was a—"

Jessica pressed a kiss to Pearl's rubbery head. "You're *my* monster, darling. Remember that, if nothing else."

Jessica hummed as she worked, getting Pearl settled into her chair, the broad, flat one covered by stains of oil and mud. The chair smelled like Jessica's house, though – lavender and roses. Jessica's old-lady voice warbled through familiar songs as she sewed up the bullet hole with quilting thread. It didn't hurt. Pearl had lost feeling in the end of her tail after cutting it too close with a train a few years – well, some years ago. Pearl wasn't sure how many anymore.

When the wound was closed, Jessica led Pearl into the bathroom with the extra-large tub. Thorough as ever, Jessica made sure Pearl was fully clean before getting out the old ice cream bucket that sat in the closet, filled with rich brown dirt.

"Wait," Pearl said, catching her arm, and Jessica let herself be tugged forward into a kiss.

This Pearl remembered. Right now she could even remember their first kiss, shocking to both of them, under a clouded night sky, in a field lit only by fireflies. They'd been so tentative, Jessica opening her smaller mouth above Pearl's larger one. Jessica had dissolved into giddy giggles, blaming the sour taste of raw fish for her flushed face. She'd gotten used to that taste, and quickly.

Jessica kissed her now, their lips moving by muscle memory. She sat forward, parting her legs, so that Pearl could reach between them with her short arms. Pearl drank up her little gasps, murmuring thank-yous against her mouth, for the bullet wound, for the bath, for the caring.

Later, when the dirt had been added to the tub, Jessica touched Pearl between her legs with hands just as silken and smooth as the mud. Jessica's hands were so familiar to Pearl that they seemed as much a part of her as her own large pink eyes, scaly legs, and six-toed feet.

"They said I was from outer space," Pearl said after the bath, as they skipped dinner and ate freshly-made cookies instead. *We're old enough,* Jessica said. *We don't have a bedtime either, you know!*

"Well, that's uncalled for," Jessica said, her mouth full of chocolate chips. Her cookies were the tollhouse variety. Pearl's were corn meal, sardines, and M&Ms.

"Said I had three legs."

"It's the tail."

"I know it's the tail." Pearl blinked her eyes in the dry air of the house. "I scared a little boy. And stepped on his foot. His dad had a shotgun."

Jessica had a look of pain on her face, the one Pearl hated, the one that made her mouth wrinkle. The first time Pearl had seen that look was some weeks after the field and fireflies, after the kiss. *It won't work,* Jessica had said. She hadn't called Pearl a monster, but Pearl had been terrified that she would. Pearl had run off alone, back to the swamp.

A year of misery had passed, of watching the farm house in Enfield, watching the corn be seeded, grown, and reaped. Watching Jessica's fiancé become her husband. Seeing Jessica for the first time with a black eye. Then with a broken arm.

Jessica had come back to Pearl one briskly cold night with that awful look of pain, and Pearl had thought she was seeking protection from her husband. Pearl was ready, willing to defend Jessica to the death, but that hadn't been what Jessica wanted. She'd still been too afraid of him. Instead, Jessica had kissed Pearl, pressed her down into the autumn leaves, whispering *I missed you, I missed you* against Pearl's mouth, her thick neck, the patches of dirt on her arms, her breasts, her waist, everywhere. Afterward, Jessica sat curled in Pearl's lap and they made promises to each other.

Jessica's husband had lasted another six months until he put Jessica into the hospital. Jessica came home after being discharged and he was gone. They both knew he wasn't coming back.

Their post-bath meal of cookies was interrupted by a knock at the door. Jessica had been expecting it, Pearl could see that in her eyes. Jessica moved quietly through the kitchen and opened the pantry door for Pearl, who shuffled in, pulling her tail around her rubbery feet, sitting on a cushion that had long since been molded to her shape. Jessica turned on the dim lamp inside the closet and shut the door.

Pearl had good hearing: you had to, in the swamp, where things were muffled. She could pick up Jessica's soft footsteps, and then heavy boots, the clink of handcuffs on a belt.

"We've had a report of a – well, something," the police officer said. Pearl couldn't remember his name, but he sounded familiar. "Wondered if you'd seen anything."

"You might want to be a little more specific," Jessica said, sounding amused. "Would you like a cookie?"

The police officer spoke next with his mouth full, so Pearl assumed that Jessica had offered him one of the chocolate-chip and not the fish. "Thanks. I don't know. A monster. An ape. Something with three legs."

"You know," Jessica said, conversationally, "I heard once that kangaroos look like they have three legs. Because their tail is so large, you see. They can even balance on it, I think."

"We're in Illinois," the police officer said, with a hint of condescension.

"We have zoos," Jessica said politely. "Perhaps you could call Chicago?"

"Sure. It was at your old house, is the thing. Just like there used to be, all the time, with the weird footprints. And there have been a couple of sightings around here, since you moved."

"Yes, I remember your visits well," Jessica said. "And I know what you're going to ask. So no, I haven't seen anything. I don't have a dog. I don't have a kangaroo, either, by the way. I don't have a chimpanzee. I don't sneak around the countryside in an ape costume scaring little boys and men with shotguns. That doesn't seem like a fun hobby to me."

Pearl caught her breath. There was a moment of silence, and Pearl could imagine Jessica's face, realizing that she'd slipped.

"I don't think I said that part," the police officer said. "Little boys and men with shotguns."

"Word travels fast," Jessica told him.

"Uh-huh." The officer's voice was suspicious.

Pearl heard Jessica sigh. "I suppose I could come clean with you," she said. "Officer Jones, I – maybe it's time."

There was a pause. Pearl scarcely dared to breathe. Because she knew that voice of Jessica's.

She knew that when her wife started speaking, she was going to have a hard time not laughing.

"I have a lover," Jessica said breathlessly. "A wild, swamp-dwelling thing with a tail and beautiful pink eyes. We've been lovers for sixty years! Mad, passionate, swamp lovers." Jessica's voice dropped a little lower. "I tell you, my dear, I have had mud in places you can't even imagine. Oh, yes – and it's a female monster. We're *lesbians.*" Jessica drew out the word, making it sound properly salacious.

There was a silence in which Pearl managed to muffle her laughter by shoving both hands into her wide mouth. Then Officer Jones said, "Thanks for the cookie," and Pearl heard his boots walk back out to the front door.

Jessica opened the pantry door a moment later and they both laughed. Jessica sat on the floor with her and then had a terrible time getting back up again.

Later, while Jessica swept the kitchen floor of Pearl's dirt, she said, "I was thinking." Her voice was light and wavering. "We could go somewhere."

"I'm having trouble remembering this place as it is," Pearl said morosely.

"Yes, but – you don't live here." Jessica reached out to brush away a crumb from at the corner of Pearl's wide mouth. "You live in the swamp."

"I have to live in the swamp. Dry out too much otherwise."

"I know. But what if we did it another way? Something new." Jessica looked brave, the way she did sometimes, like she was staring down the world, waiting for it to flinch. "There's land for sale in the next county over. There's a plot with a bit of swamp. I looked – good frog population. I know how fond you are of their singing. And I own this house, you know. I could sell it, get a mobile home. I could park it on my land – *our* land. Next to the swamp." She reached out and grasped Pearl's gnarled hand. "You'd never get lost, do you see? House, swamp, right next to each other. You'd just have to go from one to the other, you'd always be able to see where you were going, where you'd just been. You'd always be able to find me."

Pearl looked down at the counter, at the floor, at Jessica's tidy house, at Pearl's claw scratches on the linoleum.

"No little boys, no shotguns," Jessica said. "No train tracks. No Officer Jones."

"I'm going to forget you," Pearl said, and the words hitched in her throat, coming out with a sob.

"I know." Jessica's voice sounded even more mournful than Pearl's.

"I'm sorry," Pearl whispered. "I don't mean to. I don't want to."

"If you ever truly forget me–" Jessica squeezed Pearl's hand. "I'll still sit with you by the swamp. I won't leave you alone. I won't let you get scared. You might not know me, but you'll know you're with a friend."

There were muddy tears falling on the countertop now, and Pearl pulled Jessica into her arms. She was careful, she always was, with this fragile human body, now brittle with age. The dirt from their embraces never showed on Jessica's clothes. For sixty years, she'd worn only dark colors.

Moving to the new land felt like going on a vacation only to realize when you got there that it was home. Jessica had been right. The frogs did sing beautifully there. The fish population was plentiful, and Jessica drove her old pickup into town to buy anything else they needed to eat. There was a freedom here that they'd never had before, on their own land, on their own.

There was no one to see them at night but the fireflies. Jessica fell asleep on the grass one warm summer evening, with Pearl's shoulder as pillow. The next night, they had to drag out an air mattress to cushion their old bones, but it still felt like freedom, because Pearl didn't have to sneak off before the sun came up.

When it got hot during the day, they could both go into the house for lemonade, Pearl striding up the mobile home steps as plain as you please in broad daylight. They had their silly arguments out loud instead of in whispers. They made love loudly for the first time ever. Jessica took to walking about without her clothes on, just like Pearl. She bought a floating pool raft and laid on it while Pearl swam about in the swamp water.

Some nights Jessica popped popcorn and told Pearl memories like they were stories. Sometimes Pearl heard them afresh, and sometimes they were there in hazy form, just needing to be sharpened. The time they'd danced in the rain until Jessica got too chilled and Pearl took her into the swamp to warm up. The times they'd sneaked into town and set all the dogs barking. The occasional Halloween when Pearl had been brave enough to be seen beside her wife. The night Jessica had thrown her husband's ring into a corn field and turned her back on it. The night Pearl had given her a new ring.

There were sad memories – the due date of the baby Jessica had lost to her husband's beating. The night Jessica had met Pearl's family and they'd run her off. The night Pearl had told them goodbye forever.

Pearl's favorite story was the night they met. This one never quite faded out of her mind, like a track in the dirt that had been visited so many times that grass could never grow over it. It had been snowing. The frogs were hibernating, and it was so clear and cold that it felt like you could hear sounds from miles away.

Pearl was twenty, and Jessica nineteen. Jessica was alone in her parents' pick-up truck on a gravel road rutted with ice and snow. She'd been sober – Jessica was never much of a drinker – but she'd been young, a new driver on an old road. The pickup truck had skidded into the ditch and sunk into the snow, tail lights glowing red. There was no hope of moving it.

There weren't cell phones back then. No one knew about the accident. It started snowing again, heavily. Jessica had hit her head, and thought it was better to leave the truck and strike out for home. It was a stupid, addled decision. By the time the cold woke Jessica up fully, it was too late. She was lost in the snow, alone, and cold.

Pearl had seen the bright red taillights shining off of the road, and had come out of the warm water to investigate. She'd found human shoe-prints leading into an open field. Pearl's six-toed tracks trailed after them, half-erased by the drag of her tail. Jessica was wearing a red coat, and that was why Pearl saw her, sitting in a field and shivering.

Helping Jessica had been a stupid choice, they both knew that. Pearl was, in absolute fact, a monster. She was a cryptid, a creature, a demon, a beast. Jessica, upon seeing her for the first time, took her to be exactly that. There was no deception in their meeting.

But Jessica was different too. She was not sharp and acidic like some people, not harsh, and caustic, and afraid. Jessica was open and soft and sweet and lonely. She saw a monster and she wasn't afraid, even when she heard the monster offer her shelter in a half-frozen swamp, even when she heard the monster promise (and Pearl had never lived this down) not to eat her.

"You can't eat me," Jessica had observed. "I'm bigger than you."

(It had taken Pearl four days to eat Jessica's husband.)

Pearl met her soulmate that night in a snowy field. She took her back to the swamp, stripped off her clothes, coated her in mud and sat her under the water so that just her nose and mouth were clear. They sat that way all night, with Pearl's body heat keeping Jessica alive. They talked. They laughed. Pearl fell in love. She loved so strongly she thought the swamp might boil with it.

Jessica, telling the story to Pearl now, said she loved so strongly she was surprised she didn't melt all the snow.

That was something they had been afraid of, the love. But eventually they'd walked through that door and come out somewhere new, together. And even if nowadays Pearl didn't recognize the place they'd ended up, even if she didn't always know the name of the friendly white-haired lady with the fish cookies and soft kisses, she always knew where home was. Because home was not a place or even a person. It was a feeling of love, and that Pearl could never completely forget.

Give a Fish a Man
B F VEGA

There is an urban legend about the bodies. It says that if you dump a body in Lake Tahoe it will never be recovered. The water, they say, is too cold for bacteria. The lake is too deep for divers. The underwater caves and cliffs are treacherous. But some bodies are never recovered for an entirely different reason.

Marion VanZimm was a recently divorced woman somewhere over 40 but below 70. Her perpetually-dyed platinum curls and artfully reconstructed nose, lips, cheeks, brows, boobs, and buttocks made putting an exact age on her difficult. She enjoyed the bar at the golf club, the lounge at the ski resort, and the tennis instructor at the country club. Living on the California side of Lake Tahoe, she didn't gamble as much as she would have liked. She did not get the four-wheel-drive Rover in the divorce, and the snow-covered roads that led to Stateline and its casinos were not suited for her vintage Porsche. Still, when her girlfriend called one snowy February evening, inviting her to a bottomless mimosas brunch at the Montbleu resort the next day, she deemed that it was worth the trip from her cabin above Tahoma Meadows.

The next morning an alert CHP officer noticed swerve marks heading toward the icy cold lake near Emerald Bay and called in not only local law enforcement, but also the Tahoe Emergency Search and Survival unit. I had only been a member of TESS for a little over two months and this was to be my first lead assignment.

We reached Emerald Bay a little after two in the afternoon. The short winter day meant that the sun was already on its descent behind the Sierra Nevadas, and its long rays on the choppy water glistened invitingly. That was one of the things that creeped me out about the lake. Even in below-freezing temperature, there was something hypnotic about the waters. In my first week, I had done two separate ride-alongs where a tourist had inexplicably thrown off all their clothes and jumped into the glacial lake. We had rescued one and they were in the hospital for three weeks dealing with the after-effects of hypothermia. The other wasn't found. My mentor Bob Dressler, a local Washoe man, had said that sometimes Tahoe feeds. I had shaken that unsettling suggestion off.

As I stood there looking out, I saw a ripple out in the water. It seemed to be moving counter to the natural wind chop of the lake. I would have put it down to the wake of a boat but there were no boats anywhere near it.

I dismissed it as I went to join the sheriff. The crime scene technicians were taking photos and imprints of the tire treads.

"Good afternoon, sheriff."

"It's about time you Tess people got here. I have better things to do than to watch Tessie feed."

"Well, it's a good thing for you that Tessie is a myth then," I answered, giving him a big smile and batting my lashes at him.

Tahoe is a very wealthy and conservative area. The sheriff, an older fatherly man, obviously didn't know how to handle a hot young man like myself making eyes at him. He stomped off as my assistant Sarah joined me, laughing.

"I don't think he'll ask you to prom," she said.

"Meh, he's not my type anyway. Okay, first big question. A car drives off the highway and down this slight embankment, through this mud, and hits the water. Why didn't it stop?"

"Maybe the driver was asleep? And their foot was on the gas pedal."

I nodded, it was a plausible theory. I walked to the edge of the water again. Tahoe is a very clear lake. Today, with only a slight chop, I could see the bottom for maybe fifty yards out before the lake dropped down one of its many dramatic underground ledges. Even if someone had been asleep at the wheel, hitting the water should have jarred their foot off the pedal. And the depth of the water should have kept the car on the shore side of the ledge. I should be able to see the car, but what I could see were more tire marks heading straight for the ledge.

We would need to dive to recover the car. There was no rush though. If the driver had still been in it, they would have died from the cold before they died from the water. We headed over to the marina where a TESS boat was waiting for us. I donned my thermal wetsuit and by the time we got to the area above the ledge, I was ready to dive.

I had originally earned my diving certificate in the navy, doing deep-sea diving before discharging and switching to specialty aquatic search and rescue. I had dived in some of the most dangerous conditions possible; Lake Tahoe is not a highly technical dive, it is a highly dangerous one. The average depth of Tahoe is 1000 feet and the deepest parts have been measured at over 1600 feet, making it the third deepest lake in North America.

My diving partner and I started the long trek down. We were finally able to make out a blue shimmer that was a little more metallic than the world around it. We headed in that direction to find a vintage Porsche Boxster sitting on the lake bed as if it had been parked there. We swam over to attach a buoy on a long cord so that the rescue ship could locate us and drop the winching cables. As we waited, I swam to the driver's door to look inside for a victim. There was no one inside the car.

I was perplexed by this and started to look around, but the winching cables were dropping and I needed to help my partner secure the car for recovery. Right before we headed back up though I took one last look around. The sediment that had been around the car was disturbed from the recovery operation, but off to my left toward the center of the lake, I saw something that looked odd. I signaled to my partner to wait one more minute while I went to check it out. He continued to take underwater photographs of the scene since he had a moment. As I got closer to the odd shadow, I saw that it was two human footprints, as if someone had been standing barefoot on the bottom of the lake. Around them, I saw a large circle in the sediment. It looked like a huge coil of rope or cable had been laying there.

By the time we got back to our office that evening, the report had come through that the car in question belonged to Mrs Marion VanZimm. I took the manila file handed to me and the cup of hot coffee Sarah had ready, and headed to my office, to go over the report on the car.

So far not much had been found forensically, but no immediate damage was apparent. I shrugged and booted up my computer to see if the images we had taken of the lakebed had been uploaded yet. They were and I started clicking through them. For the most part, nothing remarkable jumped out at me, other than the unexplainable fact that a car had somehow driven itself almost a mile into the lake and then lost its driver. I was just about to give up and get more coffee when I saw a faint shadow in one of the photos. In the picture I am looking at the footprints, but beyond me there was a dark smudge. I wondered if it was maybe my partner's thumb. I maxed out the resolution and zoomed in. The item was still blurry, as if it had been moving in the second it took to take the picture. It looked a lot like a snake, but there are no aquatic snakes in Lake Tahoe.

I was so riveted by the picture that I jumped and squealed like a kid when there was a knock at my door. I looked up and was rewarded with a view of Connor Dressler, nephew of my mentor and co-member of Tess. He was laughing at me.

Connor was not my usual type; I usually preferred my men a little older. Connor was my age but looked younger than his twenty-eight years. Smooth tan skin and dark eyes spoke of his Washoe blood, while his ginger hair and beard proclaimed the Scottish mother that sent cookies to any newcomers in the office.

I was crushing on Connor hard, but I knew better than to start anything at work. I had learned that lesson the hard way.

"Hey, what's up?" I squeaked out, cursing my voice's tendency to break during high-stress moments.

"We were heading out to grab drinks. You coming?" He said, before slinking his way over to my desk.

Connor always seemed to be slinking. Not in the evil-sneaky way, it was more like his joints were greased with some sort of zero friction oil. He moved so seamlessly and effortlessly it was like watching water sometimes. This time he came around behind me to look at what I had been so interested in.

"I had no idea that you were so into worms," he said

"It's not a worm. At least I don't think it's a worm."

"What? You think your driver was eaten by Tessie?" His eyes sparkled and though I knew he was teasing me, I answered truthfully.

"I don't know what to think. Something or someone had to have driven that car into the lake and then had enough strength to push it to its final spot after the engine flooded. And where did the driver go? Your uncle believes in Tessie," I reminded him.

"Yeah? My uncle also believes in Sasquatch. Oooh maybe bigfoot drove the car and the woman into the lake as a Valentine treat for Tessie." He smacked me on the shoulder with the back of his hand. "Now come on, unless you want me to tell that cute bartender you couldn't come because you're hunting Tessie".

I rolled my eyes but shut down my computer. I could use a drink after this day, and the bartender was stinking hot.

The next morning Sarah and I visited Marion VanZimm's 'cabin.' Like most of the Nouveau Riche in Tahoe, what Marion had called 'the cabin' was actually a mansion cleverly disguised as a ski chalet.

"I hear that she got shafted in the divorce," Sarah said.

"This is shafted?" My eyes were round.

"It is when your ex-husband is the acting CEO of a certain oil company, who just acquired the rights to place a pipeline through Tahoe National Forest."

"How in the hell did they get permission to do that?" I looked at Sarah.

She shrugged. "It was a last-minute favor from the Trump Administration."

"Don't we have a hard enough time keeping the lake clean with just the garbage normal humans bring? Why do we need to add a gross polluter?"

"Hey, I'm just the messenger," she said and started up the steep drive.

I followed, seething that people cared more for money than nature. But I knew I was being naive. The whole reason I had a job was because of the thousands of tourists who came to Tahoe every year and got into trouble. I pushed that thought aside as we started looking for anything which might explain what happened, and more importantly, where Marion VanZimm was now.

Her living room had been done up in native art from a mishmash of tribes and nations. I was by no means an expert on Indigenous art, but I had spent my fair share of time in various cultures around the world and I knew that the 'Indian Maiden' paintings individually illuminated on the walls had nothing to do with either real Indigenous women or the Amazonian blowpipes that someone had made into a frames for them.

Sarah found VanZimm's book and the journal. The journal was the standard stuff of an old, rich, and embittered white woman. How much she hated her ex. How she knew he was having an affair. But then in early January the entries changed. In one she describes being down by the lake and seeing a wake with no boat nearby. She had grabbed her binoculars and saw three distinct humps stick out of the water before the thing dove back down.

The book found alongside her journal was entitled *Legends of Tahoe: The Terror of Tessie*. It had been heavily underlined and the description in her journal closely fit the description in the book.

"This is what happens when you read too much garbage, you start seeing things," I said.

"No, look. The date on the journal entry is January sixth."

"And?"

"She's using the receipt for the book as her bookmark. It's dated January seventh."

"She saw it first and then went to find information?"

Sarah and I just stared at each other.

Later I was in my office, and Connor slid in. "How's your worm lady going?" He said with a familiar gleam in his eyes.

"She saw Tessie before she disappeared," I said, expecting him to tease me.

"Everyone who disappears in the lake sees Tessie first."

"What?"

"My uncle didn't tell you? It's part of the legend. But look, it's only a legend. That lake is plenty dangerous without a monster." He left without telling me why he had been there. I asked Sarah to bring me the files for the two men that dove into the lake that first week when I was shadowing Bob.

The files stated that the men had reported a Tessie sighting within twenty-four hours of their icy plunges. It occurred to me that if 'it always happens,' as Connor said, there must be some sort of record or file. I started with our files, though TESS as an agency is only about thirty-years-old.

I noticed a rash of disappearances that were marked with 'Tessie' in the first two years of the agency's existence, and then there were almost twenty years with no Tessie sightings. The people lost to the lake during this period were always found. Their bodies washed ashore or divers found them nibbled by fish. Then two years ago the disappearances started again. This time, instead of being marked Tessie, they were just marked with a T: unknown. I needed more information.

I knew that Bob wouldn't talk about Tessie, it was considered bad luck to do so. I picked up the book we had found at Marion's cabin; in the bio of the author, it mentioned that he ran the Tessie research center, and there was a phone number to contact the center. An hour later I was in Truckee, sipping an old-fashioned from a tumbler, listening to the old man talk.

He started in on his Tessie encounter and I must have rolled my eyes or something because he stopped, looked at me, and said, "Son, I was a marine biologist teaching at UCSD. I know what should and what should not exist in the water. Tessie, like all the other lake monsters worldwide, should not exist. Tahoe is not large enough for a breeding colony of monsters. I was up here on an expedition specifically to prove just that. Lake monsters are myths.

But they aren't. I remember the first time I saw Tessie. He looked at me with those huge brown eyes before diving back down so deep our radar couldn't pick him up."

"He?"

"They might be a hermaphrodite species of course. I would need to see more than one of them. Which is the problem. You never see more than one of them."

"Almost like it's the same monster in every lake." I grinned into my whiskey.

"You may not be wrong."

"Come on. How could a single monster get to all the lakes? Tahoe only flows into Pyramid Lake, never into open water."

The old man got out of his recliner and tottered out of the room. I thought I had offended him but he came back a moment later holding two large pictures. Without a word, he handed them to me. One was a yellowing reproduction of what was obviously a tintype. The other looked modern. They showed the same thing.

"How long have the marks of the feet and coil been on the bottom of Lake Tahoe?"

"The yellow picture was taken during a drought at Lake Champlain in the late 1800s. The modern picture was taken by Soviet-era biologists in Lake Baikal toward the end of the Cold War. As far as I am aware this pattern has never been seen in Lake Tahoe."

Driving home from Truckee that night I couldn't get what the man had said out of my mind. I had just turned onto Highway 89 when I saw movement down by the lakeshore. I pulled into one of the hundreds of scenic turnouts and parked. I grabbed my big emergency flashlight from my glove compartment, and got out of the car. I thought I had seen a human, and no human should be diving into the lake on such a frigid night. I walked carefully over to where I had seen the person; there were bare footprints in the mud. I shined my light around but there was nothing. I shifted to shine it up the embankment and the water splashed behind me. Quickly turning, I saw a ginger head disappearing beneath the surface.

I ran to my car for my cell phone. Only my phone was gone. I had left the door open. The front seats and floorboards were soaking wet and a long round trail of water and mud led from my car back to the lake.

"Why in the hell would Tessie want my phone?" I yelled out onto the quiet lake. Of course, nothing answered me. By the time I got home and had put in a call to Bob via the landline, I was soaked and pissed.

"What's wrong?" he asked.

"Too much. Do you know where Connor is? I, uh, lost my phone and don't have his number on my contact sheet, but I thought I saw him fling himself into the lake. That's stupid right?"

There was silence for a heartbeat too long. With a terse and forced voice Bob answered, "Yeah, he's here. He's with me. I would put him on, but he was at the bar, and…"

"It's cool. As long as he's safe. Good night Bob."

"Of course. I'll let him know you were worried and you care about him when he comes to." He hung up. I had never heard him use so many words in a sentence before. Bob believed lying was almost a cardinal sin. So why was he lying to me?

It didn't hit me until I was in the shower 15 minutes later that he was going to tell Connor that I cared about him. I was so grumpy I told myself that I didn't care. But it took a long time that night to get my stomach to stop twisting every time I thought about Connor figuring out how I felt about him.

The next morning I was awakened by pounding on my front door. It was Sarah with a large coffee, a new cell phone, and the news that Marion's ex-husband had shown up and wanted to see us.

"How did you know about the cell phone?"

"Bob called. He said you had a slight accident at the lake and lost your phone."

"Something like that," I muttered before taking a too-quick sip of the piping hot coffee. "Ow! Okay, where are we going?"

"Marion's cabin."

When we pulled up to the cabin, the driveway was filled with a large, eggshell-white Rover with barely any snow on the tires and a bumper sticker that said, "Keep Tahoe Blue."

"Driving that beast isn't going to keep anything blue," Sarah noted.

The man who greeted us at the front door was like his Rover, large, white, and impossible to ignore.

"Bout time you people got here. Where is my wife?"

"Good morning Mr. VanZimm. We would love to know the answer to that question. Do you have anything that you would like to add to our investigation?" I smiled sweetly at him. Batting my eyes a couple of times to let him know I couldn't care less about his bluster.

"Oh, you're one of those," he said with a slight lift of his left nostril. "Well, come in and tell me what you know so far."

"I'm afraid that we can't do that." I stood my ground and discreetly held my hand out a little to keep Sarah still as well. "You are not her next of kin. In fact I seem to remember a document we were given stating that you were not even to be informed if something were to happen to her."

"Damn Mari! Of course she would do such a stupid feather-brained thing! Listen here, young…man…I am Anthony VanZimm and I could have you fired for talking to me like this. Do you know what company I run?"

"Yes, and Mr. VanZimm I would like to remind you that, as you have no legal authority to be in Mrs VanZimm's house, I could call the sheriff and have you arrested for trespassing and illegal entry." I turned to Sarah, indicating she should get her phone out.

"Wait! Wait! Wait! Wait!" The big man stuttered. "Let's be reasonable. I'm just worried about my beloved Marion. Look, I'll help anyway that I can."

"Was Mrs VanZimm suicidal at all?"

"No. Mari loved life. She was looking forward to a vacation she had planned to the Maldives next month." VanZimm smiled. "That was my Mari. She loved being among cultures that were bordering on extinction. She said it made her feel alive. God, why did I ever leave that woman?" He was looking up at the blue sky, projecting all the honesty of a southern lawyer defending a crooked sheriff.

"You left her because you're gay and she found out," I said and turned on my heel to walk back to the car.

When we got in and had pulled onto the road Sarah started laughing so hard that she was crying.

"Okay, first. There is no order against him. You know that. Second, how in the hell did you know he was gay? Did you see his face? It turned purple!"

I shook my head a bit chagrined. No matter how mad I was I had no right to out someone else. "I don't like bullies and there is nothing that says that we can't lie to people. And I knew because he frequents a very exclusive escort service in San Francisco. I asked the Sheriff to send over the VanZimm's divorce papers and I recognized the name from one of her complaints."

"Recognized?"

"Have I ever used it or been of use to it? No. Do I know the owner? Yes." I put my sunglasses on so I couldn't see the slight gleam in her eye.

The day passed with no new developments and without me seeing Connor at all. I tried his cell a couple of times but it went straight to voicemail. I wondered if he was avoiding me.

That evening, just as I pulled into my driveway, my cell phone rang. It was VanZimm.

"You have to help me. There's something outside and I don't know what it is and I can't—"

"I'll be right there." I put the car in reverse and drove as fast as possible to the VanZimm cabin. As soon as I pulled up I knew what was wrong. The Rover had been destroyed. It looked like it had been put in a vice and all the handles tightened. I had no idea what could have done that to such a well-built car. As I got out and looked at the driveway I saw again a large round trail of mud and water heading up from the lake. The entire area around the car was soaking wet, and in the broken mirror of the front passenger side I found one red hair.

I grabbed my cell phone and ran up to the front door. VanZimm pulled me into the living room.

"It hurt my car. That stupid monster hurt my car."

"Where is Tessie now?" I asked, no longer trying to pretend it could be anything else.

"I don't know. I looked out and saw it. I shouted at it, but it ignored me. I grabbed my .22 and fired at it, but it still crushed my baby. That's when I called you."

"You shot it?"

"It was a giant monster crushing my car!"

"Okay, fair."

He looked past me out the big picture windows that looked out on the driveway and to the lake beyond. "Hey! There it is!"

I turned in time to see a tail slither past the street lights and into the lake. I say tail, but the thing was as long as my arm and twice as thick.

"Stay here. Lock the doors. Do not shoot anything!" I was out the door before he could protest. I didn't really have a plan, but I knew I needed answers and that meant getting to the lake. I heard VanZimm huffing his way down behind me despite what I had told him. When I got to the edge of the lake, I turned to admonish him. And was looking straight into his gun.

"If you want to catch big fish you need big bait," he said, shoving me into the lake with all his might.

The cold hit me with the force of a semi hitting a brick wall. I had a lot of cold water training and knew I only had moments in water this cold before my organs failed. I tried to surface. The bullet missed me by millimeters. I dodged it looking up. VanZimm was on the edge of the lake holding the handgun.

He was shouting. I had no idea what. All I knew was that I was trapped in the freezing lake. The second bullet went wild as the surface of the water broke all around and a large serpentine head reared up over me.

VanZimm now changed targets to the monster. I saw a bullet hit its thick hide and a small waterfall of blood gushed into the water.

My lungs were on fire. I surfaced as the monster reared twenty feet straight up out of the water. In a lightning fast move, Tessie dove onto VanZimm, opening its great maw and swallowing the man whole.

I took a deep breath. I wasn't even cold anymore. I closed my eyes.

Something jarred me. I started shivering and coughing. I opened my eyes to the stars above Lake Tahoe. I was on something buoyant, warm, and scaled, shaking so hard I could barely fill my lungs. Tessie deposited me on Fannette Island, then the giant monster slithered up onto shore and formed into a coil around me. The heat of the great body warmed me enough that I was able to move my fingers to take off the sodden, frozen clothing that was making me colder.

I put my undershirt over the monster's bullet hole, which was still leaking blood, and put the rest of the clothes on the ground. Tessie moved their great head so I could see one big brown eye. They laid their head on top of their body, forming a little hive structure for me. I laid on the rocky shore and slept. I woke up somewhere around 2 am, my clothes, now dry, were lying beside me. As I shivered my way into them I looked for the great serpent. Near the shore a huge coil mark encircled two human footprints. I started to understand what that mark meant.

As I scanned the water wondering how I was going to get back to my car and home, I saw a light headed toward me. A small speedboat pulled up to the beach, Bob at the helm. He secured the boat and hopped out with a thick blanket, which he wrapped me in before guiding me to the boat.

"Are you okay?"

I nodded, "Bob. VanZimm shot the monster. I saw the bullet hole."

"Yes, I know," Bob said. "The monster will recover. We need to get you to the hospital."

The doctors told me I was lucky. I should have died in the water. I should have gotten frostbite on my extremities. They credited my training. I let them think that. The local sheriff showed up to find out what had happened to VanZimm.

"He shot at me. I ran toward the lake to get away from him. He followed and fell in. I tried to save him, but could barely save myself."

The sheriff shook his head. "Another body in the lake we'll never find."

The day after I was released from the hospital, I finally saw Connor again. It was late afternoon and I was on my porch looking toward the lake. Connor appeared on the beach looking up at me. He crossed the highway and walked up my steep drive. His hair and clothes were wet and his right arm looked stiff. When he climbed my steps I noticed he didn't move it.

"Hey," he said, not quite looking at me.

"Hey yourself. Is that a bullet hole in your shoulder or are you just happy to see me?"

He pulled down the neck of the t-shirt to show me the ugly fresh scar.

I nodded toward the empty chair beside me and waited until he had sat down before saying, "I'm sorry I couldn't do more to stop the bleeding. It was, if you'll excuse the language, fucking cold out there."

"There is no other word to describe how cold it is. Do you have any beer?"

"In the fridge. Bring me one too. Oh, and there are towels and a bathrobe in the bathroom."

He got up slowly and I watched his well-toned muscles showcased by the wet clothes slide past my chair. He returned with a bottle of double IPA in each of the bathrobe pockets. He handed me both.

"I'm having a hard time using both hands. Someone was being a damsel in distress and I had to save them."

"Ha! You didn't have to destroy his car," I said, popping both beer caps off and handing him one. "You're not a thousand years old or whatever? Right?" I asked after a long pull of the beer.

"Dude, way more than that. Tessie is as old as Tahoe. But no. It's a family gig. Every twenty years the next generation of water protectors is chosen from the family." He walked to the edge of the deck and leaned on the railing looking out onto the lake.

I joined him. "And are you also Nessie and Ogopogo and Champy?"

"Dude, you almost made me spit beer through my nose!" he said when he could breathe again, "No. Every great lake used to have a family. We are born with the lake and of the lake. Very few of the families exist anymore. Oddly, the current Nessie is my first cousin because of my mom, but that doesn't normally happen."

"Why don't you just tell people that the lakes are protected by your family? Wouldn't that be easier than having to eat people?"

He was very still for a moment. "The family that used to protect Lake Baikal were called the Khans. The Soviets were building a nuclear power plant at the lake; it was killing everything for miles around. Baikal is the oldest lake in the world, and in a four year span it was in danger of becoming a dead lake. At first, the Soviets didn't believe the old legends about Usab-Lasun Khan, the 'Master Water Dragon.' When the protector attacked the power station for the second time, the soviets managed to capture him. We can only keep our 'monster' form out of water for about twenty minutes tops. He was hauled on shore and when he turned, well... they took the whole family, and everyone that had ever had close connections with the family. I'm told that the 'experiments' went on day and night for over a month. Then everyone was taken into the Siberian wasteland. They put them all in a large wooden shack. Then they tested a nuclear weapon on the shack."

"How did the whole world not hear about that?"

"It's called the Dyatlov Pass accident. The 'hikers' were actually government operatives who misjudged how close the explosion was going to be. The youngest member of the family was eighteen months old. They didn't kill her. She was put in a cage in a lab, like a rat. When she hit puberty they attempted to 'mate' her to form some sort of monster hybrids I guess. She died in the process.

Horribly, and in pain. She was twelve." There were tears on his cheek.

I wondered how he knew all this, but instead of asking, I took a long pull on my beer and asked, "You think the same sort of thing would happen here in the US?"

"My father was shot with a tranquilizer by the army special forces in 2000. We are not lizards. We need to breathe. He suffocated on the bottom of the lake. The only reason they didn't succeed in capturing him is because my uncle called in the special units as poachers. By the time the feds and the locals had gotten things figured out, the TESS squad had been able to drag my father's body into one of the underground caves. The Baikal incident is partly why my uncle established TESS you know. The feds didn't figure out that Tessie is a shapeshifter. Lucky for me I guess."

I nodded and looked out at the ancient waters in front of me. I was quiet for a long time. Finally I finished my beer and asked the question that I had been avoiding. "So, being a water protector-shape-shifting- monster-thing. Does that mean you can only date other water-protector-shape-shifting monsters?"

I didn't look at him. I was focusing really hard on the lake. I felt him move closer and his left hand covered my right. "There are easier ways to ask me out than getting shot at, almost drowned, and becoming involved in an ancient legend," he said, and finished his beer.

No, We're Not Getting a Bog Hound: A Monologue by Your Irish Mam

CARMAN C CURTON

A Madra Síochána? Go away with that, will ya? I don't care if Mrs. Finnerty across the way *is* getting one.

Firstly, I will be the only one who feeds it, ya know that as it's true.

Second, it'll always be me who's returning harvested souls after the full moon.

And finally, who do you think is going to get trucked back and forth to Hell every fecking All Hallows Eve for all eternity? Not me. And that's that.

And don't even get me started on how we'll never keep it out of the good room.

Dancing In the Shallows
ALI COYLE

I don't remember how old I was when I first decided I was going to leave home and live above the brine. About eight, perhaps? Anyway, I didn't get far. I hadn't put the thought into it that such a big step deserves and I was found on the beach, trotting along with my shiny, blue-black hooves kicking up the sea-foam to sparkle white against my ebony hide, and my mane, usually glossy like polished jet, whipping wild in the wind. I hadn't mastered changing my form yet. There was a human child playing with the wet, firm sand, building it up into a little tower that collapsed when the wavelets washed its foundations away. The little russet-headed yearling giggled and raced to build a new tower before the next wave smoothed his work away to nothing. I watched him until he waved at me and called out excitedly about the "horsie in the sea," but I was shy and I swam out until the water was deep enough to hide me. I could hear the alarmed shouts of his mammare and sire as they galloped to stop him from running out and being swept out and sucked to the depths by strong, dangerous currents. They weren't to know that I would have been proud to carry the little one on my back to safety had he followed me under the waves.

Here's a thing I have not admitted to before: I'd got a fright and I was glad I was found before any more humans saw me, despite the telling off I got from my sire and grandsire and grandmare for going up the shore on my own when it wasn't safe.

I planned after that. Under the waves, deep beneath the Coire Bhreacain, through the roiling gyre that marked the entrance to a world that fit me like last year's shoes, I dozed off dreaming of that human child who would surely grow up to be my friend. When I woke at night with only the soft glow of startled jellyfish to relieve the inky dark, I made elaborate plans. And in my waking hours, I learned what I could about life above the brine from those who'd been there.

"Waste of time," my sire said. "Dreaming your life away, Donall, ye daft colt. What've they got up there that we huv'nae got down here? You'll not find your mammare, if that's what's in your head."

I'd've bared my teeth, if I'd dared. I knew Mammare had left us as soon as I was old enough that Sire and Grandmare and Grandsire could raise me without her. I didn't remember her at all, and I didn't want her if she didn't want me, I'd decided. A hardened heart is harder to break, Grandmare had said. But the reminder of that first rejection still stung. I shuffled my back hooves and swam away to find my cousins, and dance the nodding-head and flowing-tail and ballet-hoofed dance of my tribe. I'd learned about ballet from Grandmare, who'd danced on stage until she met my grandsire and faced her own decisions about her life. And, like Grandmare, dancing calmed me. Grandmare said it was in my blood. I swore I could feel it pulsing like the beat of the music she'd sing and stamp for me.

My second bid for freedom came when I was a dozen years old and I knew everything. With the confidence of someone who truly has no conception of the things they don't know, I trotted up onto the beach one day, wise thoughts in my head of walking to town, finding the theater, and presenting myself as a dancer like Grandmare. I was convinced they would love me. I would be a sensation, the most graceful dancer to ever flutter nimble toes on wooden boards. In my fantasy, the little one I'd seen on the beach, all grown now, would be in my audience and we would become best friends.

I got a little further than my first foray to the land-bound world of humankind. I changed, with a lot of huffing and snorting and one sound that began as a whinny and ended as a laugh, into my human form. I raised my head to sniff the breeze, filling my lungs with the warm, resiny-sweet scent of the gorse and the scrubby trees beyond the sand and the shingle, and the dusty smell of the road. Then I set off lurching away from the sea on strong legs which I was sure would be endowed with the same grace as my hooves before I reached the theater. The wind dried my hair into a thundercloud and my soft feet ached on the gritty track and my bald skin chafed, and all my optimism bled away.

I decided to go back to the brine to refine my plans. As I turned, a family of humans came along the road, two younger ones with chestnut manes, like Grandmare's only shorter, glinting russet in the sunlight, running ahead on legs as spindly as a brittlestar's. Two older ones were hanging back, watching like codfish concerned there might be a sharp-toothed selkie nearby.

"Oh my God, are you okay?" one of them yelled.

The taller of the two-legged colts called out, pointing at me but looking over its shoulder at its mammare and sire. "Mam, they've got no clothes on!"

I wished I could change right there and canter back home from the shame of it. But the sire and mare ran to me, ungainly on their two legs, and threw a checkered rug around me and told their colts to stand still and behave and not wander into the water. I wondered if I looked that off kilter when I walked on my human legs, too.

"What happened, are you okay?" the mare asked, words tumbling all at once, tucking stray roan hair behind her delicate ears.

"Do we need to call the police? Or the doctor?" asked the sire, leveling his pale face with its blue eyes and thin yellow forelock with mine, speaking loud and slow as if either I was stupid or he was.

I shook my thundercloud and summoned some sunshine to my face. "No," I said, calling up my lessons in the language we all learned, just in case we ever needed it. "I'm fine. Can you give me directions to the theater?"

Well. They said there wasn't a theater and that I should go with them to the doctor's or the police station, then they asked me my name. But I did not want to go anywhere that wasn't the theater and I was about ready to weep with the disappointment that these humans were not as understanding as the human friend I'd invented in my daydreams. So I did what any worldy-wise twelve year old would do. I turned and ran.

By Great Cailleach Bheurra, it hurt my feet! And my chest burned, but I did not look back, I did not stop, I threw myself down the shingle to the sea and into the shallows where the salt nipped my skin as a punishment, then deeper and deeper and deeper until the cool water smoothed out my mane and eased my muscles.

Maybe they said something. Maybe the ungainly, two-legged colts saw me change back and dive under the waves. Maybe news got around above the brine as well as below it, for a few days later I was paddocked in the kelp fields to Think About What I Had Done.

I thought it better to behave myself after that. I still planned and soothed myself to sleep with fantasies of a chestnut-haired human companion to be a firm and faithful friend in my new life. I dreamed of dances as light as the air I'd breathe, as graceful as golden sunbeams through trees. I did not want to remain in the depths with my kelpie clan where water dulled the sunlight and leached the colors from its glorious spectrum. I did not want to do as my grandsire had done and find a human lass to tempt under the water with beauty and grace and promises, to marry and bear the family a foal.

Grandmare laughed at me once, when I demanded, in a fit of petulance at being told 'no' when I sorely wanted to be allowed to poke my head above the water and see the humans on the beach again, to know why she fell for a kelpie's spells. She looked fond for a moment, dreamlike, and said that my grandsire, who was uncommonly handsome, offered her more lasting beauty and more sincere grace and more honest promises than any of the young human men who showed interest in her. So when my grandsire had revealed his truest self to her one night on the beach, the warm scent of the earth mingling with the sharp tang of brine, waves roaring and crashing then foaming and splashing over their bare feet, watched from up high by a waxing moon and twinkling stars, she had said yes.

"Just yes?" I asked, aghast that such a romantic moment only deserved a single word in Grandmare's telling.

"Ye ken ask yer grandsire," Grandmare had replied with a sparkle in her eyes. "He's a one for the fancy words, so if ye ask him he'll maybe tell ye the full story. I did dance for him, though. He said, 'Mhairi, dance into the waves wi' me,' and I said, 'Aye, I'll dance wi' ye, Aonghus,' and we danced in our bare feet in the shallows, and when the dance was done I was in the Coire Bhreacain. It was so cold! I remember the shock as I was pulled this way and that when I went under the gyre, but I climbed on his back and held on tight to stop me being scared, and he carried me home. Here." She winked at me and leaned in close. "Five months later yer own mammare, was born."

I almost choked in shocked laughter. "You married my grandsire because you were pregnant?" Somehow I didn't yet realize everything that this meant.

Grandmare laughed and nodded, and I could see in her joyful face that she would go back and do the same thing all over again if she had the chance to relive those times. I said as much and she regarded me with the calm, thoughtful look that always made me feel like she was reading my soul.

"I suppose I was born for this life," she told me, "only I had to be human first. I wouldn't have met your grandsire if I hadn't had two legs to dance on the firm, fresh sand when the tide went out. He appeared out of the waves like a god or a devil, and I was so smitten with the sight of him and so exhausted with everything else that I didn't care which one he was. But." Grandmare shook her head and her chestnut mane waved in the currents her movement made. "Maybe you're like me but backwards, Donall, my lad. Born a kelpie, but out of place in the water."

I cried at that. I didn't realize I'd known it my whole life, this sense of being out of place, and that it wasn't part of us all. I hadn't known that a vague sense of ill ease didn't color all of my sire's thoughts, nor did a nebulous feeling of wrongness tinge my cousins' dreams. I'd been holding it back for so, so long that I bawled until the salt of my tears stung my eyes, then joined the brine and mingled and cooled and was diluted away to nothing.

She let me cry until my personal tempest passed, leaving me as empty as one of the skeleton hulls that poked wooden and rusting metal bones out of the sea bed. But even shipwrecks can provide shelter and sustenance for other lives, like the merfolks that scavenge them, and when my heart was empty of the need to pack the life I wanted down to the exact size and shape of the life I had, new plans, better plans, gestated in the light and airy space I felt within my ribs.

Grandmare would teach me how to dance on two legs like the humans do. And when I was ready, I would dance on those wooden boards on feet as light as feathers.

I was six years wiser, and more, before I broke the surface again on my own and cantered along the strand for the sheer joy of solitude, filling my lungs with sharp, cold air, turning and laughing at the sight of my hoof-prints fading and five-toed footprints emerging. Then the next wave, every seventh a big one, washed the white sand clean again. I had studied hard and learned well from Grandmare. I knew how to walk and talk in a way that fitted my human form. I knew how to care for my appearance so that I would not be noticed until I wanted to be. I knew about ferries and buses and trains and money and, when I was as sure as I could be that I wanted it, I would leave my home and find another above the gyres. I'd be Grandmare in reverse, leaving my family under the Coire Bhreacain and finding a new family on the warm, dry earth.

Of course, I had only the faintest conceptual understanding of how all this would happen. My six-year-old imagination and my twelve-year-old arrogance were tempered by my eighteen-year-old caution. This was not my world yet. With dexterous, practiced fingers, I smoothed my mane before it dried to a cloud, my black locks dark and shiny as tar in the wet, and braided it, secured with a loop Grandmare had made from strong, leathery kelp strands. I had clothing this time, brought down by Grandmare and kept safe in case she ever wanted to go back to her old life. Her 'emergency bag,' she had called it when the family gathered to see me go, and Grandsire kissed her and called her his magnificent mare. My cousins wished me well and some gave me gifts – a spell for bringing good luck, another to help me tell truth from lies, and a silver chain bearing an amulet that the youngest swore would make me see sense and return before Bheurra's breath blew frost over the land and churned the shallows into slush.

My own sire had the saddest face, for he knew me best of all. "I wish you'd be happy here," he told me in the small hours, as I fretted and huffed to be gone. "I wish you would find a kelpie to love you and stay with us. I wish." His voice hardened. "I wish you weren't so human. Your grandmare gave you that through your mammare. It's her fault. They should've been careful not to have a human child."

"What are you on about?" I asked, confused, my mind I suppose too preoccupied with my journey to the beach and my goodbyes and my confusion brought indignation. "Mammare was as kelpie as you and I and Grandmare and Grandsire," I said with annoyance. "Everything I know about the world beyond the waves comes from the stupid, scary stories in the legends you tell all the yearlings to give them a safe shiver before bedding down, and Grandmare's stories from before she knew Grandsire. Which version do you expect me to believe?"

Sire was quiet at that and I saw in the flare of his nostrils and the flick of his ears that he regretted his harsher words. "Promise me something, Colt," he said, reaching over to groom the side of my neck like he used to when I was barely more than a foal. "If you find a good human who'll love you, bring them home. Make them one of us first."

Sire's shuffling hooves and stiff ears made me laugh. "I know," I said with a bubbling whinny. "Make them kelpie and bring them home and bed them as a kelpie out by the wrecks and the sandbanks and make a new generation of little kelpie foals." Grandmare's confession popped into my mind as if it had been hiding behind one of the wrecks, waiting for me to notice it and connect it to Sire's angry words. Open mouthed, I looked Sire right in the eyes. "Grandmare and Grandsire made a human, didn't they? My mammare wasn't born kelpie."

"Your grandsire was in human form when your mammare was conceived, and your grandmare hadn't been made kelpie yet. The baby was born on land," sire told me, shaking his head slowly. "Your grandmare had to go back above for the birth, and to nurse. Maybe that's why your mammare never took to being kelpie. She always had her head above the brine from birth. She wanted me to go back to the land with her and live as one of them, but I couldn't bring myself to leave the clan. And you turned out more like her than like me. But they don't live as gently as we do. They don't value what they have above what they want."

I knew that last comment was aimed at me but I bit back my annoyance and sighed instead. "I wish you would tell me good luck," I said. And Sire nibbled my ear and told me to be careful and that I could come back as soon as I'd had enough.

So there I was, walking up the beach to the road, this time with clothes on my back and shoes swinging by their laces from my hand, uncertainty nibbling at my innards. I muttered my cousin's spell for luck although I didn't believe in superstition, and took one last look out over the Coire Bhreacain.

"Hi, hello there…you?"

The voice called me as sweetly as the song of a siren. A human sat a little way off, by the road, in the shade of the wind-crabbed trees, soft shafts of yellow light hitting their mane and setting a fiery glow to the red that shot through the chestnut strands.

"Hi," I said, hanging back, wary, all Sire's old, childish warning tales spinning around my head.

"It's you," the human said, getting to his feet. I tensed ready to gallop back to the safety of the sea, but I felt no threat. "I wasn't making you up. All that time ago. I seen you here. You was naked. You asked my da—"

I took in the short, chestnut hair and the slim build and the pale skin and I recognized the voice, uncertain and excited all at once. I nodded my head. "I asked how to get to the theater."

"And then you ran away. I ran after you and I seen you run into the sea and you…you weren't human any more. Or you were gone and there was a big, black horse. Then it was gone too. I was scared you'd drowned."

We stood and weighed each other up while the gulls cried alarm all around, and the waves crashed behind me and I wondered again if I should run back home. I thought of Sire's certainty that I'd fail and Grandmare's hours and hours of lessons, and I felt my pride swell that I could be as human as anyone born on the dry earth. I watched the human and uttered my cousin's spell for telling truth from lies. When another minute passed, I let my shoulders drop and my spine straighten, and I smiled.

"I got paddocked for a month because someone told that I'd been seen changing. Was it you?"

The boy blinked rapidly and covered his face with his hands. He took a heaving breath, and then another one, and another. He uncovered his face again and looked at me with red-rimmed, greenish eyes. "You're still here. You're real. I'm not making this up."

"I'm still here," I confirmed, taking a few steps closer. "I'm real. Look." I held out my right hand, like I had been shown by Grandmare. The boy slowly lifted his right hand too and grasped mine, then he flung himself onto me. I was knocked backwards, we staggered under the force, but he clung to me with both arms around my neck and somehow we didn't fall.

"They told me I dreamed it," he said. "Or I was a liar, Mam and Da and my brother. But I knew you was real. I've thought about you every day since you ran away into the sea and changed. I've come to Jura every year that I could. I've come to this beach and watched the waves, and wished and wished you'd come back too. You're a kelpie, aren't you? I looked it up. I read all the legends."

I bared my teeth in a grimace. "The legends aren't written by kelpies. Anyway, I'm human," I said. He stiffened. I put my arms around him too. "This is my human form. I'm going to be a dancer in a theater, like my grandmare." His arms relaxed and he put his head on my shoulder. We leaned against each other for a few moments. I murmured, "My name's Donall. What's your name?"

"Iain," he replied. He released me and stepped back with a soft, nervous laugh. "Sorry. You probably think I'm weird or something."

"Honestly," I said, shaking my head at how badly I wanted to put my arms around him again. "I have no idea what's weird and what's not for humans." I shuffled my feet, side to side. "Maybe you can show me how to be human."

"Maybe I can," he said, and took my hand. "A dancer?" he asked. "Will you dance with me, Donall?"

"Aye," I said. "I'll dance with you, Iain." And I didn't know why I did it, but I took off my littlest cousin's pendant and put it around Iain's neck, and kissed him.

"–and that's why we always came here on holiday," I said. "Until we saved enough to move. I thought I would never go back under the brine and Iain was afraid of it, but he loves us and I missed the rest of my family. We'd come here and I'd visit my clan and we'd talk about all the things that had changed since my grandmare danced with my grandsire on this beach."

Disbelieving hazel eyes peered at me from under a chestnut fringe. Mhairi-Aonghus smiled then laughed. "You were never a dancer, Dad. You run a B&B in Taigh na Creige."

I smiled at our daughter, old enough to be a mammare herself if she desired it, and nodded to Iain, wading in the shallows, his hair turned salt-white by the passing years although he was far from old in my eyes. "I was never a dancer on stage," I admitted with a laugh. "Although I did dance. Sometimes plans don't work out. And sometimes they do. And sometimes they need a little help."

We sat and watched the waves come in and the tide go out, a low orange sun grazing the horizon to our left, the scent of gorse and heather behind, the gyres of the Coire Bhreacain ahead of us.

"Grandsire!" Mhairi-Aonghus pointed at a shadow in the sea and yelled excitedly, shot to her feet and ran into the water. I followed at a sedate trot, grabbing Iain's hand on my way past, laughing, swinging him around in a happy waltz. We watched Mhairi-Aonghus swim out to greet my sire with a soft bump of her white-flashed nose against his tarry black.

"I'll hold you through it," I said, thinking of Grandmare and Grandsire, too old now to breach the surface of the brine, waiting to greet their namesake under the gyre like they did every summer since the first time she'd run into these shallows on two legs and emerged on four. They were waiting to meet my Iain for the first time. "Like I promised I would. Get up on me and hold on tight."

Iain clambered up onto my strong back, wrapped his arms around me and kissed my neck, and together we dived.

A Heavy Hug
GRIFFIN RAYNOR

I first notice it while sitting at my desk, working. I've felt something strange for days, now, if I'm being honest. I had tried to convince myself that it was nothing, that I was just jumping at shadows.

But when I do finally see it, I don't jump. There's a chill running through me, and I can feel my heart pounding a little harder, but it feels somehow far more like awe than fear.

There is a dark corner in my room, and the shadow cast across my walls and carpet is far larger than it should be, far deeper than it usually is. There's no new addition or lack of light in my room, and the curtains are closed as they often are. I grab the small lamp from my desk and wave it towards the shadow, but while the very soft edges of it ripple and clear, the core of that dark corner shows no sign of fading. I stand up, hesitant, my legs a little wobbly, and bring the lamp closer. Still, even with me thrusting this bright fluorescent light almost into the shadow, it doesn't quiver. It remains dark and solid.

I fumble back. The room is warm, far warmer than it should be in early May. I can feel my AC vent blowing gently at my head and back, but it does nothing to offset this humid, enclosed feeling.

All of this should be unpleasant…but it's not. The dark is heavy and deep but somehow it doesn't seem menacing. The warmth that drapes around my shoulders – it feels like going out on a particularly warm day and feeling the sunlight rest firmly on my skin. It's weighty, it's insistent. But it's also…comforting?

Should that *be* comforting, or should it worry me more? I sit down in my desk chair, putting the lamp back down in its place, and stare at that dark corner. I've never believed in demons or spirits, and even now I'm half convinced that I'm imagining this odd little phenomenon. But…I suppose I'm equally convinced that *something* is in here with me.

I pick up a pen to nervously twiddle between my fingers and frown at the dark corner. "If you're evil or something, please at least wait until I'm done with this project to kill me. Okay?"

The shadow doesn't respond.

I tilt my head, rubbing my shoulder experimentally. There's nothing there but the strap of my tank top, but the warm feeling doesn't falter. The shadow seems to stare into me. "You can't hurt me," I murmur. I'm not sure if it's a question or an assertion. But the room seems even warmer, and while the shadow still doesn't diminish it somehow seems less like it's looming and more like it's just…there. Like a blanket draped over a chair, or a dark gnarled little tree that's just living its life. I feel utterly safe, if still confused and bewildered.

I let myself relax and turn back to my laptop, getting back to my project, though I glance over at the shadow every so often. It remains there all night, watching over me.

Whatever it is, it shows up the next night, while I'm sleeping. Trying to sleep. It doesn't help.

It's almost fully dark in my room now, but that deeper, inkier darkness seems to be standing about a foot from my bed. I feel extremely warm, even when I kick off my comforter and throw blanket. I sigh and turn on my side, sitting up on my elbow so I can peer and frown at it. "I'm trying to sleep."

There's no response. I pick up my phone from beside my pillow and light up the screen, waving the bright blue-white light at the area of darkness. Again, the shadow doesn't move or creep away, even as the darkness around it does. My attempt to banish it just illuminates a dark shape like a column of shadow. My chest tightens, heart pounding.

I set my phone down and scoot back a little on the bed. "I'm done with my project. Does that mean you're gonna kill me now? Or possess me or whatever?"

The warmth grows, then instantly retreats. I can't be sure what it means, but it feels comforting. "I guess not. I guess…are you friendly?"

There's another surge of warmth, and this time I feel it touch my face, just barely. It's like sunlight, or a brief caress. Then it retreats again.

I sit there in quiet surprise for several seconds. Then I find myself smiling. "Well, okay then. I guess there's no reason you can't stay, at least for tonight." *Not that I know how to get rid of you, anyway,* I think. I lay back down and pull my comforter to my chin. "Just give me some space so I can try and sleep, okay?"

I feel the warmth recede a little more, and the dark patch of room ahead of me seems to relax. It still takes a while, but eventually I drift off, my peculiar companion watching over me.

Within a few days, I become quite used to my new darkness. It hangs around my room at all times of day while I sleep, work, and enjoy my free time. Sometimes it stands right next to me, gently bathing me in its warmth. Sometimes it's just there.

I keep talking to it. At some point I start saying 'good morning,' and 'good night.' On the fourth day when I watch TV on my laptop, I look over to the corner by the door where it hovers and wave it over. "Do you like anime?" I ask, and it glides to me and curls around my shoulders.

I should be afraid of it, I think. If this was a horror story, it would eat me, or snap my neck, or crawl inside me and take over my body. But instinctively I seem to know it's not going to do that. It's done nothing and wanted nothing except to keep me company. It seems happy when I talk to it. When it leans on my shoulders, I feel it radiating warmth in a pattern, and I imagine it's purring.

I wish I could be as easily happy. The darkness makes me smile, but neither it nor anything else I do chases away the edges of sadness and exhaustion in me. I feel a little silly relying on a shadow for smiles, but I can't help it.

I've begun to need it.

It's on a rainy Sunday morning when I realize how much. I've been lying in bed crying since I woke up. It's only been a few minutes, but it feels like an hour. I'm far past the point where I want to be crying. When something first happens, it feels okay to be sad for a little while. Your family holds you up, and you know that you have a right, even a duty, to mourn when they pass. But then it's supposed to end.

I haven't moved on, though. I still can't sleep. I still cry for no reason. And in a way, the last thing I want right now is comfort.

But the darkness, it seems to understand. It's hesitant as it approaches me, sliding a little closer at a time, its warmth flooding near. I feel it wrap around the one hand that's lying on the bed and not covering my face.

I still a little, getting a few breaths in between sobs. I flex and then relax my held hand, craving that warmth all around me. "Please."

My gentle darkness settles across my body, covering me from head to toe. Without a sound or a shift in the mattress, it's now over me like a weighted blanket, enclosing me in its warm pressure. I open my eyes and I can't see anything. It's a darkness I can't even adjust to, just absolute blackness. I close them again and relax.

I don't have to be happy, I realize. I don't need to be strong or brave. The darkness will do it for me. Comfort seizes me as I surrender to the dark, heavy hug.

In the warmth of my shadow, I am safe.

Author Bios

ALICIA K ANDERSON *(Special Interest)* determined to use her autistic special interest for good, is a PhD Candidate at Pacifica Graduate Institute in the field of Mythological Studies and Depth Psychology. Her short stories and fairy tale retellings have been printed in the World Weaver Press anthology *Grimm, Grit, and Gasoline* and in Three Crows Magazine. She can be found at @A_K_ Anderson on Twitter, for all of your burning unicorn questions.

ALI COYLE *(Dancing in the Shallows)* is a science educator by day, a fiction writer by night, and has been an unapologetic daydreamer since birth. Whilst studying physics at university, Ali chose to interpret the "scientists can't write" stereotype as a personal challenge and has been writing down their daydreams ever since. Ali has an extensive back-catalogue of fanfiction and currently writes as "Rudbeckia" on AO3. Ali can also be found at @alicoylewrites and @rudbeckiaSun on twitter, and at https:// alicoylewrites.wordpress.com. They are very fond of folk tales, mild horror, romance, and cats.

ATLIN MERRICK *(Emerge…)* is the commissioning editor for *Dark Cheer: Cryptids Emerging* – this anthology – as well as for Improbable Press. She's the author of hundreds of articles, features, and essays, as well as two short story collections: *Sherlock Holmes and John Watson: The Day They Met* (writing as Wendy C Fries) and *Sherlock Holmes and John Watson: The Night They Met*. She's beyond excited by the amazing stories Improbable received for this anthology. She can be found on Twitter as @atlinmerrick, same goes for Tumblr.

AUBREY ZAHN *(Cursebreaker)* is a Brooklyn-based artist, activist, and attorney who decided to try her hand at writing something other than legal memoranda. Her most recent microfiction was published in Queer Science Fiction's *Ink* collection. She is currently working on her first full-length fantasy novel, *The Eyes of Eternity*.

BAILEY BAKER *(The Name of the River)* Bailey (she/her) lives in Northern California, keeping a wary eye on the dubious standoff between Nature and Civilization. She likes detective stories, musicals, and action movies, and looks forward to being able to travel again someday. She's written and posted some fanfiction here and there, but this is her first publication. Chat her up at @BaileyBWrites on Twitter.

B C FONTAINE *(Stitches)* Brooksie C. Fontaine's love of storytelling dates back to her unusual yet idyllic childhood. As a homeschooled student, she could often be found in the uppermost branches of a tree, reading or scribbling in a notebook. Fontaine was accepted into college at fifteen, into graduate school at nineteen, and is now enrolled in her second MFA program. Her work has appeared in a plethora of literary magazines, most recently *Eunoia Review* and *Quail Bell*. Her portfolio can be viewed via thecaffeinebookwarrior. com. By day, she works as a tutor and art instructor, and is caffeinated most of her waking hours.

B F VEGA *(Give a Fish a Man)* is a writer, poet, and theater artist living in the North Bay Area of California. She is an associate member of the HWA. Her short stories and poetry have appeared in various anthologies most notably: Nightmare Whispers, Dark Celebration, Infection, The Cauldron Anthology, Extreme Drabbles of Dread, Haunts & Hellions, and Good Southern Witches. She is still shocked when people refer to her as an author – every time. Facebook: @B.F.Vegaauthor Twitter: @ByronWhoKnew.

BO STARSKY *(Alfhild)* In 1996 a creature emerged from the void and that creature was named Bo. Today, twenty odd years later, that void creation is a gay ass author who can be found lurking in the valleys of Norway. Their gender is a question mark, but like a hot one. In their spare time they do not enjoy long walks on the beach, more like short walks to the fridge for more snacks.

BRETT STANFILL *(Raising Thom)* spends his time loving life in northern Indiana surrounded by his amazing husband, daughter, dogs and, of course… cornfields. When he isn't writing, you can find him nose down in a horror book or taking photos of bugs, slugs, worms and spiders. His other work includes various horror and speculative anthologies and online publications.

CARMAN C CURTON *(Caution!; The Price of Everything; No, We're Not Getting a Bog Hound: A Monologue by your Irish Mam)* consumes caffeine while writing a series of microstories called QuickFics, which she leaves in random places for people to find. You can find her on Twitter and Facebook @CarmanCCurton.

CEALLACH DECLARE *(A Place Where Wings Can Spread)* Ceallach is a human who is dry on the outside with four limbs and opposable thumbs. For the past 30 years they have successfully woken up, done stuff, and gone to sleep again on a regular basis. They especially enjoy sleeping; having done so in such notable places as Japan, Canada, and Ireland where they love to travel. This is their first published work after decades lurking on fanfiction sites.

CHERYL SONNIER *(Investigating the Sea-Hag Menace)* lives in Yorkshire, where she and her army of cats are plotting to bring down the patriarchy. Yes, there are only two cats; you have to start somewhere. Cheryl is studying for an MFA in creative writing at Manchester Metropolitan University, and works full-time as a Virtual PA. Recent short story publications include *The Invisible Collection* anthology from Nightjar Press, and Wyldblood Press – *Wyld Flash*. You can find her on Twitter as @Cheryl_ThePeril and on Instagram as @sonniercheryl.

CHRISTOPH WEBER *(Hunting el Chupacabra)* is an author and orchardist in Hilo, Hawaii. A prior life as a firefighter took Christoph into the West Texas backcountry, where he may have glimpsed el chupacabra, just beyond the flames. Christoph's short fiction has appeared in *Nature* and *VICE's Terraform*, among other publications, and won the Writers of the Future Award. Follow him at christophweber.com to stay apprised of his stories, including *Hangman*, his debut series about a near future we share with de-extinced ancient humans, from massive Denisovans and Neanderthals to diminutive *Homo floresiensis* "hobbits." What could go wrong?

DAN FIELDS *(Halyards of Black and Silver)* is a writer and musician from Houston, Texas. He has published over two dozen stories with the likes of Novel Noctule, Sanitarium, Pseudopod, Nocturnal Transmissions and more. He released his first full-length story collection, entitled *Under Worlds, After Lives*, in July 2021. Please visit www.danfieldswrites.com for more details, or follow @dlfTheCritic on Twitter for updates and snide comments.

DAVID M DONACHIE *(The Changeling)* is a writer, artist, programmer, and games designer, who lives in a draughty Scottish garret with a cat, a frog, four mice, and a large number of reptiles. His short story collection The Night Alphabet released in 2018, and his first novel, the mesolithic fantasy The Drowning Land, in January 2021. If you want to know more about him, visit: https://bit.ly/ddonachiewriter or check out DavidMDonachieAuthor on Facebook.

D VALENTINA *(Resurrection)* (he/they) is a biracial, nonbinary and transmasculine writer with a focus on horror with romantic elements. They live in the mountains with their cat, plants, and growing collection of books, romanticizing villains, pursuing an education in gemstones and divination, and crafting strange stories.

DANNYE CHASE *(The Enfield Monster)* Dannye Chase is a writer of queer romance, fantasy, and horror, all of which often contain monsters. Dannye and her family just moved to the US Pacific Northwest, where they are excitedly awaiting their first Bigfoot encounter. Dannye is much easier to find: check out DannyeChase.com, and @DannyeChase on Twitter & Facebook.

E SAXEY *(Bird, Dust, Wine)* is a queer Londoner who works in Universities. Their work has appeared in locations including *Apex Magazine, Queers Destroy Science Fiction*, and *Best of British Fantasy 2019*.

EMMIE CHRISTIE *(The Mechanic)* Emmie's work tends to hover around the topics of feminism, mental health, cats, and the speculative such as unicorns and affordable healthcare. She has been published in Intrinsick Magazine and Allegory Magazine and she graduated from the Odyssey Writing Workshop in 2013. She also enjoys narrating audiobooks for Audible. You can find her at www.emmiechristie. com, or follow her on Facebook at @EmmieChristieFiction.

FRANCES OGAMBA *(Tree People)* is the winner of the 2020 Inaugural Kalahari Short Story Competition and the 2019 Koffi Addo Prize for Creative Nonfiction. She is also a finalist for the 2019 Writivism Short Story Prize and 2019 Brittle Paper Awards for short fiction. Her fiction appears or is forthcoming on *Chestnut Review*, *CRAFT*, *The Dark Magazine*, *midnight & indigo*, *Jalada Africa*, *Cinnabar Moth*, *The /tƐmz/ Review*, in The Best of World SF, and elsewhere. She is an alumna of the Purple Hibiscus Creative Writing Workshop taught by Chimamanda Adichie. Twitter: @francesogamba.

FRANK ORETO *(The Worms Turn)* lives and writes in Pittsburgh, Pennsylvania. His work has been featured in, or is upcoming at, F&SF, Flame Tree Press, and Pseudopod among many other venues. When not writing stories Frank spends his time creating elaborate meals for his wife and ever-hungering children. You can follow Frank's exploits both literary and culinary on twitter @FrankOreto or on his Facebook page fb.me/FrankisWriting.

GRIFFIN RAYNOR *(A Heavy Hug)* is a writer and editor from Texas. They enjoy all kinds of fiction, and have lately been drawn to horror and all manners of darkness. Griffin is also a big fan of games, science fiction, and making and collecting weird jewelry. You can find them on Twitter @ERaynor1 to see more of their rambling and occasionally, writing.

IRENE TOUISSANT *(Coming Up From the Wilderness)* lives in the Pacific Northwest with her husband, child, cat, and dog. Sometimes mass hysteria ensues. Irene began writing in 2014, and short stories are her specialty. When she isn't writing, she's a voracious reader, of both published works and fanfiction, as well as an avid moviegoer and costumer. She was a nerd before they started calling it geeky, lettering in band and quiz bowl in high school, and still embraces her nerdiness. Her other hobbies include making liqueurs, experimental mixology to find ways (excuses) to drink those liqueurs, and adding chili powder to almost everything. P.S. The versus in the story are from Song of Solomon: 5:11, 5:13, 5:14, 3:1, 5:16, 6:1 and 7:10.

JAMES DICK *(Paper Mite Revolution)* is an author, actor, screenwriter, and director from Toronto, Ontario. He debuted as a short fiction writer in 2020 with the initial publication of his story, "Paper Mite Revolution", in the March issue of Blank Spaces Magazine. Since then his work has appeared or is soon to appear in Blank Spaces, Ghost Orchid Press, and Dark Dragon Publishing. His short horror-comedy film, "Clucked", was shortlisted by the panelists of the 2020 Toronto 48 Hour Film Challenge. He also writes for @bitesizebreakdown on Instagram, a critics' collective that reviews film and television in 100 words or less.

JEANNE MORAN *(The Spouses' Club)* once worked at a roadside stand serving hotdogs to hungry cryptids. She writes fiction and nonfiction surrounded by vinyl records, countless books, and innumerable dust bunnies. http://jeannemoran.weebly.com.

JOANNA GERBERDING *(What We Become)* is a recent graduate of the University of Michigan, Ann Arbor. She enjoys writing heartwarming twists on creepy topics and making the mundane charmingly absurd. She has been collecting owl-related items since she was two years old. This is her first published work.

JOYCE FROHN *(Vengeance is 9)* is married with a teen-aged daughter. She also shares a house with two cats, a lizard and too many dirty dishes in the sink. She has been published in "Writer's Resist", "Nothing Ever happens in Fox Hollow" and "Strange Stories" among other places.

KAITEE YAEKO TREDWAY *(Slide)* is a writer and puppeteer. She has always lived in New England: in its mountains, cities, and suburbs. She loves big, explosive magics and magics small enough to live inside of walnut shells. She is happiest when tangling herself up in new threads spun from old tales. Big thanks to Manuscript

Manufacturing and Winding Circle for every moment of support. You can find her on Instagram: @kaiteeyaeko.writes.

KASPER D P WILDWOOD *(More Precious Than Gold)* is a writer and gardener living in Kentucky with his partner and one sweet, adorable cat. He usually goes by the name Falcolmreynolds online, primarily on AO3 and Discord and very occasionally on Twitter.

LAURA SIMONS *(Home)* is a Dutch writer with some Antillean mixed in, who is deeply enamored with all things folklore and fantasy. She is a storyteller of all sorts, which is why she has a podcast, a webcomic, and a blog to share her original fairy tales, novellas, and short fantasy stories. Her podcast Patchwork Fairy Tales is filled with original, inclusive stories with intentionally diverse casts. It includes both typical fairy tales and light urban fantasy stories and can be found on most podcasting apps. All Laura's work and social media can be found at her website laurasimons.com.

MAGGIE DAMKEN *(Promises to Keep)* is an emerging writer of fantasy, surrealism, and magic, whose work has appeared in *Strange Horizons, Daily Science Fiction, Baffling Magazine*, and other literary magazines. "Promises to Keep" originally appeared in *Cease, Cows*. Follow Maggie on Twitter @shelleyisms for more strange content.

MARA LYNN JOHNSTONE *(Bedroom Shadows)* grew up in a house on a hill, of which the top floor was built first. She split her time between climbing trees, drawing fantastical things, reading books, and writing her own. Always interested in fiction, she went on to get a Master's Degree in creative writing, and to acquire a husband, son, and three cats. She has published two books and many short stories. She still writes, draws, reads, and enjoys climbing things. She can be found up trees, in bookstores, lost in thought, and at: MaraLynnJohnstone.com; twitter.com/MarlynnOfMany; MarlynnOfMany.tumblr.com.

MARIAH BARKOVITZ *(Caution!)* – animal-loving writer, reader, and college student – spends her time dreaming up magic and monsters. She loves to write fantasy fiction in her free time.

NARRELLE M HARRIS *(The Volcano and the Butterfly)* writes crime, horror, fantasy and romance. Her 30+ works include vampire novels, erotic spy adventures, het and queer romance, and Holmes/Watson romance mysteries. Her ghost/crime story *Jane* won the 'Body in the Library' prize at the 2017 Scarlet Stiletto Awards and her collection *Scar Tissue and Other Stories* was nominated for the 2019 Aurealis Awards. Narrelle was commissioning editor for *The Only One in the World: A Sherlock Holmes Anthology* (2021). Discover more at www.narrellemharris.com.

RACHEL JOHNSON *(In the Woods, a Soft and Tender Thing)* is a lawyer whose fascination with ecology, archaeology, and oceanography inspires the subjects of her writing. As a queer/non-binary, chronically ill, & culturally Jewish creator, Rachel's work centers the characters and experiences she rarely saw in media growing up. An inveterate experimenter, Rachel dabbles in game design, carpentry, cooking, illustration, and countless assorted crafts that catch her fancy. She lives with her wife Carly, a fellow lawyer & writer, and their cat Pippin, who has an advanced degree in getting into trouble.

RHIAN BOWLEY *(Pebble-mouth)* is a Welsh writer, runner, photographer, gardener and cat slave, not in that order. She lives by the seaside and this is a true story. Find more of her fiction at www.rhianbowley.com.

R J K LEE *(Stone Shaper Tanukis Estranged)* is a native Oregonian residing in Japan where he plays games with his children and works as teacher, proofreader, and voice actor. As a new author, he has two stories published: *Stoner Shaper Tanukis Estranged* in *Dark Cheer: Cryptids Emerging* and *Memo from the Jolly Overlords* in the *Weird Christmas Podcast* 2020 flash fiction contest episode. His awards include a silver honorable mention (Writers of the Future contest, 2021) and a third-place fiction award (the University of Oregon KIDD contest, 2005). Follow his posts on where to creative works at https://figmentsdiehard.blogspot.com/ or @rylandjklee on Twitter.

RYAN BREADINC *(Brave)* is a queer author from Bunbury, Western Australia. He found his passion for writing through reading gory horror stories and cheesy supernatural romance drivel when he was far too young for it. Now he makes his *own* gory horror stories and cheesy drivel, but with characters that mean something to him, and to other people that don't quite fit in the box that society's built. You can find him rambling about ideas for his next story on social media (@breadincbooks) or on his website: https://www.breadincbooks.com. He also writes comics!

SHERRI COOK WOOSLEY *(Gargoyles of Prague)* holds a master's degree in English Literature with a focus on comparative mythology from the University of Maryland. She's a SFWA member, and her short fiction has recently been published in *Thrilling Adventure Yarns 2021*, *Once Upon a Dystopia*, and *DreamForge Magazine*. This story combines her experience of living in Prague as an English teacher and being a mother to a child with cancer. Find her online at www.tasteofsherri.com, @SherriWoosley, and Insta: Sherri.Woosley.

TAMARA M BAILEY *(Ghosts in the Forest)* is the award-winning author of the children's series starting with *Lintang and the Pirate Queen*, published under the name Tamara Moss. She can be found on Twitter and Instagram @TamaraMBailey1. *Ghosts in the Forest* is Tamara's first published adult story.

THERESA TYREE *(Will-o-the-Wisp)* (she/they) grew up in the Oregon woods, dreaming of magic amongst the trees. She lives there still, with her platonic life partner and their cat, and puts the magic she dreamed of into her stories. As a nonbinary queer women, Theresa's favorite tales to tell are speculative queer stories that offer more representation and give her readers hope. You can read more of her work on her website, theresatyree.com. Follow her on Twitter at @theresatyree.

TONY RAUCH *(the goombees (are moving in down the block))* has four books of short stories published: "I'm right here" (spout press), "Laredo" (Eraserhead Press), "Eyeballs growing all over me…again" (Eraserhead Press), and "What if I got down on my knees?" (Whistling Shade Press). He has been interviewed and/or reviewed by the Prague Post, the Oxford University student paper in England, Rain Taxi, the University of Cambridge paper, MIT paper, Georgetown University paper, The Adirondack Review, and the Savanna College of Art and Design paper, among other publications. He is looking for a publisher for titles he has finished and ready to go. Find him at: http://trauch.wordpress.com.

ZANNE SUTER *(Thicker Than Water)* Zanne lives in beautiful, sunny Southern California, which is ironic since she tends to avoid the sun like it might incinerate her on the spot. While her colleagues often refer to her job as zookeeping, the technical title is actually middle school teacher. She writes in order to fund her travels and to buy books. Her most current release is *Red Hood*, a sexy reenvisioning of a favored childhood fairytale, but intended only for adults! You can find her at www.zannesuter.com, on Goodreads, and (hopefully) on your bookshelf!

Dark Cheer: Cryptids Emerging (Volume Silver)

For the lovers of things that go bump in the night

Here be stories of
South African grootslang
and bayou grundylow,
tales of elementals, jackalopes,
and flying motels.

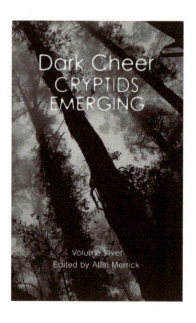

Within you'll find tiny leviathans
and rock whales,
cambion and kelpie,
a girl between time,
and a man who saves a gun's life.

These are stories of cryptids who
sing or swim or save us, living
side-by-side so often unseen
...and then seen.

When we look.

Tags: Urban fantasy, speculative fiction, LGBT+, disability, BIPOC

Order Volume Silver, the second *Dark Cheer* anthology, at:
https://improbablepress.com or online from most book retailers.

Get More Great Stories

ImprobablePress.com

From ancient gods rising, to road trips on the trail of cryptids,
from romance to mystery to adventure,
Improbable Press specialises in sharing the voices and tall tales of
women, LGBTQIA+, BIPOC, disabled, and neurodiverse people.

Come along for the ride.

Sign up for our newsletter *Spark* at improbablepress.com
Find us on Twitter @so_improbable
Instagram @improbablepress